Also by Amanda Bouchet

THE KINGMAKER CHRONICLES

A Promise of Fire

Breath of Fire

Heart on Fire

NIGHTCHASER

AMANDA BOUCHET

sourcebooks
casablanca

Published by Sourcebooks Casablanca, an imprint of Sourcebooks, Inc.
P.O. Box 4410, Naperville, Illinois 60567-4410
(630) 961-3900
Fax: (630) 961-2168
sourcebooks.com

Printed and bound in Canada.
MBP 10 9 8 7 6 5 4 3 2 1

This book is for my sister, Alexis.

The lights in the night sky aren't the only kind of star. Here on Earth, they don't shine much brighter than you. I love you.

CHAPTER

1

I SAT BACK IN MY CAPTAIN'S CHAIR AND BREATHED, slowly and deeply, letting my body adjust to traveling at a normal velocity again. It was risky to come here, but maybe we'd finally get a break. We needed one. So did the ship.

Outside the bridge's large window panels, stars winked back at me from the endless Dark. The view didn't look much different from anywhere else we'd been in the galaxy lately, but no one in their right mind would be here. I was counting on it.

It never ceased to amaze me how vast space was—and yet not a single corner of it was free. No technology existed that could get us beyond the Overseer's reach.

A red light sputtered to life on my console, and I shot forward in my chair and stared. Communication open/outside channel blinked back at me.

My heart rate went from normal to warp speed so fast it hurt. "Who the hell is in Sector 14 with us?" I demanded, turning to my first mate.

Jaxon's space-pale complexion whitened even more

as his eyes jumped between me and the flashing button. I figured I looked just as ghostly, and not only because we hadn't seen direct sunlight in weeks.

"No one's ever in Sector 14," he said, sounding worried and pissed off. "Half of it's the Black Widow."

"Well, someone's here now," I answered sharply, days of high stress and almost no sleep adding extra bite to my voice.

We both eyed the blinking red com button again. This part of the galaxy was off-limits. Usually, I was the only one not following the rules.

I scanned the views outside the multiple windows again, not seeing the ship that was reaching out to us. I did see a portion of the gigantic ring of darkness everyone tried very hard to avoid and felt a little queasy, only part of which I could blame on the long jump we'd just made through hyperspace.

The Black Widow was the reason we'd come to Sector 14. Choosing the dicey location was a last-ditch effort to lie low and recharge after three days and seven Sectors of hot-on-our-tail leapfrog with hostile Dark Watch vessels.

I wasn't an instant pessimist, but this couldn't be good. The *Endeavor* was almost out of juice, and the Sectors were crawling with government spacecraft out looking for the vaccines we'd stolen. Only the elite and the military were given access to cure-alls. Someone needed to redistribute more fairly. But when patrol ships had started popping up all around us, instead of emptying the contents of the floating lab we'd found into our own cargo hold as usual, I'd nabbed the entire thing with a vacuum attachment. Now, the extra hunk of ship was sticking out like a sore thumb, weighing us down, *and* about to get us all sent back to jail. Or worse.

I even had an enormous, leather-clad, bearded man who'd accidentally come with the floating lab. *Shit!*

My fingers tensed around my armrests. There was no way I was reaching for that com button. Whoever was hanging around Sector 14 and a freaking *black hole* was going to have to talk first.

Or maybe they would fly right on by…

"Cargo Cruiser model 419, please identify yourself." *Damn it! They talked.*

I stared at the panel in front of me as if it were a poisonous snake from one of the green planets. They had water and pretty plants, but they also had all the nasties I didn't like to think about. That was what happened when you grew up in a metal box—nature scared the crap out of you.

"I repeat, Cargo Cruiser model 419, please identify yourself."

I almost recoiled at the tinny, no-nonsense male voice that burst out of my console again. Interference from the Black Widow made the communication shriek like the five o'clock wake-up whistle in prison. I'd hated that whistle. It'd made my stomach hurt.

"Answer him, Tess," Jax hissed, nodding to the flashing button. "The longer you wait, the more suspicious they'll get."

"They're already suspicious." Only a ship up to no good would be anywhere near here.

I looked from Jax to Miko. Miko's good hand still hovered over the navigation panel, her dark-brown eyes bigger than I'd ever seen them. She looked like she hadn't moved a muscle since typing out the coordinates for Sector 14—where *no one* was supposed to be.

Swallowing a curse, I turned back to my controls and pressed down on the blinking red com button only long enough to transmit a response. "This is Cargo Cruiser model 419. It's only polite to identify yourself first." Even space had etiquette. Granted, I usually ignored protocol, but I could still cite it when necessary.

Jax groaned softly. Miko looked like she was about to pee her pants, which was odd, because I knew just how hard-core she could get when push came to shove.

The same sharp voice came through in immediate response. "This is *Dark Watch 12*. Captain Bridgebane speaking."

Shock jolted me. So did fear. Battleship 12? And Bridgebane? He was a high-ranking galactic general and part of the Overseer's band of science freaks who had come close to carving me up when I was a kid. All the higher-ups had wanted to know what made me tick differently from everyone else.

Maybe it was having a freaking heart.

I shot a look at Jax, who shot me one back. This whole mess had just gotten exponentially worse.

There was no doubt in my mind that Bridgebane would recognize me. I'd grown up, but I hadn't changed that much. I still had the same straight reddish-brown hair, wispy bangs, unusual height—which now put me eye to eye with most men—and blue eyes that stood out from a mile away. Before she died, Mom used to tell me that my eyes made her dream of the great oceans and blue skies she'd never see. And she never did. Dad kept us both under lock and key.

And now ancient history was coming to bite me in the neck and shake me hard. *Dark Watch 12* was one of the Galactic Overseer's premier warships and could blow my faithful little *Endeavor* to pieces with only two or three direct hits. It was a fully armored beast. And I knew my way around it. If not for my oddities—and my conscience—*DW 12* might one day have been mine.

"Please identify yourself," Captain Bridgebane ordered, "or we will be compelled to board your ship and ascertain your identity ourselves."

And there was the galactic military in all its glory—polite, even while putting a gun to your head.

Boarding us was out of the question. There was nothing on my ship that wasn't stolen. Hell, even the ship was stolen. Even the *crew* was stolen because, well, *jailbreak*.

I reached out and pushed the communications button without letting my hand shake. "This is Captain T. Bailey. You're looking at the *Endeavor*," I answered in the flattest voice I could muster.

"Captain Bailey, Sector 14 is a no-fly zone. What are you doing in this area of the galaxy?" Bridgebane asked.

I wanted to ask him the same question but managed to refrain. I pressed the com button again and calmly said, "Taking in the view. The crew wanted a peek at the Widow."

I lifted my hand, cutting off all sound from our end, and the longest few heartbeats of my life passed in total silence as the bridge crew stared at me, waiting for their orders.

My mind bounced from one possibility to the next. I'd given my usual false name—any Bailey, especially with only a first initial, was extremely hard to pin down since it was one of the most common surnames in the galaxy—and the *Endeavor* had fake ID numbers stickered on both sides. I could peel them off and get new numbers up in less than forty-five minutes, even with the necessary spacewalk. But I couldn't do it with Bridgebane watching.

"Power up, Jax. Time to jump us out of here." The only problem was, we hadn't found a safe Sector in *days*. "Miko, move us closer to the Outer Zones."

"We can't, Tess." Jax shook his head as he examined the data readings on our current energy levels. "We don't have enough power left to get us out of 14. And they've locked on to our com channel now and can follow short-range leaps, even if we use warp speed to stay out of sight and jump around the Sector."

I stared at my first mate. I'd known we were low on juice, but that was very bad news.

He pivoted the screen portion of his console in my direction, showing me just how fucked we were. Repeatedly hauling the lab at warp speed had put a huge strain on the ship's energy reserves, and that last, big jump had drained even more power than I'd anticipated. We'd come here to try to *fix* our power problem, not make it worse.

"Can we get close enough to the nearest star to recharge the *Endeavor*'s energy core as planned, not fry, and still keep away from the Dark Watch?" I asked, knowing what Jax would probably answer.

He winced. "Even short jumps to stay away from the warship would drain our reserves faster than the solar panels could build them up again."

I winced, too. "We'll end up a floating duck."

He nodded.

"We already have a target on our back, and this is the end of the line." Usually softly lilting with Sector 10's melodious accent, Miko's urgent words flooded the bridge with the near panic I was trying hard to keep at bay. "What choices do we have?"

Bad ones. Without recharging, our already crippled capacity for warp speed would fizzle to nothing in no time, and simply flying away wasn't going to work, either. A Dark Watch vessel could chase a lot faster than a cargo cruiser could run.

The red com button flashed again before I could even begin to analyze our terrible options, and Bridgebane's clipped voice came through to the *Endeavor*'s bridge as clearly as if he were sitting right there. "We see you have three cargo holds and a vacuum attachment that looks like the lab that was recently stolen from the Lyronium System. Prepare your starboard port for a boarding party. Any lack of cooperation on your part will be taken as hostility, and we will not hesitate to fire to recover the lab by force."

The communication went dead, and my heart slammed so hard against my ribs that it left me short of breath. I leaped out of my chair as I switched to a mapping screen on my console to get an idea of just how close they were.

My eyes widened. *Dark Watch 12* was right behind us—and looking straight at the stolen lab.

"Jax! Power up with what we've got. And tell Miko her jump range the second you know it," I said.

"It won't do any good." Jax started flipping the necessary switches anyway. "They'll just follow us and start shooting."

I glanced at my controls again, at the terrifying digital image of the mammoth battleship hovering on our tail, and then pressed my lips together, trying to hold back what was probably the worst decision of my life. "Then jump us closer to the Widow."

"What?" squeaked Miko. "We'll get sucked in."

"Well, don't jump us *that* close!" I kicked the lock on my chair and shoved the whole thing back and out of my way. I didn't plan on sitting down again while taking four other lives into my hands and also protecting the vaccines that could save thousands of people from the diseases that still ran rampant in the galaxy's civilian populations.

I watched to confirm that Miko's hand was flying over the navigation controls before I punched my own hand down on the yellow internal communications button. "Shiori! Get to the bridge. Fiona! You, too! Do *not* stop to collect your plants. This is an emergency."

I swung my eyes back to Jax, nerves riding my spine like an icy comet. "Tell us when we've got the juice."

"We're good to go," he answered. "At least to Miko's new coordinates."

I nodded. Now we waited for the other two. Usually, I'd just have told them to brace themselves for a jump, but right now, with the Dark Watch threatening to fire on our back end, I wanted everyone up front on the bridge.

The bridge was also where we could access the ship's escape pods, if it came to that—not that I believed they'd do us much good.

Every second lasted an eternity with the warship *DW 12* and Captain Bridgebane breathing down the *Endeavor*'s comparatively minuscule neck. I stood there. I didn't shake. I didn't move. My head felt numb. But I wanted to scream at the top of my lungs. Not in fear, although there was plenty of that, too. No, it was *rage* boiling in my chest.

Shiori rushed through the bridge doors, her fingers gliding along the wall. Miko ran to her grandmother and quickly guided the older woman toward my abandoned chair. With her good arm, Miko practically threw the tiny Shiori into my captain's seat, strapped her in, and then locked the chair back down, not leaving me much room at my console.

Miko raced back to her navigation controls. Shiori reached out to me blindly.

"I think I got us into big trouble," I said, taking her fragile hand.

Her skin felt paper-thin and dry and looked almost unhealthy, the creamy tan shade of it having faded into something pasty from lack of sunlight. The veins stood out, and her tremor seemed worse, but Shiori squeezed my fingers with surprising strength. "We've been ghosts for five years already, child. You gave us many more days."

The heat of unwanted emotion crawled up my throat just as my console delivered new information with a warning signal. `Incoming cruiser—starboard side. 200 meters.`

I glanced at Jax. "We can't wait." Fiona was going to have to deal with taking a fall.

He nodded, and I grabbed the edge of my console for balance.

"Go!" I cried.

Jax hit the small, round button that had saved our lives countless times, and everything went dark and weightless as the *Endeavor* shot through space. My bones seemed to crunch and shudder and then pop back to normal again as the ship slowed almost immediately. That was the shortest jump of my life.

I shook my head to clear it and then studied the view outside the bridge's windows again.

Mighty Powers That Be… The Black Widow was all I could see.

"You're certifiable, Tess," Jax murmured.

Yeah. I kind of had to agree.

I swallowed hard. "They won't follow."

The outside com blared like that awful prison whistle again, sending through Bridgebane's now-furious voice. "Captain Bailey, you are under military arrest. Jump again, and all crew members on board the *Endeavor* will be deprived of a trial. Our boarding cruiser jumped after you, and *DW 12* followed. Prepare for entry on your starboard side."

I cursed. How could I have forgotten that Bridgebane would do anything for the Overseer?

Fiona burst onto the bridge, spitting mad. She was barefoot and wearing leggings and a tank top, which probably meant she'd been in a hazmat jumpsuit only a few moments earlier. If she'd had to get out of it before leaving her secure experimentation lab, it was no wonder she hadn't shown up in time for the jump. At least she'd listened to me and hadn't stopped to collect her specimens. Botanists got really attached to their plants.

"What the hell is going on?" Fiona stalked toward me, her high, dark ponytail swinging angrily as she walked. "I just cracked my head on the wall when you dragged me out of my lab and then *jumped* without even telling me to brace myself. And just when I was getting close to making a breakthrough with those new cure-alls, too. I'm even wondering if they can cure Shiori's blindness. They're full of good stuff—like, superpower stuff."

"Those vaccines just got us followed practically into the mouth of a black hole," I said, motioning toward the bridge windows.

Fiona looked around, and her eyes widened at the sight of so much absolute darkness.

"Holy shit!" She gaped at me. "Are you crazy?"

I gave a small shrug. "The Dark Watch was breathing down our neck."

"The Dark Watch is always breathing down our neck!"

"Yeah. Well, this time, they're trying to board the *Endeavor* as we speak, and a warship got close enough to get visual confirmation on the stolen lab."

"So jump the hell out of 14!" Fiona cried.

"We *can't*. We've been leaping almost nonstop for three days, and the *Endeavor*'s power is too low to do anything other than play cat and mouse around the Sector until we completely run out of juice."

Fiona snapped her mouth shut, her usual space-rat pallor taking an abrupt dive toward ashen.

"And then they'll either board the ship or blow us up," Jax added solemnly. "Either way, we're toast."

I caught Shiori's serene expression out of the corner of my eye as I nervously tucked my bangs behind my ear. Shiori was always asking me to meditate with her and Miko, but I never wanted to sit still. Maybe I should have. She looked a lot calmer than I felt.

The *Endeavor* jolted from the hard bang of *Dark*

Watch 12's boarding cruiser latching on with a vacuum seal. Obviously, we hadn't opened the port.

"Starboard side has our most solid door," Miko said. "It'll take them a while to break through."

I nodded. But break through they would. They had all the tools.

"I don't get it," I muttered out loud. The intensity of this chase was baffling. Vaccines were important, yes, but the military was acting as though this particular batch were liquid gold.

I turned back to Fiona. "Has the big guy said anything about the vaccines?" He hadn't threatened the crew in any way after we'd carted him off by accident along with the floating lab. He hadn't tried to reach the bridge. He hadn't complained about the near-constant jumps. He hadn't so much as asked for food or water or a freaking loo in the three days we'd had him. I'd offered him the basics more than once, but he never took me up on anything. He was big, quiet, and stoic in the extreme.

I liked him. And I'd better go get him.

Will he even fit into an escape pod?

Fiona shook her head. "He left the lab only once, and I couldn't stop him from poking around the cargo holds. He wanted to know where we were taking everything."

Nowhere anymore. At this rate, those things had no chance of getting to where they needed to go. The food and seeds were for the dirt-poor colonies out in Sectors 17 and 18 that would never recover from the war. The books were for the Intergalactic Library's rare and archaic section, and the drop-off I'd planned would have been stealth itself. The vaccines were for Starway 8. Orphanages never got cure-alls. I would know.

"What did you mean by 'superpower stuff'?" I asked, suddenly zeroing in on what Fiona had just said about the vaccines.

"I meant give a few rounds to Jax, and he'd be unstoppable. Strength. Speed. Boosted healing." Fiona huffed. "Hell, give some to Shiori, and she'd kick ass like she was twenty years old again."

I felt my jaw loosen. "An enhancer?" *The* enhancer? I'd thought that was a myth. Or a bad dream. Or something that would never work.

And then it hit me. No wonder the lab had been so discreet, so empty of personnel that it shouldn't have drawn a single eye while it floated around out in bumblefuck Lyronium. That was how the Overseer worked. Hide your best science. Destroy what you don't understand.

Shit! I'd almost genetically modified thousands of kids.

"We can't give that to orphans!" All those shots clearly labeled as cure-alls were in reality the abomination the galactic government had been working toward for years.

Fiona shrugged. "You can if you want to call the concoction a vaccine and turn people into super soldiers without telling them."

I gasped. Wasn't the military already unstoppable enough?

An earsplitting hammering started on the starboard side just as the edge of the Dark Watch ship came into view. It was immense and intimidating. Too bad I couldn't incinerate it with just the heat of my glare.

Apparently, the galactic generals weren't only lying to civilians anymore; they were lying to their own.

Furious on behalf of just about everything that lived,

I slammed out a combination on my console. "I won't give it back. I'll die before the Overseer gets his serum back and uses super soldiers to terrorize the Outer Zones even worse than he already does."

The bridge lights flickered from the sudden power drain, and the hammering abruptly stopped.

"I just electrified the whole starboard side," I announced. Best-case scenario? I fried their jackhammer, and they'd have to return to the warship for another. Worst case? We were pretty much already living it.

Bridgebane's voice barked across the com again. "You are now accountable for an attack on the military, three burn victims, and a damaged Type-4 Heavy Armor Hammer. Galactic records show no Captain T. Bailey and no cargo cruiser matching your ID numbers or called *Endeavor*. We've definitively identified the floating lab. We will fire on the bridge if you continue to resist."

Jax looked at me. "They can blow up the bridge and still recover the lab."

I watched the behemoth warship hovering over our starboard side. *DW 12* definitely wasn't behind us anymore. "If they board, we're dead."

They'd consider us all repeat offenders simply for breaking out of prison. Now I had the vaccine heist and an attack on the military against me as well. There'd be no jury, no trial, and no more wasting food and space on a criminal like me. Jaxon was in the same position, but not for theft. I called what he'd done in the Outer Zones heroic. The galactic government called it murder— because they'd won.

Shiori had never technically been arrested, but Fiona

was a bio-criminal who'd created at least three major airborne plagues when she'd been fighting alongside the rebels out in 17, just like Jax. And Miko had cut off her own left hand to get out of shackles, so I was pretty damn sure she didn't like being chained up.

I glanced at my navigator. Miko's glossy black hair, fine-boned features, and delicate-seeming beauty had landed her in a position she didn't want to be in when she was nineteen years old. I could only guess at the details, but Miko's sporadic comments about the violent appetites of powerful men spoke volumes. And Miko's death sentence spoke volumes about her violent response. She'd escaped with her grandmother's help the day before she was slated to die. Shiori went where Miko went, even if that was a galactic prison—or a cargo cruiser that looked like a good place to hide.

Five years together now—Jax, Fiona, Miko, Shiori, and me—and my obsession with kids and their health was about to get my loyal band of misfits killed. If I hadn't taken the lab, no galactic warships would have been out looking for us. There wouldn't have been a Dark Watch frigate in Sector 14. Nathaniel Bridgebane would have been stalking someone else.

I looked out the front and portside windows at the looming Black Widow and curled my hands into fists. Almost the entire view outside the ship was darkness, the stars that edged the rim of the black sphere so startlingly bright in comparison. I wondered how long it would take before they were swallowed up, and then the whole Sector, and then the neighboring ones, too. How far could oblivion expand? Such nothingness was terrifying. I could almost feel its unholy pull.

I should have stayed away from the vaccines—the *super soldier serum*. I should have known the almighty Galactic Overseer could never produce anything good or pure. But I'd been so set on giving the orphans on Starway 8 a defense against some of the things that killed in silence, since I could do very little about those that did it loudly.

The ship lurched—the Dark Watch's boarding cruiser latching on again with new equipment. Probably insulated this time. My tricks never worked twice.

"I'm getting some of those vials before it's too late," Fiona said, racing for the door. "I can work backward and figure out the organics, I'm sure!"

"Stay put." My voice rang out loudly over the bridge. "I'll get the samples. And the big guy."

Fiona pulled up short. At least everyone here listened to me. When I said stop, they stopped. When I said move, they moved. My father might have stripped me of my identity and tried to get rid of me when he couldn't figure out what was wrong with me, but I'd obviously inherited his imperial vibe and knew how to use it, despite eighteen years of abandonment and four Sectors of separation.

I looked at my crew one by one. At my friends. My real family. "Anyone preparing an escape pod when I get back can take their chances with the authorities. If you choose to stay on the ship, you're dying today with the *Endeavor*, me, and a hell of a lot of super soldier serum. You have five minutes to decide."

CHAPTER

2

I QUICKLY WORKED MY WAY THROUGH THE AIR LOCK and vacuum seal at the back of the ship and then strode into the stolen lab, spying the massive man immediately. He was a head taller than anything else in the room, including the dozens of refrigerated shelving units jam-packed with *vaccines*.

I took him in, surprised all over again. Not many people were naturally that big. Considering I'd found him with the lab, there was a good chance he'd been shot up with the super soldier mixture, and this was the result.

He looked over at my entrance, his dark eyes seeming to swiftly scan for threats. Probably in his midforties, he was a ruggedly handsome black man. Short, curling hair was barely graying at his temples, but the grizzled streaks became more pronounced as they trailed down his thick, somewhat shaggy beard. The beard seemed neglected. It wasn't neat and trim, as though he wanted it. It was bushy, as if it didn't belong.

Just like the previous times I'd come into the lab, he

watched me with neither hostility nor apprehension, but I couldn't say he looked exactly friendly, either. More like he was reserving judgment.

Slowly, he lowered the vial he'd been inspecting, the movement drawing my eyes to the capped test tube in his hand. The liquid inside looked like blood.

"Where did you find that?" I asked. Between jumps, I'd searched the lab and seen nothing of interest besides the false vaccines in their prepared syringes.

He tilted his head toward one of the refrigerated units. "I just uncovered a whole tray of identical blood samples in there—under a false bottom."

I wanted to blame the sudden dread surging inside me on the frantically wailing alarms, but it felt more like the panic of being forcibly strapped down, pricked with needles, and *examined*, inside and out.

My gaze darted back to the test tube. That label couldn't possibly look familiar. *Could it?*

Swallowing, I held out my hand. "May I?"

He handed over the vial, and I turned it so that I could read the label. The bold-print *Q.N.* lunged out at me like a punch to the solar plexus.

"This was part of the lab?" My breathing shortened as I tore my eyes away from my own initials and Sector 12 citizen matriculation number.

The man crossed his arms over his massive chest. "An important part, considering how well it was hidden. Not many samples left."

"You just said there was a whole tray." I felt light-headed. My heart hammered.

"Ten vials, all labeled the same way. I didn't find more of that same thing *anywhere* else."

From his tone, I knew he'd looked hard—and maybe not just here in this lab.

Horror scraped through me as the word *component* stumbled out from somewhere deep in my memories of blurry-headed days in the Overseer's lab—along with whispers of an enhancer. For the first time in as long as I could remember, I let my thoughts dive right into my childhood nightmare.

My blood. Component. Enhancer.

Terrible understanding clicked into place. They'd used one abomination to create another.

I couldn't stop the slight tremor in my fingers as I set the stolen piece of myself down on the table next to me, my pulse booming like the noises echoing around the cargo areas as Bridgebane's lackeys worked on breaking into the *Endeavor*.

"Is that something to worry about?" the big guy asked casually. If he hadn't glanced in the direction of the central cargo bay right then, I would have thought he meant the blood, not the relentless hammering.

A high-pitched sawing started up, and a second set of alarms squawked out of the central computer. My insides pitched sideways. We needed to hurry.

"And that?" he added, his eyebrows lifting.

"Yeah. Those…and a hell of a lot of other things." In fact, I couldn't think of one thing that *wasn't* a problem right now. "Head to the bridge if you want to live."

I'd told Fiona I'd get some samples. It made me queasy to carry through on my promise now that I knew the serum was probably based on my blood, but I grabbed an insulated medical satchel stamped with the galactic government's seal anyway and started filling it with false cure-alls from the nearest temperature-controlled unit. I didn't take the sample of my blood or try to find the other vials. Drawing attention to them somehow seemed worse than leaving without them.

While I gathered syringes, the man watched me, his gaze so heavy and intense that I was pretty sure he'd memorized the placement of every freckle on the bridge of my nose by the time I finished filling the bag and zipping it closed.

I mentally gave him ten seconds before I turned on my heel and left. He could stay or go, but I hoped he'd come. Like Jax and Fiona, the somewhat prominent vowels and lightly rounded tones of his speech practically screamed Outer Zones, and he had the same slightly weathered look they did, as if once upon a time, he'd spent a lot of his life outdoors.

Those weren't the only things about him that appealed to me. His nonthreatening calm had just prevented me from completely losing it. It wasn't every day you realized your mortal enemy had most likely made a weapon from your own blood. And with Bridgebane doing everything he could to get it back, my freak-out time was limited.

I beckoned with my free hand. "Move it, Big Guy. We don't have long." His ten seconds were up, and it was time for him to squeeze his big, bearded, and possibly genetically modified self into an escape pod.

Hesitating, he studied me with uncertain eyes. They shifted to the bag I was holding.

I tightened my grip on the strap. "Look, I don't care if you're military or civilian or a scientist or a victim or whatever," I said. "You came with the lab by accident.

The Dark Watch is about to board my ship, so unless you're one of them, you'd better get off it if you want to live."

"Are you offering me a pod?" he asked.

I nodded, wincing as what sounded like a different saw scraped its serrated teeth right over my frayed nerves. "Let's go."

"You take a pod," he said, not moving. "I can't let those Dark Watch goons get the lab back."

Not only did he sound like a rebel from one of the trampled Sectors, but he acted like one, too. I knew I liked him.

"They won't," I told him. "I know exactly how to take it out of their reach. And a captain doesn't abandon ship."

Something in his eyes glinted, as though he might have approved.

With that, I thought we'd reached an understanding, but as I turned to leave, he leaped forward and snatched the medical bag from my hand. He'd moved fast. Super soldier fast.

I swung around with a glare. "I need that." If Fiona opted for a pod and actually managed to escape, I had no doubt she could eventually figure out how to use the samples for something good, like helping invalids left crippled by the war.

Shaking his head, he tossed the bag onto the metal lab table behind him, blocking my access to it with his huge body. I tried twice to grab it again, but he was incredibly quick and like a freaking building— impossible to get around.

"You're wasting time," I ground out, unable to ignore the screeching that was coming from the starboard door.

It was getting louder. They were probably most of the way through.

"Get it later…if there is one." He jerked his hairy chin toward the exit in a get-the-hell-out-of-here type of way.

Metal cried out as though in pain, and the *Endeavor* gave a sickening groan. *Later* seemed entirely unlikely right now, especially given my plans.

To hell with it. I didn't reach for the bag again.

"Let's go," Big Guy said, herding me toward the door.

I was pretty sure that was my line, but we were headed in the same direction anyway.

We worked our way through the vacuum seal and air lock, closing them behind us again before hurrying toward the bridge, our footsteps accompanied by a deafening chorus of ship-wide alerts, hammers, and saws. The bridge doors slid open at my voice command, and all four of my crew members looked over at Big Guy and me—even Shiori, who couldn't see.

Emotion lodged in my chest. This was it—and not one of them was positioned over a pod hatch, let alone setting up for a scrambled, last-hope escape in one. They'd chosen, and I couldn't tell if my heart soared or sank. It definitely swelled.

"Where are the samples?" Fiona asked.

"Still in the lab." I strode to my console and silenced the blaring alarms, leaving only the visual readouts.

I looked pointedly at Fiona again. "And they don't matter if you're not gearing up an escape pod right now."

She opened her mouth to argue but then shut it. I'd

announced that it was a pod or death, and my crew knew I always meant what I said. The two were likely synonymous anyway.

"I won't let the military take back the serum. They've been working on that enhancer since I was a kid, and if we stole their secret lab and their only batch, there's a good chance it'll take them years to create it again." And if my freakish blood really was the base ingredient, and they'd used their entire supply to produce those thousands of fake cure-alls, which my gut feeling told me they had, then they were about to be shit out of luck.

Fiona's brow furrowed. "How do you know they've been working on that serum since you were a kid?"

Ignoring her question, I informed them of my decision. "I'm taking the *Endeavor* and the false vaccines into the Black Widow. If you don't want to come with me, you need to get out *right now*."

The crew all looked at me with little surprise. In addition to categorically needing to keep the enhancer out of the Overseer's hands, we were out of time, and we'd run out of chances to get away. Capital punishment or, if someone was feeling *very* generous, life in jail were our only future options. It was really a no-brainer, at least for me.

The ship groaned again, and my console flashed to indicate a breach at the starboard door. Dark Watch goons were inside the air lock. They still had to break through the safety entrance, but that door was nothing compared to the outer wall.

Bridgebane's voice barked over the com. "I'm taking the Overseer's lab back, and you're all going to be court-martialed in Sector 12."

"Tell him who you are, Tess," Jax whispered, the scar on his cheek whitening from the tension in his jaw. "It'll stop him. Your father…"

I laughed. It burst out of me, awful. Then I squared my shoulders and told my best friend and first mate the one thing he still didn't know about me.

"My father handed me over to Bridgebane when I was eight years old, and only three days after my mother died, with strict orders to keep me in an air lock on *Dark Watch 12* until the ship was out of my home Sector and then float me into space."

Jax's jaw dropped. Miko gasped. Shiori stayed silent.

"Who the hell is your asshole father?" Fiona asked.

I glanced at Big Guy, who was staring at me. I didn't mind that he was here for the truth, but maybe that was because I wouldn't have to worry about it for long.

"Bridgebane is the one who took me to Starway 8, but he said if he ever saw me again, he'd do what my father first asked."

Jax cursed. "So Bridgebane is the good guy in all this?"

"Bridgebane is a bastard. And my name will only get us all killed faster than we're already going to get killed anyway."

"Who the hell is your asshole father?" Fiona practically snarled.

I wanted to snarl back what had always been in my heart. *That man has never been my father!*

"Who the hell are *you*?" Fiona demanded.

My pulse pounded so hard I heard it in my ears. Tess Bailey was about to die along with the rest of us. "I'm Quintessa Novalight."

My friend stumbled back against Jax's broad chest. That was the power of a name.

The blood visibly drained from Fiona's face. "As in *Galactic Overseer* Novalight's dead daughter?" she choked out.

Clearly, not so dead after all. Yet.

Nodding, I owned up to the name I hadn't used in years and to the family I wished I didn't have. "Daddy is the evil overlord of the galaxy, and Bridgebane is my uncle."

Everyone stared in shock, even Jax, who already knew who I was.

"So... No one's leaving?" I eventually asked, not surprised, but not happy, either.

No one spoke. The *Endeavor* rattled like a sick metallic animal and then groaned again hard.

"We're as dead out there as we are in here," Miko finally answered. No one contradicted her, so I figured she spoke for them all.

"Big Guy?" I asked, turning to the bearded man.

He just shook his head.

Fine. His choice, although I had no idea why. Maybe he was as wanted by the Dark Watch as we were.

"Power up, Jax, and get ready to punch it. Miko, set us ninety degrees to the left." Portside was nothing but the Black Widow. Devoid of all light, the huge, empty circle interrupting the stars looked like a bottomless pit and gave new meaning to the oft-used expression "endless Dark."

I turned away from the window, my stomach knotting. I feared the unknown as much as anyone else.

Focusing on my friends again didn't help. I had zero

expectations for an afterlife. I'd never see them again. This was it.

I cleared the lump from my throat. "Strap in. Don't strap in. It doesn't really matter at this point," I said.

We'd never been much for emotional speeches, so I didn't give one. Shiori unbuckled herself from the captain's chair, got up, and felt her way to Miko. The two women stood side by side near the navigation controls, holding hands. Fiona and Jax stayed close together. I was alone. Except for Big Guy. He stayed pretty close.

My gaze returned to the black hole, as if drawn by its massive gravitational force. Twenty-six years, and it hadn't been a bad life, even if a lot of it hadn't been fun. I'd wreaked more havoc on the galactic government than most rebels could manage in five lifetimes. With the help of my crew, I'd kept the Outer Zone colonies from true starvation for years. And everything else I ever had, I gave to the kids on Starway 8. I didn't regret a thing.

And I was a Novalight. I wouldn't go out like a sigh in the Dark. I'd go out like a fucking bomb.

I reached for the external com and opened the line to Bridgebane. "Your boarding crew has thirty seconds to detach. After that, I'm taking the *Endeavor* and your *vaccines* into the Black Widow. Everyone on this ship would rather die than see that serum back in the hands of the Galactic Overseer." I lifted my finger but then pressed firmly down on the button again. "By the way, this is Quintessa, and you can tell my tyrant father that I hate his fucking guts."

I pulled my hand off the com. The line went dead, then blinked red again.

"Quin?" Bridgebane said.

I counted down in my head. *Thirty, twenty-nine, twenty-eight...*

"Let's talk, Quin," my uncle said. "Give me the lab, and I'll see what I can do."

Fifteen, fourteen, thirteen...

"I saved you, Quin. You owe me."

Five, four, three, two...

I turned to Jax, seeing the Black Widow looming through the wall of windows behind him. I felt a lurch and hoped it was the boarding cruiser beating a retreat.

"Quin!" Bridgebane yelled over the com.

A second later, the Dark Watch frigate fired on us. The resulting jolt nearly knocked me off my feet. Silent alarms flared all over my controls—pressurization compromised in three zones. Another blast like that, and they could disable us enough to hold us in place.

I gripped my console to steady myself. The *Endeavor* was a good ship. It was too bad I had to take her out.

Each beat of my heart felt like an explosion inside my chest.

Some ends are just a new beginning...

My mother's words to me, when she'd gotten so sick. Too sick for anyone to save her.

The Black Widow stretched before us, ready to snare us in her web. Nothing escaped a black hole. Not light. Not matter. Maybe not even a soul.

Slowly, I exhaled. Some ends were just the end.

"Hit it, Jaxon." I nodded crisply to my first mate.

Jax looked at me one last time. Our eyes met, and seven years of shared history struck me in a bittersweet rush. Then he grabbed Fiona around the waist and threw the hyperdrive switch with a cosmic roar.

I inhaled sharply. Everything blurred. My bones crunched, and my chest folded in on the thousands of things I'd still wanted to do as the *Endeavor* shot toward the event horizon—and the end of us all.

CHAPTER

3

THE DARKNESS *FELT* CRUSHING, BUT THERE WASN'T A single thing that actually changed. I was no science freak, but as far as I knew, we should have been compressed into nothing by now—the ship, the crew. Everything.

"Hold on," Big Guy rumbled next to me. He snaked a powerful arm around my waist.

Who am I to argue? I wrapped my free arm around him and tightened my grip on my vibrating console.

The damaged ship rattled around us, noisy and frightening, but I had faith in her. The *Endeavor* would hold tight until something happened. Because something was bound to happen, right? You didn't fly into a black hole and then just…nothing.

Boom! Tiny pinpricks of light streaked past us. I did a double take. *Stars?*

What was happening? It looked and felt exactly like flying through hyperspace.

Holy shit! We hadn't set a destination. We could race straight into a moon, a planet, an asteroid belt. A fucking star!

"Jax!" I screamed.

Jax bellowed something incoherent and took us out of warp speed without the usual slowdown, which was already jarring enough. My feet flew out from under me, but Big Guy stayed upright and kept me upright, too. I lost my hold on my console and swung in his grip, my upper body smacking against his chest while everyone else fell down like dolls with floppy legs.

I got my feet back under me faster than a shooting star when my console started flashing out emergency warnings. Damaged circuits—bridge sector. Living quarters—oxygen at 57% and falling. Starboard door—open.

I hastily typed out the command that would close the safety hatch to the lower deck and cut off the bedrooms from the rest of the ship. They would lose their air, but we wouldn't. The outer starboard door probably had a hole the size of Bridgebane in it, but the rest of the air lock was still intact. We could fly like this, as long as the engines didn't conk out.

"We're not dead!" Jax leaped off the floor, whooping like a maniac and pumping his fists in the air. "We're not fucking dead!"

We all took a second to absorb that. It was unbelievable. Shock and amazement left my limbs trembling and weak. At the same time, it felt as though someone had just slammed a shot of adrenaline straight into my heart. Numbness gave way to a burst of life, and we laughed and screamed together, jumping up and down. We were completely hysterical.

Except for Shiori, who sat up facing the wall. And Big Guy. Nothing seemed to surprise him at all.

His lack of a reaction calmed mine, and I pushed my

hair back with shaking hands. My smile shrank. The Black Widow hadn't eaten us, but that didn't mean we were safe.

No one had reached out to us yet, but I used radio waves to verify that we were alone. Nothing came back to me, and the monitors weren't picking up anything unusual other than low levels of blackbody radiation.

"I'm seeing Hawking radiation behind us. It looks like a small black hole," I said. Had we come through that? Was it like using a front and back door?

I craned my neck to look around us, but the views outside the window panels seemed perfectly normal. No rip through space, no bright tear, no vast nebular cloud. There was nothing out of the ordinary, and my best guess as to how we'd gotten here was something I could barely wrap my mind around.

Whatever luck had come our way, though—I would take it.

Relief breathed new life into my lungs, driving out some of the remaining fear and tightness. "The Dark Watch didn't follow." We'd stolen the serum, we weren't dead, and the fact that no one knew where we were anymore was the sweetest frosting on this whole messed-up cake.

"We just went through a black hole," Fiona said, disbelief still heavy in her voice. "And lived."

Jax gave her a rare, big smile, one that actually stretched his face. "And left those goons in the dust."

"Maybe the Black Widow is only masquerading as a black hole." Excitement glimmered in Fiona's expression. "Maybe it's using similar properties to camouflage something else."

"Wormhole?" I suggested, voicing my unlikely thought.

"Yes!" Fiona's eyes widened. "A shortcut with two mouths."

If that were true, how had no one figured it out? "But there have been experiments. Probes. They never reappeared anywhere else."

"Maybe it had something to do with going in at warp speed?" Jax offered.

I shrugged. "Could be." That was as plausible as anything else.

Everything about this was fascinating and mysterious, but right now, figuring out our new location in the galaxy was more important.

"Where are we?" I asked. We needed to land in a place where we could repair the *Endeavor* and get new numbers up on her. Then we'd be anonymous again, just one more lonely cargo ship making its way through the Dark.

"From what I'm seeing, it looks like Sector 2." Miko grabbed the old and yellowed manual to double-check the coordinates that were popping up in rows of green numbers across her controls. "Yes, definitely somewhere in 2."

Shiori finally turned and groped for Miko's unoccupied chair beside the navigation console. A thin line of blood trailed down the center of her forehead and curved along the side of her nose.

Damn it. She must have hit something when she'd fallen. She was conscious, though, and looked calm, which was more than I could say for myself.

Miko reached out to steady her grandmother and helped Shiori into the navigator's chair. Shiori wiped the blood away when it dripped to her chin, leaving a smear of red across the back of her hand.

Miko shot her grandmother worried glances while still dealing with our most pressing issue—locking down our exact location in the vastness of Sector 2.

I tore my eyes away from them.

"Fiona, can you do the honors?" I pulled the first aid kit out from under my console and handed it to our resident scientist. I could fix Shiori up myself, but Fiona could do it better.

Using sterile compresses and saline solution, Fiona started cleaning Shiori's cut and wiping the blood off her face, all the while telling the blind woman what she was doing in a quiet voice. Shiori was really a grandmother to us all, and Fiona treated her with a gentleness she showed to no one else.

While she worked, I turned my mind back to our new location, a good *half a galaxy away* from where we'd just been, give or take a few solar systems. Sector 2 wasn't beaten and battered like the Outer Zones, but it wasn't exactly a thriving hub of civilization, either. I'd only been here twice before and had never lingered. I didn't know the Sector well, and I was still a little bowled over by recent events. Ideas weren't coming to me clearly. A big part of me was still stuck on the fact that we weren't dead. We were possibly the only living beings to know that the Black Widow did not, in fact, kill you. It spat you out in Sector 2.

The hypothetical wormhole had just gotten real. I was pretty sure we should keep that to ourselves. Having a handy escape route only we knew about was like winning the galactic lottery or raking in all the chips from the biggest game of poker ever played. This could be our future ace in the hole.

I glanced out the windows, still uneasy for several reasons. A random Sector was fine. Leaving *Dark Watch 12* and Captain Bridgebane behind was more than fine, but it was too bad we didn't have enough power left to get us back to a place we really knew.

"What's in Sector 2?" I asked, hoping someone else's brain was already up and running better than mine. "We need a place that can sustain life and has a bright enough sun to recharge the *Endeavor*." Unfortunately, there weren't that many. Asking for a sunny, habitable planet was a tall order.

"Flyhole," Jaxon suggested.

"Full of criminals," Shiori declared from behind Fiona's ministrations.

Well, technically speaking, so was the *Endeavor*, but no one mentioned that.

And Flyhole wasn't a planet. It was a spacedock orbiting a barren moon. It had decent sunlight, though, and would have what we needed for repairs, just not at an acceptable price. Also, the *Endeavor* was as likely to be stripped by space rovers as restored to working order.

Fiona deftly patted down the sides of the sterile tape she'd used to seal Shiori's cut, her steady hands those of someone who'd patched up plenty of people.

"Good as new," Fiona said.

Shiori murmured her thanks.

"What about Nickleback?" Fiona asked, straightening as she tossed the bloody compresses into the trash.

Nickleback. Nickleback. What do I know about Nickleback?

Oh, right. "Isn't that the place with the giant carnivorous spiders?" Another one of the Overseer's science experiments. The modified arachnids had been supposed to help aggressively control the growing pest population on one of the galaxy's more productive crop planets. If I remembered correctly, it had worked for about a dozen years. Then the spiders had begun to breed into something bigger, scarier. Now natural selection was at work, and the humans on that planet weren't coming out on top.

"Oh, yeah." Fiona grimaced. "Forget Nickleback."

A bright electrical snap from my console sent me jumping back so fast I slammed into Big Guy's solid frame. My controls went utterly black for the first time ever. Every whir, bump, and groan that was the constant music under my fingertips went silent, and my throat tightened so abruptly it closed.

Holding my breath, I looked over at Jaxon's control panel. It was still functioning, thank the Sky Mother.

I exhaled slowly. I needed to get the *Endeavor* docked and resting fast, or she was going to die on us. And if she died, we all died, too. There wasn't enough light from the distant stars to impact our solar panels, and the ship's energy core would eventually drain completely. We'd end up floating. The air-renewal apparatus would shut down along with all the other systems. Without any power, we'd suffocate. I'd seen ghost ships like that, and I'd rather blow up than have a gradual, helpless death be my fate.

I cleared my throat. "Jax, you've got control."

He nodded, and my brain started storming for answers again about where we could go—in a radius we could actually reach.

"Air. Water. Sunlight. Supplies. New parts," I muttered. What had everything we needed to get us rolling again?

"Albion 5," Big Guy said.

I tilted my head back to look at him. The colossus was still right next to me, all big and bushy and weirdly reassuring.

Albion 5... I closed my eyes, trying to picture a map of Sector 2 in my head. One system stood out from the rest as having at least two planets the right distance from their sun to sustain life. The smaller rock had required terraforming and was still a work in progress. The larger one had been inhabited practically since the first Earth exoduses had begun. It would have everything we needed, including anonymity.

I opened my eyes again. "It could work." I looked at my crew for their opinions. "What do you think?"

"I think we can get there." Miko immediately searched for and then started typing in the coordinates. Once they were actually set, though, she winced. "It's going to be close."

That was what I'd feared.

"I'll redirect all power to the engines," Jax said, his big hands moving rapidly over his console.

A moment later, the bridge went dark except for the main control panels that were still functioning. Even the low hum of the air recycling system stopped, and Jax's console beeped out an oxygen-levels warning.

"Even if we don't make it all the way," Jax said, "we should still get close enough to Albion 5's sun to recharge."

Fiona huffed a little sourly. "Let's hope so," she said under her breath.

I was hoping for better than that. For the first time in

five years, I was desperate to land, get off my ship, and breathe air that hadn't been filtered and recycled a thousand times over. And then I wanted to get the *Endeavor* repaired while I figured out what the hell to do next.

My father thought the battle was over. For all intents and purposes, he'd imposed his science and his law across the 18 Sectors, but there were still insurgencies to crush all over the Dark. The human spirit was not so easily controlled. For many, the conflict was ongoing and would be until they either won or died. What could those rebels do if I gave them the serum? Turn the tide of war?

But there were already places hovering on the edge of survival, where extinction was a word to fear. Could I live with myself, knowing I might be launching the galaxy into a whole new generation of rampant bloodshed? Knowing I could be changing people's bodies? Knowing they could evolve into something else, like those giant carnivorous spiders had?

For all the sterile labs, careful experimentation, and strict controls, science was still just a big guessing game. Sometimes, you guessed wrong. And I only knew one thing about those false vaccines: if they were based on my blood, then they were built around whatever was genetically *wrong* with me. And the more people who found out I was an anomaly, the more hunted I'd be.

"Tess?" Jax questioned.

His voice brought me out of my brooding thoughts. I may have been eleven years his junior and a few inches shorter, but I was the captain, and he waited for my orders.

"Brace yourselves for hyperspace." I sat in my locked

chair and gripped the armrests. Big Guy, who now knew half my secrets, stood next to me. When everyone else looked stable, I nodded to Jaxon. "And go."

CHAPTER

4

OUR CRAZY LUCK HELD A LITTLE LONGER, AND WE made it to Albion 5's exosphere with half a power bar to spare. Jax turned all our solar panels in the right direction the second we came out of warp speed. We still might fall apart, but at least we were recharging.

After a rattling and frankly terrifying descent toward the capital city on the planet's surface, we called in and were offered a docking port in exchange for a small fortune on the bizarrely named Squirrel Tree. I doubted there was a squirrel within a hundred-mile radius of Albion City—if there were any at all on this overpopulated rock.

We landed on our designated platform on the immense docking tower and then powered down, all of us drooping a little in relief. It had been a hell of a day. After a moment, though, the quiet became almost as nerve-racking as listening to the *Endeavor* whine and groan about the holes in her walls. Tension snapped through me. I hated being confined when we weren't moving.

I popped out of my chair and left the bridge. The

second I could slap my palm down on the interior lock, I opened what was left of the starboard doors and breathed. A few deep inhales and long exhales helped settle my nerves. Seeing my mangled air lock nearly undid the good the fresh air was doing me, though. The outer door was utterly destroyed.

Despite the obvious and extensive damage, it was surprisingly easy to refocus. I'd worry about repairs—and how much they were going to cost us—soon. Right now, I was just happy to be alive. Once again, and against all odds, the five of us had somehow made it through.

I leaned out of the ship and looked around. The view from the high-up platform was spectacular—if you liked glass and metal and rock. Sprawling, spire-filled cityscapes were fine with me; I wasn't much for green. Flora and fauna were about a million miles out of my comfort zone. I did like healthy, breathable atmospheres, though, and the sky here was clear and blue, with hints of pink and purple hazing the horizon. Three visible moons hung over the city, and a small planet hovered in the distance—the one that was undergoing terraforming, I presumed.

I sniffed a few times, savoring the mix of freshness and warmth as faint sounds from street level drifted up to blend with the low hum of crafts and transports flying around and above the maze of docks. The sunny, midday air seemed free of heavy smog and gritty particles. They must have been doing something right in Sector 2, if the lack of pollution was any indication. Not all early colonists had been concerned with sustainable development, thinking there were infinite planets out there to appropriate. There weren't, but some people hadn't figured that out before driving their new homes into the ground.

The crew and Big Guy came up behind me, taking their turn at relishing having an open door—inhaling, testing out the atmosphere on their senses, taking in the view, and squinting against the brightness reflected off Albion City's countless windows.

Fiona sucked down air until her chest lifted and expanded so much that even Jax had to look. "Well, that does a body good," she announced.

I nodded. The air on Albion 5 didn't smell bad at all. Not as good as anywhere in Sector 12. Better than on Hourglass Mile. About like Starway 8, thanks to the orphanage's first-rate ventilation system.

Behind us, the *Endeavor* belched out the recycled air we'd been breathing for months. My lungs felt different already, expanded. It was time to renew. Rebuild. Figure out life. I rolled my shoulders to relieve some of the tension. Maybe I'd even understand myself one of these days.

I left the others to enjoy their first taste of Albion 5 while I ducked back into the ship to change out of my flight suit and wash my face. What I found in my room was even more of a mess than the ruined starboard door. There was a big hole in the wall, and many of my belongings had been sucked out into space. I'd lost bedding, books, and a lot of clothes. Anything that hadn't been screwed down or locked in the closet was gone.

I pieced together a decent outfit from what was left and then turned my back on the shambles of my once-tidy living space. I refused to mutter even a single curse. We'd survived. Period.

We needed to know what we were dealing with in terms of time and cost, so I steeled myself for a thorough look around the *Endeavor*. An hour later, I couldn't fathom how we'd survived. Shot full of holes, we'd traveled at warp speed and then put the ship through the heat and pressure of atmospheric entry. Not to mention the fact that we'd jumped right into a *black hole*.

The repair budget was going kill us, even if the Black Widow hadn't.

From Jaxon's colorful language as he inspected the inside and outside of the ship along with me, I was pretty sure he agreed. Big Guy came along, too, looking stoic. He grunted every now and then. He seemed to know his way around electronics and fixed a few things while Jax and I took inventory of the more significant problems.

I limited the list of issues to actual structural damage on the *Endeavor*, although it seemed as though it should have included a lot more, like how to take back having revealed my true identity, and what the hell to do with the stolen lab.

Miko found us finishing up in Cargo Bay 3 and insisted that the *Endeavor* wasn't the only one that needed recharging. We ate a quick meal all together and formed a plan. I would head into the city immediately to see about parts and repairs while Jax got busy on the damaged circuits. No matter how exhausted I was, there was no waiting until tomorrow to find a repair person for the *Endeavor*. Whether we stayed a while or left Albion 5 quickly was fluid and would depend on how things went. Being *able* to go was a must, which meant patching holes and fixing the electrical problems.

Fiona opted to stay on board and set her lab to rights after all the hard bumps we'd just experienced, and Miko and Shiori almost never left the ship. The *Endeavor*, or right next to her, was where they felt the safest.

Everyone came to see me off after lunch, even Big Guy, who'd declined to eat with us. Anxious to get going, I hopped down onto the platform and then bounced a little, getting used to the gravity level here. It wasn't far from the universal standard used on ships, but there was a slight drag on my weight that would take some getting used to.

The heat from the dock's dark surface rammed into me from the feet up as I reached into the shadowed doorway to grab the go-pack I'd snagged from my closet. I double-checked the pack for essentials as I squinted against the early-afternoon sunlight, both bothered by and enjoying the rare-for-me sensations of planet-dwelling life.

Big Guy jumped down next to me while I rummaged in my bag, my eyes watering and my skin already feeling baked. I knew from experience that the impression of being shoved into a big, bright oven would pass. Objectively, Albion 5 wasn't that hot. It was reputed to have a pleasant climate overall, and I'd seen forests and an intriguing large body of water as we'd dropped down from the Dark. It was simply that I'd been a space rat for so long that being on the ground again took some getting used to.

We made occasional stops, usually in big cities, and there was always an adjustment period to get used to the inevitable variances from one place to another. I didn't long for a planet home, but I did enjoy coming down. Being on the ground reminded me of my mother.

"You got everything you need?" Jax asked.

I nodded, zipping up my pack again on the bottle of water, snacks, a sweater, a few implements for basic hygiene, a fold-up multitool that looked harmless enough but actually contained a very sharp knife, and some universal currency. Everything I needed in case I couldn't come home tonight.

There wasn't anything conspicuous about me now that I'd ditched my all-gray, full-length flight suit for more typical civilian clothing. My fitted black pants, ankle boots, and pale-yellow tank top were more weather-appropriate anyway. I figured I'd be fine, despite the Dark Watch's chilling propensity to arrest people for little or no reason.

"Are you sure you don't want me to come with you?" Jax asked, crouching in the sawed-open doorway. He rubbed the back of his neck in that way he had when he was torn about something.

"No, thanks," I answered, meaning it. I was competent in any huge galactic city full of tech and crawling with anonymous faces. It was anywhere natural that freaked me out. "Just work on whatever's wrong with those electrical circuits, like we said—especially anything leading to the bridge. And guard the ship," I added.

Jax nodded. He never argued with that last part. It wasn't so much the ship he'd worry about if he left it unprotected by either me or him; it was the people on it, people he thought of as his own. It left deep, invisible scars when you came back from a battle that had really only been a diversion to find your home burned and your family incinerated inside it. Wife. Kids. Everyone and everything—*gone*. There had been nothing left, except for a trap. That was when they'd taken Jax and locked him up.

Huge, scarred, been-to-the-other-side-and-back-of-just-about-everything—that was Jax. He wasn't paranoid. He was vigilant with the people he loved.

"So, Big Guy…" I turned to the not-so-stranger who was more of a big beast of a man than even Jax. "You got a name?"

"I do." He clapped me on the shoulder so hard I might have shrunk an inch or two. He squeezed, and my shoulder went numb. If it hadn't been for his friendly smile, I'd have thought he was trying to break my bones. "It's See-You-Around."

With that, he sauntered toward the elevator tube that would take him down the many levels of the massive Squirrel Tree to the streets of Albion City.

I stared after him without a blink. A moment later, he was gone.

Shit. A man full of my secrets had just walked away, and short of gunning him down, there wasn't much I could do about it.

I glanced up at Jax, who now stood leaning against the doorframe. He shrugged, not seeming too worried.

"That was abrupt," I said, my words making me realize that worry wasn't my primary feeling, either. I was stung.

I'd gotten used to having Big Guy around. He was clearly no fan of the Dark Watch, and I'd been about to offer him a spot on our crew. He'd stuck with us when the going got more than tough, and that meant something to me. Truly scary and adversarial situations were the sieve through which real friendships were formed, where the watery and weak washed through and away and those left standing beside you were the solid units a person could count on for life.

Or in Big Guy's case, for a few harrowing days.

"He was weird," Fiona announced from alongside Jax in the doorway, shoulder to shoulder. Well, more like head to triceps. Fiona was a foot shorter.

"He was awesome," I argued. He'd gone into the Black Widow with us. He'd kept me on my feet. He'd fixed the lights in the central cargo bay. And I had a feeling he'd keep my secrets. "He had no bodily functions. How cool is that?"

Miko's brow wrinkled in thought as she leaned against the other side of the open doorframe. "Maybe he was a cyborg or something."

"My vote's for super soldier," I said. "They must have tested that enhancer on someone."

"If that's the case, I don't think he was a willing lab rat," Fiona said. "One time when I checked on him in the lab, he was glaring at those syringes like he wanted to destroy them."

Odd then, that he'd just walked away from them.

"Maybe the Sky Mother sent him to us," Jax said in a low voice.

My immediate denial died on my tongue. Jax was the spiritual one of the two of us, although he'd never tried to convert me or anything. I still usually naysaid him right away. This time, I couldn't. There *had* been a lot of inexplicable things about Big Guy. Still, I had trouble believing the Sky Mother was anything other than a big fat sun.

"Sent him for what?" I asked.

Jaxon looked at me, a challenge in his coffee-dark eyes. He rarely pressed these points, but I could tell he wanted to now. "Maybe to keep the Black Widow from crushing us into nothing."

There was no denying that something strange had happened in Sector 14. Going into the Widow, I'd fully expected to become less than dust. And yet here we all were—alive. I was more likely to look for a scientific explanation, though. Something involving physics, not religion.

"The Sky Mother is all-powerful," Shiori said from just behind Miko in the shadows of the ship. Stepping forward, she emerged into the sunlight next to the others, turning her sightless eyes toward its warmth.

Miko stopped her grandmother when Shiori got too close to the edge, the blunt end of her severed hand crossing the older woman's middle as she cautioned her to be careful.

Shiori clearly wanted off the ship, if only for a few minutes, so Jaxon jumped down and then lifted her to the platform. We almost never put down the stairs. Waiting for them to fold and unfold never seemed worth it.

As soon as she was steady, Jax let go of her, and Shiori lifted her face to the sun. She breathed deeply through her small, somewhat flat nose. The white hair that had escaped the bun at her nape fluttered on a breeze I'd hardly noticed before, reminding me of the images I'd seen of the tattered flags of the old nations as they'd been ripped down and the galaxy burned into one.

Shiori spoke again, her soft, musical accent lending an almost prophetess quality to her words. "The Sky Mother balances everything. From the center of the galaxy, She sends out Her rays of light."

Yeah. That's because it's a freaking star, and they're bright.

And if *She* and *Her Powers* really balanced

anything, they would have kicked my father off his throne a long time ago—maybe before he'd murdered millions in the night.

"I'm off, then," I said, slicing through a conversation I wasn't entirely comfortable with. Besides, there were more pressing matters than debating theology—like finding someone to repair the *Endeavor*. And I loved both Jax and Shiori too much to try to rattle their faith with my own bitterness and doubt.

"Watch your back out there, partner," Jax said with a single, solemn nod.

My heart clenched a little in my chest. Jax didn't use that name for me much anymore. Partner. That was what we'd been back in the mines, when there'd been a different type of overseer with a whip at our backs.

I nodded to him, but as I walked toward the elevator tube, hiking the strap of my bag up over my shoulder, I couldn't help remembering that first day on Hourglass Mile, when rough hands had thrown me at Jax. He'd been a man already, thirty years old and no mistaking it. I'd been nineteen and scared to death.

They'd brought us in on the same day, Jax half insane with grief and me still stunned that I'd been caught, neither of us having any idea that the warden's bright idea was to pair male and female inmates off together for daily work in the mines. The warden had figured the fraternization would help keep the peace, which it did, I supposed. Once pairs were formed, that was it. No changes were made unless someone's sentence was up or someone died. Some people, like Fiona, ended up with a lover. Other women got an abuser. And some, like me, found a friend for life.

Lady Luck had been with me that day, too. Maybe she wasn't such a fickle bitch.

CHAPTER

5

Two people on the avenue at the bottom of the Squirrel Tree both directed me to the same place: Ganavan's Products and Parts. It wasn't too far—still in the docking district and within easy walking distance—so I figured it was a good place to start.

I found the shop at the base of a towering, warehouse-type structure. It was recessed into the ground a few feet, requiring me to take a short flight of stairs down to access it from street level. A bell tinkled over the door when I swung it open, surprising me with the light, merry chiming. I couldn't help appreciating the quaint touch in the otherwise industrial setting of the city's sprawling, somewhat dingy docks.

Inside, the shop was bigger than I'd expected and crowded with metallic shelving packed with more *stuff* than any space rat could ever possibly want. It was almost overwhelming—and half of it was covered in dust. Motes twirled in the air, floating in the sunbeams streaming in through the high-up windows that let in most of the shop's light.

I didn't see anyone behind the register to query about repairs, so I walked the aisles, looking for anything that might be of use. I picked up forty rounds of LW-9 bullets in a sleek metal case for our Grayhawk handguns, but I didn't really need things like the rest of this—gadgets and doodads and crap. I needed reinforced metal panels and someone who could weld them onto my ship.

I scanned the shelves for fuses and wiring, too, but didn't see anything. The *Endeavor*'s electrical components weren't in great shape, even with Big Guy's brief help, and my console was currently dead. I'd have to see, but I hoped Jaxon would end up being enough of an electrician to fix it. When it came to a ship's central power grid, I had some skills myself.

"Can I help you?" a man asked.

I turned and watched the speaker walk toward me from what looked like a back office, his steps silent and almost prowling. Despite his height and imposing physique, I might not have heard him coming if he hadn't made his presence known.

Was this Ganavan? He was tall, with at least a few inches on me. He was wide, too, but mainly in the shoulders. His body looked healthy and trim. Like me, I thought his origins could probably be traced back to pre-exodus Caucasian. Unlike me, he had a healthy tan.

The fact that he was tall, dark, and hot didn't stop my usual default mode from kicking in—to assess any stranger I met and determine how I would try to bring that person down in a fight.

I came up with a defensive scenario before he got too close. A ducking spin as he came at me, his own weight hopefully throwing him off-balance as I slid out of the way. A quick, hard kick to the back of a knee to get him lower than me. A sleeper hold from behind with my arm in a tight V around his neck, cutting off the blood flow through his arteries. With any luck, I could knock him out without ever touching his windpipe.

Unfortunately, looking at him, I estimated my chances of success with any of that at about eight percent, which made me glad there was no reason to think he was unfriendly.

He watched me, too, his brown eyes like lasers. I'd rarely been subjected to such a steady stare, especially from a gaze that held definite hints of interest and appreciation. My body started to heat from more than just the sunlight filtering down from the high windows. The light hit him at an angle, turning his eyes a tawny amber, like those of a jungle predator.

No. A jungle animal would scare me, and this man didn't, despite his obvious physical advantage. His eyes were more the color of dark honey, appealing, all warm and tempting in the sun.

My taste buds seemed to burst to life with the memory of sweetness on my tongue. Starway 8 was one of the few places left in the galaxy with an actual apiary, and the liquid gold the director sold to the wealthy elite in Sector 12 was the main source of revenue for the orphanage. This man's eyes looked just like honey number seven—my favorite. Almost the darkest. The darker honeys had more flavor.

He stopped a few feet from me, and those honey-brown eyes dipped, taking me in from my head to my toes. My clothing was skintight, and I felt a blush flare under his slow inspection.

Finally, he looked up. "Just checking for weapons."

I snorted. "Really? Weapons? I haven't heard that one before."

He winked at me like the scoundrel I highly suspected he was. "We're inventive out here in 2. Where're you from?"

"What makes you think I'm not from here?"

"You're a 12-er. I can hear it in your posh voice."

Time seemed to slow down as my mind processed his words one by one, even though it only took a second. I hardly spoke to anyone besides my crew, and they didn't care what I sounded like. Blurring my trail outside of the *Endeavor* meant it was time to work on a new accent, though. It was too bad. The precise, cut-glass diction was one of the only things I liked about Sector 12.

I crossed my arms, one hip jutting out as I shifted my balance. "If you already knew, then why did you ask?"

He shook his head as though dismayed, his close-cropped brown hair glinting in the slanting, mote-filled rays. His hair spiked a little haphazardly in front where some cowlicks seemed to have minds of their own. My fingers twitched with the sudden urge to reach out and smooth them down.

Strange. I usually resisted all forms of uniformity in conscious protest of the oppressive galactic order. And wanting to touch a total stranger was weird in itself.

"Why. Did. You. Ask." He enunciated each word pointedly, although even that didn't mask the slight drawl in his voice or the humor underlying it. "Hear that? You've got to slide it all together, fancy pants. Like this: why'd'ya'ask?"

Fancy pants? I arched one brow—high—and then dutifully parroted, "Why'd'ya'ask?"

"Good." He gave a quick nod of approval. "Now lose the imperious look, and you might fit in around the docks."

I gaped—inwardly, at least. On the outside, I just stood there. *What the hell?* How had he pegged me so fast, and so freaking well?

"I haven't been to Sector 12 in a long time. I'm from 8, if you really want to know."

"Really *wanna* know," he corrected.

I didn't parrot this time. He was exaggerating. Except for a few prolonged vowels and slightly sloppy articulation, his speech sounded perfectly neutral to me.

He pursed his lips, looking deep in thought. "You can't be full 8. I know what the rats out there sound like."

So he'd been around the galaxy. So had I.

I took a deep breath and uncrossed my arms. "You Ganavan?" I asked.

"Might be. Who's asking?"

I had the strongest impulse to say Quintessa Novalight and blow his fucking world to bits because he was ticking me off, but I wasn't stupid enough for that. "Tess Bailey," I answered, resurrecting her from the dead.

"And what are you looking for in my shop, Tess Bailey?"

His gaze dipped as he said my name, as though he were stamping the letters onto my body, or somehow imprinting them right into both of us. I got the feeling this guy never forgot a thing, and I suddenly wished I'd made up something else. Why didn't I ever just blurt out Jane Smith?

"Do you have more of a name than just Ganavan?" I asked, ignoring the heat tingling up my spine. Part of it was habitual nervousness, but there was also something else. Something I hadn't felt in a long time.

"Shade Ganavan," he answered, looking dead serious for the first time since we'd met. The rascal was gone for just a moment, and in his place, there was a man whose deep voice and assessing eyes caused a slight tremor to go through me.

I couldn't tell if I wanted to step closer to him, or get the hell out of his shop. Usually, I wasn't conflicted about that type of thing.

I opted for staying where I was. "Well, Shade Ganavan, I need someone to repair my ship. Do you know of anyone who has at least eight standard tiles of reinforced, space-worthy metal, welding equipment, and a way to get it all up to the three-hundred-and-fourteenth level of the Squirrel Tree?"

His head reared back. "You're in the fucking Squirrel Tree? Shit, princess, I guarantee they're ripping you off."

I bristled. "It was the only place to land."

"Says the guy who controls the tower, who's paid off by the guy who owns the Squirrel Tree."

He looked genuinely annoyed on my behalf. It was nice. I couldn't remember the last time a stranger had stuck up for me simply on principle. This guy was such a contradiction. Shade Ganavan had oodles of arrogance, oodles of charm, and oodles of something that made me want to kick him in the nuts.

"So?" I prompted.

"I can take care of your ship for you."

"You? Yourself?" I asked.

He spread his hands. "I'm a man of many talents."

"There's no shortage of cockiness, in any case."

"Oh, there's nothing short about my—"

I held up my hand. "Women from Sector 12 don't like hearing that kind of talk."

He grinned, a slow, sex-on-a-stick smile that made heat spark low in my abdomen. "Then what kind of talk *do* they like?" he asked.

"Squeaky clean," I answered, amazed that I kept a straight face while telling an enormous falsehood—in my case, anyway.

He smirked. "You mean boring as hell?"

My lips twitched. The scoundrel was back, and my pulse accelerated in response. I didn't mind dirty talk, and I would have bet good money that Shade Ganavan did it really well.

"And I thought you were from 8," he added abruptly.

My smile died. *Shit*. He had me there.

"How do you know so much about accents?" I asked, suddenly curious to know more about him. And also anxious to change the subject. It never hurt to shift the focus to the other guy, especially when he probably loved talking about himself.

"I travel, working, picking up stuff." His eyes cruised over the crowded shelves on either side of us.

Mine did, too. But while he looked satisfied with his jumbled collection, the brief glance around us just raised questions in my mind. There was too much stuff here, and a lot of it looked like it hadn't been touched—and by that, I meant *cleaned*—in months. It didn't appear his business was doing very well.

"Picking up things for your shop?" I asked.

He shrugged. "Goods. Odds and ends. Some jobs. You know how it goes."

My eyes narrowed. That was vague. And the quality of his clothing didn't match the neglected feel of his shop. He wore rather technical-looking dark cargo pants and a snug-fitting black T-shirt, neither of which looked cheap or worn. His boots were solid and in good condition as well, with soles that looked thick enough to help him kick down the *Endeavor*'s current starboard door.

Thinking about the thin safety hatch that was left, I was shocked all over again that we'd made it out of today's terrifying events alive. All things considered, maybe Jaxon was on to something with his Sky Mother beliefs.

In any case, Shade Ganavan was making money somewhere—even if it wasn't here.

Uh-oh. "Don't tell me you're a pirate. Is all this stuff stolen?" I asked, thinking about Flyhole and all its corrupt bandits only a short jump away.

His mouth turned down. "Not a pirate, sugar. More like a space rogue."

"A space rogue?"

He nodded. "A phenomenal one, at that."

My eyebrows shot up. "Space Rogue Phenom? Really? Maybe I should call you SRP."

His dark eyes glittered as though I'd just thrown down a gauntlet, and he was more than ready to pick it up. "Only if you want me to call you RLCA."

Don't ask. Don't ask. "And what's that?"

"Rosy Lips, Cute Ass."

I stared at him, my heart going berserk in my chest. He stared back.

His brow suddenly furrowed. "Holy shit, you're

turning bright red." He looked pissed off again. "Doesn't anyone ever flirt with you? You married or something?"

He sounded aggravated on all counts, as though he thought it was horrifying that no one ever flirted with me, and even more horrifying that I might be married.

He also seemed concerned that I was so obviously flustered, while at the same time, he was the one who had been completely provoking in the first place. The whole thing just flushed me hotter—and I'm sure turned me redder.

Despite having declined a few offers here and there, I hadn't felt this aware of male appreciation in more than seven years. Well, there had been Dagger Bently, but scrubbing off his lewd looks and comments with industrial-strength prison soap sure didn't count.

"No. And no," I finally answered, my voice sounding as though it grated across sandpaper in my throat.

He watched me for a moment from under lowered brows, and then, thankfully, Shade Ganavan, Space Rogue, let the subject drop.

"So what happened to your ship?" he asked, nodding vaguely toward where I thought the Squirrel Tree must have been from here. "The Dark Watch blow it full of holes?"

Nerves exploded inside me. It was a joke. He was joking. I forcibly calmed my racing heart. "Unexpected asteroid belt."

"You fire your navigator for that?"

I shook my head. "It wasn't her fault."

He nodded, his hands moving to his hips. I noticed scars on his knuckles and wondered how many times he'd split his skin open punching someone in the face. I had a few of those myself. Prison brawls. They happened.

For his part, Shade Ganavan watched me like a hawk, and I wasn't quite sure why. I could tell he was interested, but this seemed to go beyond normal awareness. I could have sworn he took in my every blink and breath.

Finally, he said, "I might not have the metal you need for a few days, sugar."

"You might not have your tongue if you call me 'sugar' again."

His expression flared with a heat I felt branch out into every part of me. The man definitely liked to be provoked, and for some reason, I liked provoking him. I think I even liked it when he provoked *me*.

His countenance changed suddenly, sharpening. "You know how to carry through on a threat?" he asked quietly.

I frowned. "You *want* me to slice out your tongue?"

"I want to know if your sharp edges can actually cut."

"Why?" He'd lost me. Was this kinky talk, and I wasn't getting it? I wasn't a virgin or totally inexperienced. There had been Gabe. But then he'd run one way that day and I'd run the other, and we'd never seen each other again.

Shade's voice came to me on a low whisper over the tinkling of the bell I'd just noticed, but there was nothing seductive about it. "Because the Dark Watch just followed you into my shop."

CHAPTER

6

PANIC ICED ME OVER, AND I FROZE. IT COULDN'T BE. How did they know?

"Who?" I mouthed more than said aloud.

Shade's eyes flicked over my shoulder. He gave a slight shrug, speaking so quietly I essentially had to read his lips as well. "I don't know every goon they've got."

"Uniform?" I breathed.

"Black," he mouthed back.

I exhaled. A trooper, then. If it had been my uncle coming for me, he would have been wearing red.

I lifted the shiny metallic cartridge box I still had in my hand. "You're sure all forty rounds are in here?" I asked in a normal voice again, angling the box to reflect what was behind me. I saw a soldier I didn't recognize. Probably just some Sector 2 guy in here looking for a knickknack or spare part.

I tried to act casual, even though adrenaline was making me jittery underneath. My relief was cerebral. My body hadn't caught up yet.

"How much for this?" I asked.

"Fifteen," Shade said, taking the box of bullets from me. "I'll ring it up."

I followed him to the register and then paid, only once darting a glance at the soldier who was perusing the shelves a good twenty feet from me. When Shade handed me back the cartridge box and my change, our fingers brushed, but I was too nervous to appreciate the brief contact.

Chuckling, he said, "I thought you were going to walk off without paying for that."

What in the galaxy made him think that?

"I'm not a petty thief," I said, coolness creeping into my voice. When I stole something, it wasn't measly cartridges for guns we hardly used. It was cure-all vaccines and food for the starving and prisoners of war.

"I was teasing." Shade cocked his head to one side, looking almost sorry.

I blinked. *Oh.* All right, then. Clearly, I needed a manual on flirting. I felt myself turn crimson again.

"You remember where to find me when you have those parts?" I asked.

He nodded. "See you soon…"

His sentence seemed unfinished. He might have been about to add *Tess* or another antagonizing *sugar*, but he chose not to say anything else when the soldier came up beside me and plunked a shaving kit down on the counter.

Ducking my head, I turned and left Ganavan's Products and Parts, not looking up or slowing down again until I'd reached the base of the Squirrel Tree.

The Dark Watch was on Albion 5, just like they were everywhere. And where there was one, there were many.

CHAPTER

7

SHADE FLIPPED THE SIGN TO CLOSED AND LOCKED THE door. He didn't care who might need a spare part today, tomorrow, or any fucking day. He cared about Tess Bailey and her little stream of lies.

Unexpected asteroid belt. He shook his head.

Under her pale skin, her firework of a blush, and her rabbiting pulse, there was a woman running scared. She looked like she'd been that way for a while, like she never stopped. Never came down. No one got that white unless they spent all their time in the Dark.

Shade's blood still pumped harder than usual from certain parts of their exchange, and something a little crazy had happened in his chest when she'd looked so terrified of the Dark Watch. Her poker face had sucked, but then she'd managed to pull it together and be as cool as a cloud after the initial shock and assessment had passed.

He'd seen that there had been just one soldier, a man like any other poking around the shelves. A lot of the men and women who joined the galactic military wore their uniforms all the time because it gave them a power trip—always knowing people would get out of their way, say they were right, and look at them like they were a sight. The guy probably hadn't even been on duty, not if he was shopping for razors in the seedy district around the docks.

Shade had been testing her when he'd said the Dark Watch had followed her into his shop. And her reaction had told him exactly what he'd wanted to know—she was definitely in the hot seat right now.

But he'd gotten more than he bargained for. Her chest had stopped—no breath—and her blue eyes had gone so wide they'd practically swallowed him whole. And then she'd asked the same question he would have. *Uniform?* Not how many, but what echelon. She'd wanted to know if there was someone important at her back.

Some of the blood had come back into her face when he'd said the uniform was black, which meant that whoever was looking for Tess Bailey wasn't just some grunt solider; he or she was a higher-up.

But the savvy space rat hadn't taken his word for it, had she? She'd held up that cartridge box to use as a mirror and checked for herself. She'd made sure it wasn't someone who knew her, and then she'd paid for her bullets like nothing had happened, even getting all high and mighty again when he'd teased her about walking off with the ammo.

He had no idea why he'd done that.

Shade ran a hand through his short hair, still not used to feeling it so close to his scalp. The movement wasn't very satisfying without anything to shove back.

He strode into his office, still seeing the freckles across Tess's nose. They weren't very dark; she'd have needed more sunlight for that. She also had a few on her chest. They'd looked like a constellation, a pattern to follow between her straight collarbones and the upper swells of her breasts.

Tension like he hadn't felt in a while whipped through his body. Rosy lips and a cute ass were just the start of it. He hadn't been crass enough to add NT to the acronym, but he'd noticed her nice tits as well.

Shade frowned as he tugged out his chair. She was attractive all over, but blue eyes, freckles, and an atomic blush were what had left him feeling like he'd been punched in the chest.

Sitting at his desk, he pushed aside the remnants of the late lunch he'd been eating when Tess had come in and then powered up the tablet that might give him some answers about his latest guest. While it got going, he rummaged through some paperwork, not really seeing it. He was still too focused on the way Tess had frozen, going from a little flirty and confused to petrified all at once.

Who had she pissed off? Some galactic officer? Was she a deserter? A rebel? Despite not having much of a game face, she'd seemed ready to put up a good fight.

And then there was the fact that she'd bought ammunition, when not that many people had guns. LW-9 bullets were for Grayhawks, and there was nothing illegal about buying them, but it sure as hell raised questions in his mind.

Shade wanted to call her scrappy, but it didn't quite fit. For the spirit maybe, but not for the physical part. She'd been tall and strong and fit. Her eyes had looked older than the rest of her, though, like she'd already been to hell and back and made choices most people never had to face.

Determined. That was it.

She'd looked like she could take care of herself. So why did he have this itch under his skin, like he wanted to make sure she wasn't in trouble too deep?

When the tablet was ready, he typed in the pass code to the secure database only he and about a hundred other people in the galaxy had access to. This was where shit went down. This was where he made his money.

He scrolled through the latest entries first to get them out of the way, but his mind wasn't really in the right place to check them out. Rebel. Rebel. Rebel. Escaped convict. Kidnapped scientist. Rebel. Priest.

Priest? His eyes stopped for a moment. That was unusual. Not many people fucked with the Powers, just in case they were real.

"Not interested," Shade muttered.

Going to the search bar, he typed in Tess Bailey.

No matches came up for a current job. No bounty. No info.

Adjusting the search criteria, he typed in just Bailey. Again, nothing.

He tried Baylee, Bayleigh, Bailee, and Baileigh, all without a hit.

Good. She wasn't anywhere on the up-to-date Wanted or Retrieve lists. That brought a little relief to the tension in his gut.

Shade switched databases and widened the hunt to birth records, telling the search engine to ignore any hit from more than forty years ago and to eliminate all males from the results. There was no way she was forty—more like twenty-five—but he was working large out of caution.

After an interminable wait, about five kabillion Baileys popped up.

He sat back in his chair and scrubbed his hands down his face. He'd need a year to sort through all that.

He narrowed the search to birth records for women under thirty. Still too many. He used the same criteria for just Sector 12 and got Baileys under a number of different spellings, but no Tess to go with them. Same thing for Sector 8.

He groaned. She'd probably given him a false name anyway, and this was a wild-goose chase.

"Well, shit. Who the hell are you, starshine?"

Shade hadn't expected his tablet to answer, but all of a sudden, there she was, filling his screen as a new message came through from the first window he'd opened to the restricted-access database. His eyes widened, and adrenaline ripped through his blood.

He stared at the enormous WANTED above her head and felt his stomach twist.

The sum below her picture of *two hundred million* in universal currency made his jaw drop.

Shade stood up, thunking both hands down on his desk and glaring at the tablet. He leaned over for a better look—and to make sure he was reading this right.

He'd never seen that much money offered for anyone. Ever. If he was seeing this new post, other people were, too. There wasn't a bounty hunter with access to this list that wasn't pissing his or her pants right now with excitement, but Shade felt like he was about to throw up.

His shoulders tensed as he pushed away from his

desk to pace. Those others, though, they didn't know where she was. The *exact platform* where her severely disabled ship was currently docked. They had no idea where to start looking for *Captain T. Bailey* in the whole fucking galaxy, but he could walk right up to her, and she wouldn't even wonder why he was there.

Shade swallowed the bad taste in his mouth. *Two hundred million*. He could buy back his birthright and live like a king forever on that. Never compete for another job in his life.

Stopping, he studied the picture again, impatient for the rest of the job info to pop up. There had to be more than this, something to go on.

The image filling his tablet wasn't an exact likeness. He'd seen ones like it before often enough. Someone had taken a picture of a kid—less than ten years old, if he had to guess—and then used algorithms to transform it into an adult woman. The computer program had gotten the blue eyes, straight brown hair, and almost heart-shaped face right, but it had erased her freckles, like they'd never even been.

He scowled at the screen. The pinkish, uniform skin looked all wrong on her.

More text finally appeared.

Names may be false.

He snorted. Always a good place to start.

Shade glanced at the bottom of the screen to see who'd sent out the post. Captain Nathaniel Bridgebane, Galactic General, *Dark Watch 12*.

For fuck's sake, this just kept getting worse. They'd

brought out the big guns. Bridgebane was the Overseer's right hand. His brother-in-law. And he either had no idea who Tess was, or he knew, and he didn't want to tell anyone.

> Captain T. Bailey.
> Cargo Cruiser model
> 419—Endeavor.
> Subject presumed dead.

Shade frowned. "Then why are you sending this out?"

> Last seen in Sector 14 in
> possession of highly sensitive
> government materials.

His eyebrows nearly flew off his head. He'd seen hints of fragility in Tess, but she must have had balls of steel if she'd been zooming around Sector 14 with the Dark Watch on her heels.

> The bounty will be doubled for
> recovery of the stolen goods. Live
> capture preferred—substantial bonus.

Shade's heart stuttered to a stop. He reread. Holy Sky Mother, the galactic government wanted Tess and whatever she'd taken more than it had ever wanted anything since its inception, as far as he knew.

And they preferred her alive.

Some of the sick feeling inside him eased.

Unless they just wanted to torture her for answers?

The sick feeling grew again.

What had she taken? Bridgebane didn't want to say outright; that much was clear. He was dangling bait, and the hunters had to figure it out for themselves. If they found her, they probably found it.

Tess's coolly spoken "I'm not a petty thief" came back to him, and he almost choked. He'd teased her about stealing a box of bullets? When she stole, she obviously stole big.

The photo and information disappeared, and Shade lunged for the tablet, picking it up again. Bridgebane couldn't have been taking down the job already. No one could have found her that fast.

A sort of rage-filled panic started drumming beneath his ribs, but then another window opened with a new image to take the first one's place. Same text underneath. The photo was a mug shot from Hourglass Mile, one of the most severe and secure places in the galaxy. They'd traced her to where she'd been—he looked at the date on the prison photo—seven years ago.

Tess Bailey. It might not have been her real name, but she'd been using it for a while now.

He looked at her birth date, too. A quick calculation told him she was twenty-six.

He cursed and started pacing again.

Fucking *nineteen years old* and sent to Hourglass Mile. What had she done to get herself locked up in that place? He knew what they did to the inmates there. The mines. The whips. The pairings.

The lunch he'd eaten earlier turned to lead in his stomach. Who had they forced on her? What had he been like?

How the hell had she gotten out?

The sentence stamped in red across her mug shot said *Life*.

Then he remembered the explosion about five years back. A bunch of prisoners had died. In the confusion, some had managed to run away, making it to the docks and stealing supply ships. No bounty had ever been offered for any of them, no names given—not on the regular channels and not on his. The galactic government had probably been too embarrassed by the massive amounts of chaos at one of their maximum-security prisons to post.

Beautiful. Ballsy. And brave.

A wanted criminal.

Fuck!

He worked on the fringes of the law, dipping his toes into the murky side of the system, but he was still part of the galactic machine of all-encompassing order. He knew who signed the checks. One big job like this, and he could leave it all behind.

Indecision clawed at Shade's chest. He'd never agreed to help someone before only to screw them over. He didn't get to know his targets. They were just prize money, a means to an end.

But Tess Bailey with her little freckles and her mile-long legs was everything he needed and more to finally buy his life back from that scumbag Scarabin White.

His mind worked. He knew where she was.

The easiest nab and grab of his life was waiting for him on the three-hundred-and-fourteenth level of the Squirrel Tree. He could land two hundred *million* in his account.

Double that if she still had the goods.

CHAPTER

8

I WAS SURPRISED TO SEE SHADE GANAVAN SHOW UP the next morning practically with the sun. I hadn't even had my coffee yet, but there he was on the platform, looking ready to work.

Actually, he was checking out the lab attachment. From the outside, it looked like any other piece of space equipment, most likely an additional cargo hold, and luckily, there were no holes in *that* part of the ship to give him a view straight inside.

I kept to the shadows of the *Endeavor*'s open doorway, watching him. He moved on to examining the rest of the ship, and unless he had X-ray vision, I wasn't going to worry about the lab attachment too much.

I'd destroyed the test tubes of my blood, flushing the contents and boiling the labels into oblivion before trashing the empty containers via the compactor. That evidence was gone, and I hadn't found any other hidden compartments with more samples. Just like Big Guy had said, that was it. With any luck, that was it in the entire galaxy, apart from what was pulsing through my veins.

Once I'd eliminated the samples, I'd sealed up the air lock leading to the attachment. Only I knew the pass code. No one was getting into that lab but me, and even I didn't want to go back.

Shade eventually reached the gash in the hull at the level of my bedroom, which was pretty barren and torn up. There, he *could* see straight in, and he ducked down for a better look.

Even with Albion City starting to buzz and hum far below, I heard him mutter something about *major repairs* as he ran his fingers along the blackened edges of the hole.

A sinking feeling dropped through me. Whatever Shade did was going to cost me an arm and two legs. On top of that, we needed to resupply, and I had some unexpected shopping to do. Space had eaten nearly all my underwear. And plenty of clothes as well. I was too tall to share with Miko, Shiori, or Fiona, and I swam in Jax's things. I had no choice but to buy new outfits if I wanted to blend into civilian settings, like here on Albion 5, or anywhere we might go for whatever jobs came next.

Shade's entire upper body disappeared into my bedroom. He looked like he was about to crawl in.

"Morning!" I called out, not really comfortable with him inspecting my unmade bed.

He ducked back out of the damaged ship, straightening as he looked over. Sunglasses masked his expression and reflected my own image back at me.

Squatting low, I braced one hand against the *Endeavor*'s floor and vaulted down onto the landing dock about four feet below. It was always a bit of a scramble getting back up again, but letting down the ship's stairs was an unnecessary use of power as far as I was concerned, especially while we were recharging.

"I thought you needed a few days to get the reinforced metal," I said, moving toward the man who had occupied far too many of my thoughts since the previous afternoon.

"I had two tiles in stock." Shade turned away from me, resuming his careful perusal of the *Endeavor*. After a long silence, he added, "Figured I'd get to work while I waited for more to come in from my supplier."

I nodded, although he wasn't looking. He seemed to have an expert eye and was wholly concentrated on the ship.

I thanked him anyway, and he grunted something in response, poking his head into another hole.

I watched him, and Shade ignored me. He was distant to the point of making me wonder if I'd imagined the flirting yesterday. Had the warmth and interest all been in my imagination? It wouldn't have been the first time I'd dreamed up something false. Today, his flat expression behind dark glasses wasn't telling me much. Or maybe he just wasn't a morning person, which made me wonder why the hell he'd shown up so close to the crack of dawn.

"We never talked about payment," I pointed out when he emerged from the damaged hull once more. After he'd added up materials and labor, I hated to think of the total cost.

"The metal is twelve hundred per tile, and you'll need nine, not eight."

"Twelve hundred!" My jaw practically hit my chest. "It's only eight fifty on Rhylight!"

He turned to me, finally taking off those reflective shades and slipping them into his back pocket. His honey-brown eyes looked dark. "You're not on Rhylight, starshine."

I took a step toward him. "Don't 'starshine' me, you crook. I won't pay a single unit over one thousand in universal currency."

Watching me, he seemed to think about it, his big hands resting on his hips. He apparently liked that pose. I could see why. It made him look even wider and showed off his menacing knuckles.

"Factor in five hundred a day for labor," he finally said, "and you've got yourself a deal."

I breathed through the panic of my rapidly depleting funds and did the math in my head. I had that much. There would be next to nothing left over, but I could pay his fee. And five hundred units a day for some pretty hard and heavy labor wasn't unreasonable.

Finally, I nodded in agreement. "How long do you think it'll take?" *Not more than a week. Please don't say more than a week.* And even that long in one place seemed awfully dangerous. What if Bridgebane found out we were still alive? With the lab intact? Being on the run required the ability to actually *move*.

Shade looked at the ship again, his eyes sweeping over the partially blown-out hull. He scratched at the dark stubble that had sprung up on his jaw overnight. "All week." His laser stare cut back to me. "And I'll need to hire someone to help me lift the tiles into place."

A glance toward the two tiles Shade had brought up on a hover crate confirmed that they were thick metal monsters. Just what I needed. "I—"

He shook his head, cutting me off. "Not you. You look plenty capable, cupcake, but you're not strong enough to lift this stuff."

"I know." My glare and tone hopefully conveyed just how much I *loved* being cut off. And called cupcake. "I have someone who can help. He's very big and strong," I added, just in case Shade needed convincing.

Something flashed in his eyes. *Annoyance?* Did Shade Ganavan like being the biggest and strongest around? Well, too bad. I had Jax.

Frowning slightly, Shade moved between the ship and me and then ran his fingers over what was left of the ragged edge of the outer starboard door. "What the hell happened here? Has this been…*sawed*?"

He glared at me over his shoulder.

Geez. Really not a morning person.

I shrugged. "Might've been."

Turning, he leaned against the doorframe and stared at me. I stared back. We did a lot of that. It was very awkward—at least for me.

"Can you fix it?" I finally asked.

He shook his head, pushing off from the ship and pointing to different parts of the messed-up door panels. "A patch won't work here. Or here. You need a whole new door."

Dismay settled in my stomach like lead. "I can't afford that."

"Your ship's useless then. The other repairs won't matter without a door."

I swallowed. What did I have that was worth something? What could I sell or… "I can barter with food," I said. Nothing we had was fancy, but we had a big supply, all of it purloined and military issue. I felt no guilt whatsoever. The galactic government wouldn't let its soldiers starve.

"Do I look like I'm hungry?" Shade countered.

My nostrils flared. *Fine.* "I'll fly with just the safety door, then."

"No, you won't."

My head jerked back and down into my neck, probably making me look at lot like a turtle. I'd read about turtles. Hadn't seen one yet. "*I won't?*"

"An inner door is to provide an air lock and to hold you together in an emergency until you can get the outer door fixed. It's not meant to take reentries and jumps on a regular basis."

I knew that. Did he think I didn't?

Shaking my head, I shrugged. "No choice."

Shade lifted one hand and rubbed the back of his neck, just like Jax did when he was torn about something. "I can get you a door at half price," he eventually said.

My heart wound up like a crazy clock in my chest. "Really? That's amazing!" I could make that work. I hated to do it, but I could sell the precious books I had in my possession instead of giving them to the Intergalactic Library like I'd planned. If I found the right buyer for the books, and if the door was really half-price, we could be up and flying out of here in a week. And I'd still have the food for the Outer Zone colonies. When it came down to it, I'd rather keep the provisions than the books. It wasn't even a choice.

Shade looked away from my big, fat, grateful smile as though it offended him or something. I felt it die on my lips.

A little stung but still appreciative of the generous offer on the door, I moved to the edge of our docking platform and looked out over Albion City. A sprawling latticework of tall buildings spread endlessly before me, all soaring metal, polished stone, and bright, shiny glass.

The morning sun reflected off the millions of windows, almost blinding me. I wondered about all the people behind those windows, about their daily lives. So different from mine. And probably from each other's as well.

The Sector 2 city looked settled, maybe even like a nice place to live, if you could deal with the regular Dark Watch patrols. Then again, those were everywhere, from the mansion-lined avenues of Sector 12 to the crumbling slums of the far reaches of the galaxy. I only knew of one place where the Dark Watch couldn't come knocking— and that was because they didn't know it was there.

A ship could slip completely out of sight in the Fold, and if we'd had enough power left yesterday, I would have tried to find it instead of diving headfirst into the Black Widow. In retrospect, I should have gone there first and avoided the whole chase, but I'd always managed to outrun the Dark Watch before, and I'd had no idea how important the lab was, or how vigorously the military would come after it.

It didn't help that the Fold was a bitch to find, even for those who knew how to look. I never would have known about the rebel hideaway if Jax and Fiona hadn't trusted me with the secret first. No one found the Fold unless they were brought there. And enemies that somehow made it in on rebel ships… They didn't come out again.

The pocket between the stars knew how to protect

itself, and for some, it turned into a one-way trip. Others were born, lived, and died there, their existences revolving around a single cause. The Fold was home to them, the only safe one around, but it was just an occasional stopover for Nightchasers like us, rebels running people and supplies around the Dark.

Thinking in terms of a safe place to dock made me want to do a quick flyby of Starway 8, but unless I had something vital to contribute to the huge galactic orphanage, I would never risk drawing the military there. Kids liked to run their mouths, and that never ended well. And Mareeka was too much of a rebel at heart to ever let the children under her care get pushed around by the Overseer's goons. Publicly, she dotted her i's and crossed her t's, and the Dark Watch patrols mostly left her alone.

And it was a damn good thing. If my father knew even half of what went on in that place—the chaos and joy and illicit learning of the old texts—he'd probably blow the whole orphanage up, kids and all.

Looking down from our Squirrel Tree perch, I sniffed the quickly warming air, which was already thickening with the brighter light of the climbing sun and with the droning sounds of the city waking up around us. It was going to turn into another hot day on Albion 5, but at least it didn't smell half bad here.

I lifted both arms above my head and stretched, trying to work out the muscle kinks sleeping on my hard, thin mattress had left. When I turned back around, Shade's eyes darted quickly away, as if he'd been watching me.

Heat stole through me. I wished I could figure him out.

Jax's head poked out from the open doorway.

"Coffee's ready, Tess." He scowled at me. "*Please* come away from the edge."

I immediately moved closer to the ship. I knew how it freaked Jax out when I spacewalked or went anywhere near someplace where there was even a remote possibility of my falling off or slipping away or simply…being lost.

"You must be the muscle Tess was talking about," Shade said.

Jaxon turned his head. "You must be the guy with the parts."

The Shade from yesterday would have at least smirked at *the guy with the parts*. Today, all he did was hold out his hand to Jax, and the two men shook.

"Do you want to come in for some breakfast?" I asked Shade.

"No, thanks. I'm going to take stock of the damage again," he answered. "Start making a plan."

It should have sounded good to me that he was serious and getting straight to work. Instead, an odd feeling of disappointment seized the place that should have been for relief.

Nodding, I said, "Just call out if you change your mind."

"I already ate," Shade answered.

Well. That was final.

And I shouldn't have cared. I was out of here in a week.

I reached up, and Jaxon gripped my wrists and easily lifted me back onto the ship. If Shade had needed a demonstration of Jax's strength, he'd gotten one. Not many people could haul a nearly six-foot woman straight up.

Together, Jax and I headed for the smell of strong coffee. Jax made the best cups.

We met Fiona in the entranceway to the kitchen. Her

hair was still damp from her shower, and she looked fresher than I'd felt in days. It had been her turn today. Miko was next. I'd get a shower again after that.

Maybe Shade knew where to buy half-priced water and discounted recycling tanks. In the meantime, luckily for all of us and our noses, extra-strength deodorant was cheap.

"Who's the tall set of muscles poking around our ship?" Fiona asked me with a bit of a grin.

"Shade Ganavan."

Her eyebrows slowly went up. "Got anything more to say about that?"

I fought my own grin and started with the most obvious. "Easily six foot two, two hundred pounds, dark-brown hair, light-brown eyes, flirty in the afternoon, grumpy in the morning."

Fiona laughed. "Maybe he needs some coffee."

Maybe. Or some rest. The guy looked like he hadn't slept a wink. He definitely hadn't changed his clothes or shaved.

Something uncomfortable slid sideways through my chest. Had he flirted with me and then gone off and been with some other woman all night?

I forced the slight pang to keep going and slide right on out. None of my business.

Miko had eggs, bacon, and potatoes on the table for her and Shiori already. Jax was pouring the coffee for everyone, so I got his, Fiona's, and my plates while Fiona peeled our daily orange and doled out the parts.

Oranges were often hard to split evenly into five, and if there was an extra wedge, Fiona always made sure that Shiori got it. Grandmother was the only one who couldn't see that she was getting more than the rest of us, and no one ever told her.

"So how much are the repairs going to cost us?" Jax asked.

I told them, and everyone stopped eating. They'd go back to their meals eventually, but for the moment, they were absorbing the fact that our safe was about to get cleaned out.

"Are you sure this guy's prices are reasonable?" Miko asked. "Maybe you should shop around before you let him get started."

The idea of making multiple inquiries left me uneasy. The less any of us talked to other people or walked around Albion City—or anywhere, for that matter—the better. I was already going to have to go down to street level again to try to sell those books. I just hoped there were some people on Albion 5 who still liked reading old tomes. Even though the official ban had finally been lifted on many of the surviving texts, most people were still too nervous to pick up anything without the galactic seal of approval on it. Approved books were all propaganda-filled, glory-to-the-Overseer, brainwashing hogwash, but at least they didn't get you harassed.

"It's a little steep," I answered about Shade's pricing. "But I don't think I'll find much better anywhere else on this rock."

Jaxon agreed, and he knew metal and labor costs even better than I did.

"Besides," I added. "Shade offered to find us a new armored door for half price."

They all stopped eating again. Jax looked at me as if I'd lost my mind.

I frowned. "What?"

"A guy doesn't just *give* you an armored door," he said.

"I didn't say he was *giving* it to me. I said it would be half price."

"It's practically the same thing," he muttered, setting his coffee mug down a little too forcefully. "There must be something wrong with him. Or…" Jax's eyes narrowed on me.

"What?" I asked again.

"We're leaving this place, Tess. Don't get attached."

I did that turtle thing again. Turtles were on to something with their retractable heads. "You're crazy, Jax. I don't even know the guy."

"If he's giving you a deal like that on a reinforced door, he wants to know *you*."

Low down, my belly clenched. *Is that true?*

"And what's the harm in that?" Fiona asked. She pushed her untouched mug toward me. "Why don't you take him a cup of coffee and see what you think of him."

Jaxon swung an incredulous look on Fiona. "Don't encourage her, Fi!"

Fiona rolled her eyes, somehow managing to make her ponytail swing without even moving her head. "Just because *you* never want to see anyone again in your whole life apart from the four of us doesn't mean that Tess has to stay shut up in this metal box."

True. Although I liked my metal box.

Jax waved a hand through the air, whispering, "Everyone out there is looking for us."

"Not *everyone*, Jaxon." Fiona met his dark eyes with some pretty fierce eyes of her own. They were green, like her plants. "And not everyone is looking to take her from you. From us."

He quietly set down his fork and sat back in his chair when I thought what he really wanted to do was throw the utensil across the kitchen and break his plate. "You never know when they'll strike," Jax said so flatly it hurt my heart.

"You're right. They could strike anytime," Fiona agreed quickly. "That's all the more reason to *live*!"

Jax flinched, and Fiona looked momentarily horrified, as though she feared she'd gone too far.

"We're careful, Jax. We're all careful," I said, although I didn't know if I should have been soothing him or helping Fiona to rile him up. I was pretty sure some smashed dishes and an explosive bellow would have done him a galaxy of good. Sometimes, I wished he would fill his lungs with his pain and fury and shake the ship with them.

"Good," he finally answered, his face turning into a wall—flat and blank.

Fiona's expression went in the opposite direction, bursting with emotion, and they stared at each other for a moment before Jax disconnected, shifting his gaze to the side.

Sadness crept through me, and irrepressible Fiona suddenly drooped, although she probably thought she was hiding it. Some things were only secrets here because nobody talked about them, and I wanted to scream at Jax to look right in front of him, instead of behind.

"You know who Tess is now." Jax picked up the conversation again in a monotone that reminded me of the grieving man on the Mile, the one who might never let himself get over his dead wife. "There isn't a single person alive who doesn't know who she is."

"Yeah. And they all think she's been dead for the last *eighteen years*," Fiona shot back.

"That's a good point," I said. Everyone in the galaxy thought I'd died from the same mysterious fever that had taken my mother, when in fact, I'd never been sick a day in my life. Not even when the other children in the orphanage had been dropping all around me, killed off by infections and diseases with cures.

"There are more people searching for our Tess than for a ghost," Shiori said, looking across the table at Fiona but not quite hitting her mark. Her milky eyes landed somewhere between Fiona and me.

"Exactly," Jaxon agreed, turning a pointed look my way. His expression regained only enough life to look satisfied that Shiori had helped prove his point. "People everywhere—looking for Tess."

Well, I doubted that Shade Ganavan, Space Rogue, was one of them. And I hardly thought *Tess* was that important. The great rebel wheel was full of cogs, and I hardly signified. At most, I was worth a lethal injection, and the Overseer had plenty of those.

That said, I didn't want to get caught. But I also wouldn't stop doing what I needed to do just because I feared the possible consequences. Fear was something I could accept. Abandoning the galaxy to a group of despots was not.

"I have a plan for how to pay for the repairs." I stood up, finishing my portion of the orange and then grabbing Fiona's and my mugs. "Thanks, Fi."

She nodded since she was chewing her food.

"Tess…"

I turned back to Jax from the doorway, the two mugs in my hands, and gave him my most reassuring smile. He'd lost his sister to the heat and murderous roar of the galactic military's flamethrowers that day, too. She'd been visiting, helping out with the newborn.

Some days, I thought he forgot I wasn't her. Most days, I was glad he thought I was.

"Don't worry, partner. I'll be careful. He knows this place, and I have to pick his brain about where to sell some rare books."

Jax pressed his lips together and didn't say anything else. It was Miko who surprised me, because I knew she'd dropped out of the conversation and crawled into herself the moment Fiona and Jax had hinted at Shade wanting anything more from me than universal currency. Miko liked to pretend that no one ever had urges, because they scared her half to death. If I were ever to take up praying again, I'd pray that someone, someday, could show Miko that intimacy could involve tenderness instead of violence.

"He used to kick his dogs." She looked my way, but I didn't think she was seeing me, or any of us. "Why would anyone kick a dog, Tess?"

My chest tightened as I shook my head. He'd kicked Miko, too, I'd have bet. I was glad the bastard was dead. "I don't know. There's no reason for that."

"Don't trust anyone you think would kick a dog," Miko said.

She still looked as though her thoughts were focused far away, but she knew what she was saying, and it was solid advice.

CHAPTER

9

I HANDED SHADE THE MUG, HOPING THE DARK LIQUID inside was still hot enough—and that he didn't prefer it with sugar. We didn't have any, although we did still have a little of Mareeka's valuable honey.

"Coffee," I said. "Good stuff. It'll put hair on your chest."

His lips curved up in amusement. The surprised smile faded quickly. "You think I don't know what coffee is?"

"I think you've never tasted *this* coffee. It's the best in the galaxy."

He took a sip. "Yeah, it's good. Thanks." He drank again.

I smiled. This already seemed easier than earlier. Maybe he'd just needed coffee to brighten him up.

"So, what about the damage?" I asked. "Still thinking the same as before?"

His gaze roamed over the *Endeavor*, over the holes the Dark Watch had blown in her hull. Shade Ganavan sure did like to stare. At me. At my ship. Maybe it was a Sector 2 thing.

Had his eyes just snagged on the fresh-looking stickers?

He obviously didn't miss a thing, and they did seem a little too new, with none of the slightly raised numbers battered yet by space travel. I'd meant to beat on them with a chain this morning, but then Shade had shown up too soon.

"I can patch her up for you," was all he said.

"Still thinking a week?" I asked.

He nodded. "Unless you mind seeing a whole lot of me."

Actually, I was pretty sure I didn't.

The heat of a blush spread across my chest and neck. I willed it not to hit my face. "I probably won't be around much anyway," I said.

His eyes seemed to sharpen on me. "Why's that?"

"I need to sell some rare books." I figured I should just outright ask him what I wanted to know rather than beat around the bush. Or in this case, the *Endeavor*. "Do you know of anyone who likes the old stuff? You know, bindings and pages and all?"

His face remained fairly expressionless, although there was no way I could call him bland. "Stamped or not stamped?" he asked.

He wanted to know if my books had galactic approval. Tamping down the nervous twist in my belly, I shook my head. "No seal, but they're not seditious or anything. Just novels."

"Just novels?" Something wry colored his tone. "What's more seditious than the imagination, Tess Bailey?"

A chill swept over me. A little from the way he said

my name, a little from the fact that I was putting way too much trust in someone I didn't know, and a little from Shade's unexpected and almost daring question. He was right. The free mind was both a wonderful and a dangerous thing. My imagination was betraying me right now. The mutinous little beast was envisioning having all sorts of interesting conversations with Shade Ganavan over the course of the week.

I lifted my mug and took a sip. The coffee's enticing aroma curled around my senses while the idea of getting to know Shade better heated my insides, possibly making me reckless.

My eyes flicked up, meeting his. "Rabble-rousing comes to mind," I answered.

He cautiously nodded, as if he hadn't expected me to come right out with something like that. Maybe I shouldn't have.

"That means agitating something in here." He tapped his chest over his heart with the hand that wasn't holding his mug. "Why do you think no one writes novels anymore?" Shade asked.

Was there a hint of regret in his voice? Of nostalgia for a time when people could say what they wanted? Neither of us had been alive then.

The obvious answer was to avoid harassment or possible imprisonment for something the authorities, even erroneously, might consider subversive or inflammatory, and especially anything they might see as dangerous to their hold on power. But Shade already knew all that.

"Because novels stir feelings, wishes, and the heart," I said. "Not all ideas and thoughts need to be proven, or even can be, and the Overseer is only interested in—no, only *allows*—what can be measured and quantified and put in a neat little box."

Shade looked at me hard, and I replayed what I'd just said in my head. It was fact. I hadn't said anything truly rebellious, nothing that should have earned me such a stern look.

"Do you talk to just anyone like this?" he asked.

"I don't talk to anyone."

His brow creased, and I wished I could take that back. Being a total recluse probably wasn't an attractive quality to a man who lived and worked in the swarming docks. And despite the situation, and Jax's completely rational cautioning, I wanted Shade to like me. It had been so long since I'd been kissed.

I swept my bangs behind my ear, adding, "Except for my crew. I talk to them."

Shade moved away from me, taking another sip of coffee. "Do you think science is incompatible with creativity?" he asked.

I relaxed a bit with more distance between us—and because he'd chosen to continue the conversation, despite its slightly dangerous undertone.

I shook my head. "Some new discoveries are accidents, but most come from a person's vision, from having enough inspiration to imagine the next step."

And yet the Overseer constantly tried to stomp the imagination out of life. He wanted everything to be clinical, uniform, as boring as the brown clothes he always wore. For such a competent, smart, and horrible man, it was surprising he didn't see that there couldn't be hypotheses and experiments without imaginative thought.

Shade looked pensive.

"What do you think?" I asked.

He didn't answer right away. Then, "I think life would be damn dull without good books in it, and there's a great little place in Windrow that might want what you've got."

My heartbeat took off with a sudden burst of speed, and my smile couldn't help but go along for the ride. "Windrow?" I asked.

"The bookstore is about twenty blocks south of the docks—on the corner of Baxton and Lorn. A woman named Susan owns and runs the place. It's called Flipping Pages and has quotes by Vivica Vot all over the front. You can't miss it."

"I love Vot." Vivica Vot was a poet and philosopher who'd taken a spot on board *Exodus 2*, the second mass transport to definitively leave Earth to explore the galaxy and look for safe places for humanity to plant new roots. Her poems were full of the fear, hope, and wonder that accompanied the first irreversible leaps toward new horizons.

Shade nodded. "Who doesn't like Vot."

It wasn't really a question and didn't invite further discussion. That was too bad. I loved talking books.

I mentally filed away the name and address of the bookstore. "Thanks. That's a really big help."

Shade rubbed the back of his neck again. He took another sip. "How come you're the captain?" he asked.

I bristled a little at the question. "Why wouldn't I be?"

He shrugged. "Just asking how it all came about."

Most of the truth was off-limits. I chose my words

carefully. "When we first got together, I was the only one who knew how to fly." It was an honest answer. Innocuous, I thought.

"And the one who knows how to steer the ship ends up steering everything else?"

I thought about it. Fiona was really only interested in her plants and the possible damage they could do to some—and their potential benefits to others. Miko and Shiori just wanted to survive one more day until the inevitable end. And Jax... Jax didn't care who was in charge as long as it was someone with a conscience who listened to what other people had to say—which was what he'd been fighting for his entire life.

"I think we steer together," I told Shade. The crew only listened to me because they chose to, and that was how it should be. When I gave an order, they obeyed, but that was because loyalty and trust had been earned, not imposed in any way. If one day I asked them to do something they didn't want to do, they wouldn't. And I would respect that choice.

Shade didn't say anything.

I finished my coffee. "Well, I'm going to let you get to work while I go see about those books."

He glanced toward his bag, a smallish brown thing he'd brought up along with his heavy equipment. He went over to it and rummaged around. When he came back, he flopped a hat down on my head.

"You're so pale," he said, adjusting the brim to shield my face. "You're already getting sunburned."

My whole chest clenched tight, as though two big fists had grabbed on to my heart and squeezed out an *oh!* and a *my!*

"Thanks," I said a little hoarsely, resisting the urge to fiddle with the hat myself. It was good having something to shade my eyes. And hiding my face from possibly prying eyes was never a bad thing. My heart still raced.

He held out a small box to me. "And take one of these today, and one in three months."

I took the sealed box from him and read the label. "Liquid vitamin D?" I asked.

Shade sniffed, his hands falling to his hips again. He looked off into the distance. "You've finally got some sunlight. Might as well stick some calcium to your bones."

"That's…" *Incredibly nice*. I didn't think he wanted to hear that, though. He was scowling. "Thanks," I said again, pressure growing beneath my ribs.

"How many are you?" He looked at me again. "The whole crew?"

"Five," I answered. No one but Jax had come to the door, so Shade hadn't seen any of the others yet.

Shade nodded. "There's enough for everyone."

He'd thought of the others? That was even better. "Wow. Okay. Great. I'll pay you back for this."

He shook his head.

"I insist."

"No." He barked the word as if he were angry or something. Again.

Surprise and gratitude and confusion all jumped inside me like solar flares, heating me up. Shyness had been burned out of me in the first few weeks of incarceration with the help of Hourglass Mile's communal showers and vermin-killing soap, but Shade Ganavan was one-man proof that I could still get embarrassed.

I took a step back. Then another. I climbed on board the ship, having let down the stairs for once. It had been more practical for carrying coffee.

"All right. Thanks," I said from the doorway.

I turned and moved deeper into the *Endeavor*, hoping the shadow of the hat's brim had hidden the bright flush across my face.

***

I gathered a small selection of books while Shade got to work filing down the rough edges of the hull where he'd eventually attach the reinforced plates. I said goodbye to the people inside the ship and then to the person outside. Just before I stepped into the elevator tube to head toward Flipping Pages, Shade called out, "Keep your head down, Tess."

I nodded, figuring he was serious about that, since he hadn't called me buttercup or some other crap.

There wasn't an inch of me that didn't think Shade Ganavan knew his way around his city and most of what was going on in it. And he'd seen how I'd reacted to that Dark Watch goon in his shop, since playing it cool hadn't really cropped up. I doubted I'd hidden a single moment of my panic, fear, and flight from Shade, and if he was telling me to keep my head down, he probably meant that Windrow was a district that soldiers patrolled—maybe more than others. It made me extra glad to have his hat. With it, I could look around but still have a shadow on my face.

With five of the rare books in my bag, vitamin D in my body for the first time in years, and sunlight on my bare arms at least, I wound my way out of the docks—noticing plenty of spare platforms on towers other than the Squirrel Tree as I went.

Damn swindlers. Shade had been right.

Ground level was busy—busier than on the previous day. But it was also earlier. The pedestrian lanes were clean and wide, especially the farther I got from the docking towers, and there were even some small trees and shrubs planted here and there to break up the endless monotony of man-made constructions.

The city teemed with people, machines, vehicles of all kinds, some robots, and, weirdly, a whole lot of cats. I'd seen cats before, but only in live-stream videos. The felines were usually stalking birds, running from dogs, or doing what looked like death-defying acrobatics. These cats weren't doing much of anything, though. They were just walking around or sitting there in the sunshine, watching this world go by.

Making it to Windrow wasn't the same thing as finding the bookseller I needed, so I typed Baxton and Lorn into one of the interactive Albion City assistance stands on a busy street corner. A grid pattern instantly popped up on the screen in front of me, mapping out the best route to get there. I turned and walked on, learning the neighborhood as I went.

Flipping Pages already looked special from the outside with the Vivica Vot quotes decorating the storefront, but once I opened the door, it was pure magic. A window into something else. My heart hung suspended for a moment, waiting for the rest of me to catch up.

The first thing I noticed was the bell over the door, just like at Shade's place. Then it was the high shelves lining every single wall, filled to capacity with a jumble of mismatched books. And then it was the comfy chairs and well-used couches toward the back, with *wooden* tables between them, all of them strewn with magazines and books. Paper. I'd never seen so much of it in my life. And the heavy books and glossy pages weren't even in neat piles or stacks. They were haphazard. I loved it. I loved the whole place on sight.

How did Shade Ganavan know about this store? It was obvious he liked it—and books. Was he as drawn to the happy disarray in here as I was? He seemed like the kind of guy who liked to muss things up, and if the heat in my belly when I thought about him was any indication, I wanted him to get a little messy with me, too.

Disheveled. Tangled. Warm. Just like his shop and this place. I'd bet Shade didn't give clinical touches or neat, dry kisses. No, he would lick, devour, and suck.

My pulse surged like that moment when an engine ignites. Thoughts of Shade were distracting me, though, and I blew out a quick breath, trying to get my mind back on track. I was here to sell rare books, not wonder about what that man did in bed.

"Hello?" I called out. There didn't appear to be anyone here.

After a moment, I heard scuffling on stairs, and a woman I assumed was Susan appeared behind the register, having evidently come up from a lower level hidden behind the counter. She was probably in her mid-to-late fifties, a little on the short side, and totally unruly, just like her shop. There wasn't a piece of clothing on her that matched the rest. And nothing in the galaxy could ever have matched the flame-red hair that stuck out in corkscrews all around her head.

"Sorry." Smiling, she made a useless attempt to smooth down her hair. "Just feeding the cats."

"No problem," I said. "I like cats." *In theory, anyway.* I'd yet to touch one, in fact.

I slid my fingers under the strap of my bag, shifting its bulk a little. *Now for the fun process of trying to foist off stolen goods.*

I didn't feel guilty about having taken the books—they'd been completely underappreciated in that billionaire's sterile basement—but I did feel guilty that the library wouldn't get them. If they ended up here, though…

I looked around again. *Wow.* This place was nice.

"I know, I know—the shop's a little untidy." Susan's gaze darted around, turning tenser. "I-I'll straighten up soon."

"No! Don't!"

Her eyes widened at my sudden outburst.

I settled my voice back into a normal volume. "I mean, it's great. It's great just the way it is."

She smiled again, her grin so big I could see the insides of her cheeks. "Are you a kindred spirit, then?"

"Uh… Maybe?" I wasn't quite sure what she meant.

Her eyes narrowed, dipping up and down to look me over. I couldn't figure out her look. It wasn't hostile in any way, but she was still sizing me up—and very obviously, at that.

"White, gray, or black?" she asked.

It would have been a lot easier to answer her question if I'd had any idea what she was talking about, but I decided to just go with it. "None of those colors are much fun by themselves," I said. "Mix them up?"

She nodded. "Stripes, then. Stripes it is."

Huh. Well, weird and wonderful as that was, because anything inexplicable that didn't kill you was actually pretty damn cool in my opinion—the Black Widow, for instance—I had business to conduct. I pulled out one of the books.

"Would you be interested in anything like this?" I asked, turning it over in my hands so that she could admire the old-style hardcover binding. The artwork on the cover jumped right off the page, looking like something straight out of a fairy tale. I hated to give it up, especially before I'd read it, and the kids on Starway 8 would have salivated over something like this, all of them impatiently waiting their turn. Mareeka or her partner, Surral, might have borrowed it from the library for them. I knew of at least one eleven-year-old boy whose eyes would have lit up like starbursts. Coltin loved a good adventure story, and I brought him one whenever I could.

"Hmmm." Susan took the book from my loose grip and looked it over. "No seal?"

"I don't think it ever went through the rounds." And by that, we both knew I meant not only the stampings of approval, but the burnings as well.

"That's unusual." She looked at me, her fingers still lightly tracing the bold, gold lettering of the embossed title. I noticed her fingernails. They weren't dirty, but they were definitely a little unkempt, just like the rest of her. "It must have been in a very secure location to go unnoticed," she said.

I shrugged. Luckily, I was good at getting into secure locations and decoding locks, especially the fancy ones. Also, the galactic government didn't seem to be actively hunting and destroying these kinds of relics anymore.

They must have figured they'd gotten the bulk of them in the beginning and could let slide the spread-out, occasional, hard-to-find rest. Otherwise, places like this shop and a small wing of the Intergalactic Library would have been goners.

"If you like that one, I have four more with me today, and I can get you sixty-seven others. Really good stuff."

She hummed a little under her breath. "So many. Did you steal them?" she asked.

First Shade with his bullets, and now this? *Do I look like a thief?* Apparently, yes.

I lifted my chin. To hell with it. I was always living on the edge. And from the looks of this place, the utter lack of order, I was pretty sure I was safe. "I heard about their unjust imprisonment and liberated them from an unappreciative source."

There was total silence for a moment, and then a laugh cracked out of her. "Anyone who talks that way about books is definitely a kindred spirit."

I was beginning to understand what she meant by that. A slow smile spread across my face. "Can you take any of them?" I asked, hope for my new armored door bubbling inside me.

"I…" She shook her head in what seemed like pretty easy surrender. "If they're all as beautiful as this one, they'll be hard to resist."

Yes! "I need five thousand in universal currency," I said in a low voice.

She sucked in a sharp breath. "That's…not easy." The book lover's gleam in her eyes turned into distress.

"I know. I'm sorry. I would *give* them to you if I could, but that's my best price."

She leaned toward me, her soft waist pressing into the counter, her even softer brown eyes pleading with me to drop my price. "Why? Why do you need that much?"

All the frustration and want and hope and sadness inside me punched out, seeming to blow holes right through the slots between my ribs. "So I can repair a door, fly off this rock, and liberate more things that need freeing." I didn't confine my mission to books. As much as I loved and appreciated them, other things ranked higher than novels on the list of *what to deliver from tyranny*.

Susan closed her eyes and took a deep, long breath, her hair like a halo of fire around her head. When she opened her eyes again, I could have sworn they were wet. For some reason, that made a hint of tears burn behind my own eyes, when I hadn't cried in years. This amazing place—and woman—were wreaking havoc on my heart.

She finally nodded, her look saying it all. *How can I? But how can I not?* Her skin seemed to scream it from every pore.

"Bring me the rest in two days," she said, "and I'll have what you need."

Relief sang through me. That was perfect.

Her eyes suddenly darted to look at something beyond my shoulder, and she shoved the book under the counter, whispering an urgent "Get behind here."

Years of living on the run honed certain instincts in anyone. That tone of voice—low and brittle, with rising panic just underneath—I knew it so well that I didn't hesitate for one second. In two steps, I was around the counter and diving down faster than a comet about to inflict Armageddon on some poor, unsuspecting planet.

CHAPTER

10

THE BELL TINKLED LOUDLY JUST AS I LANDED ON ALL fours behind the counter. Susan stayed close to the register and used her foot to nudge me toward the stairs, sending me oozing down the steep, tight spiral. I held the bag of books against my middle, trying not to make a sound. I stepped quietly, hardly even breathing, and ended up in what must have been her living space, although it closely resembled the bookshop.

My heart racing, I eased backward until I was out of sight entirely but could still hear the conversation above. It sounded as though three, possibly even four people had come in. They were loud—of mouth and step. Military-issue boots always hit the floor with a distinctive thud.

I glanced around to make sure I was alone. I was—except for cats. Cats were everywhere.

I darted anxious looks from side to side and up and down. Cats occupied much of the available space, even sitting atop furniture and bookshelves.

Did they bite? How many colors did they come in?

There were some bright-orange ones draped across the back of a tattered couch, parts of the animals almost pink, especially their noses. The rest of the felines mostly came in whites, grays, and blacks.

Susan's odd question suddenly made more sense. Had she been talking about cats?

A striped one approached me and weaved between my ankles, rubbing against my legs. The sinewy motion reminded me of a snake. Not that I'd ever been around snakes, either. In fact, the only living thing I knew how to deal with besides people was bees. How weird was that?

I stood there, still and quiet, nervous about what was above and nervous about all these unfamiliar creatures below. I tried not to startle the felines or seem threatening in any way. If they ganged up on me, they would totally win.

The smallish cat continued using my leg as a head scratcher while I gazed up, listening for clues as to what was happening overhead. Customers wouldn't have freaked the owner out. But the Dark Watch... And those boots...

My gut clenched. I'd had my back to the door and a bag of stolen, unstamped books in my hands.

Bad move, Tess.

Did Susan get visits like this often? A military patrol banging into her shop?

"When are you finally going to clean this place up, Susan?" a woman demanded. I heard a chair clatter and scrape across the floor, as if roughly kicked aside.

My hands fisted at my sides. I was going to have a fit if they touched those wooden tables.

"Oh... Um... Soon. I've been meaning to." Susan went quiet for a moment. "I got distracted by a book and...forgot."

Someone snorted loudly. A male. "And what book had you so interested that you couldn't clean up this shithole like we told you to last week?"

Shithole! This was the most amazing place I'd ever seen besides the apiary on Starway 8.

I swallowed the rage and protest burning up my throat. Now wasn't the time to shout them out.

I could tell that Susan was moving out from behind the counter, probably drawing them away from me. She must have walked over to a shelf. "This one. It's... it's a bit older. All about the legends that sprang up around Mall Hall after its orbit changed and its moon drifted off."

"No seal on it," a third voice said a moment later.

"Oh? Yes, well, look at that. I'm not sure anyone minds so much about that anymore," Susan said.

"The Overseer minds," the man grumbled.

Actually, I was pretty sure the Overseer had bigger fish to fry, like the rebel squad that had just found and destroyed the unmanned probe that had been sneaking around Sector 17. It had probably been gathering information about the possible location of the rebel base.

Asshole goons. They'd never find what didn't want to be found.

Even from downstairs, I heard the Dark Watch soldier scrape the saliva out of his throat with a vulgar grating sound and then spit. I didn't have to see it to know he'd spat on one of Susan's beautiful books, and it was all I could do not to tear upstairs and spit on *him*. If I hadn't been outnumbered and armed with nothing but four books and a clingy cat, I might have tried it.

"Well, now it's got somethin' on it, doesn't it?" the man drawled.

"It does," Susan agreed without a hint of animosity in her voice.

Feet stomped, trooping all over the floor above. "Now clean this place up before we come back!" the first man growled. "Or we'll double the fine from last time."

The bell chimed violently, and then they were gone.

My pulse continued to roar, at odds with the new quiet in the bookstore. The cat still wove between my legs with long, sinewy caresses. The feline was small. Not a baby, I didn't think, but slight and lithe. The rumbling vibration coming from its body was curiously soothing and helped to settle my incensed spirit and rattled nerves.

Susan wound down the spiral staircase and located me in the maze of cats. "Sorry about that. They were just…"

"Harassing you?" I supplied.

She nodded, adding a fatalistic shrug that told me this had happened before—and would happen again. Everything about the movement said *it is what it is*.

But something in her eyes seemed suddenly forlorn. Not defeated, but unsure and maybe a little scared. I put a hold on the rebellious rhetoric I wanted to spew with angry and justified words. She was already fighting in her own way, bravely, and I had no right to try to persuade her into more. The reason more people didn't rise up was because it just meant getting beaten down. That kind of life was something a person had to choose.

Fucking Dark Watch. Damn Overseer, with his tyrannical—no, maniacal—vision of the galactic ideal.

"Your bookstore isn't a shithole. Far from it." I wanted to reassure her, since I hadn't been able to defend her. If they'd turned physical, I wouldn't have been able to stop myself, but apparently, bullying and verbal threats weren't enough to make me take a risk with myself anymore, and I wasn't sure I liked what that said.

"No," she agreed. "But it's untidy—at least for them."

Chances were, those goons probably wouldn't have cared about *untidy* at some past point in their lives, and maybe they would have even liked it. But anyone who joined the galactic military was eventually brainwashed into believing the Overseer's jargon and garbage.

"Untidy isn't the easiest path these days," I pointed out. Expressing her desire for more personal freedom through mildly subversive means like a riotously disorderly bookshop made Susan a target for fines and intimidation. That took guts.

She still looked shaken, but a sense of pride washed through me. For her. For me. For everyone who consciously drew their own line in the sand and refused to cross it.

"For what it's worth, I like your form of protest," I said, finally getting up the nerve to squat down and pat the cat. It immediately turned its small, striped head into my hand and rubbed enthusiastically. Its fur was soft and short, its nose wet, its whiskers wiry. The rumbling sound got louder.

"And for what it's worth, I like yours," Susan replied with a significant look, holding up the book I'd shown her and that she'd hidden behind the counter.

I nodded my thanks, knowing that the level of defiance the crew and I embraced wasn't for everyone. We knew the consequences of our actions. We'd already lived them. We still did.

Susan's *kindred spirits* remark came back to me. For some reason, it made me think of a huge web connecting everyone who fought the oppressive regime in whatever way they could, big or small. The image morphed into stars, bright spots of hope and courage winking all over the Dark—one giant constellation, spread out, but strong. Stronger than the Overseer thought.

I scratched under the cat's chin, where fluffy white fur led down to a slim chest. It seemed to like that and offered me better access, tilting its little head to one side and closing its eyes into contented slits.

I smiled. This little beauty had a small body but a big personality, if I had to guess. I wondered if all cats were like that, or if this one was special and different from the rest.

"What's that noise?" I asked. "It's like this cat has an engine inside it. It's not an android or something, is it?" I'd never heard of robotic cats.

Susan laughed. "He's quite alive. It's called purring. It means he likes you."

I straightened, the feel of the cat's stiff whiskers lingering on my hand. I rubbed the tickling sensation away. "I thought it was a her." I hadn't seen any obvious evidence of *himness*.

"Oh." Susan made a snipping motion with her fingers. "Can't have *more* cats, you know?"

Ah. Poor little guy. I think I did know.

"He's yours," Susan said.

I blinked. "What?"

"He chose you. That much is clear." She nodded

toward the cat at my feet. "Plus, he's gray, white, and black. All mixed up—just like you wanted."

Anxiety shot through me. I hadn't had a clue what she'd been talking about. "I'm not equipped for a cat."

"Not to worry." Susan flitted around her living room before coming back to me with a small metallic tray— kind of cat-sized—and a bag of sand.

"The litter renews itself," she announced. "Very handy. Only needs refreshing once a year or so."

She shoved everything at me, clearly intending for me to take it. I removed the remaining four books from my bag, set them on the nearby table, and then slipped the tray and litter inside my carrier in their place.

Crap, that was heavy. It seemed I had a cat.

"What's his name?" I asked.

Susan glanced around her wonderfully disorderly, cat-strewn home. "I don't really name them anymore. Too many." She scooped up one of the big, furry, orange ones. It was four times the size of my new companion. "If I want them to come, I say, *Here, kitty, kitty*, and if I want them to listen, I say, *Hey, you!*"

In a timely demonstration, she called out, "Hey, you! Get off the table!" and a slinky black cat jumped down with a light thud from apparently the one piece of furniture on which they weren't allowed.

Susan shook her head. "The paw prints they leave all over that glass top…" She turned back to me, smiling warmly despite the wry resignation in her voice. "I may not like to conform, but I do like a clean place to eat."

I nodded in agreement. I was enthralled, fascinated, and somehow completely at home, even with all the unfamiliar cats.

"Would you like some tea?" Susan asked.

I wished I could stay, but I still had clothes to buy, and I didn't want to be gone so long that the crew started to worry about me. I kept both explanations to myself and politely declined.

"Maybe next time, then." Susan made it feel like a real invitation, one she genuinely meant.

"Thank you." I'd be back in two days. Maybe I'd take her up on the offer then.

She glanced at my new cat. "You can name him, though."

My eyes widened. What did you name a cat? "Um…"

She shook her head, making her sunburst hair move. "No, 'Um' is too vague. It won't work."

It took a second for understanding to sink in, but once it did, I burst out laughing, startling *Not*-Um into a low crouch. He looked at me a little warily for the first time, his black-tipped ears flattening back.

So, no startling noises for my cat. He was going to love a high-speed, shoot-'em-up, jump-around space chase, for sure.

"I think I'll name him Bonk," I finally decided, tilting my head to look at him.

"Bonk?" she asked.

"He spent five minutes bonking his head against my ankles." And now he was doing it again, bumping and rubbing like my legs were the best things around. "What's that *W* on his forehead?" I asked.

"People usually see that as an *M*. Most tabbies have it."

I swiveled to see him from the front instead of from above. "I was looking at him the wrong way, I guess."

Susan picked up Bonk and gently slid him into my bag on top of the cat equipment. He immediately sat and poked his head out. She gave him a final pat.

"Not the wrong way," she said to me. "I think you just see things from a different angle than most."

My heart warmed, understanding that for the compliment it was. I had a feeling Susan saw things from a different angle, too, and maybe in brighter colors.

✳ ✳ ✳

After leaving Susan with the promise to return in two days' time with the rest of the books, I went to a couple of the large clothing emporiums I'd seen while walking through Windrow on my way to the bookstore. I didn't linger, even though personal shopping was a rare treat for me—something I remembered doing with my mother in fancy buildings with beautiful light—and I could hardly feel guilty about using a small part of our dwindling funds to replace some of the essential items I'd lost. The real reason I moved quickly was because I'd had to zip Bonk into my bag to keep him out of sight, and I was scared he'd freak out. Or suffocate.

As it was, he stayed calm—and fine—but I ended up checking on him every minute or two, panicking when I didn't feel him moving around.

Luckily, I didn't need much. Having been locked in the closet, my flight suits and spare boots had all survived the hole-in-the-hull carnage, and I really only had to pick up some underthings and a few civilian pants and tops. I'd taken the spare bedding off the never-used cot in the brig but left our four-bunk guest bedroom intact in case we needed the extra beds. We mostly moved food and chose our own missions, but sometimes we were needed to transport rebels between operations, with our orders coming directly from the Fold.

On my way back to the docks, I started to get the prickly sensation of someone watching me. I couldn't look around too much without being obvious, so I took the most winding, convoluted path I could manage without getting myself lost, trying to shake the feeling—and whoever it was, if there really was someone. I didn't underestimate the strength of paranoia. It was entirely possible my twitchiness was all coming from my own head. As Shade and I had said earlier, the imagination could be a powerful thing.

Just before I reached the docking towers, my anxiety finally faded. Maybe that chafing feeling on my nerves had just been because of the multiple Dark Watch patrols I'd seen around the city, some on foot and some in armor-plated hover cruisers. I'd kept my head down, Shade's hat on, and stuck almost uncomfortably close to groups of other pedestrians, pretending to be a part of them. Guards were more likely to overlook harmless-seeming civilian groups than anyone walking alone.

When I finally strode onto our platform on the three-hundred-and-fourteenth level of the Squirrel Tree, Shade Ganavan was just packing up for the day. A welding mask and various other pieces of equipment now occupied the hover crate where the two metal tiles had previously been.

"Hello, SRP," I called out as I looked over the progress Shade had made, presumably with Jax's help to fit the heavy tiles into place. It was impressive, and I was beginning to think he might deserve his nickname. He'd patched up my bedroom entirely in one day and gotten a good start on another hole.

"Sugar." Shade acknowledged me back with a slight smirk.

I let that go. He'd done good work.

"Thanks for the bookstore recommendation. Flipping Pages was perfect."

Shade nodded and then took a long drink of water, draining half a bottle in one go. More stubble had grown on his jaw since this morning, giving his already attractive features a rougher look I liked even more.

The rest of him looked grubbier, too. There was a black streak of oil down one corded forearm, and he was covered in the sticky evidence of a hard day's work. His short, dark hair looked damp and crushed, probably from being under his welding helmet. Sweat slicked his neck. I watched a bead roll down the thick tendon that began just behind his ear and angled toward the base of his throat. The drip caught on his collarbone and stopped.

My mouth went suddenly dry. I wanted to lick the drop off.

"What's the matter, starshine? Never seen hot and dirty before?" he asked.

My eyes jumped to his. He hadn't put even a hint of innuendo into his voice. I couldn't tell if he was flirting or not, but desire still surged inside me like an electrical pulse. Warmth simmered between my legs, and *hot and dirty* played on repeat through my every thought.

"Seen all kinds of things," I eventually said.

His expression seemed to harden somehow. "I'll bet you have," he muttered under his breath.

I felt that little crease form between my eyebrows, the one that was quickly etching itself into my first permanent wrinkle. The heat swirling through my abdomen dissipated, leaving only confusion instead. The weirdest things seemed to tick Shade off.

Bonk broke the tension by poking his delicate head out of my bag and letting out a croaky little meow. The still-sleepy, wake-up sound was immeasurably cute.

Shade frowned at my bag. "What the hell is that?"

"A cat," I said. "They're all over the place."

"Yeah, but you don't just pick up any old one. It could have vermin. Or be totally wild."

"He's not *any old one*," I said, leaping to Bonk's defense. "He's Bonk, and Susan gave him to me."

"She gave you a fucking cat?" He looked so stunned it was almost comical.

"Jealous?" I asked. "She's never given you a cat?"

His hands landed on his hips. Machine oil and scarred knuckles flashed at me.

Damn. I liked those hands.

"I don't want a cat," he said.

"Sure you don't." My tone conveyed just how much I believed *that*.

Unzipping my bag all the way, I took Bonk out and lifted him up onto the *Endeavor*. He started sniffing around immediately. I hoped he wasn't about to pee. I still needed to set up that box.

I turned back to Shade. "You can pat mine if you'd like."

His eyes took on a sudden glint, and a blush exploded across my face, burning up my pale cheeks.

I waited for Shade to follow up with something,

anything, hoping he would, even if it was a lewd joke. He just turned back to my cat instead. He'd apparently lost all interest in flirting with me.

Internally dealing with my disappointment, I produced the metal tray and sand from my bag. "Any idea what to do with these?" I asked.

Shade took both, setting the tray in the ship's open door near Bonk—who immediately looked interested. He tore open the top corner of the bag and dumped a thick layer of sand into the bottom of the tray before nudging the whole thing toward Bonk.

Bonk climbed in, squatted, and peed.

"Well, that was easy," I said, impressed.

Shade folded the top of the bag over to close it and then put it down next to Bonk's tray. "Susan gave you the good stuff. You don't even have to clean it. It cleans itself."

A nearly maintenance-free pet sounded good to me. I had my hands full enough as it was.

"How do you know Susan?" I asked.

"She want your books?" he asked in lieu of answering.

I nodded. "I'm bringing her the rest in two days." I immediately wondered why I'd said that. Anything beyond the fact that there was going to be a transaction wasn't information Shade Ganavan needed to know.

He stared. I stared back.

Great Sky Mother, we have to stop doing that.

Shade finally reached a hand out to Bonk. After a few careful sniffs, Bonk leaned in, looking ready for a scratch. Shade obliged, muscles he'd probably overused today standing out firmly under the thin layer of his cotton shirt. The dark material stuck to his upper body in places, revealing contours and revving up my apparently uncontrollable imagination. I couldn't recall ever having had such a strong urge to reach out and touch.

"I'll see about getting you that new door, then," he said, letting his big, grease-stained hand drop.

I nodded again, but that didn't seem like enough. "Thank you, Shade. Really. I'm glad I found you. I mean...your shop."

I nearly bit my tongue. *I'm glad I found you?* Who *said* something like that?

Clearly, two years in a maximum-security prison and then reclusive living with the same four people in a confined space severely eroded a person's social skills. I appeared to have none left.

I stood there, my chin up despite my embarrassment, which seemed to be a permanent state around Shade Ganavan. Who the hell could still fluster a woman who'd been used as a science experiment, abandoned, imprisoned, hunted, and chased through a freaking black hole, for fuck's sake? It must have been Shade's super-power. *Great.*

He didn't respond to my thanks, and the awkward silence grew so heavy that I could have sworn gravity doubled right then and there on Albion 5.

"Here's your hat." I took it off and handed it to him, trying not to wonder how crushed my hair was and in which directions my bangs were sticking out.

He took it from me only to flop it back down on my head. "See you soon, Tess Bailey. When I've got the rest of your stuff."

Shade turned, and I watched him walk toward the elevator tubes, Bonk already bumping my shoulder and jaw with his little head, hitting whatever he could reach from his new perch on board the *Endeavor*.

The transparent tube Shade had entered whooshed down, taking him out of sight, and I felt on edge and unsatisfied, as though he'd just left in the middle of something I hadn't finished yet.

Maybe there was nothing left to say. I'd get his money. He'd get my door and the other panels. Transaction complete.

Shade had definitely flirted with me in his shop. It had been exciting and nice, but maybe I wasn't the type of woman a man stayed interested in. Except for Bently. He'd had staying power. The slimy jerk had offered every morning for two years to keep me out of the mines for the day in exchange for hard and fast and rough against the prison cell wall.

I scoffed. As if I'd ever have chosen that over a day with Jaxon, even if the mines had meant breathing in toxic fumes, risking the explosions, and breaking my back under the heavy loads.

At least Dagger Bently never tried to force me. He was a beefy, power-abusing turd, but he wasn't a rapist, which had made me glad he was my cellblock guard.

I leaned into Bonk, and he rubbed against my chin, making that running motor sound again.

"We're home," I told him. I rubbed back with my nose, and he purred louder. I hoped that meant he liked his new digs.

As Bonk and I got better acquainted, I couldn't help wondering why Shade hadn't answered my question about how he knew Susan. Had he just been more interested in confirming that he'd get his money for the armored door? Or was he hiding something I might want to know?

Speculating was useless, but the turn of my thoughts brought home how little I knew about the man who was going to be all over my ship for the next week.

CHAPTER

11

"WHAT DO YOU SAY WE FIRE UP THE TABLET AND SEE what's going on out there?" I asked about forty-eight hours after our perilous descent onto Albion 5.

Jax looked iffy. Miko wrinkled her nose.

"We encrypt everything," I reminded them. "What could go wrong?"

"Famous last words," Jax muttered, sliding out from under my console and wiping his hands on the rag he'd tucked into his belt. Between the two of us, we'd managed to fix the ship's electrical systems, and the *Endeavor* was running smoothly again—or at least without sparking and spontaneously shutting down sections of the bridge.

Better still, with Albion 5's steady sunlight on our solar panels, we were up to almost a quarter of our power capacity again after only two days. Life was good, all things considered.

It would be even better as soon as Shade Ganavan came back with a big pile of parts.

I scratched between Bonk's ears, listening to him

purr. Bonk had conquered the entire crew in less than a day and was now king of the *Endeavor* and grand master of the bridge, despite the fact that his main activity was to curl up on one of Jax's old sweaters and sleep.

"What a tough life you've got, Bonk," I said, smoothing down the white fluff under his chin. He tilted his head for better patting, and his little motor sped up. "Do nothing and still rule the roost."

We'd already seen significantly more of Fiona and Shiori on the bridge, when Fiona usually stuck to her lab, and Shiori preferred the kitchen or her bedroom to the busier section of the ship. Such was the appeal of Bonk, his Feline Majesty, Lord Tabby. I was seriously contemplating hanging a sign over his sleeping sweater that read *Pat here to feel good*.

I smiled, enjoying my cat's steady rumble. He was so slight that the sound made his whole body vibrate.

So far, I'd fed him the same food we'd eaten. Some beef stew. Cooked vegetables. Rice. He seemed to like it. And it was convenient, just scraping leftovers onto his plate. None of us ever wanted to reheat the canned stuff anyway. It wasn't good enough for that.

Earlier, we'd all followed him outside when he'd leaped down from the ship and started exploring the docking platform. He'd had a grand old time chasing a twirling feather around, and we'd all laughed our asses off at his springing, stalking, and pouncing until his antics had taken him too close to the edge, and then we'd all freaked out and started shouting at him to come back.

Hey, you! had worked like a charm, thank the Powers for that.

I'd heard that cats always landed on their feet, but I seriously doubted that applied when falling from three hundred and fourteen platforms up the Squirrel Tree.

Now Bonk was safely back inside along with the rest of us, and I was ready for some news, especially from Starway 8.

I logged on to the right channel and then sent a message to Mareeka, asking how things were and sending my love to her and Surral. While waiting for a response, I scrolled through various articles. There wasn't anything about a stolen lab, missing *vaccines*, or a confrontation in Sector 14. Of course not. Those things would never have made it into the public feeds.

There was something about a natural gas explosion half-destroying a weapons plant on Switchtide, and then there was a long article about troop deployment on one of the large inhabitable moons just outside of Sector 17.

Reading between the lines, I saw a rebel attack on a galactic armament facility and then a clear message to the insurgents hiding in the Outer Zones. *We're here. We're watching. We control you.*

But in fact, they didn't. Despite forty years of hardcore looking, the military still had no idea where the rebel stronghold was. That was the cool thing about thinking outside of the Overseer's tight little box: you could find a hole.

A message back from Mareeka pinged and popped up on my screen.

Viral epidemic. Possible quarantine
in sight. STAY OUT OF SECTOR.

I sucked in a sharp breath, tapping her message and making it full-screen. It still said the same thing, only bigger now.

"What?" Jaxon asked, frowning over at me.

"Disease on Starway 8."

His mouth thinned. "It's either something new, or…"

"Yeah." I nodded, my stomach knotting up.

With our efforts, our thefts of cure-alls over the last five years, the director and other personnel on Starway 8 were fairly well-protected against disease. So were many of the children. But we hadn't managed to get any inoculations to them in almost a year. That meant this was either a mutated strain of some already-known sickness, which would make it even more dangerous; something entirely new that could hit anyone; or something that had been around for a while, and it was the newcomers and the little ones who were dropping like bees covered in pesticides.

My heart turned over like lead. There had to be something we could do.

I sprang up, disturbing Bonk enough for him to crack open one greenish-yellow eye. "You want this?" I asked Jaxon, holding out the tablet.

He shook his head, so I powered down and then slid the tablet back into the cubbyhole under my console.

"Where are you going?" Jax's question, or rather the wariness in his voice, made me hesitate midstep.

"Nowhere." I glanced at him over my shoulder, my hand already reaching for the touch panel adjacent to the automatic door. "Staying on the ship. I'll be back soon."

He nodded, and I let myself off the bridge, heading for the lab attachment I'd closed up tightly two days earlier. My heart pounded a little harder with each step I took along the *Endeavor*'s corridors, across the central cargo bay, and then through the rear air lock and accordion-like vacuum seal. *What am I doing?*

Then again, I'd acted on some pretty bad ideas in the last several days. Why stop now?

The second I entered the stolen lab, the stale air hit me like a dirty sock in the face. My breaths tasted like crap on my tongue and didn't quite satisfy my lungs.

I shut the door again and cautiously sniffed, adjusting to the stuffiness. We'd kept the lab sufficiently ventilated for Big Guy's sake, but I'd stopped doing that when he'd left, and I hadn't thought anyone would be back in here, least of all me.

The oxygen levels seemed okay—although definitely not ideal—and if I hadn't been about to do the unthinkable, I'd have gone back and opened all the doors to let in some fresh air again. Being locked inside a silent metal can with rank O_2 and no systems running was totally unnerving, but there was no way I was risking an accidental audience for this.

In finding the concealed test tubes with my initials and ID number on them, Big Guy had helped me link the enhancer to my blood. I never got sick, and Fiona had said the false vaccines boosted healing. What if I could boost healing at the orphanage without giving the children something invasive, altering, and possibly dangerous like that military-engineered cocktail? The Overseer's serum did who-knew-what to a person, but what if Fiona could use her knowledge or her medicinal plants to make something less risky out of one of the serum's main ingredients?

At least, I hoped it would be less risky. I didn't know what made my blood different, but I'd been carrying it around inside me for twenty-six years and it hadn't killed me or made me sick or insane. Chances were, it wouldn't harm the kids, either.

All those days in a frightened haze, all those vials of blood stolen from me, and no one had ever told me what they'd found; they'd just taken. And my knowledge was as incomplete as ever, because I hadn't let anyone near me with a needle since the day my father decided I was no longer worth keeping around. Not even Surral had ever gotten a blood sample out of me, and she was my doctor.

Maybe it was time to finally find out what the hell was inside me. It would be worth it if I could help Starway 8.

Shoving aside remembered whispers of "foreign," "inexplicable," and "unknown" that still made my hair stand up with a shiver, I went directly to what I needed and opened one of the drawers I'd taken stock of during a previous exploration of the lab attachment.

Bingo. Needles. Vials. Blood bags. Everything in sterile cases.

It was too bad I'd dumped the test tubes Big Guy had found, or I wouldn't have to do this.

Trying not to overthink my actions, I pushed up my sleeve before I could change my mind. I grabbed a rubber strip and tied it just above my elbow with the help of one hand and my teeth. Then I sprayed the inner part of my elbow with a disinfectant, feeling more and more detached the further I got into the process.

I knew exactly what to expect. The cool dampness on

my skin that would almost instantly evaporate. The eye-stinging, nose-wrinkling odor of antiseptic. The sharp prick and then the steady flow of blood. Sometimes, they'd drained me straight into oblivion.

I paused, the syringe in my almost-steady hand. I'd never drawn my own blood before, and I had definitely never given it voluntarily. But doing this on my own terms, for my own reasons, was different and somehow empowering. I didn't know if I was making a good decision, or the right one, but at least it was mine. *My* choice.

I looked down at my pale skin and at the needle poised over my inner elbow. My heart raced, and the tourniquet felt tight and uncomfortable.

Who could this hurt? I'd kissed people, had sex with Gabe, bled on just about all of my crew members, and whatever was different about my blood or fluids had never harmed them. There was no reason to think my body contained anything damaging to other people, at least not in its natural state.

I forced the slight tremor from my hand. If I was going to do this, there was no sense in mucking it up with the jitters. I'd seen my blood drawn often enough to have the right idea about technique, and I went straight for the vein I knew worked the best. Maybe it was more the feel of the process I knew by heart? In any case, I got blood flowing into the syringe on only the second try and then filled up a whole blood bag before calling it quits.

Sliding the needle out of my vein, I held a sterile compress to my arm until blood stopped welling from the tiny hole I'd made. I wondered if I felt a little woozy. I couldn't tell. It might have been my memory supplying everything about how I thought I *should* feel after something like this—how I often had.

In the end, I decided it was just the ghost of the past haunting my imagination. I stood and felt fine. I pulled my sleeve down, not bothering with any kind of bandage, and then threw the used needle and syringe into the covered biohazard trash.

The clear plastic bag full of my blood lay on the metal lab table. I picked it up and held it away from me a little warily. With all his wealth, resources, and experiments, I wondered if my father had ever figured out what was different about me.

Actually, *what* probably wasn't an issue at this point. The questions that remained were why? And how?

I started toward the series of doors that would lead me out of this airless trap, powering down the lights in the lab attachment when I reached the exit.

The problem was, even if dear old Dad knew the answers to any of those questions, I still didn't.

***

After giving the blood sufficient time to cool down in one of our cargo bay refrigerators, I made my way to Fiona's lab and called out a greeting to her. She turned, her goggles and mask in place and a tiny eyedropper in one hand. Rows of test tubes sat lined up in front of her, all color-coded and carefully labeled. Floral-toned liquids bubbled in beakers behind them.

"Are you back to distilling essential oils?" I asked. She'd been working on naturopathic cures for Starway 8 since we hadn't found anything pharmaceutical to give them in ages. I'd thought our luckless streak had finally ended, but taking the lab didn't exactly work out like I'd hoped.

She nodded. "They're pungent. You might want to stay back."

Taking her word for it, I hovered near the doorway to Fiona's leafy green domain. Her plants had a significantly larger living space than I did. The strong, almost overpowering odor of whatever she was working on reached me a moment later, and my eyes started to water.

"Wow. What is that?" My nose already felt burned up and hollowed out.

"Celioptolix. It'll clear up a stuffy nose like that." She tried to snap her fingers but just produced a slight rubbing sound because of her latex gloves.

"A drop of that in the ventilation system might help everyone breathe better," I said.

Fiona nodded. "The most direct method for dealing with the sniffles is a small dose of this in very hot water and then inhale the steam."

I'd seen Jax and the others do that, and it seemed to bring them some relief, although only temporarily. Despite progress in medicine and science every day, some of the most basic infections had no cure. The common cold was still a huge pain in the neck, but at least here on the *Endeavor*, and thanks to Fiona, the crew could suck up some highly concentrated celioptolix and at least be able to breathe more easily while they waited out the virus.

Fiona set aside her equipment and took off her mask and gloves. I seriously doubted they were dealing with a common cold on Starway 8. Not if there was a possible quarantine in sight. Whatever had hit the orphanage must have been far more dangerous and highly infectious.

I wondered what could have brought on a virus like that. Mareeka kept her ventilation system cleaner than anyone else in the galaxy, Surral was a top-notch doctor, and a good portion of the kids had already been inoculated against the really bad stuff.

Unfortunately, viruses mutated, and vaccines had to be updated annually. The crew and I hadn't always found the most recent inoculations—or had enough for everyone.

"What've you got there?" Fiona asked, eyeing the blood bag in my hands.

I held it out. "I found this in a hidden refrigerated unit in the lab. It was labeled Point Zero, so I think it could be the base ingredient in the super soldier serum." I did my best to ignore the guilt dragging my heart toward my feet. I hated lying to Fiona, especially now that she knew more of the truth about me than ever before.

Her eyes seemed to brighten as she took the bag and studied it. "Blood. I knew it. Usually serums are a saline and chemical cocktail, but there was so much organic in that one that I knew it had to be different."

"Looks like you were right," I said, starting to feel sick to my stomach. The psychosomatic symptoms of lying to your only friends really sucked.

She glanced up from the bag. "I thought you'd searched the lab and found nothing but the serum?"

I shrugged. "Big Guy must have distracted me. And everything was such a panic and a rush with the Dark Watch chasing us that I obviously didn't look carefully enough." All that was true, at least. "This time, I found that."

"Do you want me to study it?" she asked hopefully, microscopes practically dancing in her eyes.

I nodded, almost wishing that Fiona wasn't so easily taking my word for everything. I was already a liar. Her faith in me made me feel like a real jerk, too.

But there was a reason for all this. A good one, I thought.

"The kids on Starway 8 are getting sick. Some kind of really bad virus. Didn't you say the super soldier serum could boost healing?"

"Yeeesss." She dragged the word out, looking at me strangely. "But it could also turn them into huge battering rams that no one can control. Don't really know," she said, frowning.

"I'm not talking about giving the kids those false vaccines," I hastened to assure her. "I'm wondering if this organic component—point zero—could be useful to boost healing, though." I'd never been sick, *ever*, not *once*. There had to be a reason for that. "What if you mixed it with some of your medicinal plants? Maybe it wouldn't even have to be a shot. Just ingested or something."

Fiona looked skeptical. She turned the blood bag over in her hands. "I've already got a few purifying herbs distilled in fairly high quantities. Detox stuff. I could do some experimenting, but without an actual sick person to test anything on, I'm not really sure what it'll be worth."

I nodded. "I get it. I won't get my hopes up. Just see what you think of that ingredient by itself and then think about what might help slow or stop a viral infection." I shoved my hands into my pockets, trying to look casual and probably failing. I never put my hands in my pockets. What a time to start.

"Sound good?" I asked.

"I'll get right on it," Fiona said, starting to seem eager, despite her warning about the chances of success.

Maybe it wasn't the best idea, but I added, "There's more where that came from. Just let me know what you need, and I can get it."

"Okay. Great." She moved toward her lab station and put the blood into a small cooling unit before using an antiseptic wipe to clean off the shiny metallic surface of her worktable.

"Did you ever think that if there's an outbreak on Starway 8, it's to draw you there?" she asked without turning around.

Unfortunately, the thought had crossed my mind. I was trying not to let it stop me. "Bridgebane thinks I'm dead."

"Bridgebane knows you were after large quantities of vaccines. He also knows where you grew up, because he's the one who put you there."

I rubbed my arms, feeling chilled. "Could anyone really do that? To children?" It was despicable.

Fiona turned, her brows lifting in question. "You know him better than I do. Could he?"

Infect thousands of kids with something awful just to draw me out on the off chance I hadn't been squashed by the Black Widow?

My last meal churned in my stomach. "Yeah. I think he could."

Funny how I still remembered a time when he hadn't seemed like such a terrible person. He'd brought me toys. Played with me. Talked with Mom. Maybe it had taken a while for my father to brainwash him.

"Then going there is a bad idea," Fiona said.

A bad idea had rarely stopped me. My only fantastic idea had gotten me caught and locked up.

"Just see what you find, and then we'll discuss," I said.

Fiona nodded, already setting up her most powerful microscope. "I'll let you know if anything looks promising." She straightened, her face brightening again. "And once the *Endeavor* is up and running again, we could always slip into the Fold and then get someone else to take the solution over to Starway 8. Someone no one is looking for."

That wasn't a bad idea. I hated sending anyone else into danger, but I also knew that a lot of rebels lived for this kind of thing—the daring deed that made them feel as though they'd accomplished something in the endless fight against the Overseer's regime.

But who could get into the orphanage more easily and safely than I could? I knew the gigantic structure like the back of my hand and could run through the whole place blindfolded. Also, *I* wouldn't get sick with whatever was raging through the children.

"Asher. Frank. Macey…" Fiona looked at me over her shoulder again. "Caeryssa's always up for anything."

When they weren't out wreaking havoc, Fiona's old friends from 17 would lie low in the Fold, popping in and out, just like we did. They were Nightchasers, too, moving food, weapons, equipment, sometimes people. Undertaking anything on a deadline was incredibly stressful, though, because you never knew if you'd find the Fold quickly, or if it would take days and days of searching. But the Fold's random movements were part of what made it so safe, one of its inexplicable self-defense mechanisms.

"Coltin is Asher's nephew," I said. Coltin's health as a young child had been really iffy, which was why Asher hadn't adopted him. He'd wanted to, but things had been so touch and go at first that he'd known Coltin had a better chance of survival with Surral looking after him.

Surral had done the doctoring, but I'd ended up doing a lot of the rest. That was how things worked on Starway 8—the older kids stepped in when and where they were needed. I'd been helping out in the orphanage's sick bay and had seen a young man dropping off an infant. He'd looked so devastated about it that I hadn't been able to walk away. From the day Coltin had arrived at six weeks old to the time I'd left when he was nearly three, I'd spent more time with him than with anyone else, even Gabe. He'd just seemed to need me. I'd fed him. Rocked him. Heard his first words. Seen his first steps. It had almost been like being a mother.

"Asher could go to Starway 8, then," Fiona said. "If a patrol stopped him and things started to get sticky, they could verify the connection—no problem."

That was if Asher was around and easily found. And thinking about Coltin in a box full of sick people made me nervous enough to want to check on him myself. He was healthy enough now, but his breathing was always a bit labored, even when he was just sitting still and listening to a story.

"I'll keep it in mind," I said, touching my hand to the panel that would open the door.

For some reason, Shade Ganavan also came to mind. Mr. Space Rogue Phenom was probably pretty good at getting in and out of sticky situations without getting himself stuck.

CHAPTER

12

SHADE WONDERED WHAT THE HELL HE WAS DOING WHEN he went back to the Squirrel Tree before he had Tess's parts. He also wondered why the hell he was even getting Tess's parts. He kept telling himself it was a waste of time to fix her ship. He didn't mind hard labor, but it was a pain in the ass to do it for no reason.

Unfortunately, he hadn't quite been able to slap the cuffs on this one yet. It was more than just having met Tess before he saw the job. That first day of repairs, he'd been willing to put in some work just to scope out her ship, her crew, and how things were on the three-hundred-and-fourteenth level of the fucking rip-off Squirrel Tree. He'd wanted to see if he could figure out anything about the stolen goods. But then she'd brought him coffee, and they'd *talked*.

He couldn't remember the last time he'd had such an interesting conversation with anyone. Maybe with Susan, but she was more like an eccentric aunt, fluttery and easily distracted. Tess made his blood heat and his mind soar back to the things he used to dream about before he'd gotten himself into a situation where he needed to make a lot of money. His legacy was falling apart in the hands of Scarabin White, and he needed to buy it back before the asshole ruined everything his family had built. Some of the older docking towers were barely safe at this point. Without repairs, people's lives could be at stake.

Shade zoomed up to the *Endeavor* in the elevator tube. He stepped out when the lift opened and looked around the platform. No one on watch. The ship's door wide open.

How the fuck did these people stay alive?

At least the stairs weren't down, as usual. He knew the crew hardly used them, because he'd been keeping watch. He'd started to feel like a stalker by the fourth flyby of Tess's platform today, but he'd needed to make sure things were still quiet, and that none of the other bounty hunters had sniffed her out.

A scowl pulling at his face, Shade walked to the open cargo cruiser and rapped hard on the metal floor, calling out a hello as he did.

A small woman showed up a moment later, her long black hair swinging when she leaped back at the sight of him.

Was he that scary?

She set her jaw, looking almost like she was gearing up for a do-over, and then stepped forward again.

"Is Tess around?" Shade asked.

"Name, please," she said like some clerk at a reception desk. Her hand hovered over the panel that would slide the inner door shut, leaving him closed out on the dock.

"Shade Ganavan."

He thought she relaxed. "Do you have something for the ship?" she asked.

He shook his head. "No, just a question for Tess." He'd decided that instead of just watching her, he should try to talk to her. Maybe it would help him figure out what to do next.

The woman pursed her lips, not moving. What was she? The damn gatekeeper?

"Wait here." She finally turned on the ball of her foot, not inviting him in as she left.

She came back with Jax. The big man didn't look happy.

Nerves suddenly bunched in Shade's belly. "Tess isn't here?" Had she gone out when he hadn't been looking and not come back?

Jax answered with a question of his own. "You got some parts to drop off?"

"Not tonight. As I told…" He looked in question at the woman, whom he now realized was missing a hand.

"Miko," she supplied.

"…Miko, I'm looking for Tess."

Jax glared at him, then around at the fading light. Dusk was falling fast. "Why?" he asked.

Well, this was going well. Jax had seemed a lot friendlier when they'd been working together. But that hadn't been about Tess.

"I thought I'd show her around the city." Actually, getting *out* of the city sounded better right now. He felt stifled. Having nothing but bad choices always made him feel like he couldn't breathe.

Jax's eyes narrowed.

"If she wants," Shade added.

What *he* wanted was to get to know her better. He

needed to make a decision. His damn docks were on the line. What had been a slow work in progress only two days ago could turn into tomorrow's reality with just a bit of rope and a call to Bridgebane.

"Oh, it's SRP," a new woman said, showing up in the doorway and crossing her arms as she looked down at him. She had spitfire written all over her.

Shade felt heat rise up his neck. Tess had talked to her about him?

Jax turned to the brunette, looking incredulous. "*Now* is when you leave your lab, Fiona?"

She shrugged, but Shade could see the humor in her green eyes. "Since you two are the perpetual *wall of no*, I guess I'll go get Tess myself." She turned, her high ponytail swinging as she strode away.

Miko's mouth flattened into a line. She trailed Fiona into the ship, not looking like a happy gatekeeper.

Jax followed the women with his eyes before turning back to him. "Could you get that door you promised?" he asked.

Shade nodded. "Ordered it yesterday."

"Half-priced is half-priced," Jax said with a low growl in his voice. "I hope you're not expecting extra payment."

What was he talking about? "A deal's a deal," Shade said.

Unless he turned Tess in and ruined their lives.

A bitter taste flooded his mouth. He doubted any of them would be worrying about a new door after that.

"Shade." Tess arrived in the ruined doorway, tucking her hair behind her ears and looking slightly flushed. "Did you bring something for the ship?"

He supposed it was normal for them all to think he was here about the *Endeavor*, but couldn't a guy just show up?

"No. I thought you might want to explore for a bit. If you have time," he said.

Her face brightened. "That sounds like fun."

"The city? You sure about that?" Jax asked.

Tess seemed to waver. "Actually, I should probably stay in."

Disappointment squeezed Shade's lungs, jarring him. *Shit.* This was worse than he'd thought.

"Forget the city. We can go to the beach," Shade said, trying to tempt her. It wasn't a secret between them that she was interested in discretion, so he added, "There shouldn't be anyone around once we get past the casino."

Her eyes widened. "A beach? With sand?"

He nodded. "And water. Waves. Fish. The usual things."

Tess looked both excited and petrified. Had she never been to the beach before?

"I can't swim," she admitted, seeming to deflate.

"Wasn't planning on it." Shade almost shuddered at the thought. "The water's too cold for that."

Visibly relieved, she turned to Jax, grinning. "Jax. The beach!"

His answering smile was resigned, but genuine. "Enjoy it, partner."

Partner? Shade instantly knew what that meant. They'd been paired up on Hourglass Mile.

A stab of jealousy struck him square in the chest, surprising him with its sharpness. Had they been lovers? Were they still?

Realizing he was being irrational and even an ass-hole, considering his own agenda, Shade still replayed any interaction he'd seen between them in his head. They were close, and seemed to understand each other without many words, but they didn't look at each other like they were anything other than friends.

Whatever relief he felt was tainted. He couldn't imagine what they'd been through, and yet here he was, poised to rip them apart. He could even do it tonight, with her coming willingly. Unsuspectingly.

Shade started to feel a little nauseous. Was this who he was now? He didn't like this man much.

"Do I need anything?" Tess asked. She frowned. "Currency units?"

Shade shook his head. He knew she didn't have a unit to spare. "Just a sweater. It's cooler outside of the city."

She nodded and disappeared back into the ship.

Jax stared at him, and Shade waited for the home-before-midnight-hands-to-yourself speech. He hadn't heard it since he was a teenager, but he knew that look well enough. It was timeless and universal.

"Tess makes her own decisions." Jax squatted down, bringing their faces closer together. "Just be careful what you do with her good faith."

That was more spot-on and hit harder than the lecture Shade had been anticipating. Jax flexing a big hand between them like he was ready to wrap it around Shade's throat and squeeze was exactly what he'd expected.

Shade didn't step back. Jax had to know he would put up a good fight.

Tess reappeared quickly and hopped down onto the platform to join him. Her slightly hesitant smile always seemed to knock the air from his lungs, and this time was no different. Shade once again had to wonder what the hell he was doing, especially since there was attraction between them. Was he moving toward a decision, or just making everything worse?

His questions didn't stop him, and they turned and walked toward the elevator tubes together. Shade glanced furtively at Tess. He couldn't remember a time in his adult life when he hadn't had to shorten his stride to accommodate a woman.

"Bye, Jax!" Tess called as they stepped into the next available lift.

Jax grimace-smiled at her from the *Endeavor*. He waved just as the elevator doors shut.

"He hates me," Shade said as they whooshed toward ground level.

Tess laughed. "He's just protective. He's…lost people."

The smile that had managed to start budding on Shade's lips died. "You seemed to like the idea of the beach," he said, wanting to change the subject.

"I saw what I thought was an ocean when we flew in. I was curious."

"Not used to water, then?" he asked as they exited the elevator, and he guided her toward his small private cruiser. It easily fit two, though not many more. It was space-worthy, but he also used it to get around Albion 5. It was a hell of a lot safer than the public shuttles run by the planetary authorities. He knew that for a fact.

"I'm used to metal, metal, and more metal. Honestly, when I hit water, I might rust."

Shade chuckled, opening the door for her. "I don't think it works that way."

Tess slid into her seat, seeming entirely at home in any kind of spacecraft. "I'll let you know after the beach."

Her words gnawed at Shade's conscience as he rounded the cruiser to his side. What if there wasn't an after? What if there *was*? He was feeling less and less inclined to make a decision tonight.

But if he didn't bring her in soon, then someone else would. She had a massive price on her head. He knew of at least one couple that was bound to be searching high and low for Tess—and they'd be a lot less gentle with her than he would. And Solan and Raquel weren't the only ones. There were a dozen skilled hunters that could be on this right now, and a dozen others that might just have dumb luck. The end result would still be the same for Tess, but he would be out two hundred million units—everything and more that he still needed to buy back his docks.

Shade opened his door a little too forcefully. *His* docks. Who the fuck was he kidding? They hadn't been his for ten years. And if he turned his back on the bounty for Tess, chances were they wouldn't be his for ten more.

He powered up and took off, staying low to avoid traffic. Tess watched the city go by, seeming to appreciate it but not looking overly impressed. Her Sector 12 accent made him think she'd grown up with enough privilege to make Albion City look pretty basic. So what had turned her into a rebel and a thief?

"Sector 12 has all the best planets and the nicest resorts. How come you've never been to the beach?" he asked.

She glanced over. "I told you, I'm from 8."

"And yet you speak in tones of the galactic ideal."

She paled and turned back to the window. "I abhor the galactic ideal."

Shade could tell. "Yeah, me too," he said.

Tess swung around again. "I do. You do. There must be other people who do, too. Why is it winning? Why is *he* winning?"

Shade shrugged, going for levity. "I guess people don't like having to think for themselves."

"That's bullshit," Tess said, leaning toward him.

"Because he has bigger guns?"

She snorted. "Because he doesn't fear using them."

Shade felt sweat prick the back of his neck. For fuck's sake, they'd been in the cruiser for five minutes, and she already had him talking like a Nightchaser.

He tried to steer the conversation to safer territory. "The Overseer brought order."

"The Overseer brought *murder*, and I'll jump out of this boat right now if you start trying to convince me otherwise."

Shade blew out a breath. This wasn't a path he'd wanted to go down with her tonight. He already understood that she was radical to the core. "You do realize that most people would report you for a statement like that?"

"Are you most people?" she challenged, facing him straight on.

He hoped not. He sure as hell didn't want to be. "You got a parachute?" he teased, since she'd just threatened to jump out.

She didn't look impressed.

"I control the locks, Ms. Bailey."

Her chin went up. "I can override any lock."

Interesting tidbit. Was that how she stole the good stuff? "Since the locking mechanism is on my side, good luck overriding me first," Shade said.

Her eyes narrowed as her razor-sharp gaze shifted over the lighted panels. Her mouth thinned, and she *hmphed*.

Shade grinned. This was turning fun again.

Tess had spirit. She made every sentence feel like a dare—like she was daring him to be different. To be more. He'd wanted more from the women he'd dated in the last decade, but all he'd found were people trying so hard to conform that they'd left him feeling frustrated and unsatisfied. Even in private, no one was willing to make a ripple for fear of where that wave might wash up—and who it could drag under. He didn't blame them, but there was nothing exciting about it, especially in bed. The galactic ideal was boring as fuck.

Tess finally grinned back. "You're just trying to rile me up."

"Guilty," he said with a wink, although that hadn't been entirely it.

The city disappeared behind them, giving way to green fields and then to a tangle of foliage. They flew over the forest, and Tess inched away from the window while still avidly staring down. She looked like she couldn't decide if she wanted to jump in with both feet or run away screaming. It was cute.

"We have dragons," Shade said, nodding toward the darkening treetops. "That's where they live."

She gasped, and her head whipped around. "What? Really?"

Damn. He couldn't help smiling again. "Just kidding."

"Why would you do that?" Tess's hand snapped out

and thumped him hard across the chest. "Dragons don't exist."

His lips twitched. "Maybe they did—at one point."

She shook her head. "Next you'll be telling me there are mermaids in your ocean."

Shade sighed. "Ah, wouldn't that be nice. I'd come to the beach every day, if that were the case."

He thought she muttered *men* under her breath.

Tess looked like she was having fun again. So was he. That was a problem—and yet he didn't want it to stop.

The cruiser's com buzzed, and Shade glanced at the caller ID. His pulse surged. Solan and Raquel.

He reached over and rejected the communication.

"Do you need to answer that?" Tess asked.

Shade shook his head. "Nothing important." Now, if he could just convince his hammering heart of that.

A few minutes later, the casino resort came into view. Tess pressed up so close to the window that it started fogging up, and she had to use her sweater to wipe it off.

"The shore is amazing," she breathed out. "Such pretty lights."

"What? The torches?" Shade asked. They lined the long stretch of beach.

She nodded. "It looks so…ancient and exotic."

That was what he'd always thought. Every time he saw them, he half expected prehistoric tribespeople to materialize with their body paint and drums and start dancing beneath the moons.

"It's pest control," he told her. "There's a scent that keeps insects away from the beach."

"It's beautiful," Tess murmured, sounding like she was caught in a dream and just waking up.

Fuck mermaids. Tess had a siren's voice that sent his blood rushing south. Shade shifted in his seat. "Let's go down for a closer look."

She turned his way again. "Not to the casino, though, right? Just to the beach?"

Shade nodded. Every wily rat in Sector 2 frequented the Star Palace Casino, and there was no way he was bringing Tess into it. He'd gone in exactly once and lost everything. He hated that place.

Next to it, though, was the only safe stretch of beach on this side of Albion 5. Most of the coast was rocky and lined with sheer, often-crumbling cliffs. And here, the waters were all netted off. Nothing that might eat you could get through.

Shade requested a docking space, paid electronically, and then brought the cruiser down to his assigned platform in the beehive-like structure adjacent to the resort. Landing here put them closer to the casino than he liked, but there was no other choice. This was all Star Palace land for as far as the eye could see, and the owner didn't tolerate anyone on his property for free. The minimum to set foot on the private beach was forking over the docking fee.

With a smirk in Tess's direction, Shade very point-edly unlocked the doors. Tess smirked back and hopped out, but he didn't miss the humor in her eyes. It made him feel both warm and cold.

The com buzzed a second time, drawing his attention away from Tess. Solan and Raquel. *Again.* Couldn't they leave him alone? Figure things out on their own for once?

Or not, he revised, glancing at his companion. He knew what, or rather *who*, the hunters were after.

Tess grabbed her sweater. "They're not giving up. I'll let you take that while I wait by the railing." She nodded toward the edge of the platform before shutting her door again.

Tess was clearly a woman who valued privacy and didn't begrudge him his. Could she be any more perfect?

WANTED flashed through his mind. Yeah, he supposed she could.

Then again, she probably wouldn't have been half as interesting if she'd been your typical law-abiding citizen.

They were docked one-hundred-and-seventy-two levels up and over a cliff, but she still went straight to the edge and leaned against the barrier, looking out. An ocean breeze tossed her loose hair around, and Shade thought he'd never seen anything so beautiful in his life as Tess framed by a dusky, dark-blue sky and the first stars of the night.

Bzzzz. Bzzzz. Bzzzz.

Scowling, he crushed his finger down on the com like he wanted to pulverize it. "What?" he barked.

"Why the hell aren't you out on this hunt, man?" Solan asked in response.

"How the fuck do you know where I am?" Shade asked.

"Raquel might have added a little something to your cruiser the last time we met up."

Shit. That called for an immediate sweep for tracking bugs. "Met up? You mean when you followed me and stole my target and my reward."

Solan scoffed. "Lighten up, Shade. You get all the good ones."

Shade clenched his fists, wanting to punch something. These two had sunk to a new level. "That's because I work. Not because I swoop in at the end with illegal weapons and screw colleagues out of what's theirs."

The call went to video, and because they were on his contact list, it happened without him having to accept. He glared into Raquel's resort-tanned face. Solan hovered behind her, the black man a little far back to clearly see in the grainy video feed.

"I have books about how to play nicely with others," Raquel told him. "They're for a five-year-old, so probably right at your level."

Shade snorted. It was hard to believe that Solan and Raquel had a child. They were the ones who needed to learn about fairness. And fucking safety. The kid probably played with knives and drank poison.

Solan's teeth flashed at his wife's jibe. They were in their cruiser—so anywhere in the galaxy. *Great.*

Their daughter was doubtless at home in Sector 6 with a caretaker, probably setting the house on fire.

"You want to lecture me about playing nice?" Shade asked, incredulous. "You threw a fucking firebomb at my head!"

Raquel's don't-give-a-shit shrug came with a little smile. "Your hair will grow back."

It hadn't been long to begin with, but it hadn't been *this* short.

"What do you want?" Shade asked, his molars grinding in the back. "I'm busy."

"Too busy to go on the biggest hunt of our lives?" Solan asked.

Shade knew he needed to come up with a good

excuse right now for not having moved yet, or they'd swoop down on Albion 5 and Tess. "I'm working on something already. It's about my docks."

"*Your* docks?" Solan asked.

"Fuck you," Shade said.

Raquel glanced over her shoulder at her husband, tutting. "You know how sensitive he is about those towers."

Solan barely had eyebrows, but they still went up. "All the more reason to go on this hunt. He could buy them all back tomorrow."

Shade darted a look at Tess. They had no idea.

And Solan clearly wasn't buying his story. He needed to add a layer.

"Since you've obviously put a tracking bug on my ship, you know I'm at the Star Palace Casino. I've got a meeting with Scarabin White."

"Why? You don't have the money," Raquel said.

"I've got enough to make a decent offer," Shade lied. "If he accepts, I'll buy what I can on Albion 5, forget about the rock next door, and get out of the hunt. Never liked it anyway," he muttered.

Solan leaned closer to the camera. "Or you go on one last hunt and buy it all. We can work the case together. We each take a third. With this prize, you can have everything you want and more."

Not true. A third would only be enough if they doubled the bounty by turning over whatever it was that Tess had stolen.

And then there was the bonus for a live capture…

Shade shook his head. It didn't matter. There'd be no splitting of anything. If he chose to, he'd take it all.

"If you're calling me with that offer," he said, "it means you have no idea where this woman is located."

Raquel's face pinched. She had two expressions: bland and bitch. He didn't like either. "You're the best tracker," she grudgingly admitted.

"You need me," Shade said. "I don't need you. This conversation is over."

They muted their voices but didn't disconnect. Shade thought about hanging up on them, but they'd just call back.

"Half," Raquel said when they unmuted the conversation again. "You get half, and we bring her in together."

"That's a pretty hypothetical half, since no one has a clue about the target," Shade said. His eyes wanted to find Tess again. He forced them not to.

"Really?" Solan asked dubiously. "Nothing? No research? You haven't been looking *at all*?"

"No. I told you, I'm working on a deal with White."

Someone striding out of the elevator doors caught Shade's eye. *Speak of the devil*. The scumbag himself had just walked onto their platform and was making a beeline for Tess.

Shade couldn't even be surprised that White had shown up immediately, although he'd hoped to avoid him for once, despite resort security keeping track of any ship that docked here. Scarabin White took every opportunity to grind Shade's face into what he'd lost. Tonight would be no different.

"I gotta go," Shade said. "He's here." No lies in any of that. He even angled the camera to catch the property mogul in his flashy white suit. That fucker had never done him a single favor—until now.

"I would say good luck, but I don't really care," Raquel said. "And when we find her, you won't get a cut."

"If this deal goes south, *I'll* find her, and you can stay the hell away from what's mine this time," Shade growled before cutting them off. He disconnected the entire com unit for good measure, watching as White took Tess's hand and planted his foul mouth on the back of it.

Tess didn't shrink away, but she did look like she wanted to snatch her hand back. She obviously knew a snake when she saw one. Too bad he hadn't been as smart in the days following his parents' death, when he'd discovered problems he'd never expected, and been forced to deal with things that went well beyond the devastation of losing his family. But instead of giving himself time to sort it all out and find solutions, he'd piled all his dumb into one night and was still paying for it.

Shade locked up his cruiser and strode over to them, trying to keep his temper under control. A fist in Scarabin White's fleshy face might feel really good right now, but it wouldn't serve his long-term goals.

White looked his way, his slimy smile in place. As a name, *White* fit him. White suit, white skin, bald, white head. Even his light-blue eyes seemed colorless. Inside, though, he was every shade of conniving ass.

"My security cameras picked up your cruiser. I thought I'd take the opportunity to say hello." White turned to Tess again. "I see you've brought a lovely guest. I'd be happy to provide more appropriate attire if you'd like to enjoy the casino."

She flushed bright pink. The asshole had just unwittingly embarrassed her. Shade stole her hand from White's and kept it in his.

"We only came for the beach, which doesn't require dressing up." He looked at Tess. "Ready?"

She nodded, moving closer to his side and clearly away from Scarabin White, almost as though she were using him as a buffer.

Damn if that didn't make Shade feel strange. And powerful. It made his heart thump.

He squeezed her hand, and she stopped just behind him. He was pretty sure Tess could take care of herself in a lot of ways, but she obviously saw no benefit in forced bravado. If he was right about Jax having been her partner on Hourglass Mile, Shade thought she must have learned this behavior there. Fight when you had to. When you could, hide behind the bigger animal.

"Before you go, I wanted to give you this." White held out a silver money clip engraved with a long-extinct songbird's head. "The hotel staff found it under a piece of furniture. I believe it was your father's."

Shade felt a muscle in his jaw twitch. Not only his father's. That went back generations. Centuries. It went back to Earth.

He took it, knowing everything White had just implied.

Your father had a gambling problem.

Your family was rich and powerful—before two generations ruined it all.

He also knew that White hadn't found the silver clip under any piece of furniture. Ten years or more forgotten in a corner would have tarnished it, and the clip was perfectly polished. The bastard had kept it—along with everything else.

Shade turned the unique piece over in his hand,

wondering how long White had been waiting to get in this particular dig. He'd probably been holding out for an audience, and here Shade was, on what looked like a date.

Too bad it wasn't one—and that Tess was in an even shittier position than he was.

Shade pivoted and hurled the family heirloom into the ocean, not even looking as it plunged toward the surf.

Tess gasped. "Shade!"

"Fix the lower levels of Cardinal before the whole fucking thing collapses," he ground out, already walking away and towing Tess.

Tess didn't once glance back at White, which made him want to kiss her. Hard. On the mouth. He almost did after the lift doors closed and they started zooming downward, but he was afraid it would feel more like punishment for both of them than anything else.

"Are you okay?" Tess asked, freeing her hand from his and lightly touching his arm instead.

"I'm fine!"

She reared back, a yeah-not-so-much look on her face.

"I'm sorry," he said, forcing a calming breath.

"It's okay." She didn't step closer again. "That was beautiful. Why did you throw it away?"

"I didn't want it," he said.

"Maybe someone would have. Someone in your family."

He didn't have a family. "Then someone can have it," he said. "When it washes up."

Tess nodded, her expression still somber with concern.

They stepped out of the lift when it reached ground level, and he guided her toward the shore, taking a path lined with fancy shrubs, potted trees, and colorful blooms. There was no denying the beauty of the resort, despite the ugliness of its owner, and Tess trailed her fingers over velvety, exotic-looking petals, stopping to smell a few of the prettiest flowers. She didn't say anything else about the money clip.

There she went again, being all perfect, knowing when to let something go.

They eventually stepped onto sand, and she turned her face into the breeze, sniffing the damp, briny air. She stomped her feet a few times, getting used to the feel of the shifting grains beneath her shoes.

They walked farther along the beach than Shade had intended, but the long stroll gave him a chance to cool off. Tess seemed happy to just soak in the scenery and didn't say much, besides commenting on the flickering light from the torches again, their subtle scent, and how the paths from the three moons glittered across the now-dark water like rippling starlight. He thought she didn't want to talk a lot, but rather listen to the surf.

Finally, when the brightly lit casino looked small in the distance, she chose a dune and sat down on the side of it. Sea grass swayed behind them, rustling. The waves rolled in and out with a soothing rhythm. Shade leaned back on his elbows and watched Tess more than the ocean. She was the better sight.

Tess suddenly laughed. "Stop."

"Stop what?" he asked.

"Stop looking at me."

Shade smiled. "You're fun to watch."

She bit down on her grin, but he still saw it tugging at her lips. "Do all the people on Albion 5 stare? Are you a planet of starers?"

His eyebrows went up. "Starers?"

"Yes, like this." She leaned closer and locked eyes with him.

Shade chuckled. No way was he looking away first.

"Damn, you're good at this," she eventually said.

So was Tess. Shade shot out a hand and tickled her ribs.

"Ah! That's cheating!" she cried, laughing and curling into a ball.

"I win," Shade said.

She gave him a sidelong look that promised retribution. "Fine. What's your prize?"

Prize? The word sank into him and stuck in his gut. "Nope. You win. I cheated. You claim the prize."

"Okay."

Her quick agreement made him nervous. *Retribution, here we come.*

"Put your feet in the water," she said.

Shade groaned. "That water's cold, Tess."

"I'll do it if you do." She looked so hopeful that it was immediately clear to him that she wanted to touch the water but was afraid of going anywhere near it by herself.

"We'll be wet and barefoot for the whole walk back," he cautioned, half-heartedly starting to slip off his shoes and socks.

She immediately did the same. So much for his attempted warning.

Shade rolled up his pants to keep them dry and then helped Tess wiggle her tight-fitting pants up as far as they would go, adding his strength to the final few tugs to get them past her knees.

When they finally succeeded, Tess puffed out a

breath in exaggerated exhaustion. "I should have worn a miniskirt," she joked.

Heat flooded his abdomen. Shade sat back on his heels, putting some distance between them. Her legs were shapely—and so space-pale they practically glowed in the moonlight. If this had been a date, he might have smoothed his hands down her legs to see if they felt as soft as they looked.

"No backing out," Tess said, popping up and racing for the surf. She stopped just at the water's edge and then leaped back, shrieking happily when a wave chased her up the sand.

Shade stood and moved closer. He didn't join her yet. It was too much fun watching her scoot back and forth, laughing and getting out of the way just before the next wave caught her around the ankles and froze her feet.

Something expanded in his chest, pushing out hard. Tess wasn't afraid to show enjoyment or enthusiasm. To be herself. He couldn't imagine her ever approaching life timidly, or just moving quietly from one day to the next.

She finally stood still and let a wave rush over her. Water swirled around her ankles and then sucked and bubbled its way back down the slope, pulling sand out from under her feet. She sank a little into the beach, wiggling her toes. The next wave crashed up her shins, and Tess threw back her head and screamed. It was pure joy—discovery, delight. Probably the cold. Shade loved every second of it.

This wasn't a woman who kept her head down, playing it safe. Tess lifted her face and yelled to the stars. How many people did that these days?

She turned to him, grinning.

Unable to resist, Shade moved toward her, preparing for the inevitable toe freeze. "What do you think?" he asked.

"I love it!" Her eyes were brilliantly bright, even in the near dark.

"What about the cold?" He suppressed a shiver as the soles of his feet touched wet sand. The foam was even worse. The next wave hit, and Shade sputtered a curse.

"You call this cold?" Smiling, Tess kicked some water at him, splashing his lower legs with tiny beads of ice. "Cold is when you get a tear in your spacewalk suit, and you think, *Oh fuck, I'm going to die!* This…this is wonderful!" She spun around, raising her arms to the sky.

Shade stared at her. How many times had Tess been on dangerous spacewalks? How many times had she thought, *Oh fuck, I'm going to die*?

"That happen often?" he asked, frowning.

She shrugged and went a little deeper, bouncing up with every wave in a hopeless attempt to keep her pants dry.

"Don't go much farther," he warned. "The drop-off is steep and sudden, and I don't want to have to dive in after you."

Tess inched back, turning to him with a crease in her brow. "That seems awfully dangerous for a resort beach."

"It's better closer to the hotel and casino. Safer for families. This part of the beach is mostly for walking."

"Did you learn to swim here?" she asked, jumping another wave.

Shade shook his head. "In a pool. A *heated* pool," he added.

"A pool," she said wistfully.

Shade watched her splash back toward shallower water, where she let the waves roll over her feet again.

Was he wrong about Sector 12? Tess had the accent, but nothing else. No pools, no beaches, no brainwashing into a life of boredom. She showed zest for life. She said what she meant. It was unbelievably refreshing. No one had a fucking opinion these days. Or if they did, they didn't share it.

He'd been like that, too—until his parents had died and he'd lost everything. Then he'd figured he was free to be himself. Why not? He'd had no one left to impress. The problem was, no one else impressed him, either.

Tess glanced at him, her head tilted to one side. "'The ocean my secrets keep, its waves whispering echoes from the deep.'"

"'Mysteries abound; mysteries profound,'" Shade continued for her, his heart speeding up.

"'Until currents carry them to their final sleep, and then the abyss may them reap.'" They finished together, her smiling, and him feeling like he'd been hit by a wrecking ball.

Was he going to have to hand over to the Dark Watch the only person he'd actually *liked* in a decade?

"You've read Tynhill?" Tess asked, beaming.

"Hasn't everyone?" Shade sounded hoarse.

"No." She laughed. "And most people can't recite her poems, either."

"Yeah, well, those are good ones," he said, rubbing the back of his neck.

A small, dark animal waddle-ran across the sand and plunged into the water near Tess's ankles.

She yelped and jumped behind Shade, clinging to his shoulders. "What was that?"

Shade peered at the water. Whatever it was, it was gone. "I don't know. A flerver?"

"What the hell is a flerver?" Tess cried.

"You're scared of a flerver?" Shade couldn't help it; he started laughing.

"I don't know what a flerver is, you idiot!"

"Small. Brown." He grinned at her over his shoulder. "Webbed feet. Semiaquatic."

"Do they bite?" she asked, not letting go of him.

"Yes. Very hard."

"What?" She practically jumped on his back, knocking into him.

Shade slid to the side, wrapped an arm around her waist, and propelled her toward dry sand. His feet were freezing. "Just kidding. They're harmless."

Tess whirled on him, scowling. "Why do you do that?"

Because teasing her was the most fun he'd had in years.

He reached out and tucked her hair behind her ear, letting his fingers linger just a little longer than he knew he should. "I know you're brave. Why are you scared of a little animal?"

She shivered. "We're all scared of something, right? It's only human."

He nodded, the levity draining from him again. It had been like that all evening—highs and lows until he felt like a yo-yo. "Yeah, you're right."

As they collected their shoes and socks and got ready to walk back to his cruiser, Shade realized he was starting to feel pretty damn terrified himself.

For the first time in a long time, he had no idea what to do.

CHAPTER

13

I LEFT THE SQUIRREL TREE AT DUSK AFTER AN
uneventful day with no sign of Shade. My anxiety level
amped up the second I hit the streets with a large hover
crate full of contraband books. I wasn't sure what made
me more nervous as I headed toward Susan's bookstore—
the fact that the books were all unsanctioned by the galactic authorities, or the fact that they were all stolen.

Only the latter would get me into immediate trouble,
but the former wasn't great, either. It could leave me
open to questioning and eventual holding—all of which
could lead to an arrest.

Using a small wireless remote, I guided the crate
through the darkening streets of the docking district before heading into more open and welcoming
Windrow. I cultivated a certain walk as I went, throwing
the vibe I needed off me like radio waves. It straddled
a line somewhere between *I'm perfectly normal, there's
nothing to see here* and *Don't fuck with me, or you'll
be sorry.*

I'd learned the nuances of both in prison. No one

wanted to be the weirdo, all alone, that people ganged up on. And everyone wanted respect. I'd started thinking of effectively blending the two attitudes into one as a difficult but achievable art form. Mastery of *the walk* had given me something to aspire to on Hourglass Mile—with the added benefit of usually keeping me safe.

I heard the three long electronic beeps that signaled a public announcement and stopped along with everyone else, keeping a hand on my crate as I let it touch down. The whole city seemed to hold its breath, waiting. My stomach clenched when the Overseer's live image appeared on the huge visual display unit attached to the front of the building across from me. He was in his office, a room I knew well for having been summoned to it more than once for long, sometimes violent lectures.

As usual, he wore plain, dark clothes. In fact, he was a plain, dark-haired, dark-eyed man. And every time he popped up on a building-sized screen to project his propaganda across the galaxy, his bland uniformity anchored itself a little deeper into the collective psyche as the galactic ideal.

Tonight, I was as guilty of conforming to his stark, unembellished image as everyone else. My tight black pants, low-heeled ankle boots, clingy dark top, and drab little vest made me look just like any other woman my age. I remembered playing with some of the dresses my mother had kept from her youth—clothing with integrated lights and materials that changed colors when you moved. They'd made me dream about laughter and parties until my despot father had found them and thrown them in the garbage. Neither Mom nor I had been allowed out of the house for a month, and from one day to the next, everything in our closets had been replaced by clothing of the Overseer's choice.

"Citizens of the eighteen Sectors," the Overseer began. "You live in a time of peace and prosperity. Of great discovery and progress. Despite that, there are still misguided people who would take from you your life of ease and security, who would destroy the orderly society we've worked tirelessly to build and shatter it into warring, lacking factions that can't see past their own selfish wants and needs."

Well. There would be no easing into it today, it seemed. Something must have royally pissed him off.

Losing a lab full of enhancers perhaps?

"You must root them out. Dig out and destroy this rotten fruit whenever you can. *Wherever* you can. *Every single one of you* is responsible for protecting the life the galactic government has built for you."

He paused to let that sink in, and it felt as though whatever passion and warmth was in the air got sucked right out of it as people froze, wondering if someone might point a finger at them next. It didn't take more than a half-assed accusation to get carted off by the Dark Watch.

"Your personal choices reflect on who you are—and on what you can become."

On that, at least, we agreed.

"Excess of any kind is to be avoided. Immoderation shunned."

Funny how that didn't apply to wealth, when some had so much and others not enough. Or to violence. I sure hoped the Overseer didn't actually believe he set an example of restraint when it came to ruthlessness and brutality.

He pointed a finger right at us—at everyone across the entire galaxy. "Know. Your. Enemy."

Oh, I did. It was him. The man who'd streamlined learning to eliminate the arts and chosen to censor books and other information, imprison protestors, kill dissenters, condemn lifestyle choices outside of his highly limited box, and blow up democracy to replace it with himself.

He went on for exactly five minutes, no more, no less, his main purpose seeming to be to remind people to control themselves—and others—to his satisfaction and to not hesitate to inform against their friends, neighbors, and whoever else. The subtext being *or else*.

I listened, just like the citizens of Albion 5 around me, wondering how many people were buying into this, and how many people wanted to throw rocks at his gigantic face as badly as I did.

The screen finally went dark, but nobody moved at first, an odd push and pull in the air between the undercurrent of fear and the displays of allegiance as some people started clapping, forcing everyone to do the same or risk being singled out.

Some brave soul eventually took a step, and the city groaned back into motion after the Overseer's latest speech. I dropped my eyes to my remote, got my crate moving, and started walking again, keeping pace with the other pedestrians and not letting on how shaken I was from seeing my father's face and hearing his voice.

Everyone kept their heads down after that, and no one looked at me sideways. My hover crate could have contained a week's worth of groceries for all anyone knew. I was just a person like anyone else.

No one stood out any more than I did, and I realized that we'd all perfected the art of blending in and avoiding notice. Maybe Hourglass Mile had nothing to do with it, because the whole galaxy was a freaking jail. Not everyone needed bars to be locked up, and what I saw around me was evidence of entire populations falling into complacency for the sake of personal peace.

Because there was peace—for most. It was drab, dry, and sterile, and often a little scary when the Dark Watch was around, but not everyone wanted to be washed in color, especially if it was the purple-yellow of bruises, or the red of blood.

A good portion of the galaxy had already tried that—and lost to Overseer brown.

Only the Dark Watch generals wore crimson now, and it was hard not to read *massacres* into that. I was pretty sure their uniforms were meant to remind the entire galaxy of how the war had finally ended with the near-total destruction of the Outer Zones.

The crowd that had gathered for the announcement thinned, and the overhead street lamps got brighter as I moved farther into Windrow, their cozy pale-yellow glow driving some of the darkness and anger from my thoughts. The neighborhood was tucking itself in for the night, with shops and businesses closing at street level and turning off their lights. The number of pedestrians steadily diminished, while small personal cruisers and public shuttles started accumulating overhead, their safety lights flashing and their engines droning with a calming buzz.

Turning a corner, I found myself alone on a quiet street and tilted my head back, watching the tall buildings brighten toward the tops. Windows were lighting up throughout the residential towers, blazing warmly as people returned from their jobs and settled into their home lives. A gentle breeze swirled down the street from behind me, and I drew in a breath that tasted of humidity and summer. We tended to forget about seasons on board the *Endeavor*.

Determined to enjoy the rest of my walk on such a warm, pleasant evening, I steered my crate around a bunch of cats all lazing on a quiet section of the sidewalk. They made me smile, even though the big dark-gray one eyeing me looked as though he would give me one hell of a fight if I disturbed them.

Cooking smells snuck down a side street and made my mouth water. A cat meowed. Music came from somewhere. It was too bad we had to leave Albion 5 so quickly. I wasn't quite sure why exactly, but I liked this place better than I'd liked any planet in a while.

Maybe it was Susan and her devotion to old books, or the anonymity of a huge city, where I could both hide and get lost. Maybe it was the warmth and sunshine and the infinite adorableness of Bonk.

Or maybe it was Shade Ganavan, Space Rogue, the first man in ages I'd wanted to undress.

Walking steadily but without hurrying, I mulled over the disappointing unlikelihood of undressing Shade, given that he hadn't made a single move in that direction the previous night. I'd thought he might, that he'd been about to, but then he'd gone quiet at the end of our outing and quickly dropped me off.

I would get over it. I'd certainly gotten over worse.

I eventually reached the bookstore and quietly knocked, since the lights were dimmed and the door was locked. Susan opened up for me, took one look at my large hover crate, and directed me around to the back.

Once there, I steered the crate through a double-sized loading door and into a mostly empty storeroom, let it touch down, and powered off. Susan closed and locked the door again, and I finally relaxed. I was off the streets. I'd arrived without incident.

Susan shifted from foot to foot, seeming giddy with anticipation and looking ready to tear open the crate. Her eyes shone brightly under the harsh overhead lighting, and her sunburst hair bounced. Her eagerness put a smile on my face and fed my own excitement now that I wasn't so anxious. I'd already looked at the books myself, but now I could share them with someone who cared and who would appreciate them just as much as I did.

I punched in the security code I'd set earlier and then pushed the button that would retract the door. Susan immediately leaned closer to see what was inside.

"Can I help you unload?" I asked, stepping back to give her more room.

She nodded, and we took turns taking the books out and stacking them into the empty bookcase that Susan had made available for them.

I'd managed to read a few of the novels before we'd stumbled onto the floating lab and all hell had broken loose, but they were new to Susan, and she looked reverently at each one, treating them like the historical treasures they were. It was our duty to preserve them.

Humanity had a rich past that spanned time and planets and that the Overseer was trying to beat out of hearts and memories because it didn't serve his goals.

"Great Powers," she said in awe, holding up a dark leather-covered tome with gold lettering. The edges of the thick paper were browning and not quite smooth, as though they hadn't been cut by a machine. It was clearly ancient, probably from a place the book had outlived by far. I'd admired it as well, when I'd discovered it in my haul.

"I never thought I'd see something like this in my whole life. I think..." She looked over at me, the book clutched like a baby against her chest. I could have sworn there were tears in her eyes. "I think this book alone is worth more than the five thousand you asked."

Despite Susan's obvious distress, her words took a big load of guilt off my chest. I'd been feeling awful for taking advantage of her preserver's spirit and charging her so much.

I unloaded another book and slipped it onto the shelf. It was actually a lot more than a simple bookshelf; it was a maximum security safe with temperature and humidity controls. Perfect for old books. Much better than the *Endeavor*'s cargo hold.

"Then it's a good thing I'm leaving it here with you, where I know it'll be safe," I said.

I'd meant to reassure her, but her expression just fell even further. "You're in danger, aren't you?"

I shrugged, letting my own fear and habitual stress roll off my shoulders for Susan's sake. "Always."

"Then you should charge someone more for this." She tried to hand the priceless book back to me, but I didn't reach for it. "Maybe the money could help you... get away."

I kept unpacking books for her, knowing she'd take her time discovering them all later. "If you want to, you can give that one to the Intergalactic Library. That's what I was going to do with all of them." I bit my lip, wishing I hadn't said that. I *was* taking advantage of her. "If I didn't have to pay for major repairs on my ship, I'd give them to you. I wish I could."

Susan looked so torn that I knew I had to ask for something in return, or I'd have a real argument on my hands.

"What's your personal water situation like?" I asked, breezing into a new subject like the previous one was already closed.

Her distraught expression blanked for a moment as she processed the sudden switch. "Good. My drain and refresh happened just last week." She lowered her voice to a conspiratorial level. "And my tank is three cubes bigger than anyone realizes."

Nice. Water that hadn't been filtered a gazillion times over AND three cubes for free. "Well, if you really want to give me something more in exchange for that nice book, I could definitely use a shower."

Susan scoffed. "That's hardly equivalent."

"But it's the only thing I need. And you can also consider Bonk as prepayment," I added. "He's like a dose of happiness in a cuddly, purring package."

A small laugh bubbled out of her. "Of course. You're welcome to use my shower."

I smiled. "I'll need soap, shampoo, and a towel, too." Too bad I hadn't brought clean clothes with me.

Although mine weren't dirty. In fact, they were mostly brand new.

"You drive a hard bargain—" She frowned suddenly. "I don't even know your name."

My heart blasted off like a rocket. We hadn't done names. I only knew hers from hearing the Dark Watch talk and speaking with Shade.

I sometimes joked in my head about wanting to tell people who I was, but I never really meant it. I'd told Jax early on because we'd both been in such bad shape when we'd met that we'd latched on to each other like lifelines, and there hadn't been room in that rawness, fear, and pain for anything but the truth. I'd spent five years with the rest of my crew and only told them who I was the moment I thought we were all about to die. In a way, Bridgebane had forced it out of me, even though his threats were what had kept me silent in the first place.

I'd owned my real name three times in the last eighteen years, once to Jax not long after we'd met, and then just recently, to my crew and to my uncle. Right now, with Susan, I wanted to be me again, the daughter my mother knew.

But could telling her put her in danger? I didn't think so. I'd be gone soon, and no one would ever connect us. The galaxy was too vast and populated for that. But if someone did, I wouldn't blame Susan for betraying me. I would never want her hurt in my stead.

I waffled, indecision plaguing me.

Susan shook her head. "You don't have to tell me. Forget I asked."

"I want to." I swallowed. "I just don't usually tell the truth."

"But the truth is something you want to tell me?" she asked.

I nodded, then laughed a little—an odd gurgle that didn't sound right. "You might not believe me."

Still holding that precious book, Susan looked at me like she had the other day, as though she were sizing me up. "I think I will."

In that case... "Quintessa Novalight," I blurted out before I could change my mind.

Susan's eyes widened, and her whole body tilted back, even though her feet stayed planted where they were. My name was a bomb. It blew people away.

"You look nothing like him," she finally said, her voice sounding thin.

I went back to carefully unloading the remaining books. The work helped to calm the anxiety sawing me in half again. "I guarantee I don't act like him, either."

That brought some of the color back into Susan's face. She smiled weakly. "Is your mother really dead?"

Her quiet question reminded me that humanity in general had liked my mother and mourned our deaths. Mostly, I thought the people of the galaxy had felt sorry for us, being at the epicenter of a tyrant's oppression. "Yes. But that fever didn't take us both."

"Why the deception?" she asked, curiosity starting to override her shock.

There was a multilevel answer to that, some of which I couldn't explain myself. I simplified and held up two of the unsanctioned books, waving them around a bit. "I'm different. And the Overseer couldn't have that."

Susan's expression told me she understood well enough. "So he hid you?"

I snorted. "My father thinks I'm dead. Only a handful of people know I'm not."

She didn't ask how I'd gotten away, or what had happened, although she did ask, "So you live your life running from him?"

Gently, I placed the last of the rare books into Susan's storeroom safe. The shelves were almost full now. "Pretty much." I turned back to her, opting for the simplified version again. "That, wreaking havoc on the Dark Watch, and liberating books."

Susan looked like she wanted to smile but couldn't quite manage it. She continued to hold that one book, still cradling it in her arms. "You remind me of the Mornavail."

I frowned. "The who?"

"The Mornavail. Haven't you heard of them?" Susan seemed genuinely surprised, but if I hadn't heard of them, I doubted that many people had.

I'd devoured every kind of book at the orphanage, all those rejects of the galaxy that Mareeka and Surral had collected over the years—just like their kids. And I'd come across some pretty rare and interesting finds over the last five years, this recent haul being the most impressive yet. The galaxy's one and only library had finally gained permission to house some historical artifacts, and anything I found and couldn't quite bring myself to put into sticky little hands went there. The rest went to Starway 8.

This was the only haul I hadn't had time to fully read before passing on, but I'd at least looked at the title of every book I'd ever touched. I racked my brain, but I was pretty sure I'd never seen or heard the word *Mornavail* before.

I shook my head to indicate that I hadn't, and Susan finally set the ancient volume down with the others in the climate-controlled safe and then went over to a different bookcase. The shelves easily contained a hundred books, many of them old-looking, although nowhere near as archaic as what I'd just produced. She ran her finger along the spines until she found the one she was looking for and pulled it out, handing it to me. It was a lot newer than the rest, but still older than I was, if I had to guess.

"Here. Take this and read it when you can. It's one of a kind, so it, Bonk, and the shower will help me to pay you back." She removed a big folded-up wad of universal currency from the pocket of her baggy sweater and gave it to me along with the book. "And this is yours, too."

I thanked her and slipped the money into my bag without counting it. If I trusted Susan with my name, I trusted her not to swindle me.

Now for the book. I read the title out loud. "*The Second Children of the Sky Mother: The Mornavail*."

I glanced up, confused. "Second children?"

Susan seemed a little sad all of a sudden. "Should she not have tried again?"

I felt my eyebrows lift. A person had to buy into theology, or somehow reconcile it with science, to believe we were the creations of the Sky Mother at all. But another species on the human level? It seemed pretty far-fetched.

A chill swept down my arms when I flipped open the newish-looking cover but then found the text handwritten in ink. The letters were swirling, extravagant, and overly ornate. The anachronistic style didn't make sense for a relatively new book. There was no cover page. The author hadn't signed the work.

Almost warily, I scanned the first paragraph.

> When the Heart of Men failed once again, the Faithful of the Galaxy prayed to the Sky Mother for aid. The Great Star answered, as She always does, this time by giving them the Mornavail, the Incorruptible who worked tirelessly to spread Her Light to the far reaches of the Dark. Her New Children made their Home in the deep pocket of the Fold—

Holy shit! I snapped the book shut. "You have to get rid of this!"

Susan looked startled.

Way to be cool, Tess. My pulse drummed like the harsh tattoo of a military march. What else was in this book? What information? If the Dark Watch saw it, could they find the Fold? Inside me, I could already feel the rhythmic thudding of their heavy boots.

"Um… This will get you arrested. It's blasphemous," I said, trying to turn fear of offending the church into an excuse for my strong reaction, even though I couldn't have cared less about religion. Still, the powerful Church of the Great Star spewed all kinds of nonsense about the Wondrous Sky Mother, but not this. In one of those bizarre contradictions, the Overseer supported the teachings of the church, spinning them however he saw fit in order to make them mesh with evidence and tests. It was just another way to obtain greater control, his one compromise, perhaps—and necessary to help gather everyone into *his* fold.

But this book was dangerous, no matter my personal beliefs. For all I knew, somewhere in the extravagantly handwritten words, it could give away the secret to finding our one safe place. It could get every single rebel killed.

The tale of the *Incorruptible* Mornavail might have been a load of bullshit, some story the faithful cooked up to comfort themselves in the face of the Dark turning *too* dark at the height of the Sambian Wars, but the Fold was no myth, and I would protect it with my life.

Susan waved a hand in the air. "No one even knows that book exists."

She did. I did. That was already a start.

And the final war only ended because my father decided that total destruction was a viable path. The darkest days were still alive in most memories. For some, they weren't even in the past.

Hope for the galaxy *was* in the Fold, but it wasn't because of some fairy-tale, human-like species that the equally fairy-tale Sky Mother had magically sprung forth. It was because regular people were sacrificing their lives.

"What if those goons had searched back here?" I asked, trying not to sound as frantic as I felt. "Have they ever tried to see what's in the back?"

Susan frowned, looking worried now. "Yes, once. But they hardly even glanced at the books."

I held my breath. "Did they look at this one?"

She shook her head, and I released the air stagnating in my lungs. They still felt tight.

I stuffed the book into my bag, hiding it mostly from myself. I was probably going to have to destroy it, but I would read it first.

Apprehension simmered along my nerves, making me sweat. The walk back with that anonymous manuscript in my bag was going to be even more nerve-racking than the walk over here with an entire load of stolen and unsanctioned books.

"How well do you know that book?" I asked.

"I read it a few years ago. It's just a story, Quin—"

"Tess," I said.

"It's just a story, Tess."

I couldn't tell if she sounded convinced.

There were tons of religious texts out there about the greatness of supposedly magnificent beings—the Powers this, the Sky Mother that. Now I could add the Fabulous and Incorruptible Mornavail to the list.

I didn't buy into it, but I also didn't begrudge anyone else their beliefs. One thing was certain, though. The Fold wasn't something you just talked about, something you wrote down in a freaking book and then let loose into the universe.

"I'm glad you showed it to me." So I could get rid of it, but I wouldn't tell Susan that.

My fingers fluttered over the outside of my bag. I pressed on the hard lump the book made, making sure it was still there, even though I could feel the weight of it on my shoulder, and I'd just put it inside.

She smiled a little uncertainly. I'd probably freaked her out.

"I'm Susan, by the way. You never asked."

I nodded. "I know. I heard the goons talking to you that first day."

"Oh. Right." She glanced at my bag. Maybe we both felt as if the book might burn a hole in the cheap material and fall right out.

I hiked up the strap. An awkward silence fell.

Susan finally spoke. "I don't know if you've already got someone working on your ship repairs, but I know a man who I think will give you a fair deal, especially if you tell him that Susan sent you."

My pulse picked up again, though not from fear this time. I had a sneaking suspicion I knew who she was going to suggest, especially since he'd pointed me toward Susan in the first place.

"Oh, yeah?" I still asked.

She nodded. "Shade Ganavan. He works out of the docks. Ganavan's Products and Parts."

Bingo. "He's already on the job," I said, warmth spreading through me. "And getting me a door for half price."

She smiled, seeming to relax again. "Oh, good. He's excellent. Very competent. And very nice."

Very nice wasn't quite how I would have described him—I liked a man with a bit of an edge—but my heart still did a little flip in my chest.

And when it came right down to it, he did seem nice. Cheap doors and vitamin D didn't lie. *Right?*

"How do you know Shade?" I asked.

"I knew his parents first. When I opened this shop, his father bought a lot of books. So did Shade's mother. Shade did, too, even as a youngster. In fact"—she laughed softly—"they might have kept me in business for the first several years."

It sounded as though Shade had family money. Did that mean he could sell or not sell the things in his shop and take on any odd job he wanted, because he was already all set?

Susan's expression gained a hint of nostalgia. "His parents were the studious sort, but Shade... He went for the novels every time."

The warmth inside me grew, gathering around my heart. "What kind of novels?" I asked.

"*Every* kind," Susan said, smiling again. "But he liked the adventure ones the best."

I smiled back. So did I. "And what does he like now?"

She arched her brows. "If he's smart, tall brunettes."

A flush hit me like a solar flare, blasting heat off my face.

"Shower time?" Susan asked, bypassing my obvious reaction as though I hadn't just turned bright red and held my breath.

"I can't wait," I admitted a little hoarsely, wondering what percentage being clean and fresh for Shade Ganavan factored into my enthusiasm—and even into my original request.

CHAPTER

14

SHADE PEELED HIMSELF OFF THE DARK WALL AND FELL into step a good distance behind Tess, wondering what the hell had taken her so long. Three *hours* with Susan. What had they been doing? Drinking tea? Having dinner? Patting cats?

He'd followed her from the Squirrel Tree, watching her slip seamlessly through the city with her hover crate. She'd moved in a way that hadn't been suspicious at all, somehow looking natural while still keeping to the shadows and melting into the coming night. She'd gone to Susan's back door to unload her books and then hadn't come out again until now. Finally.

"About time," he muttered under his breath. He'd actually started to worry that she'd slipped out, and he'd missed her. He rarely dropped the ball like that, but Tess was discreet.

She'd left her container behind, but that wasn't unusual. There was a sort of rolling galactic loan system where hover crates were concerned. You dropped one off, you picked one up. And they were cheap. Just tin cans made useful by a bit of tech.

Shade kept her in sight this time, not wanting to lose her in the dark if she took an unexpected turn. Earlier, he'd known where she was going, which had meant he could give her more space. This time, he couldn't be sure of her destination or of the path she'd take. Nothing dictated that Tess would go straight back to her ship, or that she'd use the same streets as before, even if they were the most direct.

On the surface at least, she didn't look any more nervous about moving through the city at night than she had at dusk. Everything about her screamed confidence, which made the flashes of confusion and embarrassment he'd seen in her all the more intriguing.

Considering he might ruin her life, the fact that he enjoyed bringing out that nuclear blush probably made him a real bastard. But Tess made him think all sorts of delicious and dirty thoughts. And the way she sometimes looked at him, like she was ready and willing to do wild things, sent his blood rushing straight to his cock when he really needed it in his head.

Tess drew the eyes of more men than Shade liked as she walked, but she let the attention roll right off her like she didn't give two fucks. Women looked at her, too, probably wishing they could be that tall and striking. Tess was perfectly there, and perfectly unapproachable. She was hiding in plain sight.

More quickly than he would have thought possible—must've been those mile-long legs—Tess left the crowded and residential Windrow district behind her and headed straight for the seedier, significantly darker docks. The streets were mostly empty here, so Shade made sure not to get too close. Some people who were constantly hunted developed a sixth sense about being watched, and he wouldn't have been surprised if Tess was one of them. She was clearly a professional. But a professional at what?

At theft, to start with. Those books must have been stolen, but he wasn't going to worry about that. Not his job. Although he had spent a lot of time wondering about what was in that big attachment she had vacuum sealed right onto the back of her ship. It might have been extra cargo space and nothing worth thinking about. It could also have been something Nathaniel Bridgebane wanted enough to put up the biggest bounty Shade had ever seen in his life.

Tess seemed adept at getting things done and getting out. The problem was, there was no getting out this time. Letting Captain T. Bailey slip out of Sector 2 and disappear into the Dark would be the *other* worst move of his whole fucking life. He'd already colossally messed up once and didn't plan on repeating the experience. He needed to stay on track. He had a payment to make on his future, one transaction to rid himself of Scarabin White.

He'd let that bastard rob him of his birthright when he'd been grieving and in shock over losing his parents in the shuttle crash—and facing debts he hadn't even known about. He hadn't been thinking straight. Now he was, and he wanted his docks back, even if getting them meant working for people he hated. Even if it meant ruining lives.

Unfortunately, Tess wasn't a random target anymore.

He knew her. He *liked* her. But did he like her enough to let her go?

Shade stalked his quarry past the first of the docking towers—the lower, cheaper ones that were bordering on dangerous and that would have seen a total overhaul by now if he'd been in charge. He trailed her by about half a block, always on the lookout. The Dark Watch was around, and other hunters might have been scoping out the area. He didn't know if he'd managed to throw off Solan and Raquel with his story. Lately, they'd taken to tracking *him* instead of tracking the target. The cheating fucks.

Shade sped up when Tess rounded a corner. He should nab her now, before someone else did. If anyone was going to bring her in, it should be him. She'd fallen right into his lap. It was like a gift from the universe. *Wasn't it?*

He got her in his sights again. Tess turned halfway, glancing back. She started moving faster.

Shit. Had she seen him?

Making a split-second decision, Shade veered off, hoping that would calm her suspicions. He jogged down a side street and then took a parallel avenue to Tess's path, moving fast enough to get ahead of her. He turned down the next cross street and sprinted back toward the main artery.

Reaching the corner, he put himself in a position to pop out at her from the side when she came to the intersection. He leaned forward just enough to take stock of where she was—not far away and closing fast. She was coming on steadily, but he had time to settle his breathing.

Shade quickly scanned the nearest platforms on the docks. No movement. No flash of weapons. No inky spots that might have been Solan and Raquel about to jump out at him or Tess with a freakish amount of stealth. The area was quiet, settled, although there would be the inevitable Dark Watch patrols.

He knew the area so well it was like a 3-D grid in his head. Right now, they were closer to his place than to the Squirrel Tree, and for a second, Shade wondered if he should just go home. He'd see Tess tomorrow. He had her stuff. He could fix her door.

A dread-like feeling twisted through his gut. What was he doing? He'd never hesitated to bring in a target before, and he sure as hell shouldn't have started with *this* one, a woman worth more than what he still needed to move the fuck on with his life.

Why hadn't he turned her over to Bridgebane yet? Why hadn't he gotten his money and finished it?

Tess had almost reached his hiding place, and Shade felt himself start to sweat. He needed to close the deal on this one. Make a damn choice.

But nothing about this sat right with him. When he looked at Tess Bailey, he saw what he wanted the galaxy to be like, not how it actually was. He used to dream about joining a crew a lot like Tess's, about putting up a fight. He'd have done it a long time ago if he hadn't had the responsibility of an urban empire to run.

That thought drove into him like a rusted nail. He wasn't running it, was he? Scarabin White was doing that.

The sudden, low vibration of an engine made Shade stiffen. He flattened himself against the wall, darting a look back. A Dark Watch patrol had just turned the corner and was zooming up from behind him, doing a sweep of the streets in an open hovercraft.

At the speed they were going, they'd reach the intersection not long after Tess. He'd already heard her steps.

Adrenaline dumped into his system. If she spooked and ran, they'd chase. If she kept her cool, it might be okay.

Shade's pulse pounded as his decision time narrowed to mere seconds. He despised having his hand forced. Only an idiot made important choices without reflection—he'd learned that the hard way—and he hadn't yet determined what to do with Tess himself. But if the Dark Watch brought her in now, he'd lose his chance.

He slipped around the corner just as Tess was bolting away from the engine noise. Her hair nearly whipped his face as she took off in the other direction at a dead run. He lunged and grabbed her wrist. In a blink, she broke his hold, spun, and came at him with a closed fist.

Shade ducked and used his shoulder and weight to plow her toward the wall. She grunted when her back hit, and he caught her head in his hand just before it thumped the building. She struggled against him, her whole body tensing to fight.

"It's me, Tess," he whispered next to her ear.

"Shade?" she breathed out.

"Good reaction time," he said. "Sloppy attempt at a hit."

She huffed in surprise, and then, damn him, she completely relaxed. Her whole body softened, and she lifted her head. Their cheeks brushed. Her exhale warmed his jaw, and those fingers that had been trying to shove him away only seconds earlier suddenly curled into his shirt and held on.

"Dark Watch patrol." He settled one hand on her hip and slid the other into her hair. "Gotta make this look real."

Somehow, Tess understood exactly what he meant. Her nod was so slight that he might not have noticed it if their heads hadn't been touching. But then, before he could line up their mouths, she slid her parted lips all the way across his cheek in a sexy-as-fuck move that sent hot blood rushing through his veins.

"Kiss me, Shade," she murmured, pulling slightly back before their lips could touch.

Her eyes flicked up, meeting his. His heart slammed so hard inside his chest that she could probably feel it thundering against her palms. He didn't think he'd ever had a woman in his arms who was this honest. Oh, she'd lied about a ton of shit, but there was almost more honesty than he could take in the way she looked at him right now, and how her breath hitched.

Knowing he'd started this and needed to follow through, Shade tightened his hold on Tess's head and hip, drawing her in to him. Their bodies lined up perfectly, and he ate up her little gasp when it feathered across his mouth.

Tension crackled between them like an electrical charge, almost drowning out the sound of the hovercraft turning the corner next to them. Angling his head, Shade both fought and desperately wanted what he was about to do. He had a sense of honor, and right now, he was deliberately kicking it to the curb. He'd also been dying to taste this woman since the moment they'd met.

Shade molded his lips to hers, desire sparking even more powerfully at the contact. She kissed him back without hesitation, and his mind blanked to tactics, to the

Dark Watch, and even to his docks. Everything seemed to condense into a tight little ball of him, Tess, and so much heat and pressure that a supernova had nothing on the explosion they could generate.

✳ ✳ ✳

Shade kissed me just as the Dark Watch rounded the corner. If I'd had a bomb, I might have tossed it into their loud, showy hovercraft and blown them all to bits just so that Shade Ganavan could keep devouring me in a way that was so hot I turned molten in his arms.

His hold on me tightened, and his breathing changed. I gripped his shoulders and pressed into him, kissing him back with a sweep of my tongue that tangled every part of our mouths. I wanted him, and I couldn't help myself. I knew this was supposed to be a ruse, to hide my face and allay suspicions, but it felt pretty damn real to me.

So did Shade's growing hard-on. If the goons hadn't started barking at us with their megaphones right then, I would have rolled my pelvis against it and gotten a really good feel for his length and size. I was seriously tempted as it was, even with the military right behind us, yammering about rules and regulations and the unseemliness of public displays of affection.

Things like "Bring that inside, you two!" and "No vulgarity in the streets!" rang in my ears, but I hardly even noticed. I was too caught up in Shade, especially since the Dark Watch seemed to have bought our deception.

Shade broke the kiss and turned his head, nodding to acknowledge the goon patrol's orders. He kept his hand firmly in my hair, pulling my face into the crook of his neck.

The protective tug sent heat spiraling through me. Excitement, danger, and desire all crashed inside me like some fucked-up storm that made me crazy with want. I opened my mouth and licked his neck, tasting the entire length of that tendon I'd seen dripping with sweat. He was clean now, but my imagination supplied the tang of hard work and salt. I sucked, and Shade exhaled in a burst.

He didn't move until the Dark Watch had gone farther down the avenue and away from us. Then he met my eyes and half carried, half swept me around the corner and out of sight.

With a low groan, he pressed me back up against the wall. "You're killing me, starshine."

"Don't stop." I grabbed his short hair and pulled his mouth back to mine.

He met my lips with enough dominance to send a kick of exhilaration through me. This was what I'd been missing for so long, and I kissed him like he was the key to all the thrilling, fun things no one was supposed to do anymore. Kissing Shade felt like belting out a song from a rooftop, or splashing fully clothed into a rare public fountain. It felt like freedom, like he wouldn't judge, like I could do what I wanted.

And that he would like it.

I moaned and kissed him like I was freaking dying for it—which I was. For seven years, I hadn't had the slightest interest in a man. Not sexually, at least. But then Shade had looked me up and down with his honey-brown eyes, said he was checking me over for weapons, and I'd started falling for him right then and there in his dusty, overstocked shop.

I'd only known him for a few days, but I'd been waiting forever for this kiss. I wanted more than a kiss from Shade; I was so ready. I hooked my leg around his hip and tilted my pelvis up, finally getting a good feel of his hard length. He pressed against me, almost thrusting. Heat sizzled low in my belly and flared between my legs. My head dropped back against the wall, and I gulped down a breath.

Shade trailed scorching, openmouthed kisses along my throat. "Holy shit, you're like chaos in skin."

A splash of cold hit the fever inside me. We were taught to like and value order, restraint. I'd thought he was like me, but maybe I was too wild and impulsive for him?

"Too chaotic?" I asked.

"Fucking perfect." His hands dove into my open vest, and he palmed my breasts. He lifted them, bent his head, and rubbed his face along the twin curves he'd plumped up.

Rub. Kiss. Lick. *Holy fuck.*

Little-used muscles clenched, and my breath shortened to pants.

Shade's light stubble scraped my skin. He grunted something I didn't understand. *Freckles*, maybe. I had a few. Whatever he said was husky and low and got lost in a haze of lust. My nipples hardened under his hands, and he gently squeezed, his mouth moving along the scooped neckline of my shirt.

I held on to his head, clamping him to me. I never wanted him to stop. I wanted him to touch me higher. Lower. Everywhere.

Shade kissed my chest and collarbone, my throat and the soft underside of my chin. His hands skimmed my ribs, falling to my hips, and then his lips were on mine again, yielding but firm, his tongue in my mouth, and we both made a needy sound that was volcanically hot.

I pulled him closer. He ground against me. It was both torment and relief.

A double pair of footsteps rang out on the avenue close to the intersection, and we sprang apart, both of us breathing hard. If we didn't stop, someone was sure to report us, and that would send the Dark Watch roaring back. No matter how good it felt, or how much I wanted to continue, a bout of deliciously crazy public indecency could get me into a whole lot of trouble.

I tucked my still-damp hair behind my ears, my voice coming out like a scratch. "I should get off the streets."

Shade nodded, his eyes on my face. He looked incredibly tense. Did he regret kissing me and feeling us both ignite?

The footsteps drew closer, and Shade held out his hand. Instinctively, I took what he offered, and he led me down the darker cross street and away from the main thoroughfare. His hand was warm, the skin a little rough, and I loved having it around mine. It was too bad I couldn't hold on to him for more than a few days.

My spirits sank. *Dangerous thoughts, Tess.*

There was no settling down for me yet. I had things to do. People to help. Right now, stopping the illness at the orphanage was my priority, followed closely by deciding what to do with those enhancers. I couldn't get complacent and stay in one place just because there was a man who turned me into a raging inferno and made me want to jump into his bed.

My body talked back—*loudly*—still all warm and

wound up. Parts of me, both in my head and decidedly *not* in my head, wanted to stay on Albion 5 and see what could happen with Shade.

If anything. Maybe that kiss had been it.

Or maybe there could be more—just short-lived.

My spirits sank even further. Neither possibility was my first choice.

I glanced at Shade as we walked. It had been pretty obvious that first day in his shop that I needed to avoid the Dark Watch, which explained his tactics tonight, but not much else.

"Why are you here?" I asked.

"I live nearby."

"And you just happened to run into me on the street? Literally?" What were the chances of that?

He shrugged, and I stopped.

"Shade?"

He dropped my hand and turned to me, scrubbing the back of his neck. "I followed you from Susan's. You said something about the book drop-off today, and I wanted to make sure you got back all right."

My heart started pounding like a heavy-armor hammer trying to break through my ribs. "You were worried about me?"

"You're carrying my money," he grumbled, starting to walk again. "Already paid for that door."

He had my door!

Wait. He had my door.

He'd fix it, along with the remaining holes in the *Endeavor*, and then I'd fly off this rock.

"That's, ah…great news," I said, thinking I should have meant it.

He didn't respond.

"It's creepy to follow women, you know."

He slanted me an odd look. "Maybe I'm a sketchy bastard."

I didn't believe that, especially with Susan vouching for him. "You could have just walked with me." I took his hand back, because I was a numbskull like that. "I don't bite."

What seemed like a wry huff escaped him. "Actually, I kind of hope you do."

My pulse bucked, and my lower abdomen tightened, flooding with heat again.

"Where are we going?" I asked, looking around us after I'd caught my breath once more. My attention had been so focused on Shade that I hadn't realized until right then that I didn't recognize a single thing about the area.

"It's a shortcut," he answered, leading me toward a dimly lit tunnel under a docking tower that soared so high I couldn't see the top. The network of darkened platforms rose straight up until it faded into the night. "To your ship," he added.

I bit my lip. That was disappointing. I'd begun hoping we were heading for his place.

A whole lot of awkward silence went by.

Oh, screw it. "No one's expecting me back right away," I said.

Shade eventually responded with a soft grunt. In the end, I thought it was just to acknowledge that he'd heard me. He didn't look at me or take me up on anything, even though I'd thought that was a pretty clear invitation to resume our earlier activities.

Confused and stung, I let his hand drop. I didn't understand, and I definitely wasn't used to putting myself out there like that, despite apparently going full throttle whenever I was with Shade. Our kiss had initially been a ruse to trick the Dark Watch, but he'd seemed just as into it as I'd been, especially the second part, after we'd ducked around the corner. But now, it was as though he'd taken a cold shower, while I was still hot, hot, hot.

"Did you take a shower?" he asked.

Shit. Had I said something about showers out loud? I didn't think so.

"Yeah. At Susan's. She's really nice."

"You smell like peaches." Shade glanced over at me. "I fucking love peaches. Best fruit in the galaxy."

He took my hand back, and just like that, I felt better again. I had to duck my head to hide my smile, and the silence that stretched between us after that didn't seem so awkward anymore.

Worry still niggled at me as we made our way toward the *Endeavor*, and I finally recognized some landmarks. I was starting to think that *numbskull* wasn't even the half of it. It was a little scary how this man I barely knew was starting to hold sway over my emotions and occupy my thoughts. Maybe it wasn't such a bad thing, having to get off Albion 5 in a rush.

And then maybe I could stop wondering why Shade looked like he wanted to consume me one moment, and then scowled so grimly the next.

CHAPTER

15

THE NEXT DAY, SHADE SHOWED UP WITH THE sunrise again, bringing his equipment up the Squirrel Tree on a loaded-down, front-opening hover crate. He supervised while some people from a delivery service dropped off the rest of the reinforced metal tiles we needed as well as the new—and significantly upgraded—armored door. They took care of the initial setup and heavy lifting on the door, and Shade, in definite need of Jax's special brew, watched and directed from behind his dark sunglasses, slowly sipping coffee from the mug I'd brought outside for him.

Shade had already paid for everything, and when I tried to pay him back, at least for the door, with the money Susan had given me the night before, he just shook his head.

"Hold on to it for now," he said. "I'll tally it all up when the work is done."

I put the universal currency back into my pocket with a shrug. "That seems awfully generous for a self-proclaimed space rogue."

"Like I said, I'm a *successful* space rogue."

"Ah, that's right. SRP. Wouldn't a successful space rogue take the money as soon as it was offered? I'd figured there was a bit of being mercenary involved."

"Maybe." He sipped his coffee. "But there's no rush. A few days won't make a difference."

They did to some people. Maybe my hunch about Shade having family money was correct. Or maybe he made a bunch of money doing whatever else it was he did. One thing was for sure: he didn't open up about his work.

"So, Mr. Phenom, do you often take on odd jobs like this?"

He looked over at me, his eyes hidden and his expression inscrutable. "No."

I heated up from the inside out, even though I shouldn't have read anything into what he'd just said. Little starbursts still exploded in my stomach. "Are you a sucker for a damsel in distress, then?" I asked.

He slipped off his dark glasses. "Is that what you are?" His brown eyes were intense, too serious, when I'd just been trying to tease.

Obviously, I was bad at it.

I shook my head. "I always land on my feet." Just like Bonk.

I glanced toward the *Endeavor*, all beat up but still the best ship ever. "Or fly away to fight another day."

"Fight for what, Tess?"

Crap. I needed to shut up. "Nothing. Just joking around."

Shade's eyes lasered in on the small scar on my chin. "You throw an okay punch."

"I missed."

"I ducked."

I scoffed. "It's the same thing, Shade."

"I wouldn't say that." He went back to watching the workmen fit the armored door into place. Shade would see to the finishing touches and electrical connections, but he needed both the extra manpower and their machinery to haul the massive parts up and fit them into the recessed holding slots.

"But your technique needs work." He turned back to me, bringing up my mediocre punches again. "I could give you a few pointers later on. I've got gloves and a big mat under my shop."

My pulse rocketed off into space. Work up a sweat with Shade in his private basement? Yes, please.

I pretended to think about it, then casually said, "Sure. Sounds great."

He nodded.

My heart pounded. Was that a date?

"I'm licensed in three different types of self-defense," he added. "Maybe I can teach you something useful for all that *not* fighting you might be doing another day."

I arched both brows. Clearly, I was as transparent as my punches. But I'd been pretty straight with Shade, and it didn't take a genius to look at my torn-up ship and sense that I was in deep shit. His offer just meant he wanted to make sure I could take care of myself. But anything that made my heart flutter the way it did right now… I'd call that a date.

Shade got straight to work as soon as everything was set up and the door people had left, recruiting Jax's help to hoist some of the heavier tiles into place. He was mostly grunts and grumbles after that and totally focused on the repairs. My usefulness ended at handing Shade a blowtorch once and tossing a water bottle up to Jax. I seemed pretty superfluous to the entire operation and was getting sunburned to boot, so I finally told them to just shout if they needed me and went back inside to check on Fiona's progress with my blood.

I found her in her lab—nothing surprising there. She was humming, though, which had to have been a first.

"Good mood?" I asked.

"This stuff is fan-*freaking*-tastic," she answered without looking up. "I need more as soon as possible. I was about to go find you and ask for it."

"No problem," I said with significantly more casualness than I felt. I was pretty conflicted about sticking myself again. "How many bags?"

"Five?" Fiona glanced at me over her shoulder. "You said there was more, right?"

I nodded, but *wow*, five was a lot. I wasn't sure how to explain not bringing them all at once, though, so I would probably just need to drink a lot of water and then go buy myself a steak. I knew from experience that I had a higher tolerance than most people for how much blood I could lose, and luckily, bag size had diminished over the years. I could do five without going into shock. I wasn't so sure about remaining conscious, though.

Moving farther into Fiona's lab, I approached her workstation for a better look at what she was doing. I saw red-dotted microscope slides, test tubes full of blood, and a pile of scribbled notes that looked totally indecipherable to me. Science had never been my thing.

I leaned my hip against the metal table, feeling its

coolness through my pants. "So, what've you found?" I asked.

"It's definitely pure organic," she said.

"Pure organic," I echoed. Well, that sounded good. Not souped-up or anything. "And?"

"And the super soldier serum was mixed with a ton of chemical crap to boost strength and stamina. This is just blood. It's got all the same ingredients as regular human blood."

Could that be true? Could that be *all*? Then what the hell had my whole childhood been about?

"But…" she said, drawing out the word.

My stomach clenched, and words like *freak* and *foreign* and *guinea pig* shrieked through my head. "But what?" I cautiously asked.

"The proportions are all off."

It was easy to act clueless. I was different; that was all I'd ever been told until the day my father decided he'd had enough of my oddities—and my defiance— and threw me out with the space trash.

"What do you mean?" I asked.

"White blood cells usually only account for about one percent of our total blood volume. The percentage goes up a bit when you're sick, to fight infection, but then it goes back to normal again. It's just a small, albeit important, part of our blood. In *this*"—Fiona picked up a test tube and swirled the crimson liquid around—"the percentage is up to nearly eighteen. That's *huge*. Like mega, massively huge."

"Holy Sky Mother," I breathed out. No wonder my father had called me a freak. And no wonder I never got sick. I was a walking immune system.

"Where do you think it comes from?" I asked. "You know, the origin of it?" I dreaded her answer. I was also dying to hear it, to finally *know* something.

"Human," she said immediately. "Granted, my equipment isn't the most sophisticated available, but the only difference I see is this increased white-blood-cell count. It's healthy, normal blood. There's nothing wrong with it."

For the first time in my life, I understood the idea of going weak-kneed with relief.

"In terms of the illness on Starway 8, what can we do with it?" I asked, trying not to get my hopes up. "Do you think it would be safe to inject? The imbalance wouldn't hurt someone else?"

"In large doses, like a blood transfusion, it might be hard for a person to adjust. But..." Her green eyes lit up as she drew out the word again. "Give me a few more days, and I might have a shot that'll kick that virus in the butt."

❋❋❋

I made sandwiches for the men outside and then let Bonk out onto the platform for a quick romp in the sun. When he got tired of sniffing around, I took him in and then headed back to the kitchen for my own lunch with Miko and Shiori. I told them about Fiona's experiments and asked Miko to set a course for the orphanage. I wanted the coordinates programmed in so that we could make the jump to Sector 8 the second the *Endeavor* was ready for space travel again.

Neither of them looked all that eager about returning to the Dark, and I ignored the pang in my chest when I thought about flying away from Albion 5—and Shade Ganavan.

Procrastinating because I dreaded drawing my own blood again, I cleaned up the kitchen with Miko's help and then checked in with Mareeka, who responded that the situation was getting steadily worse on Starway 8, although the Dark Watch hadn't imposed a quarantine yet.

Vomiting. Kids can't keep fluids down. Dehydration. Fevers.

Apparently, she'd hit the whole place with a massive round of strong antibiotics as a last resort, but it hadn't done a thing.

It's viral, she wrote. Surral is working hard. She sends her love. Coltin is okay for now.

I closed my eyes, picturing the handsome little boy. My heart always ached when I thought about him, and my fingers curled, as though trying to hold on to the feel of soft baby fuzz on a tiny head. That sensation was just a memory now, like Coltin's first tooth popping through, his gurgling laugh, or his chubby, spit-wet fingers grabbing on to my hair and pulling hard.

He didn't need a replacement mother anymore. Our relationship had turned into something more like siblings, even though there were fifteen years between us in age, and I only saw him a few times a year.

Coltin is okay for now…

My lunch soured in my stomach. How long would he resist? How many were struggling?

It was time to suck it up and do my part, so I made my way toward the vacuum-sealed lab attachment at the back of the *Endeavor*.

Feeling powerless was hard for me. Hard for anyone,

I supposed. Right now, I had to wait for Fiona to work her science and for Shade to finish fixing the ship. Kids were scared and suffering, but there was no way to rush to their aid like I wanted to. The only thing I could do for now was get Fiona more blood.

I had to wonder why the Dark Watch hadn't set up a quarantine yet. Usually, the military was quick with things like that. For all his faults, I didn't think the Overseer actually *wanted* disease to spread like wildfire throughout the galaxy. We had to hurry, because before too long, they were sure to cut the orphanage off.

Needles and blood bags.

A chill skittered down my arms, ending in a shudder. I rolled my shoulders and shook out my neck.

With lunch, I hadn't only been delaying. I'd needed to eat, drink, and digest a bit before doing this, or else five bags of blood could knock me out. Hell, they'd probably knock me out anyway. Jax sometimes donated blood when we were in the Fold, since that was where so many of our injured ended up, and it was usually just one bag at a time, with donations once per week, even for a big, strong, healthy man like him.

I knew I was different. I could give more. Even as a kid, it had usually taken three or four bags before I'd felt my head spinning out of control.

With detached efficiency, I locked myself in the lab and set everything up, putting the blood bags out in a row so that I could just switch them without taking the needle out. I pulled a rolling chair over to the lab table and sat. I didn't bother with disinfecting my inner arm or with a tourniquet this time. I was highly resistant to infection, and there was no way I could deal with that tight rubber band around my arm for the amount of time this would take. Strangely enough, that sticky, pinching, constant pressure was the part of this whole process I hated the most.

I inhaled deeply, trying to unravel some of the knots in my stomach.

Here goes…

I stuck myself—and missed.

Fuck. My hand shook. The air in here tasted like metal and death.

Muttering a curse, I got up and opened the whole series of doors again, renewing the air in the sealed-off lab attachment with the fresher air from the rest of the *Endeavor*. I stood at the entrance and kept watch, hoping no one would come this way and wonder why in the name of all the Powers I'd laid out a syringe and five empty blood bags.

No one showed up at the back of the ship, and after six minutes and thirty-two seconds of wide-open doors, I began the process of sealing them all up again. It smelled and tasted somewhat better in the lab now, but when I punched in the lock code and the final door barreled shut with a hydraulic *whoosh*, I still felt like a coffin had just slammed down its lid.

I took two steps before abruptly turning and going back to the lock. I changed the code to something I thought Jax could guess. It felt too stupid to lock myself in here and draw five bags of blood without the possibility of someone being able to get into the lab if I didn't come out.

I went back to my grim setup and tried again, overcoming my jitters with concentration. It was a physical effort to steady my hand as well as a mental one. Like the previous time, I got my blood flowing on the second try.

A dull lump of panic thickened my throat as I leaned back in the chair, trying not to look at the plastic bag that was slowly inflating with blood. It wasn't terrible to watch. It was actually kind of mesmerizing. But I closed my eyes and pictured open spaces instead. Quickly, that turned into picturing Shade Ganavan with his lush mouth all tangled up with mine and his big hands covering my breasts.

Daydreaming about Shade and steamy, urgent grinding and take-me-now kisses up against a dark wall helped distract me and pass the time. I kept an intermittent eye on the level of the bags as they filled up, so I'd know when to switch. By the start of the fourth bag, I felt like utter crap, and even remembering the hot, sexy slide of Shade's tongue against my night-chilled skin didn't help. I started breathing faster but felt lethargic. My heart pounded, trying to circulate my reduced blood.

Halfway through the fifth bag, I felt myself really going south. I pulled the needle from my arm, capped off the bag, and collapsed back. My vision darkened, and that was that.

***

I woke up with drool on my face and a painful crick in my neck. I wiped off my chin with a hand that shook. After a moment of blinking at the harsh overhead lighting and fighting the urge to vomit, I reached for the bottle of water I'd left on the table next to me. I was hardly able to close my hand around it, and unscrewing the top was a challenge I hadn't anticipated, one that left me panting and almost falling straight back into another nonnegotiable nap.

Once I finally got the cap off, I drained the bottle one slow sip at a time, working through the nausea that kept roiling up. Every second that passed made me more and more desperate to get out of the sealed-up metal box, but I needed to replenish my fluids first, or I risked not even making it through the first door, let alone the rest.

The next twenty minutes turned into a personal challenge in mastering the anxiety I always felt when I was shut inside a closed space but not flying. This time was made even worse by being light-headed and weak and having an actual *locked* door between myself and the rest of the ship.

Nevertheless, I sat there slowly rolling the now-empty bottle between my hands, listening to the cheap plastic crackle and staring rather blindly at the rows of temperature-controlled shelving units holding the enhancers.

Part of me wondered if I should blow them up. I couldn't decide.

Eventually, I felt steady enough to get up. My head spun as though it were orbiting my body instead of attached to it, but I didn't fall down. Deep breaths helped chase away the sparks and floaters dancing across my vision. I gripped the edge of the table for balance, still dizzy as hell. I probably should have sat back down, but getting out of the stifling room was starting to feel like a priority I couldn't ignore. I swallowed hard, gearing up to move. The moment I was able, I gathered the blood bags and stumbled out of the lab attachment, locking it again behind me.

I somehow made it to Fiona's domain, dragging my

feet and keeping a heavy hand against the corridor wall. In a small miracle that saved me from having to explain why I was barely upright, she wasn't in her lab. Maybe she'd finally remembered to eat something. I stuck the already sufficiently cooled blood in her refrigerator and left her a note. It was hardly legible, but I didn't have the energy to try again.

Before I left, I took a bottle of water from Fiona's stash but didn't open it yet. One foot in front of the other, woozy step by woozy step, I made it to my room. Thankfully, my personal sanctuary had been intact again since Shade's first visit to the *Endeavor*, when he'd fixed the hole in my bedroom wall. There was still a shit-ton of construction noise coming through the hull, but I didn't care. I curled up next to Bonk and put my arm around him.

It felt so good to lay my head on the pillow that I snuggled into it like I used to when I was a kid and my only real worries were why my father scowled at me the way he did, used me like a blood dispenser, and fought so much with my mother. I hadn't liked it, but I also hadn't known anything else existed until Mareeka and Surral took me in, just like they took in all the strays of the galaxy.

I smiled. Just like Susan with her cats.

It hadn't been all bad in the Overseer's opulent but prison-like home. Mom had loved me and done her best to protect me, and we'd had some good times with Uncle Nate before he'd become Captain Bridgebane to both of us, even in private, just like he'd already been to everyone else.

He'd eventually closed himself off to us, hardly

visiting his stepsister or her apparently mutant daughter anymore. Even an ex-hooligan from 17 could finally buy into Dad's crap. Mom had been really sad about that.

I yawned, wishing so many things had turned out differently—and not just for myself.

Bonk started purring, and sleep hovered close to my thoughts, trying to overtake them. A few fought back.

It was going to be really hard to spar with Shade tonight, but I wouldn't miss it for all the worlds.

Also, he wanted to show me some moves? I knew at least one of us was hoping they wouldn't be limited to self-defense.

CHAPTER

16

SHADE WAS GONE BY THE TIME I WOKE UP, AND JAX told me I was supposed to find him at his shop for our "workout," which he of course said with narrowed eyes and a huge amount of disapproval in his voice.

I didn't mind, and I didn't try to argue Jax into changing his. I loved that he looked out for me. He wouldn't get all growly and sullen if he didn't care, and if he had been doing something that worried me, I sure as hell wouldn't have held back. But Jax never really did anything stupid, or at least potentially stupid, like I sometimes did. The only thing that bothered me was how he spent so much time stuck in the past and never, ever planned on leaving it behind him.

As the elevator tube sucked me down to ground level, I knew I looked okay on the outside because I'd fancied myself up a bit before leaving, but I still felt like crap on the inside. My head spun with any sudden movement, and if I hadn't wanted to see Shade so badly, I'd have thought better of this whole plan and gone straight back up the Squirrel Tree to bed.

But my heart beat harder at the thought of him, and my skin tingled with an electric attraction I wanted to explore. If I only had a few more days in Albion City with Shade, I didn't want to waste them in my own bed. If he was game, I wanted to spend them in his.

On the way to Ganavan's Products and Parts, I stopped and ate a steak and a mix of mostly unidentifiable greens and nuts. I didn't feel much better after eating, though. In fact, I felt nauseous again and even worse.

I moved slowly after that, making sure I wasn't going to be sick before showing up at Shade's place. Digestion finally did its thing, the queasiness passed, and I trudged on, popping a breath freshener into my mouth a block away from Shade's building and sucking on it as I walked.

Shade had left the shop lights on, but the door sign said Closed. I knocked, and he showed up quickly to let me in. My pulse sped up at the sight of him, making me feel slightly breathless as I stepped inside. He didn't say anything, just opened the door and then closed it again, locking it behind me.

I turned, and our eyes met. Then I took in the rest of him. He looked hot as hell, dressed in a black T-shirt that pulled tight across his broad chest. It somehow made his eyes look lighter instead of darker. Simple, dark-gray workout sweats hung low on his lean hips. They were tied with a double knot. Just as with decoding locks, I was good at unraveling knots.

Slowly, I backed toward the counter with the register. Desire pulsed through me. Sparring sounded like fun, but really, I just wanted to rip off Shade's clothes.

Shade prowl-walked me straight into the counter until

my lower back bumped against the cool surface. He made no move to cage me, but I was definitely caught. Anticipation whipped through me. Did this mean we were skipping the training? I was perfectly fine with that.

"Fuck it," he muttered, cupping my face in his hands. His honey eyes hit mine just long enough to make sure I was okay with a kiss before he lowered his mouth to mine.

Heat detonated inside me. I lifted my hands and held on to his sides, kissing him back in a way that said I was totally on board and wanted more, more, more. I angled my body into his, greedy for the feel of him. The kiss deepened, and I licked my tongue into his mouth. Shade groaned, the sound deep and resonating. It sank into me and tugged hard between my legs.

We both went a little wild after that. His reaction made me feel as if I might have skills, even though I'd only ever had one partner, and that was a long time ago. It was hard to remember anything about that teenage fumbling in the dark with Shade's hands in my hair, his mouth on mine, and his big, solid body pressing me up against the counter. Shade was a man, not a boy. The feel of his erection against my lower belly set my body on fire. I wanted him inside me. I was desperate to feel him everywhere.

I slipped my hands under his shirt. I wasn't sure if I wanted to go up or down, so I just stayed there, my hands at his waistline, my fingers pressing into his warm skin.

Shade finally lifted his head and stepped back, his eyes bright and his breathing hard. "Let's go downstairs," he said.

I nodded. I really hoped downstairs had a bed.

Shade brought me through an office situated behind the counter and cash register. At the far side of the room, we took a metallic staircase that curved downward in a tight spiral and led into an immense basement. It was bright, the lighting so severe I had to squint at first—and as masculine and functional as a place could possibly get.

Disappointment washed through me. It was a workout space, with mats, weights, a few machines, a pull-up bar, and a big black punching bag with BRUISER written down the side in bumblebee yellow.

My eyes landed on a closed door beyond the mats. Unless…

"Do you live here?" I asked.

Shade nodded. "Over there." He tilted his head toward the door I'd noticed.

He didn't go that way, though. He crossed his man-cave gym to a tall cupboard, opening it by flipping a series of numbers on an old-style combination lock.

Apparently, we *were* exercising, just not in the way I'd hoped.

"Nice gym." It smelled a little sweaty down here, but not too bad. I glanced around. The equipment was good quality, even if it wasn't all state of the art. It was still a hell of a lot better than I could afford. "Needs some cats."

Shade chuckled. "Noted." His brown eyes flicked to mine.

It was a relief that some of the tension had broken, but my mind wasn't really on workouts or cats. Shade's totally unapologetic erection still taunted me from under his loose pants, making me want to wrap my hand around it and squeeze.

Shade, however, got straight down to the business of working out. He set two bottles of water on a low bench and then rummaged in his cupboard, moving things around. He dropped a pair of padded gloves by his feet and then tossed me a smaller pair that he dragged out from farther in the back.

I held them against my chest. They were heavier than the last boxing gloves I'd used, but the training gear in the Fold wasn't always the best. Standing there across from Shade, performance anxiety suddenly struck me. I hadn't gone any friendly rounds in a ring in at least two years. I'd been too busy doing other stuff.

"You don't have to wear them if you don't want to," Shade said. "I will, just in case I accidentally get too rough."

So the padding was for me, not for his hands. I couldn't decide if that was sweet or patronizing. Maybe a bit of both. At least he'd seen something in me that had made him believe I *could* spar, and that we weren't starting from scratch.

"You think I won't land a punch?" I challenged.

He grinned. "If you do, you'll want those." He thumped his chest. "Hard as a rock."

I laughed, although there was nothing false about that.

Shade bent to take off his shoes before stepping barefoot onto the large square mat. He pulled on his gloves, securing them in place as he moved toward the center and started loosening up.

I followed his lead, setting my socks and boots aside—and *whoa*, my head swam when I straightened back up. I blinked silver streaks from my eyes as I tugged on the gloves, using my teeth in the same way

Shade had to secure the second wrist strap. When I felt steady enough again, I walked out onto the mat.

"You want headgear?" Shade asked.

"How about nothing above the neck?" I said.

"Didn't plan on it, starshine." He started bouncing on the balls of his feet and throwing easy punches at the air to warm himself up. Sadly, his hard-on seemed to have disappeared, and kissing looked like it was off the table—for now.

I watched him out of the corner of my eye as I did some limbering up. He was fast and smooth, undeniably strong and fit. Shade seemed pretty easygoing overall, but there was obviously a born warrior underneath. Or one of those alpha animals. There was an innate dominance about him that he didn't really show off, but that he didn't downplay, either. It was just there, a part of him.

And he threw a wicked right hook.

I wouldn't have wanted to be on the wrong side of him in a fight that wasn't just for some training fun. There was no doubt about it; he would kick my ass. I was no pushover, as I'd had to prove a time or ten on the Mile when Jax hadn't been around, and I could get the jump on someone when I tried, but my strong suits were blending in, getting in and out of places undetected, and giving the galactic goons the slippery runaround.

Shade moved into kicks, and even just for warm-up, the strong pivot of his bottom foot and the hard snap of his kicking leg made his roundhouse look lethal to me. Cage fighting had been outlawed, but it still happened on some of the seedier spacedocks, and Shade Ganavan could probably have made a fortune at it—as long as he didn't mind having a few of his features rearranged.

The man I was falling for was powerful and skilled, and I liked the idea of having a top predator showing me how to better defend myself. Truthfully, I needed the training. I had a few good moves, but when they didn't work out, I could easily end up at a loss. *Run really fast* wasn't always a solution, either, and I had two years in prison as proof of that. It would have been a lifetime if other people's bad luck hadn't turned into my good fortune.

Shade could obviously be as big a bruiser as his punching bag, but I wasn't worried about him using his strength against me. My thoughts just kept veering off in other directions—like how much safer every day might feel with him watching my back.

I blinked hard. *Stop it.*

Self-chiding wasn't very effective, but it was a start. A modicum of effort on my part to stay reasonable and on track. I would be leaving soon, and mine were ridiculous thoughts.

Shade nodded for me to start. "Show me some of what you've got, and then we'll take it from there."

A giddy fizz of emotions effervesced inside me again. I couldn't help stupidly loving any interaction with Shade, even though physically, I still felt like a slug. I did my best to put on a good show and started circling him, looking for an opening. He kept his guard up, watching me. I threw the first punch, and Shade dodged. I tried again.

"You're transparent as hell. Try not to turn into the punch three hours before you throw it," he said.

"Three hours?" I grumbled, circling again.

He winked. "Just a tip, sugar."

I narrowed my eyes.

He moved in, and I danced back. His first punch was so half-assed that I easily stopped it with my glove. A few seconds later, I aimed a kick at his ribs. His hand swept down to block my foot, and his solid forearm sent me hopping back, off-balance.

Shade arched his brows.

Shit. I was making a fool of myself.

He came at me again like he almost meant it, throwing a punch that had me rearing back. I got out of the way in time, and his hit didn't connect, although I was starting to wonder if he would have let it. Even so, the next thing I knew, my butt hit the mat. Impact jarred a grunt out of me. I'd fallen over, and Shade hadn't even touched me.

"Tess?" He looked down at me, his eyebrows drawing into a frown.

I blinked. There were two of him. I blinked again. Okay—one.

I decided to admit the truth. "I may not be up for this tonight."

He scowled. "What the hell is wrong with you?"

"I…" I was too tired to think up a good lie. "I gave blood before coming here. I may have given too much."

"How much?" he asked.

"Five bags."

"Five bags!" Shade exploded toward me, dropping to his knees on the mat. "Are you crazy?" He tore off his gloves and then picked me up. I looped my arms around his neck as the room tilted. He carried me like I was small—and I was *not*. I closed my eyes, willing the spinning to stop.

He walked a few steps and then shifted his hold on me. I heard him jiggle a door handle. When I opened my eyes again, he was taking me down a softly lit corridor. I caught flashes of other rooms, but then he turned right, and I found myself being set down on a bed. His bed, I supposed. It was nice. Soft. The bedding was dark brown and slightly textured under my hands and bare feet.

I took stock of the room, which was pretty empty. I could smell Shade in here—or rather the soap he used. There was something fresh about it, like a forest, or the outdoors. I wasn't quite sure. I didn't know much about that.

I smoothed my foot over the comforter, liking its velvety feel. The bed wasn't huge, but it seemed just right for two people. I'd wanted to get here, though not exactly like this.

I glanced up at Shade. The only light we had came through the open door, and his expression looked dark and almost dangerous in the dimness. He leaned over me, and I sat there as he pulled off my gloves, freeing one hand and then the other with a muttered curse. Straightening away from me, he threw the pair of gloves across the room like he was pretty pissed off.

"*One* bag. You give *one*—if you give at all. Who would take that much? Where the fuck did you go? Some black-market clinic?" He scrubbed a hand down his face, exhaling loudly. "Shit. You're not selling your insides to pay for my repairs, are you?"

I went for levity, because he looked really upset. "This seems like a rich city. I'm sure I'll get a good price for that kidney."

His eyes flared. "That's not funny."

I shrugged. "Neither is needing a kidney." They were really slow to grow in a petri dish.

His jaw visibly flexed. Forcing exaggerated evenness, he asked, "Can you *please* explain to me why you gave up so much blood?"

I chose to level with him. Mostly. What could it hurt? "There's disease on Starway 8. I thought they might need blood. Sometimes, transfusions help. You know, out with the old, in with the new. It could be good."

Shade didn't look convinced. In fact, the way he looked at me made my stomach knot all up—and not in a good way this time.

"Let me get this straight. You drained yourself of blood to send it off to orphans? Just in case?"

I nodded.

"You're a fucking lunatic, Tess."

People kept saying that! I bristled. "I weigh every move I make, Shade. Don't think that I don't." That also meant my decision to be here tonight, alone with him, and I was pretty sure he understood.

Unfortunately, I'd just demonstrated that I wasn't up for even some good-natured sparring. He probably assumed I wasn't up for anything else, either.

Shade's hands moved to his hips. He took a deep breath and then ground out, "Stay here."

Without waiting for an answer, he turned and walked out the door, leaving me alone in his darkened bedroom.

***

Five bags of blood. Shade wanted to punch something.

Thank the Sky Mother typical bags were smaller than they used to be, or she'd be dead. Tess had still probably lost twenty percent of her overall blood volume, and that was way too much. Reaching dangerous levels.

What the hell had she been thinking? And then she'd come over to his place to duke it out on the mats? He'd thrown punches at her, for fuck's sake.

While he was at it, what the hell was *he* thinking? He still didn't know if his aim tonight had been to ascertain how to best bring in Tess without hurting her, or to reassure himself that she knew how to fight off whatever hunter came for her first. And then the next hunter. And then the next. Everything was so fucked up. *He* was a fucking mess.

In a rage he couldn't quite contain, Shade banged around his kitchen. Luckily, he'd held back. A lot. He hadn't wanted to get rough with her. He'd just wanted to see what she could take.

"What've you eaten tonight?" he shouted toward the open door down the hallway.

A moment later, Tess's answer floated back. "Water. Steak. Some nuts and green stuff."

He made a face. Nuts? With steak and salad? At least she had her proteins covered.

He grabbed his bag of trigrain bread. Now he needed to get her blood sugar up.

While the bread toasted, he squeezed some orange juice, getting some aggression out on the ancient contraption he'd picked up a few years ago. He usually only brought out the prehistoric juicer in the mornings, but he thought Tess might like it. The end result tasted like sunshine in a glass.

He slammed the pump down hard, mashing the fuck out of the half-rounds of fruit he'd just cut. It felt good to pound on something, and fresh juice might give her some energy back.

The toast popped. He used three times as much butter as he would have wanted for himself, sprinkled a heavy layer of cinnamon sugar onto the bread, and then went back to the bedroom, carrying a tray with the toast and orange juice on it.

Tess was right where he'd left her, propped up like a nearly six-foot-tall, pale-as-fuck queen against his pillows. They were the same color as her hair. They looked like just plain brown at first, but then you saw the russet.

It was weird seeing her there. He'd never brought a woman downstairs before. No one but him ever went beyond the shop.

He set the tray on her lap. What a great place to start—with a wanted criminal in his bed.

His scowl felt etched into his face. Incredible woman he liked and desired. Bed. It was usually pretty obvious what to do with that, but he had no idea what to do with Tess.

The arrow of guilt that speared him reminded him that he'd already done way too much, since he still wanted that money as much as he wanted Tess.

Fucking rebels. How many times had he wondered what it was like? Chasing the night. Not living by the rules. Not crunching numbers, or worrying about infrastructure he had no right to touch, or thinking about employees that weren't even his. Kissing Tess was like living a different life.

But he'd never wanted that different life enough to abandon the docks his family had built from the ground up. He'd worked his ass off, and he wanted them back.

Tess finally looked up from the tray she'd been staring at. Her blue eyes looked darker than usual in the low light. She glanced from him to the food and then back to him again. "You made me cinnamon toast?"

"And fresh-squeezed orange juice. Eat up."

She blinked a few times, and Shade thought maybe he'd been too gruff. "Here. I'll prove it's not poisoned." He took a big gulp from her full glass.

"Hey!" Tess snatched the juice away from him, smiling now. "That's mine."

She drank and then groaned low in her throat. The satisfied sound shot straight to his groin.

Shade shifted back from her. Not appropriate. The woman could barely stand up.

Among other reasons...

"That tastes amazing." She devoured the toast, making a noise that was practically orgasmic when she licked the sugar off her fingertips.

Was she trying to kill him?

Glancing away, Shade swiped a hand through his hair. He heard her finish off her juice.

She sighed. "I love landing because the food is so good. Up there, in the Dark, the fresh stuff runs out fast, and then it's just the same old canned slop over and over again until you want to throw up."

Steeling himself, Shade turned back to her. She was still just as beautiful. A light smattering of freckles across her nose, the bluest eyes he'd ever seen, hair all over the place.

"Why do you stay so long in the Dark?" he asked.

She acted like she was thinking about it, but he knew she was just coming up with a lie.

"Because everyone wants me dead."

Shade started. *Honesty?* That was a surprise. "Everyone?"

She shrugged. "Well, no, not *everyone*. But some very powerful people do, and that trickles down to even the lowest goon in the galaxy. And the Powers know, the Dark Watch is all over the place."

"Do you need help?" He nearly bit his tongue. Had he really just asked her that? He didn't want to be an even bigger bastard where Tess was concerned, but he was going that way fast.

She shook her head. "You're fixing the *Endeavor* for a fair price. That's already huge in my book."

Shade lifted the tray from her lap and set it on the bedside table. "Why are they after you?" he asked.

She laughed. "I'm not telling you that!"

"Why not?" He sat on the edge of the bed.

She huffed, tucking her hair behind her ears like she always did. Earlier, he'd wanted to push it all back himself and see her face.

"To begin with, it's a long list," she said.

"How long?" He was being pushy, but that seemed to put her at ease. She probably figured a person who was a danger to her wouldn't just outright ask questions like this. They'd use tactics and finesse. Or else brute force.

Shade tried to ignore the sickening fact that Tess seemed to trust him. He was to blame for that.

She bent her knees and tucked her legs up under her. The movement brought them closer together. "You know when it's do or die, Shade?"

Her eyes drew him in, and the sound of his name on her lips was like a drug. He inched closer, letting the 12-perfect diction of every word she said wash over him, even though it was toxic to them both.

"And you do things anyway," she continued. "Maybe mess up your whole life, because you *know* it's the right thing to do. You just know what you have to do, or you could never live with yourself again."

He nodded. He'd never had that feeling himself, but he was mesmerized by her conviction. And a little ill. Even as he listened to her, he was still thinking about taking her in. She was weak and alone, sitting right here in his basement with him. In mere seconds, he could have her tied up and completely at his mercy. Two hundred million. Maybe more. His money. His new life—or the life he should have been living already. Scarabin White—paid off and out of his future for good.

Tess was obviously a resistance fighter to the core. He'd already brought in dozens. He could bring in dozens more. But she'd just said they wanted her dead, and the problem was that he didn't want anyone touching a hair on her head.

"Shade?"

He cleared his throat. "Yeah, baby?"

She glanced down. When she looked back up, her lips were slightly parted, and a pretty flush colored her cheeks.

Shit. He was so fucked.

"Do you give nicknames to everyone?" she asked.

He forced a smile. "Ah, you like *sugar*, do you?"

Her mouth twitched. "No, actually. I don't."

"Princess, then?"

She shook her head. "Not really."

"Starshine?"

She blushed again. So that one worked.

"What do you like, baby?" he asked in a voice that unintentionally dropped.

She bit her lip, looking shy and uncertain, even though he knew she could lose her inhibitions quickly and kiss like a wildcat. "The last two are all right."

"Noted," Shade said with enough seriousness to make her smile again.

They fell into a silence that wasn't awkward but wasn't exactly comfortable, either. There was too much tension between them for that—tension he was dying to release if the pressure inside him was any indication.

As they sat there on his bed in the dimly lit room, in the quiet, Shade finally truly understood what a huge problem he had. He'd already known, but yeah... Every second he spent with Tess made it a thousand times worse. It was do or die, just like she'd said. Or more like do or don't.

He had to make a choice.

Her hand crept onto his leg. "I'm feeling a lot stronger now." She stroked up his thigh. "Much better," she said.

Every nerve inside him jumped to attention, and heat billowed through his chest. He wanted her more than he could remember wanting anyone. Hell, he could hardly remember anyone else at all with Tess looking at him the way she did, with that weird mix of hesitancy and up-for-anythingness on her face. She was a fucking dream, and arousal roared through his blood.

Shade grabbed her hand, stopping her increasingly bold explorations just before she hit where it would really count. He curled his fingers around hers. He knew he could be a selfish asshole sometimes, but there was no way in hell he'd sleep with a woman and then turn her over to the Dark Watch for a reward.

Tess froze, waiting. It was his move.

He hated his options. Even if he did what they both wanted and then let her fly away, she'd still be hunted by the others, and they were a bunch of vicious fucks. And if he satisfied this craving, she'd take off when her ship was done, leaving him, and then he'd be stuck facing another ten years of doing other people's dirty work just to get back the property he'd so stupidly lost.

If he turned her in, he could buy back every single docking tower on Albion 5 and its neighbor tomorrow. He'd run this place, just like his family always had. Just like he would have all along if he hadn't fucked up that one night.

Talk about paying for your mistakes. He was sick to death of it.

Shade lifted Tess's hand from his thigh. It was burning a hole through his pants. "If you're feeling better, then it's time to get you back to your ship."

Her face fell, and her disappointment crashed straight through him. She didn't bother trying to hide anything from him anymore, which might have been the worst part of this whole twisted mess.

He'd been clear in his rejection, though, so she pulled it together and got off his bed. Because that was what Tess Bailey did—she dealt.

CHAPTER

17

It was sheer embarrassing torture, but I forced myself out onto the platform in the morning to bring Shade his usual cup of coffee. He accepted it with thanks but then barely looked at me again. He was always a little off in the mornings, so maybe he was just being his habitual cranky self. Or maybe it was the fact that I'd thrown myself at him the night before, and he'd turned me down. My stomach still dropped at the thought of that.

I climbed back on board the *Endeavor* without trying to make small talk with Shade, but then regretted missing our usual conversation time over coffee. He was interesting and intelligent, and he went down uncommon paths of discussion without looking horrified or making a fuss, which made talking to him one of the highlights of my day.

But not today. His rejection was still too fresh, so I hid out in the kitchen with Miko and Shiori until lunch. Together, the three of us managed to generate the mother of all shopping lists, which I then uploaded to a local food and goods outlet that would deliver later in the day. I added a huge supply of cat food and some of that extra-special litter Susan had given me to the end of the list. We had Bonk to think about now.

When the total came up, I nearly blanched. With everything I still had to pay Shade, that was the end of our money. It was time to start planning a new heist, one that had to be at least somewhat profitable to us as well as useful to our friends. One thing was for sure, though: I wouldn't be selling my blood. Or a kidney. Or anything else.

Through the internal com system, I sent out a call to lunch. Jax and Fiona arrived, completing our group for the trigrain noodles I'd made with sauce. I didn't go outside to invite Shade in to eat with us. He could fend for himself.

"Plain red sauce? Again?" Fiona looked at her plate as though I were asking her to eat worms in mud.

"Sorry." I shoved a fork in her direction. "It was all we had left without dipping into the food for the Outer Zones. New stuff is coming in later today."

"I cleared a spot for it in Cargo 2," Jax said, already digging into his lunch.

I nodded my thanks. Cargo Bay 2 had plenty of free space for crates and a huge refrigeration unit that stayed cold even when the ship wasn't running for days.

"Any news from Mareeka?" Miko asked.

"I haven't checked in yet today." Wiping off my fingers, I reached for the tablet I'd used earlier to order the food and supplies. As soon as it powered up again, I shot off a quick note to the director of Starway 8.

A response came back almost immediately.

"Same," I told the others after reading the message. "Sickness but no quarantine, probably because there haven't been any deaths yet. High fevers. The kids are weak." I skimmed the few lines again. "Ships are starting to avoid the Sector as the news spreads, and food is getting scarce." I glanced back up. "Mareeka says to stay away."

"What's your plan?" Jax asked, obviously knowing we weren't staying away.

Honestly, Mareeka should have known better herself. How many times had she stuck me on ventilation-shaft cleaning duty for not following her directions? A hundred times, at least.

She'd hoped my dislike of closed, still spaces would deter me and turn me into a better listener. It hadn't. I'd just powered through my mild claustrophobia and cleaned the damn ducts.

"As soon as Fiona gives us the go-ahead on the cure she's working on, we'll bring it to Starway 8." I glanced at our resident scientist. She was doing her best to eat her noodles and sauce, but it looked as though it took a real effort and didn't make me want to touch my own lunch very much.

There were noises of consent from around the table, but I hadn't been worried about anyone backing out. I shut down the tablet and picked up my fork. I would power through my meal just like I'd powered through those ventilation ducts.

Eyeing the limp worms in mud, I scooped up a bite and aimed it at my mouth. *Bleh*. It tasted as bland as it looked.

"Have you concluded that the blood Tess found in the lab is the base ingredient for the super soldier serum?" Miko asked.

"Definitely," Fiona answered, wiping off her mouth. "But it's pure. Not only in the sense that it's undiluted, but also in the sense that nothing potentially dangerous has been added to it."

"Perfectly safe for kids? Or anyone else?" I wanted to be sure, even though I'd already asked.

"As far as I can tell, it's simply ahead in terms of immuno-defense." Fiona started to look excited and set down her fork. "Like an improved version of our own blood. If we're life-form A, for example, then this is from life-form A1. Only slightly different, and still totally compatible, but a lot better."

"So life-form A1 will survive over A?" I asked.

"Biologically speaking, it has the better chance," Fiona confirmed. "Think of it in terms of natural selection and the very slight genetic modifications of evolution that, over time, make a huge difference to an entire species."

My brain seemed to slow down and speed up all at once, bouncing between shock and possibilities. "But a beneficial genetic anomaly needs to occur first? Propelling that change?"

Fiona nodded. "In this case, the anomaly seems to have produced a person who'll never get sick."

Was I life-form A1? Human, but improved? "Genetic flukes happen all the time, though. Is this one different?" I asked.

"A little." Fiona shrugged. "It's not just a small jump; it's a big one. And it has the potential to spread—if it hasn't already."

"What do you mean?" Miko asked.

"I ran diagnostics at the molecular level. It's a change

at the genetic level, and it appears to be a dominant trait," Fiona said.

Trying to process that, I asked, "How do we help the orphans with it?"

Her tasteless meal as forgotten as mine, she said, "I was hoping at first that this might somehow inoculate them for life, but I was wrong. A1 blood will eradicate the infection, but it'll also eventually get eliminated from the host body, because it can't change the host's own white blood cells. Giving someone A1 blood just temporarily adds to what they've already got."

"How do you know this?" Shiori asked, chiming in for the first time with a question that, as usual, landed in the air somewhere between Fiona and me on the opposite side of the table from her.

"I mixed some of the test blood with some of my own and then watched," Fiona answered. "The immune cells from A1 and mine didn't merge in any way. They stayed separate. But A1 cells will help fight off sickness in the short term, like taking medicine. And that just further confirms that there's no long-term risk."

"So the shift has to happen at the genetic level?" I asked. "You have to be born with it?"

Fiona confirmed with a nod. "It was either a fluke at conception, and A1 is the first step toward evolution of the human species—*if* A1 procreates—or whoever's blood this is had at least one parent already carrying the genetic material necessary to produce a child with type A1 blood."

Holy shit! The few bites I'd eaten were about to come back up. Mom got sick—she *died* from a fever. So either I was the starting point of type A1 blood, or my father…

I couldn't recall. Had he ever gotten sick?

Noodle-and-red-sauce acid burned in my throat. If the Grand Galactic Overseer was the next step for the human species, we were so incredibly fucked.

And if he was, he'd also used me as a lab rat instead of himself. If he was *exactly* like me, I was going to wring his neck.

Horror percussed through me like the beat of a too-loud drum. If he knew, he could have saved her. All he'd had to do was inject Mom with some of my blood. Or maybe his own.

I jerked back as if slapped. *Of course* he knew. I'd never tried to find out the truth before now because I'd been running from what I thought was something alien and horrible in my blood. And the possibility of my father tracing me back to any tests and finding me had put the fear of all the Powers That Be into me. But Fiona had figured it out in just a couple of days in a makeshift lab full of pieced-together, stolen equipment on a beat-up old cargo ship. With all the technology the Overseer had at his disposal, there was no way he hadn't known. It was simply that creating enhanced soldiers with my special healing blood had been more important to him than saving Mom.

"Tess?" Miko bumped my leg under the table with her foot. "You all right?"

Rattled to the core, I said, "Yeah. Just thinking." My voice came out hoarse, and I cleared my throat.

Miko had lost her hand the day of the explosion on Hourglass Mile. No, she didn't *lose* it; she sawed it off just before the fortuitous blast. Fortuitous for us, anyway. She and Shiori found the *Endeavor* before Jax and I did. We hadn't known, or cared, who was on board when we'd vaulted up into the open cargo cruiser and raced toward the bridge. As long as there weren't guards with guns on the ship, we were good. The two small women huddled in the corner together, one old and blind and the other spewing blood, hadn't seemed like much of a threat.

That afternoon sometimes still felt like yesterday, especially when I was alone at night in the dark, and with this new, unimagined information about myself, my thoughts raced wildly, just like Jax and I had that day.

I'd powered up the ship and taken stock of the controls—luckily nothing newfangled or fancy—and been ready to take off when Jax had looked out the huge window panels and seen a pair of inmates running across the cargo-level docks. He'd yelled for me to wait, thinking they could make it to us. But then we'd watched as the man was gunned down by the chasing guards, hit in the head. The woman got hit, too—in the leg. She'd fallen, sliding through her companion's blood.

Even though we hadn't known them, Jax had run back out, picked her up, and brought her on board the ship with us, somehow escaping the hail of bullets himself. The woman was Fiona. Just like us, she and her partner had run up from the mines, making a break for it as half the prison had dissolved into chaos and flames.

We'd taken off, bullets pinging against the cargo cruiser's outer armor, and I'd jumped us all the way to the Outer Zones, somehow bumbling through the coordinates math with Jax's help, even though I'd been terrified of ramming us into a moon.

Everyone was still alive when I slowed us down in

17, and Jax and I did our best to clean and bind Fiona's wound and doctor the blunt stump of Miko's arm. Miko had been in shock, in and out of consciousness, and Shiori had been murmuring soft words and holding her close.

There'd been blood everywhere—so much that I was surprised it hadn't permanently stained the bridge. Something from the explosion had sliced my hand. I had no idea what, but it had throbbed like crazy, and I'd been bleeding, too.

Fiona had seemed like she had a decent chance of making it, but I was sure Miko would die of infection. We'd found the ship's medical supplies in a severely understocked state. No antibiotics. Some saline. Hardly enough sterile gauze.

Getting help had been out of the question. We'd have endangered any doctor or clinic that chose to assist us, and I was sure someone would see us and turn us in, even in a rebel-friendly zone. That was when Jax first told me about the Fold—a place where we could get medical treatment and disappear. He had friends there. It turned out that Fiona did, too, and that was when they discovered they had more in common than any of us could have possibly known, including a birth planet. We eventually found the rebel hideout, but it had taken days and days of searching, even for people in the know.

And in that time, Miko hadn't died. She never got even a hint of infection. Neither did Fiona. Nor did I.

I understood why now. I'd bled on their wounds from my own cut hand, which had been the last thing to get cleaned and bandaged. Digging for a bullet. Unsteady stitches. Blood-soaked bindings over a stump that had made me want to vomit. *I'd* been their antibiotic.

I turned back to our botanist—who was capable with a lot more than just plants. Unsurprisingly, plant *genetics* had been her specialty, although the force of things had set her on the path to biological warfare. Somehow, I couldn't feel sorry for those goons who'd breathed in her poisoned spores. Incinerate a planet, and you got what you deserved.

"It can't be ingested, right? The kids would need to have shots?" I asked.

"Shots, yes," Fiona confirmed. "But a small dose should be enough. I can keep preparing the injections while we get ready to take off. I've already done a whole batch, and I remember seeing a few big cases of needles and syringes in the lab attachment. Can you get them for me along with more bags of blood?"

I smiled, but it felt weak. Triumph never came without sacrifice. "How many?" I asked.

There was no real surprise for me in her immediate question back. "How many do we have?"

I hesitated. "Four." I hated the answer I had to give her, but Shade would be done soon, and I couldn't risk taking more than that in the time before we left.

Fiona recoiled in shock. "That's not enough. There are thousands of kids."

Yes, but I was only one body. "Knowing Mareeka and Surral, they've already imposed a quarantine of their own to try to minimize contagion. Not everyone will be infected." I hoped.

"Yeah, true," Fiona said. "Still, keep looking. Maybe more bags will turn up."

I nodded, my already minimally appetizing lunch turning over in my stomach and making it cramp. I ate my noodles anyway. I needed to keep up my strength.

✳

A few hours later, I delivered the blood and syringes to Fiona. I must have done a good job of pretending I wasn't about to collapse, because she didn't seem to notice anything strange about me. I made it back to my room without seeing anyone else, drank a bottle of water, and then took a nap with Bonk. Cats sure slept a lot.

When I woke up, I drank another bottle of water and ate a protein bar while I sent a message to Mareeka, telling her I had a cure and to get the sickest ten percent of the orphans ready for a round of shots.

Reading between the lines of her message back, I could tell she wanted me to be cautious, but she also wasn't going to refuse something that could save her kids. I could also tell that ten percent wasn't going to cover it. Double that, and maybe we had a chance.

Shit. I felt nauseous just thinking about it, but if I took a bag each morning and evening for the next three days, that was six additional bags we could use to prepare more shots. It wasn't the nine I'd already given, but it was more, and I could probably do it without totally incapacitating myself.

For now, though, it was time to rest.

Leaning over, I rummaged in my bag and pulled out the book Susan had given me on the Mornavail. It took a while to get used to the flowery writing, but the farther in I got, the more convinced I became that it wasn't a religious text at all, but rather a thickly veiled retelling of the final Sambian War from the winner's perspective.

The Mornavail—Dad and his goons, if I was reading

this right — were good, righteous, the answer to so many prayers.

"Nope," I muttered, scratching under Bonk's chin as I read.

Susan seemed to have taken the poetic, handwritten text literally, even though it wasn't that old, buying into its suggestion that the Sky Mother had set up some new group of people to spread her light. Personally, I saw an attempted allegory for our new "peace," who had brought it, and how it had been won.

True, order *had* been restored after decades of war, but stability hadn't been so much offered as imposed, with one freedom after another being tossed in the garbage and replaced by the Overseer's fanatical prose.

As a young man, my father had already been an imperialistic mastermind. Early in his career, he'd finished what the two generations before him had started by conquering the remaining free Sectors and bringing them one by one into the giant galactic machine, whether they wanted to be there or not. The Dark Watch was born, and before anyone knew what was happening, Dad's reign was official, and his goons were more numerous than the stars.

Narrow-minded ideas about the natural order of all things, including how people should think and act, became law. What to learn wasn't a vast choice anymore, but instead determined by statistical analysis and apparent strengths, with no regard for human interests or desires. Lifestyle choices turned limited, at least publicly, and the concept of self-determination got tossed out the door. It had already begun over the course of the previous Sambian Wars, spreading across the galaxy like a plague, but then my father had come along with the heaviest hand of all.

I sighed, stroking Bonk's soft fur. "Dad's a Mornavail," I told him. "In case you're wondering, that's a four-letter word."

Bonk purred.

Susan had said I was like them, but she must have gotten the story all wrong. She'd grasped onto the idea of the Mornavail being a light to follow. Flip the pages of recent history, though, and they grew dark with blood.

When I finished reading the book, I got up and locked it in my closet. Maybe I was wrong about it. I hadn't found a single mention of the word *Sambian* in the whole story. It was possible I was overthinking things, and this was simply the ramblings of some zealot who'd been convinced the Sky Mother and Her Powers had tried again, making People 2.0 or something, because regular people just weren't good enough.

Since I was firmly agnostic, it was a lot easier to believe the Mornavail were the winners of the last Sambian War, with my father now lording over us all from what was once the Sambian System but was now Sector 12 and the heart of galactic imperialism.

Home sweet home.

I snorted out loud, but as I stretched back out beside Bonk, I remained perplexed. The book had gone on and on about the Incorruptible, but the anonymous author also hadn't seemed to glorify mass murderers, intolerance, autocrats, or imperialistic fanatics. In the end, I wasn't sure what to think, but I was too tired to try to figure it out. Blood loss sucked.

I closed my eyes, wondering what Susan had found

so special about that book. Maybe I'd read the whole thing wrong. I wasn't tempted to try again.

I did know one thing, though. Whoever had penned that first paragraph should have shut the fuck up about the Fold.

CHAPTER

18

SHADE WORKED LIKE A MADMAN FOR THREE DAYS straight. His dedication to fixing the *Endeavor* made me pretty sure he wanted me up and off Albion 5 as fast as he could humanly make it happen. I wasn't sure if he was doing it for me or for himself, if I should be happy and grateful, or if I should feel like crap.

Feeling like crap won out, but that was also because I'd just passed over six more bags of blood that I'd miraculously "found" in a concealed refrigeration compartment. What luck!

Having given myself a couple of hours to eat, rest, and recover—*again*—I took a quick shower with our new water from the same multigoods outlet as the food and cat supplies. Refreshed and dressed once more, I towel dried my hair with Shade Ganavan's final bill staring me in the face.

It was exactly what I'd expected. No more, no less. I combed the tangles from my hair and explained to Bonk how the man's manically hard work to get me off his planet as quickly as possible had done wonders for my already fragile ego where he was concerned, but that because I was tenacious and incredibly attracted to him, I was going to give it one last shot.

"What can I lose besides pride?" I asked Bonk.

Shade had worked shirtless for most of the last few days, and we'd all gone outside more often than usual because it had been so beautifully sunny and hot. I'd snuck more peeks than I could count at his tanned skin and hard body, glad that the heat wave had given me an excuse to fan myself, especially when my needle-marked arms had meant wearing long-sleeved shirts. Shade and I had gone back to conversing easily again, although I always felt tension and desire pulling me taut underneath. He'd chatted with all of us, even talking theology with Shiori and getting Miko to open up.

Now that was a feat. In five years, I'd never seen Miko voluntarily speak more than a few words to any man except for Jax.

Fiona liked to know how things functioned and fit together, and Shade explained his process for repairing the ship whenever she asked. As for Jax, the two men worked in companionable silence for the most part, but every now and then, I caught them sharing a laugh.

When Shade had shown up yesterday with an entire case of what he declared were "the best coffee beans in Albion City," I think we all fell a little bit in love. He'd put the big box in the open doorway of the *Endeavor* and then gone about his work, not expecting a damn thing in return. My heart still squeezed happily just thinking about it.

I liked Shade. I liked so much about him, and any man who got Miko to talk to him and made Jax laugh was worth putting myself out there for. Another rejection would suck, but I would get over it. Life went on until the day you were gunned down or shot out of the Dark.

I tucked a fat bundle of universal currency into my coat pocket and then pulled on my ankle boots.

I was ready—I hoped.

I owned one nice piece of clothing, so I was using it. It was a simple, all-black dress that stopped midthigh on me and had a low-cut, square neckline and internal support that turned my breasts into perky balloons. Jax had nagged me into getting something nice for Emergence a few years ago, even though he knew I wasn't a believer. I'd chosen this dress, although with the amount of skin it showed, it was probably a far cry from what he'd had in mind.

The midsummer festival to celebrate the birth of the Sky Mother was a huge party in the Fold. I'd been to two, and they were a lot more fun than the solemn rituals I'd been made to observe as a child in Sector 12. Mareeka had made Emergence fun, but she believed in the Sky Mother and Her Powers about as much as I did, so it had been more about playing games and cooking special desserts we got to decorate ourselves. In the Fold, we got dressed up, danced, drank, laughed, and forgot for a night that we were the hunted.

That was after humbly thanking the Sky Mother for existing, of course.

But even then, all dressed up, happy, safe, and not lacking for invitations once the parties got started, I hadn't had the slightest interest in doing what I was about to do now. I didn't delude myself into believing

I'd turned down offers because I thought Gabe was still out there somewhere. I did wonder, and I hoped he was, but I hadn't held back because of him. I'd held back because I hadn't been ready to trust any of those men with myself, not with something so intimate, even though they were rebels like me and I trusted them with so much else.

Things had been done to me against my will, parts of me stolen without my consent while I fought, strapped down, small, scared, and powerless as adults loomed over me with needles, lab coats, and masks. Poking. Prodding. Taking. People I should have been able to trust had done that to me, to my body. They'd used me, and those experiences had formed me. I didn't trust easily, especially when it came to getting inside my personal space. Inside *me*.

The funny thing was, with Shade Ganavan, I wanted to trust. Tonight, I would show him that.

✸✸✸

The moment Shade heard the tentative knock, he knew who was at his door. It had to be Tess.

His heartbeat sped up, part excitement, part dread. He was so conflicted that he wanted to bash his head against the wall. Maybe then he'd either forget his need to reclaim his docks, or forget his feelings for Tess. Then he'd know what to do.

Earlier, he'd handed his bill to Jax and walked away from the Squirrel Tree without trying to see Tess. She'd slipped into the ship again at dusk carrying an exhausted Bonk. They'd played chase-the-rope around the platform until the cat had finally plopped down for a nap.

After she'd disappeared, Shade had been able to put on the finishing touches without being distracted by how much he wanted to kiss and touch Tess.

His chest had ached like it was being squashed in a giant clamp when he'd left the *Endeavor*'s platform without seeing her again, but he'd almost been hoping that Tess's thieving instincts would kick in, and that she'd fly away immediately, leaving him shafted for his labor and his parts. That would have cost him a chunk of money, but he wouldn't have chased after her, and that would have been that.

But no, she wasn't a *petty thief*. And now she was at his door.

His whole body in one big knot, Shade walked across the dimmed shop to let her in. He'd had more than a week to turn her over to Bridgebane, and he hadn't done it. He'd fixed her ship. He'd bought her half a door. Logically, that told him he'd known deep down and for a while now that he wasn't going to betray her. The question now was, did he warn her before she left? Did he tell her the truth? Did he try to keep her here, with him? How deeply fucked was he willing to get?

Shade opened the door. Tess was wearing little boots and a dress. Heat shot through him. Those long legs were just what he needed wrapped around his waist.

"Hey." She swept her long bangs back behind her ear, looking nervous.

"Hey," he echoed, stepping aside so that she could come in. Once she'd passed him, he closed the door and threw the lock again, shutting them inside.

Tess walked straight to the counter with the register and plunked down a big pile of universal currency. "I'm sorry, I had to hold back about a hundred units to pay for the Squirrel Tree docking fee earlier tonight. You were right. It was way too much."

Shade started to shrug. It didn't matter, because he wasn't going to take her money anyway. The second he'd seen her, he'd known, but she went on before he could tell her that.

"I brought you this to try to make up for it." She pulled a small but thick book from the deep pocket of her lightweight jacket and handed it to him.

Looking down, he read *Tales from the Dark*. Shade glanced back up, and he could have sworn she was blushing.

"It's not in great shape because it's old, and I've read it a lot, but you know Susan, and you seem to like books…"

Even though he wanted to have something of Tess's, Shade tried to hand it back. "If it's a favorite, you should keep it."

She shook her head and pushed it back toward him. She also picked up the money and put it on top. "I hope this will be enough. Along with my thanks for your help."

"Yeah, about that…" Shade put the whole pile on the counter next to her and then stepped back. "I don't think—"

"Please," she interrupted. "It's all I've got."

She didn't beg, but she was sincere. And strong. And beautiful.

His chest grew tight. He wanted her in his life. In his bed. He wished she'd never walked into his shop.

"Then like I said, you should keep it," Shade told her, sounding hoarse.

She blinked. "What?"

"Keep it. Keep it all," he said.

"I-I can't do that." She glanced around, as if looking for answers somewhere on the rows of shelves.

When her blue eyes came back to him, he asked, "Why not?"

She frowned. "Because I owe you."

"I say that you don't, so you don't."

Her frown deepened. "I *do*, and you have to take it."

Rebels were always dirt-poor. Why didn't she want her money back? "Look, Tess, I'm not—"

"Take it. Promise me you will." She interrupted him again, which was probably a good thing, because he had no idea how to end that sentence.

I'm not who you think I am? I'm not going to hurt you? I'm not your enemy? I'm not your friend? I'm not *what* exactly? Maybe if he could decide, he'd know.

Shade blew out a breath. "Why? Tell me why. And you're a shit negotiator, by the way."

She smiled and seemed to relax. "You'll take it? You swear?"

"Why?" he asked again.

"Just promise me," Tess insisted.

"Fine." He could always find a way to give it back later—if she lived.

A bullet seemed to plow through his heart at the thought of Tess not making it out of this.

"Now why?" he practically bit out.

He thought her shoulders went back at his surly tone, but it was only to shrug off her jacket. It hit the floor, leaving her in a little black dress.

His pulse quickened with a lurch. Slowly, she

dragged the side zipper down. The front and back of her dress began to separate until they were a lot like him—torn in half.

Tess pushed the straps off her shoulders, and her dress fell, pooling around her feet. Heat blazed through him. She wasn't wearing anything underneath.

She raised her chin a notch. "So you don't think this is in any way an offer to pay for my ship."

Shade's mouth went bone-dry. She was stunning. Every single part of her was perfect.

Except… His eyes narrowed. There were bruises and needle marks all over her skin.

"What the fuck is that?" he demanded, picking up her hand and holding one arm up to the low light.

She seemed to recoil, and he let her slip from his grasp. "Nothing you need to worry about," she said.

Was this about the orphanage again? More blood? "I hope you're staying hydrated," he ground out. That was all he could manage. His jaw had locked up tight.

Tess nodded, like she knew all about this, like maybe she did crazy shit like this all the time, and he was gripped by the sudden urge to rattle something. Not her. Just something—to get some aggression out.

"Why?" he asked, curling his hands into fists.

Her eyes flashed. "They're children."

Did that answer his question? He wasn't sure it did.

"Yeah, and they've got people taking care of them already. Why you? What does it mean to you?" He pushed for answers, for something from her, like he always did. With Tess, he couldn't seem to stop himself.

Her reaction was fast, almost frantic, and stronger than he'd bargained for. "I grew up there! I rocked some of those kids. Played with them. Read to them. Buried too many that I couldn't help!" Her breath hitched, and a sheen of tears brightened her eyes. "Didn't *know* I could help."

Shade felt like a bastard when he pushed for more. "You're from 12."

"I'm from 8!" She looked like she wanted to ball up her fist and sock him in the nose. "Eight!" she practically yelled.

Abruptly, Tess bent down and pulled up her dress. It was mostly on and she was halfway to the door before he even moved.

"Tess!" Shade sprang after her. He didn't grab her and pull her back like he wanted to. He touched her bare arm with his fingertips instead.

She turned, one dress strap on and the other drooping down her shoulder. The zipper still gaped, and her coat lay forgotten on the floor.

He curved his hands around her upper arms, hating the hurt and anger he saw in her eyes. Her skin seemed chilled, and the need to warm her rose inside him so quickly and powerfully it overwhelmed. "Don't go."

She stayed rigid for a moment while his heart thudded, and he wondered what the hell he was doing. He'd been mostly on track until now.

Her expression softened. "Don't go?"

Shade shook his head. "Come downstairs."

She swallowed, and her hands rose to his chest, light and cool and a little tentative.

"Stay with me tonight," he said.

And that was that. He'd decided, because he couldn't watch her walk out the door when he could have one more minute with her. Apparently, that was how deeply fucked he was willing to get for Tess Bailey—and he in no way meant the sex she was offering him now.

She hesitated only a second before sliding her hands up and around his neck. "No one's expecting me back tonight."

Shade couldn't help his small huff of laughter as he drew her closer. "I'll bet Jax loved that." He'd worked on and off all week with the often grim-faced man, and Shade had gleaned some insight into Jax and Tess's relationship. He let her live her life without interfering, but he was watchful, always alert, and she was the stitches holding him together, because whatever his wounds were, they were still raw and festering underneath.

"Oh yes." Her agreement was pure irony. "His side-eye was something else."

Shade leaned down to nuzzle her neck, and Tess's head dropped back, inviting more.

"You sure you know what you're doing?" he asked, brushing his lips along the curve of her jaw. He wanted her to know that she could back out if she wanted to.

"What I'm doing?" She laughed softly, rubbing her leg up his until she had it practically hooked around his hip. His cock started to swell as desire lit up his blood.

"Not really," she said. "But I know what I want."

Something about the way she said that made Shade draw back. "Are you a virgin?"

Her eyebrows flew up. "No. Would that make a difference?"

"Yeah, it would," Shade said. "It would change a lot about how I do this."

"But it wouldn't stop you?" she asked.

"Only you can stop me, baby." He looked at her hard. "Remember that."

Tess nodded. Her lips parted like she was begging for a kiss, but then she flushed a bit and ducked her head. "Maybe just go slowly at first. It's been a while."

A while? Shade took her hand and drew her toward his office. "How long?"

She didn't answer until they were halfway down the stairs. "Seven years. Plus."

He stopped, turning, and Tess nearly ran into him. He put a hand out to steady her, but she didn't need it. She had the balance of a cat when she wasn't falling over from blood loss.

"That's a long time," he said, although what he really wanted to do was ask, *Why me?*

"Well, I'm pretty sure virginity can't spontaneously grow back."

It was a joke, but he couldn't laugh. He didn't think it was funny that something about her life had kept a healthy, beautiful, adult woman completely celibate for years. Or that she'd chosen the worst possible person to trust.

Tess seemed to grow nervous in the pause left by his silence. "I'm fully vaccinated, and I have an ovulation suppression implant."

Shade stared. He figured he'd had about as many sexual encounters as any thirty-two-year-old man who worked hard and had a lot on his mind, but he'd sure as hell never heard a woman blurt that out before.

"I have protection," he said.

Tess shrugged. "I'm risk-free. But it's your choice."

He was risk-free, too, because he'd never done

anything to make it otherwise. The thought of being inside Tess with nothing between them sent lust ripping through him. He practically shook, he wanted her so much.

Shade took her hand again and led her toward his living space. He wanted to devour her in any way he could, but she'd asked to go slowly. That didn't mean he couldn't get back some of the spontaneity they'd lost.

He threw open his door, and with a tug on her hand, he jerked Tess in to his body. She gasped, and he captured the sound with a kiss that turned so hot so fast that he knew she was right back to being the woman who'd shown up at his door and dropped her clothes.

As usual, she jumped in with both feet, licking, sucking, grinding, and driving him crazy. Wildness came so naturally to Tess that he never felt like he had to try to coax it out of her and hope she got on board, instead of running from him like he was a degenerate or a freak. She was so fucking sexy, and she didn't even know it.

He grabbed her hips and lifted. She jumped, and then her legs were around his waist, the naked heat between her thighs pressed right up against him.

Shade groaned and kicked the door closed, cutting out the harsher light from the gym. The table in his hallway—the one he'd never seen any real use for before—suddenly seemed very well placed. Turning, he slid her onto it, leaning over her until she reclined on her back. They never once broke their mind-blowing kiss.

Tess arched up into him. Her knees rose, hugging his sides. She clutched his head, keeping him on top of her. Her total lack of restraint made him want to rip off her dress like a savage, but he managed to shimmy it down her long body instead. He backed up enough to get it off her and drop it on the floor.

Tess watched him, her chest rising and falling on quick breaths. Flushed cheeks. Parted lips. Bright-blue eyes that blew him away every time she looked at him. The rest of her was amazing, too. He couldn't wait to know every inch.

Shade got back between her legs and palmed her breasts. With just a little attention, her nipples stiffened, and he dipped his head, taking one into his mouth. Tess started to strain and twist, gripping his shoulders and moving her hips. She tasted fresh and sweet. He knew where she would taste even better, and just the idea of it made his cock strain hard against his pants.

He whipped off his shirt and then leaned over her again, skin on skin, his mouth on hers. She wasn't cold anymore; she was burning up. Tess sank her fingers into his back and kissed him with an intensity he'd never felt from anyone. She was like a drug. He'd never been addicted to anything before, but he was afraid he was falling down that rabbit hole right now, and he couldn't imagine how he'd ever get back out.

Shade finally lifted his head—but only because he was desperate to have his mouth on the rest of her.

He snagged her gaze with his. "Unless you tell me not to, I'm about to lick you between your gorgeous long legs until you scream and kick."

Tess inhaled sharply. Her eyes widened, glittering with anticipation, and her eager nod was the *yes* he needed to do exactly what he'd said.

CHAPTER

19

I COULDN'T BELIEVE THIS WAS REALLY HAPPENING. IT was exactly what I wanted, and Shade made me so desperate and hot that I could barely contain the shouts and moans I already needed to let out.

I gave him the go-ahead, and with two quick zips, he had my boots off. Kneeling, he brought my legs over his shoulders, so they draped down his back. Two big, strong hands gripped my hips and slid me to the edge of the table and right to his mouth.

His tongue dove straight into me, giving me a hint of penetration before coming back out and moving over me in strong licks.

"Oh my… *Shade!*" I gasped out. My legs twitched. One of my hands hit the wall beside me, pressing hard against it. I gripped the table behind my head with the other, grounding myself as I lifted my hips. This was incredible. New for me. Gabe had never done this.

Shade growled something between my legs. I had no idea what, but it made me forget all about my past and anyone in it. He was both methodical and uninhibited.

Making noises. Exploring. Gripping my hips, flicking his tongue. Finding out what made me thump his back with my feet or turn my head into my raised arm with an openmouthed gasp.

I never wanted him to stop. I also wanted to reach that peak I was climbing fast. Too fast. I wanted this to last.

He slid a finger inside me. I whimpered, almost in tears. It was too much. So good. *More*.

"Shade!" I banged the wall with my hand to get his attention, and his head came up.

I knew I'd like everything that came after this, too, but right now was my turn to feel amazing. "I don't want this part to be over so fast."

His lips tilted up, and a warm puff of breath raced over my sensitive skin. Slowly, he slid a second finger inside me, and I felt the slight stretch.

"Baby, if there's some fucked-up law that says you can't come more than once, then I'm not following it."

He went back to work, and I think my eyes actually rolled back in my head. The crest did come fast, hot and explosive, shattering me like a star at its death. There was definitely that scream he'd been talking about.

I went limp on the table, naked and out of breath. Little tremors still pulsed through me, making my body clench in places that wanted more.

"Fuck the Powers," Shade said as he stripped off the rest of his clothes. "You're my new goddess."

I laughed. I didn't care if he was blasphemous.

His eyebrows rose. "You think I'm kidding? Tess of the Table. I'm going to worship you all night."

He scooped me up before I got a good look at his body and then strode toward his bedroom.

When he set me down on his bed, his fingers slid over the scars on my back. There weren't many, and they weren't that raised, but he still felt them and looked.

His countenance darkened. Even in the whole galaxy, there weren't that many places where a person got whip scars, and I was pretty sure Shade knew that.

He didn't ask about them, and I let out the breath I'd started holding. He usually pushed when he saw something he didn't like. Tonight, though, I thought he had other things on his mind.

So did I. I got up on my knees and ran my hands all over him, loving the feel of his warm skin. He was strong and beautifully built, sculpted and muscled without being bulky or thick. There was a light dusting of dark hair on his chest, and I speared my fingers through it before running them up and over his shoulders and then down his arms to his hands. He was the most gorgeous thing I'd ever touched.

Shade let me explore him without trying to hurry me along. I loved that about him.

I had a sudden, burning desire to find out what his thighs felt like, so I did. Short, springy hair. Hot skin and solid muscle. My gaze dropped to his erection, my hand hovering near it.

"Can I?" I asked.

"Starshine, you can do anything you want to me."

His words seemed to thump between my legs. The husky rumble in his voice made me burn even hotter. Down low, muscles clenched.

I wrapped my fingers around him, lightly squeezing. Shade's nostrils flared, and his whole body tensed. I knew it was in a good way, and I stroked him from base to tip. He hardened even more, so smooth, steely, and appealing under my hand. But I needed more than this. I wanted him inside me. I wanted us to be joined. It was starting to feel as necessary as breath.

Putting one hand on his shoulder for balance, I slowly moved my leg over him, straddling him. Shade turned us so that he was sitting on the edge of the bed, his feet on the floor, stable. He kept his hands on my hips, letting me take the lead. My eyes on his, I rose up and guided him to my opening. I started to sink back down, but then stopped.

"Did you want protection?" I asked.

Shaking his head in answer, he curled his hips, penetrating me just a little. The look on his face when we came together was pure heat, and I felt scorched, inside and out.

I took my time lowering myself completely onto him. The stretch was unpleasant, and the fullness wasn't comfortable at first, but then Shade wrapped his hand around the back of my head and drew my lips to his. He kissed me hard while he gently rocked his hips, and I forgot all about the initial discomfort. Soon, I started moving faster and sinking down farther. The intensity between us built, and everything else slipped away, replaced by waves of heat and jolts of pleasure.

Nothing in the galaxy could have distracted me from the slide of our bodies, our panting kisses, our subtle noises, or Shade's hands on me. I set the pace for a long time, and he adjusted to my rhythm, using his mouth and fingers to drive me wild and move me toward that pinnacle he'd promised again.

He finally turned us so that he was on top, his weight

balanced above me. I drew my knees up as he thrust. He went so deep I gasped.

"You all right?" he asked, holding my head in his hands.

I nodded. "More than all right." I was so all right that I was ready to blurt out stupid things like *Wait for me* and *I'll come back*.

He started moving again, touching places inside me that made fireworks spark. Between consuming, soul-searing kisses, he breathed heavily against my neck.

"Shade," I whispered, wound up so tightly that I shook.

His big, hard body was a heady weight on mine. His strokes stayed long and deep but went faster. I raised my hips, spurring him on.

"You're a dream I didn't know I had," he rasped, his stubble grazing my neck.

My heart swelled. I felt the same way.

He bit down on where my shoulder met my neck. It didn't hurt, but it was feral and possessive and perfect. It made pleasure burst between my legs.

"Shade!" I dug my fingers into his back, arching up into him as I climaxed hard. It was everything the first time had been, and so much more, because he was *inside* me this time, and the connection I felt to him was starting to both amaze and terrify me. I couldn't believe how right this felt—*he* felt.

I let out a shuddering breath, sinking back down into the covers with a satisfied moan. Pulsing aftershocks rippled through me, heightening every sensation. Shade kissed my shoulder and neck and then slid his mouth along my jaw. I gripped his short hair and turned his face toward mine, claiming his lips and knowing that I was trying to imprint myself onto him—and hoping it worked.

He began thrusting again, driving himself toward his own release. I held on with arms and legs, my mouth open against his neck. I bit, too. Why not? I'd loved it. Then I sucked. Sucked hard. Shade tasted like a salty dessert. A lusty sound thrummed in my throat.

"Holy hell, baby." He shuddered above me, an exhale rushing from his lungs. Then he stopped, and I felt him throbbing inside me. Slowly draining of tension, he groaned in a way that told me he was just as lost in me as I was in him.

The moment was so perfect I wanted to stay in it forever, lovers entwined. For a few seconds, I let myself wish that could be my life.

Closing my eyes helped cut off that thought, blocking out the dim light and reminding me of the Dark. I still couldn't help the *maybe someday* that blew like a cyclone through all the doors I was trying to shut.

Shade stayed where he was, caging but not crushing. I turned my head to lightly kiss his mouth again, and his eyes opened, warm and brown.

"You're something else," he murmured with a smile. "A man could get used to this."

He kissed me back, and I flushed all over, hot with pleasure.

He eventually pulled out of me, but we stayed all tangled up together, neither of us making any effort to clean ourselves up or talk. I smelled like him, and we smelled like sex, and I wanted to hold on to that. I watched his big hand on my waist, watched his scarred knuckles, watched his thumb sweep slowly back and forth in what seemed like an instinctual, subconscious caress.

When I shivered, Shade got us under the covers and curved himself around me until I slept.

CHAPTER

20

SHADE HAD TO WAKE HER UP. TESS HAD TOLD HIM SHE needed to leave for Starway 8 today, and past a certain hour of the morning, she'd have to pay for another whole day on the Squirrel Tree. She couldn't afford that.

Lying there, she was so still. It made him realize how kinetic she usually was, always in motion. Even when she wasn't actually moving, there was a nervous edge to her, making her seem active. Not now. Not sleeping. Sleeping, she didn't look like she'd been orphaned and imprisoned and hunted and who knew what else.

Propping himself on one elbow, he leaned over her and stroked a hand down her arm. "Tess?"

She mumbled something and curled up on her side, her back to him.

"Does that mean leave me the hell alone and let me sleep?" he asked.

Her lips curved up. "Maybe." There was morning gravel in her voice.

He liked hearing how she sounded when she woke up. There was something intimate about it, like he was gaining another piece of her. He wanted to collect them all.

That terrifying thought felt like a ticking bomb inside his chest, and his heart started to pound. He'd only made one decision in his life that he truly regretted, but right now, he was afraid he was barreling toward a second one that might be even more disastrous than the first.

Tess shifted, and her hips moved against him, distracting him back to better thoughts. She went still against his groin, but then slowly rubbed, as if she couldn't help herself. His balls tightened, and his already hard cock grew heavier, filling even more. He pressed closer to her, and warmth tingled at the base of his spine. He wanted her. He couldn't imagine *not* wanting her. They were a flawless fit.

She was so greedy for physical contact. That was perfect, because she also gave. Humanity seemed brainwashed these days into thinking anything beyond tidy, boring sex and orderly touches menaced society. Sometimes, he was surprised babies were even still being made. He had no interest in that kind of dull, passionless contact and hadn't pursued a woman in so many months that his own dry spell seemed long, although it was nothing compared to Tess's seven years.

Shade swept his hand toward her belly and splayed his fingers over her abdomen, letting his thumb tease the undersides of her breasts. Dipping his head, he kissed her shoulder, inhaling her scent. She didn't smell like peaches anymore. She smelled more like him than anything else, and something possessive yanked hard at his gut.

The raw, primitive feeling reminded him of stories

he'd read about the first Earth men and how they'd lived like animals in caves, hunting and killing and fucking and dragging their women around by the hair. He could almost see the appeal of it. He basically had the cave. He could hunt for Tess. Get rid of anyone who threatened her. They would fuck. He could probably skip the hair part, although she might like a good tug.

Only a little distracted by his strange ideas, Shade slid slow, hungry kisses up Tess's neck. Her skin was warm and soft, and he nuzzled behind her ear. She started moving, writhing in place, straining in that completely uninhibited way of hers. The need to satisfy her blazed through him, and he moved his hand between her legs.

He pressed and stroked, smiling a little against her hair when he found the right spot, making her gasp and jerk. The whole back of her body was like a branding iron against his front. He knew she'd left her mark on him, and she sure as hell went more than skin-deep. There was no getting Tess out of his system. He didn't want to. He just wanted more.

Shade kept her tight against him as she jumped like a live wire, full of electrical shocks. The sexiest noises whispered out of her, getting louder the more wound up she got. He wanted to lick them up with kisses that went so deep they touched her throat.

He was about to turn her around and do his best to devour her when she lifted her leg on top of his in clear invitation, quickly derailing his last thought. He didn't have to wonder if she was on board for sex, because Tess was the one reaching down to guide him inside her. She arched back, opening herself up and taking him in. She didn't need to ask twice, or even out loud. With slow thrusts, Shade worked his way deeper, and his mind blanked to everything except for how good she felt around him.

Rocking his hips, he kept rubbing his fingers above where they were joined until she shuddered and came, gasping his name. He absorbed her tremors, feeling her body clench around him and pull him toward his own release.

Already satisfied as hell, he rolled on top of her. Tess went easily onto her stomach for him, leaving her hands beside her head and him between her legs.

Shade curled his fists around her hands and pumped into her until heat swept up his thighs, shot through his dick, and he came so hard it was like an explosion inside him. Tess cried out, her head turned to one side. He didn't know if she was climaxing again. His own throbbing overwhelmed everything else, and the thud of his pulse echoed like thunder in his head.

Sweating, his muscles spent, he bowed his head, breathing rapidly against her shoulder. His heart hammered, and he held on to her hands, not wanting to let go yet.

"Come back," he murmured before he knew what he was saying. "When you're done on Starway 8, come back here." Then he'd at least know she was still safe.

Her body seemed to soften even more under his. "You want me to come back?"

"Baby, I don't want you to leave in the first place."

She smiled. *He* made her smile. His chest seemed to grow ten sizes, and he knew he was in deep, deep trouble. He hadn't had a weakness in years, not one fucking thing he couldn't stand to lose, because everything he cared about was already gone.

Fear started to run like ice through his veins. What had he done to himself?

A second later, he realized it didn't matter—because he'd do it all again.

Shade rolled them back onto their sides and wrapped his arms around her, those few long whip scars hidden against his chest. After a moment, he threw his leg over both of Tess's, thinking that its heavy weight pinning her to his bed was about as caveman possessive as she'd let him get.

"I'll try," she finally said, not making any move to wiggle free from his near-full-body grip.

Trying was better than nothing, he guessed.

"Go to Nuthatch," he said. "It's as good as the Squirrel Tree and less expensive."

She nodded. "Why do all the docking towers have such weird names here?"

"My—" Shade cleared his throat and started over. "The person who built the docking empire on Albion 5 was a naturalist at heart, even though he ended up in urban construction and then got involved in the terraforming next door. He studied the old Earth species, those that survived the fallout and those that didn't, and even wrote a few books about them in his spare time. He was fascinated by birds and small mammals—I guess because they're tough little critters that can apparently make it through almost anything. He named the towers after them." Shade chuckled. "Avoid the Rat Hatch. It's as bad as it sounds."

"Interesting." Turning her head toward him, Tess asked, "How do you know all that?"

Shade tried to keep the glumness from his face and voice. "Read his books."

Tess seemed to accept that. It was the truth, even if it wasn't all of it.

"Thanks for the tip." She smiled. ."I'll remember—Nuthatch."

He smiled back. "Anytime, starshine."

Both their smiles slipped from their faces. *Anytime* was as up in the air for them as the stratosphere.

Shade's lungs contracted almost painfully. Tess might fly off in an hour, and he'd never see her again.

✱✱✱

That hour came fast, and as the elevator tube swept them up to the three-hundred-and-fourteenth level of the Squirrel Tree just after sunrise, Shade had no idea how he was going to let go of Tess, especially knowing the danger she was in.

She used a hand scan to open the new starboard door of the *Endeavor*. A beep sounded from somewhere deep inside the ship, signaling the door opening from the outside.

He didn't know if anyone was awake inside, but he moved Tess a little farther out onto the platform before stopping again. Their goodbye seemed more private that way.

"Stay safe," Shade said, his voice coming out gruff. It didn't seem like enough, but he didn't know what else he could add. Don't kill yourself for orphans? If you see anyone who looks like a bounty hunter, *run*? Ditch the rebellion and hide out in my basement?

As much as he wanted her tangled up with him in his bed, only a jackass would suggest that.

Tess moved forward and threw her arms around his neck. "You, too, Shade."

His arms were up and around her before his brain caught up. With Tess, he seemed to function on a primitive level with instinct driving him. Help. Protect. Fuck. Keep.

He squeezed her hard, trying to mentally erase that last part.

Their story probably ended with help, protect, fuck, and he wasn't sure he'd done any of that except for the fuck part.

"As usual, you hit the target first, Ganavan. And it looks like you went about it in a pretty *Shade*-y way," said a deep voice he hated to recognize.

Shade froze. *No. Not now. Not yet. Not ever.*

His whole body seemed to involuntarily curl around Tess.

Solan chuckled as Tess jumped back from Shade's arms, breaking his grip. Confusion flashed across her face, and then her eyes widened when she saw the gun trained on her chest.

Turning to face the other hunter, Shade grabbed on to Tess's wrist from behind and kept himself in front of her. He'd been an idiot to leave this morning without arming himself, but he hadn't wanted Tess to question him. Unless you were military, private security, or a hard-core rebel, you didn't walk around with a gun.

Solan kept his firearm raised. Over the centuries, humanity had tried all sorts of laser-based weapons, only to decide that plain old guns were still the best way to kill people. Accurate. Long-distance. Deadly. They were hard to deflect. Bullets just went through shit.

Shade's gut clenched. A bullet would go through Tess.

"What is he talking about?" Tess asked with quiet urgency. She tugged on her wrist.

Shade didn't answer. His eyes darted around the platform. Where there was Solan, there was Raquel.

"So helpful of you to do all the work." Raquel stepped out from the shadows behind the ship. As usual, she wore a tight black catsuit with a low-slung utility belt. Shade hated that belt. It was basically an exercise in how many illegal weapons a person could fit into a small space. "Just like last time, when I burned off your hair."

"It wasn't that long to begin with," Shade ground out.

Raquel strode over to Solan's side, making one more armed body between Tess and him and the elevator tube. Solan stood a head taller than his wife and was as black as she was white. They prided themselves on being able to hunt day and night—one of them always blended in. Solan knew his way around guns and sometimes shot with both hands. Raquel chose tranquilizers over bullets, but she could move like the wind and kick like a turbo blast.

Tess started tensing more and more behind him. Shade could hear her breathing turning shallow and fast. His guilt conjured up the cold rolling off her in waves.

Facing the bounty hunters, Shade felt his lips pull back in a snarl. The last time they'd fought, Solan had stolen his prize while Raquel had gone at him with her steel-tipped boots. Shade could handle a gun, but he was more hands-on, and you couldn't exactly shoot your colleagues, no matter how underhanded they were. Despite two cracked ribs from one of the more vicious kicks Raquel had gotten in, he would have beaten her and maybe gotten his target back if she hadn't pulled that mini firebomb out of her belt and thrown it at his head.

"Quite the prize," Solan said, trying to get a better look at Tess. He cocked his gun, and Shade felt fear blow through his chest.

She could die.

And she'd hate him if she lived.

"He said *alive*," Shade growled, trying to stay in front of Tess.

"He said there'd be a *bonus* for a live capture." Solan started slowly walking forward. "The way I see it, there's already more than enough. No reason to risk the hunt."

"Shade?" Tess whispered his name. The hurt and betrayal in her voice clawed him open and bit with sharp teeth.

He wasn't the only one to hear it. Raquel laughed. "Aww. Poor little girl didn't know she was in bed with the big bad wolf."

Tess jerked hard on his grip.

Not taking his eyes off the hunters, Shade started squeezing out one of the oldest codes known to man against Tess's wrist, hoping there was a tiny percent chance she knew Morse. *Safe* he pulsed out, even though she wasn't. He meant with him. She was safe with *him*.

Tess wrenched her arm from his hand.

"Stay behind me," Shade snapped, twisting to reach for her again.

"Don't touch me!" she snapped back.

Her horrified expression was enough to keep him from putting his hands on her again. He turned back around, his teeth grinding. He wouldn't touch her, but he wouldn't let Solan get a line on her, either. The other man would have a lot of explaining to do with the higher-ups if he blew holes in a fellow select hunter, and the mountain of shit a move like that could pile up on him would keep Solan from taking the shot.

Shade tried to inch them toward the *Endeavor*'s open door without touching Tess. They weren't that far from it, but Solan was a good shot. With the climb up...

Why the hell didn't she ever put down the stairs?

Tess came out every morning, gave him coffee, and talked about stuff most people didn't dare open their mouths about, making him crave their next conversation until he could barely sleep, but she didn't use the stairs. Unless Shiori came out, everyone pretended the damn ship didn't even have them.

His palms started to sweat.

"Time to move out of the way, Ganavan," Solan said with a flick of his gun. It was a Redline, Legal Weapon 10. Shade had two, and he knew the recoil was so strong that it was hard to get multiple shots off fast.

"No." Shade shook his head. For Solan and Raquel, this was just another job, part of a long string of them. Not for him. "Not this one. Move on," he said.

But even as he said it, he knew this wasn't just another job for any of them. Thanks to Bridgebane's ridiculous bounty, Tess was the monetary mothership, and there was no way these two were backing down.

"You're outnumbered," Solan informed him, as if Shade couldn't fucking count. "Either we brawl again like last time—and we all know how that turned out for you—or we go in on this one together, like we talked about."

"You talked. I shut you down." But he obviously hadn't thrown them off the scent like he'd hoped. Or he had, but only for a few days.

Raquel narrowed her eyes, and Shade could read her like a book. She was thinking about which one of her hidden gadgets she could throw at him without getting herself into too much trouble. There wasn't always an easy distinction between incapacitating and lethal. So far, though, Raquel had figured it out.

Shade cracked his knuckles and loosened up. He hated hitting a woman, but he could make an exception for Raquel. She seemed more like a machine to him than anything else.

"I got here first," he reminded them, because that was *supposed* to mean something in this profession. It was his final effort to avoid a fight.

"Don't be a bastard," Raquel spat. "You'll still be the top hunter, and two hundred million is more than enough to share around."

Behind him, Tess gasped. The sound sliced right through him. He could imagine what was going on in her head right now, and it made his insides curl up in disgust.

"You're...*Dark Watch*?" Tess sounded as though she'd never heard something so horrendous in her life.

"No!" He would never be that.

Solan snorted. "Then what do you call it when you're on Bridgebane's payroll, just like the rest of us?"

At that, Tess's breathing turned so hard and erratic that Shade could feel it punching into the back of his neck.

Don't lose it on me now, baby. He still had to figure this out.

"I can't…" Tess didn't finish, and an audible shudder leaked from her mouth.

His stomach sank. This was not going to end well.

Over his shoulder, talking fast, Shade said, "Listen to me, Tess—"

"No!" He caught a flash of her eyes—two bright-blue bombs ready to blow.

"Tess, listen—"

"You listen to *me*, Shade Ganavan." She uttered his name like a curse. "I will hate you until the day I die." She rammed her hands hard into his shoulder blades, shoving him forward a step.

She ran just as Solan sent off his first shot. Shade lunged after her, trying to stay in between them enough to mess with Solan's aim and shield Tess.

Fiona suddenly curled her upper body around the doorway and started spraying Grayhawk bullets all over the place. Solan and Raquel ran and dove behind the supply crate that Shade had left on the dock, and Tess sprang toward her ship. As if by magic, Jax appeared. She raised her arms, and he hauled her up, throwing her away from the opening and out of the hunters' line of sight.

From the cover of the crate, Solan started firing back at Fiona. His angle was nearly impossible for aiming inside the ship, but dents started showing up on the outer hull near the door. With only her arm and one eye visible, Fiona kept hammering off shots that pinged off the big metal box. Out in the open, Shade figured it was only a matter of seconds before he caught a ricochet and got hit.

Something seared his skin. *Shrapnel?* He reached up.

No, Raquel and her fucking darts. Unlike Solan, she never missed. He ripped the tranquilizer from his neck.

Shade knew he was practically in the cross fire, but he had to tell Tess. She had to know...

Safe.

He staggered, the strong sedative hitting him fast. Gunfire roared on his left.

"Tess!" he croaked, reaching for her. His hand wavered in front of his face.

From just a few feet away inside her ship, Tess stared at him, her fiery eyes gone cold, her beautiful face turned to rock.

"In or out?" Jax yelled, his eyes sweeping back and forth between Shade and Tess.

If Tess hesitated at all, Shade didn't see it. "Leave him with his friends," she answered, stepping back.

Shade felt himself crumbling, falling apart. It wasn't only the drug. He'd lost. He'd lost *everything*. Again.

A ball of fur streaked past Tess's legs and jumped off the ship, landing like a gray torpedo on the platform and racing away from the noise.

Panic replaced the hatred on her face. "No! Bonk!" she yelled, lunging after her cat.

"Stop!" Jax's bellow probably wouldn't have stopped her, but his hand grabbing the back of her jacket did. He jerked Tess back.

"Bonk!" Her frantic shouts rattled like a nightmare in Shade's spinning head.

With the last of his strength, his knees giving out, Shade lurched toward the exterior lock—because he was the asshole who'd programmed his own handprint into Tess's new door. But before he could lock her in himself,

Jax slammed his palm down on the interior control, still gripping a struggling, screaming Tess in his other hand. The door whooshed shut, ending Fiona's hail of bullets toward the other hunters and cutting Shade off from the woman he'd fallen for so hard that he'd ruined his life.

He wanted to howl in misery, but his mouth wouldn't open for anything other than breaths. He fell onto the platform, darkness crawling over him, empty and void like space.

He heard the ship take off, felt the slap of hot air and the vibration of the engine as Tess flew out of his life.

Two shadows loomed over him. Raquel gave him a good kick, and he heard his own groan as if from a mile away from this place.

He wasn't military—*exactly*—but he was close enough. There were a hundred ways to spin what he'd done as treason. It wouldn't be hard, because it *was*.

"The next time you fuck up a hunt like that just because you want the bigger prize all to yourself, we'll report you for obstruction," Solan announced.

Shade huffed, a weak sound that reflected the current state of his body. Leave it to the Heartless Duo to think he'd been holding out for the bonuses and not even realize he'd been protecting Tess. That was a relief, he supposed.

He should have known they'd come. No story, not even one about his precious docks, could have thrown them off for long or kept them from wondering why Shade Ganavan was ignoring the biggest hunt of their lives.

They'd probably been on Albion 5 just long enough to track him to this platform, wait for the cover of dark, and then try to ambush Tess when she came back. Only she hadn't come back. She'd stayed away all night and then shown up at daybreak. With him.

"There was plenty for everyone on that one, even without the live capture or the stolen goods," Raquel said in a fury. "Now, no one has anything. Bastard." She plugged him with another dart.

CHAPTER

21

FIONA RACED OFF AS I STUMBLED BACK FROM JAX, shaking. My heart felt ripped out, shattered, crushed. Bonk was gone; I'd lost him. And Shade…

Horror overwhelmed me, tearing through my chest and shredding what was left of it. The ghost of Shade's touch haunted me. I could still feel him pushing into me, holding me close.

Touches. Kisses. Words that had wrapped around me like promises. *Lies.*

I curled in on myself. Everything burned. My breath came out in harsh pants, shuddering from my lungs and then sawing back in. My head swam. I couldn't… This couldn't…

I blinked hard, trying to clear my thoughts. Trying not to feel Shade anymore. His hands, his mouth, his warmth.

"You're hurt!" Jax said.

Confused, I uncrossed my arms and tried to straighten. The pain and weight of my awful mistake were so heavy that it was hard to move. Time seemed to advance in slow, straining increments, and it was all I could do just to get from one devastated heartbeat to the next.

So much had happened in so little time, and it all clanged inside me, jarring and discordant. Shade smiling. Bonk purring. Vitamin D. Hot kisses. Shade's whispered *Come back*. Bonk curled up in my lap.

Pull it together. Pull it together, Tess.

I was rocking. I forced myself to stop. I had to figure out what Jax was talking about.

Almost as if from outside of myself, I took stock and found my right hand slicked with blood. It trembled as I lifted it. My hand was fine, besides being wet and red. I glanced at my side, where I'd been clutching myself. It turned out that Shade's betrayal wasn't the only thing burning like a deep, searing cut. A bullet had grazed me, slicing a line through my jacket and dress.

Jax dove in for a better look.

"Flesh wound," he and I said at the same time, his voice filled with relief and mine fighting its way past the tears in my throat. It wasn't the gunshot injury that hurt.

The *Endeavor* lifted off, making us both lurch.

My eyes widened, meeting Jax's. "Who the hell is flying the ship?"

"Miko?" he guessed. "Or maybe Fiona."

Well, I sure hoped it wasn't Shiori. We raced toward the bridge together and burst like a terrified storm through the doors.

"Thank the Powers!" Miko backed off the controls, looking pale and wide-eyed. Her hand shook. It was hard enough to navigate the maze of docks and interwoven platforms with two hands, let alone one. And we hadn't even gotten to the traffic of the spheres.

Jax ran to his console, and I stumbled over to mine. I took the controls, but my hands rattled too much to steer.

"Jax!" I barked.

"I'm on it," he answered. I wasn't sure he was entirely steady either after everything that had just happened, but he was a hell of a lot better than blind, one-handed, or bleeding and quaking. Fiona hadn't tried. She knew her own equipment inside and out, but she was clueless when it came to a flight console. Too many buttons she'd never tried to memorize.

As soon as Jax took over, Miko threw her arms around me.

"What happened?" She sounded both outraged and scared as she drew back.

I didn't know how to answer. So much had happened, and it was all so raw.

"Men are assholes," Fiona said.

Jax grunted, seeming like he wanted to take exception but was too busy making sure we didn't hit another ship as he guided us through the troposphere.

Shiori, who was sitting in the navigator's chair, took exception for him. "You are unfair to one who has always been good and honest with us."

Fiona grunted, as though *she* wanted to take exception. I had to agree. Jax was good—no doubt about it—but if he were honest, even with himself, he and Fiona probably wouldn't have been in separate bedrooms for the last few years.

Fiona inserted herself between Miko and me, the bridge's medical supplies already in her hands. I shrugged off my jacket, wincing at the movement, and then let Fiona cut a big hole in my ruined dress.

Her brow furrowed as she squirted me with saline.

Shit, I knew that look. It meant stitches. I sat, keeping my arms crossed over my chest and hoping she'd miss the lingering needle marks. Her attention was on my waist, and she didn't look up.

Miko joined her grandmother at the navigation controls. "As soon as we reach the thermosphere, I'll activate the coordinates for Starway 8."

"No!" Everyone looked over at me like I was nuts. "Jump us to Flyhole. We'll get lost in the crowd while I sweep for tracking bugs."

Jax's face turned thunderous. "You are *not* going on a fucking spacewalk with a hole in your side!"

"It's a scratch," I said. "And I'm not leading bounty hunters to the orphanage."

His face reddened, except for the scar on his cheek, which whitened instead.

"Jax!" I flung my hand toward the window.

His eyes snapped back to where they should have been, and he quickly adjusted our course out of the way of the huge transport that was bearing down on us.

"Argue when we're in the stratosphere if you want, but we need to sweep the exterior for bugs, and you know it." At least Shade had never come inside— something to be grateful for. But he was way too smart not to track the ship, and those other two hadn't looked dumb, either.

I gritted my teeth when Fiona stuck the suture needle in and then grimaced at the pull of thread. She did it again, and the pain actually helped to focus my thoughts and settle me. Every sharp prick drove Shade farther from my heart. Each painful tug erased his touch. This was my reality, and I didn't even have a shot to numb myself to any of it. I was stupid to have forgotten.

"Then I'll go," Jax announced.

Jax hated zero G. And he could barely cram himself into a space suit.

"I've been outside a lot more often than you have. I'll be faster and more efficient." I winced. Stitches sucked. "Really, Jax, this is just a scratch. Fiona's hurting me more than the bullet did."

Fiona half looked up, giving me the hairy eyeball.

"There's about a hundred percent chance those bounty hunters are on our tail right now," I said. "We'll lose them with a short-range jump to Flyhole that won't take much power. Then Jax—you squeeze us into some supply line or other, like we've been there all along. I'll go out and sweep for bugs and then get new stickers up, hopefully before the hunters can locate us again with any precision."

The hunters or Shade. There was no forgetting he was one of them.

A sharp ache lanced my chest. I scowled. I wanted to pummel him.

"I don't have those coordinates set," Miko said.

"Then do it," I told her, my whole body clenching from another prick. We needed to be anonymous again—*now*.

I glanced down. *How big is this scratch?* Crap. Six stitches so far.

Fiona tugged, knotted, cut. "Done."

Thank the Powers. I blew out a breath.

I sucked one in again when she slapped on a bandage with her full hand, pressing hard. She was punishing me for scaring the shit out of her and putting us all in danger.

"I'm sorry," I said to everyone.

It was Jaxon who finally spoke. "He had us all fooled, Tess."

I nodded, pretending that a lump wasn't rising in my throat again, nearly choking me, and that my eyes weren't burning hot. I blinked a few times. I wasn't going to cry over that jackass. Not today. Not tomorrow. Not *ever*.

"Get us to Flyhole." The order came out gruffly, but it was the best I could do without breaking down. "I'm going to suit up."

"Careful of your stitches," Fiona warned. "Need help?"

It was complicated to suit up alone, but I couldn't stand the thought of anyone looking at my body right now. This body had betrayed me, led me down the wrong path. I could still feel Shade all over me, *inside* me. Smell him on my skin.

I shuddered, sickened on too many levels to sort it all out. Trusting Shade had been one of the stupidest things I'd ever done, and my willful blindness had put the people I loved in danger. I'd ignored the risk to them, and to myself, because I'd wanted him. It was as simple and as terrible as that.

I hated my body right now. I hadn't deserved the lash marks on my back when they'd happened. Now, I felt like I'd earned them, and they were the only part of me that I could stand.

I shook my head, finally answering Fiona. I sounded almost normal when I spoke, probably surprising us all. "I'll change on my own. But thanks, Fi. Thanks for everything."

She smiled. "I love shooting things up."

I smiled weakly in return. Yeah, she did.

"Thanks, everyone." I glanced down, hiding the damn sheen that was blurring my vision again. "Thanks for having my back."

Without looking at me, Jax grumbled something and just kept steering us up and toward the Dark.

No one else answered. We didn't need to thank each other, but I still did.

"He fixed the ship." Miko looked over from where she sat with her old, beat-up coordinates book, looking pensive when she should have been punching in numbers as if the hand she still had depended on it—which it probably did. "Shade, I mean. Don't you think that's weird?"

I shrugged, not answering. I didn't understand anything he'd done.

"Shit. I almost forgot. Check your tablet," Miko said. "A message came through last night from Starway 8."

Dread plowed into me. Time was dangerously tight with the hunters after us, but I needed to look now in case the message told us we had to figure out a way to avoid a quarantine blockade around Sector 8.

I reached for the tablet and woke it up, quickly accessing my messages. This one was from Surral.

> Things are worse. Unless you're
> absolutely certain you can help,
> do not risk yourselves. No military
> quarantine yet, but it could happen
> at any time.
> Tess, I'm sorry. Coltin is sick.

I grabbed the edge of my console to steady myself and swallowed hard. I would lay down my life to protect Starway 8 and everyone in it, but I recognized that my deepest attachment to the orphanage could be drawn in the portraits of four faces: Mareeka, Surral, Gabe, and Coltin.

I had no idea what had happened to Gabe, or whether he was even alive. I would not lose Coltin.

I left the bridge, my heart a tight, aching knot, and turned right, rubbing my chest as I headed for the spacewalk gear in the utility room at the end of the corridor.

My mind whirred, even though I wanted to shut it off. Shade. Hunters. Coltin. Shade. I couldn't stop myself; my thoughts kept jumping back to the man I'd believed I could trust.

What had he been doing? With me? With the ship? Why?

The *Endeavor did* work. The starboard door closed and locked. We were flying. Shade didn't appear to have sabotaged anything. And the fact that he was surely tracking us right now hardly mattered, considering I was the idiot who'd told him exactly where we were going next.

I slammed my palm into the cold metal wall beside me, punishing myself for my stupidity. The sharp pain in my hand only helped for a second before hurt and betrayal and fear came roaring back.

Our choices stank. Actually, we had none. We were going to Starway 8. The kids there needed us. Coltin needed me, and I would go to him, even if it meant falling into a trap.

But that didn't mean we had to make things easy

for those bounty hunters—or for Bridgebane, if he was behind all this. First, I had to get rid of any tracking devices before that pair of hunters found us again and shot to kill. Then, we'd head straight to Starway 8.

As for Shade, I'd worry about him when he showed up, set on a live capture and looking to get the most out of his *prize*.

I growled so loudly it hurt my throat. He'd already gotten more than enough from me, parts of myself I should never have given up.

I threw open the door with every bit of the violence I wanted to unleash and stalked toward the spacewalk gear.

I had no doubt that Shade would come. He didn't strike me as the type of man who gave up, and I was worth a lot. Sooner or later, he'd find me—along with a swift kick in the balls.

CHAPTER

22

ZERO G DIDN'T BOTHER ME, BUT I HATED THE SPACE suit. It was hot and heavy and confining, a mass of bulk around me, some of it hard, some of it flexible, but all of it necessary, right down to the thick, movement-impairing gloves and the titanium-soled, integrated boots. It felt like a coffin to me every time I put it on, only it was encasing me alive instead of dead. The damn thing was my nemesis—or one of them.

My own breathing echoed back to me, loud in the confines of my helmet, a constant reminder that I had limited air and time and that even with a forty-five-pound suit on me, I was about to be weightless, and that one cut through the tether could leave me floating off into the Dark. The suit didn't have any integrated propulsion, no handy button to set off mini thrusters or little joystick to steer me around. We didn't have the money for that, only for the basic, standard suit. I would have to crawl all over my ship with a rope clipped to my waist. If I drifted away, I'd have to reel myself in from the void of space.

Fun times. The last twenty-four hours had been great.

My heart clenched, and heat blasted through me, followed by a quick shot of cold. I'd actually thought the last day had been pretty freaking fantastic—before.

"Fuck you, Shade Ganavan," I muttered as I pressed my gloved index finger down on the seven-digit code to the air lock control. A palm swipe would have been easier, but that would have required undressing, so…no.

"What's that?" Jax asked.

"Nothing, partner," I answered into the com.

The inner safety entrance to the *Endeavor* was already sealed up behind me, and I kept my arm firmly hooked around the handle next to the new starboard door. The moment it opened, space claimed the air between the two doors. The powerful pull sucked at me, and I held on, waiting for equilibrium to settle over the entrance once more.

Calm came quickly, along with silence. The slight magnetism in the soles of my boots kept me anchored. It wasn't enough to make it hard to pick up my feet or move around. It just kept me close to the ship and allowed me to do what I needed to do without having to constantly worry about floating off.

Looking out the wide-open door, the same combination of sensations as usual shivered through me: a chill, a thrill. Spacewalking was cool. It was also terrifying.

I'd already checked twice, and so had Jaxon before he'd sealed me out of the main part of the ship, but I gave the tether another hearty tug before I let myself drift out, keeping a hand on the hull to guide me.

Carefully, I started combing the *Endeavor* for bugs. We didn't have the tech for anything other than a manual sweep with the electronic wand in my hand, and it didn't immediately pick up anything of note. The device had a fifteen-foot radius, so I didn't have to touch every single part of the ship, but it was slow going to be methodical and thorough.

"Jax, when are you going to squeeze us into that supply line?" I asked. I wanted us to get lost in the other ships around Flyhole as fast as possible.

"Don't like moving when you're out there," he grumbled.

"I'm holding on tight," I assured him.

Jax bullied his way into a line of ships waiting for water renewal, but instead of just cursing us and then shrugging and going with it like ninety-nine percent of people would have, the captain behind us started flashing what-the-fuck? lights from the midsize cruiser's bridge.

Great—that would really help us blend in.

I turned and glared, wishing the asshole would knock it off. The point of cutting into a line had been to make it look like we'd been here for a while, instead of like we'd just arrived in a panic to sweep for bugs.

The other ship kept going berserk on the *Endeavor*'s rear end, so I told Jax about the flasher and asked him to try to communicate enough with the cruiser to make the aggravated captain shut the hell up.

We were in breach of unwritten rules, but as soon as I finished, they'd get their spot in line back, and all would be right in the world of Flyhole extortion.

Who in their right mind would buy water at Flyhole when Albion 5 was just a hop away? There were at least thirty ships in this line, and they'd all pay twice as much here as they would on any inhabited rock.

Whatever. Money wasn't an issue for everyone, and their loss was our gain. If those hunters got here before I was done, at least we wouldn't be sticking out like criminals on the run. We looked a lot like everyone else here. Out in deep space, with nothing else around, a tracked ship was impossible not to spot in an instant. Here at Flyhole, you had to weed through the crowd to be sure you had the right one.

My skin buzzed with nervous energy as I crawled along the hull, meticulously moving the wand back and forth. I reached the stickers on the starboard side without getting a single hit for bugs. Since eliminating possible trackers was the priority, I left the numbers up for now and moved to portside. Two minutes later, my wand beeped through the earpiece I had in my helmet, its little flashes and alarms getting more frantic and insistent as I moved left and down.

"There you are," I murmured, finally spotting the tracking bug. It was the exact same dark gray as the *Endeavor* and blended in almost perfectly.

"I've got a live one," I said, informing the crew of my find.

"Try to destroy it," Jax said. "If that doesn't work, toss it hard."

I took hold of the device and detached the transmitting bug with a sharp twist. It was a discreet, sophisticated little thing. I never would have seen it if the wand hadn't led me to the right place. It was probably Shade's, considering how well it matched the ship.

Envisioning Shade's deceitful face, I hauled off and smashed the bug against the side of the ship.

The result was thoroughly unsatisfactory. It didn't get

out any of my anger or hurt, and in space, with a big, bulky space suit on, I didn't move well enough for a really hard hit. The intact tracker kept transmitting, and my wand kept up its frenzied beeps.

Sourly, I informed Jax that smashing it hadn't worked.

"Then throw it the fuck away, Tess."

Sound advice, as usual. Too bad I hadn't listened to him about Shade.

A sharp ache sliced through me. It was hot-cold, twisting and tight, and hurt more than I wanted to admit.

Shoving aside the awful feeling, I turned, anchored myself against the side of the *Endeavor*, and then sent the bug soaring off into the Dark. It would go forever—and hopefully lead that lying shit away from us.

With that device on its way to somewhere else, I kept going, continuing my methodical search. I found another bug just as a ship materialized on the outskirts of our side of Flyhole, punching into perception after a jump.

A bad feeling burrowed through me the second I saw it, and my heart started to thud. It was small, made for speed and maneuverability. It couldn't possibly house more than two.

Two bounty hunters, if I had to guess.

I ripped the new bug off and sent it flying away without really moving, not wanting to draw attention to myself. It was possible that whoever was in that small cruiser wouldn't see me out here. My suit was a similar color to the *Endeavor*, and we blended in with the other cargo ships hovering around the spacedock. It would take effort—and time—to pick us out from the rest, especially if it was that craft's signal that I'd just sent spiraling off.

If it was Shade in that ship, though, he'd recognize the *Endeavor* in a heartbeat. He'd worked on her all week.

And what about more bugs? I still had a quarter of the ship to cover, and I couldn't stop until the job was done. There was no easy fix from inside, like hitting the ship with a hull-wide electrical charge. Trackers were always insulated, specifically to guard against just that. This was all me, all now, and there was no way I was drawing what could turn out to be a horde of bounty hunters to Starway 8. It was already bad enough that Shade, the apparent top dog of the whole money-grubbing gang, knew exactly where I was heading next.

If he chose to, Shade could steer Bridgebane straight to the orphanage. The Dark Watch general might go there anyway. A disgusted voice inside me was telling me there was a chance that infecting kids in a place he could easily guess I cared about was his plan B—if his hunters failed to bring me in.

My stomach in knots, I continued searching for tracking devices, speeding up as much as I could.

The clock was ticking now more than ever. The kids were in bad shape and getting worse. There wasn't enough time to find the Fold and recruit someone else to take the shots to Starway 8. That could take days—and cost lives. Cost *Coltin's* life. Our best bet now was to get in and out of the orphanage before Shade or Bridgebane caught up.

"Talk to me, Tess." Fiona's voice came through the com, efficient and a little clipped. "Your heart rate just jumped."

"Small ship. Portside. And a bit behind." They likely couldn't see it from the bridge, and there were so many blobs on the radar here that it would be almost impossible to pick out a little one like that. "I don't like the way it looks."

"There's too much activity on the monitors to find it," Jax said. "Foe?"

"Who's not a foe, Jax?"

"I'm not your enemy, Tess. Save it for the asshole you just left."

I tried not to leap down his throat again. "I'm not done yet."

"Forget the stickers. Get back inside. We'll jump," Jax said.

"There might still be bugs."

The small cruiser moved closer, breathing down my neck.

Jax must have gotten a lock on it once it entered our space, because he started to sound even more urgent. "Let's go, Tess. We'll jump halfway to 8 and finish there."

"That's a useless waste of power." Draining the *Endeavor*'s energy resources with an extra jump now when we might need the juice a lot more later was a hard *no* in my mind.

Jax wasn't done arguing. "The jump isn't useless if it saves your life!"

"Now who's the one snapping?" I asked.

In my earpiece, there was a deep growl followed by a crash, and I wondered what Jax had just thrown and smashed. He usually controlled his emotions, but sometimes he just…broke.

Guilt clamped down inside me. "I'm almost done, Jax."

"Hurry," he ground out.

Only my free hand and the slight magnetism in my boots kept me attached to the *Endeavor*. I pushed off, making bigger leaps so that I could cover the rest of the hull faster. The tether hung under the belly of the ship. Too visible from up close, it snaked back toward the open door I'd exited.

I took stock of my position as I swung the wand a little frantically now. *Under* was currently the long way home. The shorter distance would be to go up and over the top and hope the tether didn't catch on anything that stuck out. The portside door wasn't an option; it didn't have an air lock.

I stretched my arm as far as I could and flew along the hull, sweeping the wand back and forth. When did the ship get so big?

When you decided to add the hulking lab attachment onto the back of it that started this whole mess. Way to go, Tess.

"That ship is coming closer." The com on Jax's console was open, and Miko's voice came from a slight distance.

The back of my neck prickled, but I couldn't turn my head enough to see without turning most of my body. *Damn suit.*

"Fifty feet to go. I'm almost done," I said.

"Hurry, partner."

Partner. My throat closed up tight, like it always did when he called me that.

"Shit! They're moving in." The panic in Jax's voice sent my heart pounding against my ribs. "Move, Tess! Move! Move!"

"I have to finish!" I yelled back.

The maneuverable little ship zoomed into my peripheral vision. It was practically on top of us.

My pulse hammered harder. I started to sweat.

"Tess!" Jax bellowed, a sort of madness creeping into his voice.

"Thirty feet!" I dove forward with the wand. I could cover the rest of the ship.

"Get to the door!" They were all screaming at me now.

Their wild pleas battered my ears as I propelled myself along the side of the bridge, sweeping the wand above and below the portside window. Shiori stood right in front of me, both her hands pressed to the transparent surface we still liked to call glass. Her lips moved fast, but I knew her words were silent. She was praying for me.

Their fear amped up my panic, setting it loose inside me like a toxin that nearly rattled me off the ship. The small vessel closed in from the side, and I turned, almost hoping it was Shade, because at least he didn't want me dead.

It wasn't. They were close enough to make out through the window now, and it was the male-female pair that had tried to ambush me on the Squirrel Tree.

A hatch opened under their ship, and a mechanical arm came out, opening into a nightmarish claw at its head. The arm shot forward.

I gasped and rolled along the side of the *Endeavor*. The claw struck the portside window where I'd just been. Shiori flinched from the sound the shock must have made inside the ship, and for a terrifying second, I thought the window might break.

It held, thank the Powers. The hunters pulled the arm back, maneuvering for another grab.

"Tess! Get inside!" Jax begged. Our eyes met, and he looked terrified.

Gripping the edge of the window, I shot toward the *Endeavor*'s roof. "I'm coming!" I finally agreed; an extra jump would be way better than this.

Curses and yelling came through my helmet, and I scrambled out of the way as the claw lunged for me again. Like an animal on all fours, I crawled over the outside of the bridge, trying to get to the starboard side again. The hunters stalked. The claw extended.

I nearly jumped out of my skin when the wand flashed and sent an angry beep into my earpiece. Another bug!

Fright thundered inside me as I narrowly escaped the claw again. My frantic shimmy dislodged me from the ship, and I grabbed back on with a shout. Breathing hard, I waved the wand around like a crazy person, trying to locate the tracking device.

Beep, beep, beeep, beeeep, beeeeeeeep!

I swung around. Damn the Powers! It was behind me. I had to go back.

CHAPTER

23

"THERE'S ANOTHER BUG!" I CRIED, DIVING UNDER THE mechanical arm as it reached out.

"Leave it!" Jax roared.

Leave it? Now that I know it's here? This wasn't a hypothetical problem anymore; it was real.

The hunters would follow us almost immediately after we jumped. On Albion 5, they'd had to get back to their ship, track us, and then locate us more precisely in the Flyhole mess. All those factors would be eliminated for a hasty second jump. We'd be in the same situation we were in right now, just somewhere else.

For the millionth time, I wished the *Endeavor* had firepower. But phasers weren't authorized on cargo cruisers, and black-market stuff was way out of our budget. And bullets… They were for places with breathable atmospheres. No sparks in space.

The wand's signal beeped more frantically toward the nose of the ship, and I crawled over the front panel. Reflected in the window, I saw the small cruiser looming behind me again, the claw opening wide. My crew looked on in horror, but I hardly had time to register their distress, or how they looked like ghosts, aging with every breath.

"Got it!" The device sat just above the central window, like a target on our heads.

I ripped it off and tossed it away.

"Move. Start moving!" I shouted.

"Are you fucking kidding me?" Jax cried.

I pulled hard on anything I could grip and let go of the ship for terrifyingly long glides, propelling myself back over the top. The claw chased me. The armored tile I was gripping vibrated. I glanced over and saw a flash of retracting metal and dents not even a foot from me.

Holy shit, that was close.

Whoever was steering the claw readjusted. I sprang away before they could correct their aim.

"Drop us out of line, Jax!" Even if I managed to get inside, we couldn't jump like this, sandwiched between other ships. We needed a minimum of open space.

Fear and effort got me to the other side of the *Endeavor*, and I crawled-flew-swam toward the open starboard door. The hunters repositioned themselves, getting so close that their powerful spotlight nearly blinded me. I turned away, squinting. The claw hit just beside my foot, and I yelped, jerking my leg up.

The *Endeavor* finally dipped, and I tumbled sideways, rolling out of control until a protruding instrument caught me in the ribs. I hissed, my gunshot wound exploding in agony.

"Tess!" Jax shouted.

"Here," I panted out.

A bright light flashed near me, followed by another.

Gasping, I threw myself away from the next blast. The hunters had phasers. No surprise there; they were Bridgebane's lackeys.

My mouth stung with the acidic taste of panic. How had they missed?

They let off more shots that bounced off the *Endeavor*. They were aiming for the tether!

Shade must have convinced them to go for the live capture. If they could shake me loose from the hull and send me floating without the rope, that claw would snatch me up in an instant. I'd have nothing to hold on to, nothing to propel myself away from them.

There was too much hysterical shouting in my com now to make out any of it. I wished I could turn the damn thing off, but I didn't have control over that. My side burned as I scuttled away from more phaser shots. One grazed my suit, making my pulse explode with dread.

I held my breath.

I didn't freeze and die instantly, so my layers of protection must have mostly held. I could feel the cold starting to seep into my leg, though, and it scared me more than the phasers did.

Ignoring the pain in my calf, I kept going. The door wasn't far.

I straightened and ran, taking a huge leap to get there faster. The *Endeavor* dipped again, and the ship went one way while I went the other.

Terrified, I flailed and dropped the wand, trying to grab back on to the ship with both hands. I pitched forward, stretching my arms and fingers out.

I missed the hull and somersaulted. My feet didn't even hit as I came back around. My attempted dive sent me into a weightless spin, and I spiraled out into space, rotating again and again.

Dark. Claw. Ship. Phaser beam. Up was down, down was up. I was out of control. Petrified. Momentum carried me away, every dizzying head-over-heels inch rolling out like a mile paved in solid fear.

I screamed for Jax. Jax screamed for me back. He'd fall apart if I died. There was no one to keep him together, not when he wouldn't really let himself have anyone else.

A hard jolt wrenched my waist and snapped me to a harsh stop.

"Fuck!" I yelled.

"What?" everyone yelled back.

I sucked air through my teeth, pain ringing inside me like a slap. I blinked, trying to focus. Pain and panic were making it hard to see. I frantically tried to locate the hunters again.

There! On my left.

"Might need new stitches, Fi."

"Just get in here!" she cried, sounding like she wanted to tear me apart, not stitch me up.

My sweat-pricked gaze found and followed the line of the tether home to the *Endeavor*, and I swung my arms forward and grabbed on. Hand over hand, I began reeling myself in.

The hunters zipped around and let off a series of shots again, nearly severing the line. If it had been any thicker, they would have had it, but without anything technological for their instruments to lock on to, the tether was a damn hard target.

My heart beat like a drum in an empty cavern as

I pulled myself in. Double-crossing asshole, I-will-eviscerate-him-if-I-ever-see-him-again Shade had definitely convinced his buddies that a capture was better than a kill. So much more profitable. Either that, or they couldn't shoot for shit, but bounty hunters weren't known for their incompetence.

I finally hit metal tiles with enough force that it would have hurt without the bulk of the space suit to cushion me. Grabbing on to the hull with both hands and the help of my magnetized boots, I scuttled toward the open door again. I would get to that starboard air lock. I had to.

Another hard jolt stopped me, making me gasp and curl in on my injury. *For fuck's sake!* The actual gunshot wound hadn't hurt half as much as the rest of this did.

The hunters swooped down next to me, the claw reaching out. I sprang forward but couldn't move. Something was holding me back.

I twisted and yanked on the rope. "Jax! I'm stuck!" The tether was caught.

"I'm coming for you!" he yelled.

"No! Stay inside!" He could never suit up fast enough. Either I got inside on my own, or…

The claw twisted toward me, opening like a terrible flower. My eyes widened behind my mask—no way was that thing catching me.

I swiped at the latch on my belt, fumbling the mechanism because of my thick gloves. I tried again, shaking from the fear and adrenaline pouring through my blood. *Come on… Come on…*

The tether detached, freeing me. I pulled hard on two of the big screws holding down the armored plates and shot along the outside of the ship. The claw hit right below me, smacking my heel so hard my foot went numb.

"I'm loose! Don't move. I'm coming in." I aimed for the opening, going as fast as I could. I'd never space-walked without the tether before. It was as terrifying as I'd always imagined.

"Tess. Partner. Holy Sky Mother."

Poor Jaxon. He'd lost hair the last time I scared him this much.

I propelled myself toward the starboard door, using more hands than legs, my arms straining and my shoulders aching. Phaser shots chased me, getting closer and closer. The hunters weren't aiming for the lost tether anymore. Dead was plenty good enough again.

I reached the opening and dove inside, pain flaring again at the level of my injury as I twisted to get behind the protection of the doorframe. "I'm in! Close the door, Jax!"

Phaser shots blasted through the gap, and I huddled into the corner as the air lock lit up like a solar storm, direct hits exploding straight into it.

The new armored door whooshed shut, cutting off the barrage. All went suddenly dark and silent.

A red light flickered on. It meant no atmosphere.

"Tess?" Jaxon sounded so lost.

"I'm here, partner. I'm okay." Or at least, I'd tell him that.

Breathing hard inside my helmet, I waited for the red light to turn green, indicating the repressurization of the air lock zone. If the hunters were still shooting at us, I didn't feel it. Their small phaser wouldn't do anything against my girl, not like the heavy artillery of a Dark Watch frigate.

The instant the light changed, I punched in the code and went through the safety door and into Jax's arms.

He gripped me hard, locking me tightly against him and closing the door again with his other hand. In practically the same movement, he pressed a finger down on the com button to the bridge and yelled, "Jump, Fi!"

"I don't know how to fly!" she cried back through the speaker.

"The blue button I showed you. Hit it! Now!" Jax let go of the com panel and swept me up against the wall, bracing us both.

Pressure clamped down on me, my bones crunched, darkness came and then ultimately went—a plunge into deep night before dawn broke again.

I shuddered, sagging against Jax.

And that was that. We were in Sector 8. I was home. Alive. Ready to help Coltin and the others as fast as we could.

I exhaled. I could hardly believe it. Yesterday already seemed like a lifetime ago, lived by somebody else.

A raw sound crawled up my throat, but I didn't let it out. I wasn't even sure what it was. Relief? Rage? Hope? Hurt? Everything was all jumbled up, and I couldn't see straight, even in my head.

I struggled to find some sort of equilibrium, both emotional and physical, while Jax got my helmet off. Then we both tore at my suit. He pushed it down, and I shimmied out of the confining gear until I could step away from it in nothing but the tight, short undersuit. Blood wet my side. My bare calf was bitter red from cold.

Jax stared at me, horrified.

"It could have been worse." I was trying to reassure him, but I just sounded like I was still terrified instead.

It was Jax who made a weird, strangled sound in the end. He pulled me in close, wrapping me in a fierce hug that was still gentle enough not to hurt. His arms were so big and warm, and I was shivering, inside and out.

His embrace was exactly what I needed. I let him gather me up, and I held him back, my arms around his waist. Jax sank down as though out of strength, his face twisting into something nearly unrecognizable as I curled up in his lap.

I felt like a child, and maybe he was getting exactly what he needed from me right then, too. Someone to comfort and protect. He rubbed my back, and I sucked down breaths that hiccupped in my throat. His voice low and deep, Jax crooned soft words he might have offered to the family he missed so much—to the wife, children, and sister ripped from him, their lives so brutally snuffed out.

He cradled me, and I turned my face into his broad chest, squeezing my eyes shut. My shoulders shook as I tried to hold back.

I couldn't, and I lost it. I started crying in great, heaving sobs, blurting out, "I'm heartbroken, Jax."

He stroked my hair, my back, holding me against his chest. "I know you are."

"Why? Why did this happen?" He didn't have answers, but I still asked.

"The galaxy is full of bad people. You deserve better. I'm so sorry you got hurt."

"You were right." I gripped his shirt, holding on to him like a lifeline and keeping my head buried under his chin. "I should have listened to you."

"No, I wasn't right."

"Well, you sure weren't *wrong*," I said, sobbing again.

I felt his smile against my hair, knew it was wry from his small huff of breath. "Is it wrong to try? Maybe what's wrong is never putting yourself out there for fear of losing things you don't even have."

I looked up through lashes spiked with moisture. Did Jax mean…?

Sniffling, I wiped the tears from my face, my hand shaking. "Did you ever think…? Maybe you and Fi…?"

He swallowed. His mouth flattened into a line as he cupped my head and slowly pulled me back down against his chest again. His big fingers moved in soothing circles over the base of my skull.

I leaned in to him. He didn't answer. And I didn't press.

CHAPTER

24

MAREEKA HUGGED ME ON THE LANDING DOCK AND then scowled and snapped, "Sick bay. Now!"

"How's Coltin?" I asked without preamble.

"Alive…I think."

I froze. That was terrifying—and could only mean he was teetering on the edge.

Her blue eyes softened at my obvious distress. So did her voice. "He's stronger than he used to be. We told him you were coming, but I'm not sure he heard."

Tears stung my eyes. "His breathing…"

"Will always be a problem," Mareeka said. She frowned. "What happened to you?"

I was a mess. I'd shown up on Starway 8 in a bloody spacewalk undersuit, barefoot, and looking like I hadn't slept in a week. No wonder her face was pinched with worry.

"Nothing incurable," I said, glancing down at my side. My broken heart was another matter. "I brought those injections I told you about."

A statuesque woman with warm bronze skin and

glossy black hair rushed toward us from the side, and my heart swelled at the sight of her. Surral was from the New India Conglomerate. The water-and-mineral-rich Sector 15 system had been one of the first settled after most of the population of a whole huge country had up and left Earth, leaving it to fail without them. That was ancient history now, but the group of planets still nearly rivaled Sector 12's privileged rocks in terms of wealth and resources. Most New Indians stayed in Sector 15, where they pretty much had it all. Surral had left the day she met Mareeka, who'd been visiting there on a fund-raising trip for Starway 8.

Surral hugged me and then stepped back, scowling as well. Her stern expression clashed with the cheeriness of her rainbow-hued scrubs.

"Hey, Surral." I fought the urge to scuff my toe against the platform and hang my head. Neither of them looked happy with me.

While Mareeka had ice-blond hair and piercing blue eyes that I'd seen make galactic officials tremble, it was Surral who knew how to make me squirm when she wanted to. To the outside world, the two of them were tall, lean, hard, and the unquestioned generals of this place. To us, the kids who grew up here, they were Mom and Mom.

To each other, they were everything—along with their kids.

Surral's mouth turned down in a way I knew from experience meant displeasure in the extreme. "No one ever expects you to do things at the expense of yourself, Tess."

I stood taller, even though it hurt. They were the ones who had taught me about service, about choosing others—and what was right—over myself, or the easy way out.

"Then what's the point of living?" I asked.

At that, they both rolled their eyes, knowing any further argument was a lost cause.

"Let's go," Mareeka said, waving everyone forward.

Jax and Fiona each picked up a large case of the prepared injections. I carried a smaller bag, and Mareeka and Surral each took another case. That was it. That was all we had, and I hoped to the Sky Mother it would be enough.

I glanced back at the ship as we left the dock. Miko gave me a quick wave. She and Shiori were already busy trashing the old numbers and putting up new stickers on the *Endeavor*. Between them, they had three hands and two eyes. They could do it, although seeing them up there on that ladder was a little nerve-racking.

I heard kids calling out to me as we made our way to the medical facility on the sixteenth level. I smiled and nodded my hellos, recognizing most of the faces, even if I didn't know everyone's name.

In sick bay, we arrived more to moans than to greetings. I swept worried glances around, taking in the feverish eyes and dry lips in faces that had thinned too much. My heart squeezed at the sheer number of kids, all lined up in beds that stretched on for what seemed like forever under the long string of faintly humming overhead lights. From what Surral had said on the way up, I knew that other large spaces looked like this one, and that the whole floor above and below us had been commandeered for medical purposes as well.

A lump grew in my throat and stuck. I could hardly swallow. "There were no antiviral shots? Nothing?"

"We ran out eighteen months ago," Mareeka said.

And I hadn't found them more. I got the sudden, nearly unstoppable urge to yell in desperation. The orphanage wasn't poor. It simply wasn't given *access* to everything it needed, just like so many other places. There wasn't enough of everything. There never had been, and there never would be. So the Overseer made *choices*. He chose his soldiers, his Sector 12 cronies, his political friends, and all the rich influencers across the galaxy who wanted safe, healthy planets to live on and could give him the support he craved and needed. I wanted those people to suffer for once while these kids got the medicine they needed, the medicine those people took for granted and bought so easily with a flash of universal currency and an indifferent smile.

"The sickest ones are here," Surral said. Then she nodded to a few beds down.

Coltin.

I moved toward him, dread weighing me down. Loving one kid in particular didn't stop me from seeing the other children, too. Some of them were so heartbreakingly small. So pale, despite their variety of skin tones. So deathly still.

"Has anyone died?" I asked softly as Mareeka followed me toward the boy who was mine in a lot of ways that counted.

"We lost the first six yesterday. Three more this morning." She squeezed my wrist when I stopped in shock and horror. "You got here just in time."

I shook my head. Nine little lives lost. That sounded like two days too late, not just in time.

Crushed and starting to shake, I knelt next to Coltin's

bed and touched his feverish brow. His long lashes looked like dark fans against his pallid skin. His too-shallow breaths wheezed in and out.

"Hey, sweet bee." I brushed his sandy-blond hair back from his forehead. "It's me, Tess."

Slowly, Coltin's eyes opened. They were blue, like mine.

"I knew you'd come." His words cracked and scratched, his voice so weak I could hardly hear him.

I bit my lip, fighting tears. "Nowhere I'd rather be than with you."

"I think...I might've...seen...my mom." He panted between words, and I could hear the rattle in his lungs. That rattle had terrified me when he was a baby. It still did.

My voice thickened. "Your mom's a star, sweet bee. You see her in every sunbeam."

"No." Coltin's swallow clicked in his dry throat. "I just saw her. Just like the picture I have. But then"—he stopped, trying to catch his breath—"I opened my eyes, and it was you."

Tears sprang up and overflowed. I was glad Coltin didn't see them. He drifted back to sleep, exhausted from just a few words. I held his hand, and the agitated twitching of his fingers was the only thing keeping me from falling apart, because it meant he was still there, still alive, still fighting.

Around me, no one spoke, and the pall-like silence haunted me until a slew of nurses converged on us, jarring me back to my feet. Without needing specific directions from Surral, they organized their attack on the virus like a team of scrub-wearing soldiers, a candy-colored brigade leading their charge. There was no

Overseer brown here, no washing out of life. This was where life was injected back into people, and not only through hard-fought-for and scarce medicine and shots.

But then we grew up and left, adults seeing in brilliant color, and nothing else in the galaxy ever lived up to what we'd had on Starway 8.

For a bright, flashing second, the thought of Shade punched right through my ribs and hit my heart like a fist. He'd been colorful. If he hadn't been the enemy, he might have lived up.

I let out a slow breath, banishing Shade from my thoughts. My devastation over Starway 8's recent deaths lingered, as did the dark cloud of loss and worry for the sick, but the nurses' efficiency left little room for standing around and wallowing. They were already on to the next step.

Mareeka put everyone and everything on pause with a single raised hand and the slight clearing of her throat. "Every nurse and adult present gets an injection first." She speared the three of us from the *Endeavor* with a hard look, especially me. "It's highly contagious. No arguments, please."

Jax and Fiona obediently rolled up their sleeves and held out their arms. I hated to let anyone waste a shot on me, so I pretended to do it myself, surreptitiously giving the injection to Coltin instead. He didn't even move when I stuck him in the upper arm, but I gained slight comfort in the midst of all this fragility—the beeping monitors, wheezing lungs, and droning track lighting—knowing he'd get a double dose.

I made sure Surral saw my empty syringe as I threw it out and then pressed on my arm as if it stung.

Liberated as soon as they were vaccinated, the nurses dispersed with the cases of injections. Surral gave one to Coltin herself and then checked his vitals, scribbling numbers on his chart. Jax, Fiona, and I stayed out of the way. They would go back to the *Endeavor*, and we'd leave as soon as I could.

Mareeka swept out an arm, motioning Jax and Fiona forward and shepherding them as though they'd always been a part of her flock. "Let's get you back to your ship. Our security cameras are undergoing maintenance, and we wouldn't want anyone sneaking up on you while you're here. As soon as Tess is ready, as usual, a quick departure is for the best."

Security was down? *Great.* I knew these checks only lasted a few hours and came at irregular intervals, but the timing couldn't have been worse. Shade knew where I was. He'd be on his way. With any luck, though, it would take him a while to shake off whatever had sent him reeling like a drunkard across the Squirrel Tree dock.

I nodded for Jax and Fiona to go. We wouldn't linger, no matter how much I longed to curl up under the watchful blanket of this institution and its keepers, read, dance, and eat ridiculous amounts of liquid gold with kids who were never told that it wasn't okay to put their sticky fingers on the walls after dipping them into the honey pots.

For our own sakes as well as to preserve Starway 8, to preserve all of that, we would leave the second we could.

I waved my companions off. "Be ready to go. Set coordinates for the last known location of you-know-where." I had a lab chock-full of serum to get off my hands once and for all. The problem was, I still didn't know what to do with it. "I'll just get fixed up, and then I'll be right down."

Jax looked twitchy about leaving me, especially after what we'd just been through, but he also recognized that I knew this place like the back of my hand and had nothing but allies here.

Of course, that was assuming I'd taken all the hunters' bugs off. And that Shade was still in a stupor. And that Bridgebane hadn't orchestrated this whole epidemic just to get me to Starway 8.

Yeah, it was entirely possible we were fucked.

I gave Jax a reassuring smile. He glowered back, probably knowing exactly what I was thinking.

That was as much of a goodbye as we got. Surral, who'd personally doctored my every scrape since I was eight years old, dragged me over to a private cubicle. She swept the curtain closed behind us, cutting us off as Jax and Fiona left for the ship in the company of Mareeka, and the nursing team started administering shots.

Her profile to me, Surral snapped on a pair of gloves. The sound was oddly comforting when it was her tugging them on, even though I'd heard the same tight, elastic noises repeatedly under traumatic circumstances before she'd come into my life.

She turned to me, all medical efficiency to try to mask the worry I saw sinking delicate lines into her face. "I can't say I wish you hadn't risked yourself for all of us, but that's only because you're here with me and clearly not dead."

"I'd die for this place." And for the people in it.

"Please don't," she said stiffly.

"Surral…"

"Mareeka and I try not to have favorites," she cut in. She breathed deeply, fighting the emotion I saw abruptly glaring out of her like a too-bright light that suddenly hit me square in the eyes.

Tears burned behind my lids again, and I blinked. She blinked, too.

"I've never spanked a child, but sometimes I want to spank you."

I laughed in surprise, the movement tugging on my injury. "Really?"

Surral smiled as well, a wobbly little thing that made my chest ache. "Oddly enough, the itch grows, the older you get."

"I'm not sure you could catch me or hold me down. I'm bigger than you are."

She gave me a look that quelled both our tears and made me feel as though I was about to get sentenced to cleaning the air ducts again. Besides, I probably only had two inches on her, and one on Mareeka, and I hadn't gotten that tall until I was sixteen and went through a painfully fast, late growth spurt. Part of their easy command of this place was almost always being able to see over everyone else's head.

Back to business, Surral said, "I'm not asking you what's in those injections or how you got them."

Gingerly, I got myself up onto the examination table. "Yeah. That's probably a good idea." She trusted me and knew I had Starway 8's best interests at heart.

Her sour look was somehow filled with love. She was good at that. My sour look was just sour.

"If I had more time, I'd check it out first. But this has gone on too long, and there are too many children hovering between life and death."

And none of us wanted more kids to go the wrong way.

"I think it'll work. But if it doesn't…" That lump rose up in my throat again, and Coltin's sweet face flashed before my eyes. "It won't hurt, anyway."

"How can you be sure of that?" Surral asked, spearing me with eyes that were such a deep brown they were almost black, like the hair she always kept pulled back. That neat twist was a part of her. I'd never seen her hair loose in my life.

"Have you ever heard of the Mornavail?" I asked in lieu of answering—and trying to distract.

She nodded. "Can't ever get sick. Not subject to the illness or disease that would normally corrupt the body."

A new framework of thought clicked into place. *The Incorruptible Mornavail.*

Shit. I had to reread that book.

Realizing I hadn't changed the subject at all or even remotely diverted her from the truth, I forced out a croaked, "Can't ever get sick?"

Surral shrugged. "It's a myth."

"What if it's not?" I whispered, suddenly light-headed.

What the hell did Susan know that I didn't? Was it a coincidence? Or had she somehow set this up?

"Not a myth?" Surral looked at me and understood all too quickly from what must have been my huge eyes and probably ghostly pale face. She dropped the pair of scissors in her hand, this woman who had never fumbled anything in her life.

She stared at me. "Are you telling me that my nurses are currently shooting my kids up with Mornavail blood?"

My heart thudded. I didn't know. Was that bad? "Maybe?"

Surral bent down and picked up her scissors.

"Would that be okay?" I asked, my upper lip starting to prickle with sweat.

"Okay? It's brilliant!" She threw her head back and whooped. As far as I knew, she'd never done that in her life before, either.

Holy shit, this was huge.

"But what if it really is just a myth?" Or something else entirely, as I'd thought from the book?

"I assume you tested it in some way." Her dark eyes shone with excitement, glittering with hope. "Why else would you think it would cure the kids?"

"Yeah. Of course." It had been a lifelong test in this case. And a few incidents had proven just how well it worked.

My mind raced with a thousand questions as I stretched out on the examination table, bringing my legs up with a wince. Wiggling to get more comfortable, I kept my arms at my sides and turned a little inward to hide any lingering needle marks.

"Where did you find it? Them? What are they like?" Surral asked.

"Um…" Nervous heat stole over me. "Can I not answer any of those questions?" This was a safe place for everyone. She wouldn't push.

Surral nodded, respecting my wishes despite her curiosity.

With her scissors, she cut my undersuit in half from my right thigh straight up to my neck. She peeled the material away from me, leaving me in only a bra and underpants. I must have looked pretty bad, because her mouth pinched, and she started grumbling.

"You just came off a spacewalk?" Clearly, she recognized the now-ruined garment for what it was.

I nodded, lifting a little to help her get the undersuit out from beneath me. Surral tossed it in the garbage.

"With a..." She bent over and examined me for a moment, gently prodding my bruised and bloodied side with her gloved fingers. "Massive contusion and hastily stitched-up gunshot wound?"

"Well, the bruise really only happened after. During the spacewalk."

Her stink eye was spectacular. "How many times am I going to have to patch you up?"

"Probably until I'm dead," I answered.

"That's not funny."

"I didn't think it was."

Frowning, she took my messed-up stitches out. She didn't offer me any numbshot, probably because she was pissed I hadn't taken better care of myself.

Mareeka's voice came through the communications bracelet on Surral's wrist. "They're settled at their ship, and I'm back in my office. Have Tess swing by here quickly before she goes."

Surral confirmed through the link.

Not looking up from her work again, she said, "Don't break Mareeka's heart."

I swallowed, knowing she really meant both their hearts. For a second, I felt guilty, because I loved them both more than I loved my actual mother, who was just a distant memory now. She was a good memory, though, which was what mattered, and what I would always hold on to.

Surral unlocked an expensive-looking laser-healer thing from a rolling cabinet and started patching me up with what I liked to call magic medicine. It worked, but I didn't know how. Other than a slightly uncomfortable heat, it was much less painful than good old-fashioned stitches — and worked a lot faster, too. In mere minutes, I was as good as new.

"We pray for you daily," Surral said, running a warm, wet cloth over my now-healed side to clean off the dried blood.

I smiled, despite my own lack of spirituality. I could just imagine those who chose to pray bending their little heads over their dinner plates and chanting out thanks to the Sky Mother, Her Powers, and to Tess.

"You're giving me too much credit," I said.

"You bring health, and no one here forgets that."

"I haven't brought much of anything lately, and I was almost too late." For nine kids, I *had* been too late. I didn't dare ask who we'd lost. Right now, I didn't think I could deal with knowing. For some things, it was better to wait.

"You've always seen the bigger picture, Tess." Surral trashed the bloody cloth. "Don't lose that now, or every failure will drive you insane."

I didn't want any failures at all, especially where dying kids were concerned. "You know I think praying is just a comfort for your own ears."

"So does Mareeka, but I don't." Surral moved her

attention to the cold burn on my lower leg. "And the kids can decide whatever they want, just like you did."

That was part of what I loved about this place. Diversity of opinion was celebrated. Beliefs were presented but never imposed.

"We pray for all our benefactors," Surral added, flashing me a smile.

I chuckled. "The bees still getting a good mention, then?"

"Oh, yes." She set down her medical instrument. "They keep us in food and clothes."

Honey was pure gold. Too bad it reminded me of Shade's light-brown eyes. I'd probably never want it again.

I sat up without a twinge of pain.

"Tess, maybe I shouldn't ask, but…you're sleeping with someone?"

Surral's question snapped through me like an electrical shock.

I gaped at her, my heart pounding. "What?"

"There's a bite mark on your neck, and the particular light from my instrument revealed recent…uh…evidence between your legs."

My face flushed hot. "No one. Not anymore." My voice came out rough. To my horror, my eyes brimmed with tears.

Gently, she asked, "Is he dead?"

I shook my head and jumped off the table, wanting to run. "No, but he's a lying fuckhead."

"Then I'm assuming it's not Jax."

"What? No!" I gaped at her in horror again.

She spread her hands, a small, helpless gesture that

didn't seem right coming from her. "I just thought for a moment…that maybe…"

Surral didn't finish, but I knew what she was thinking. What she wanted to hear. *Gabe*.

I shook my head again. "No one you know." As it turned out, I hadn't known him, either.

I started to move, but Surral's hand on my shoulder stopped me, lightly pushing me back. My butt hit the examination table, and I crossed my arms over my nearly naked chest. I wouldn't have gotten very far anyway without any clothes besides my underthings. Probably only to the curtain before I realized and stopped.

I suddenly felt doubly exposed and looked around for a towel or something to cover myself up with.

"I know you're fully vaccinated, but remind me, where are you on contraception?" she asked.

I wanted to protest the whole conversation, but that was just stupid. Surral taught us what we needed to know as we grew up, and she was the one who'd given me my birth control implant to begin with, when she'd seen how Gabe and I had started looking at each other when we were seventeen.

"There's about a year left," I said.

"In that case"—she turned back to her cabinet and rummaged around—"you need another ovulation suppressor. I don't know if I'll see you again before the year is out, and it's sometimes less reliable toward the end." She looked over at me again with the sterile packaging of the tiny implant in her hand. "Unless you want children, of course."

I did. Someday. I thought. Unless it was too dangerous. What did I know? I kept getting shot at, and there

was a huge bounty on my head. But none of that mattered for the question at hand because…

"I'm not sleeping with anyone," I repeated—a little
dully to my ears.

"Maybe not now. Or again. But ten years is a long time.
Let's just replace it, yes?"

I nodded and let my doctor do her thing. Out with the
old. In with the new. I felt the slight pinch as she got the
previous implant out from under my skin and then injected
me with its minuscule replacement.

"You can remove it at any time," she reminded me.
"Any qualified nurse can take it out."

I nodded again, but right then, I couldn't imagine my
life being stable enough for kids, which made me sad as
hell. It wasn't even stable enough for a boyfriend. A good,
fun, steady guy. Not one who lied, and snuck around, and
took his blood money from the galaxy's most powerful
and dreaded Dark Watch general.

"I waited seven years after losing track of Gabe and
then slept with the absolute worst person in the whole
galaxy," I blurted out. "Yesterday."

Surral arched her brows, taking in my confession.
"Why did you choose the worst person?"

I didn't even try to hide my dejection. "Because I
thought he was something else." Shade had fooled me.
He'd made me believe he was everything he wasn't.

"Did he hurt you?" she asked.

"Yes."

She sucked in a sharp breath. I glanced up and found
Surral looking like a force of nature, ready to rip Shade up.

"Not like that," I hastened to reassure her. "Not
physically."

I couldn't help it. I rubbed my aching heart. I didn't add any details. I didn't tell her that he'd been about to act on the dead-or-alive bounty he'd been keeping a secret while he earned my trust. And I didn't explain how he'd been waiting for the right moment to haul me in to the Dark Watch and claim his prize. All that had been next on his agenda—after the beautiful sex.

She was quiet for a long moment and then finally asked, "No sign of Gabe, then?"

I would have asked her the same question soon—her or Mareeka. Now I didn't need to. If he still hadn't checked in here in nearly a decade, he was either in prison, or dead.

"Nothing," I said.

"Well, let's not assume the worst," she said, peeling off her surgical gloves.

Her words came out forcefully enough to make me think they were more for her benefit than for mine. At this point, I was pretty resigned to the worst.

"I lost my cat." While I was confessing things, there was also that.

The ache in my chest grew. Poor Bonk. I hoped he got off that platform somehow. If he did, would he go feral on the streets? Fighting for scraps? I had all that food, the fancy litter... He would have had such a good life.

"I'm sorry, Tess."

I bit my lip. "Yeah. Thanks. And I have no clothes," I added, curling in on myself.

Surral turned to another cupboard and pulled out a pair of candy-pink scrubs with lime-green trim. I didn't know where she got these things. It was as though color elves wove them during the night and then delivered them to Starway 8.

Or maybe her contacts in New India provided them. As a rich and established group with a colorful culture they'd held on to for eons, the Sector 15 planets were strong enough to get away with some snubbing of the Overseer's drab example.

I put on the scrubs. They fit like a box, but at least they were almost long enough. My bare feet didn't bother me. The floors here were never cold.

"I'd better go," I said. "There's a massive price on my head."

"Wonderful." Surral sighed. "Let's check on Coltin first."

I followed her to Coltin's bed, a mix of hope and dread churning in my gut.

"It's working!" I whispered. I could tell. He had slightly more color, and his breathing was less labored.

I felt his forehead. Still hot—but I hadn't been expecting an instant miracle.

Relief settled my stomach but left a jangling impatience in its wake. I wanted him to be better now, *really* better, before I left. I wanted him to open his eyes, smile at me, and promise to be here the next time I came back.

I curled my hand against my middle to keep from selfishly waking him up.

Surral looked at him, and then all around her. "Great Powers, I can practically feel the life coming back into them."

She checked Coltin's vitals and wrote on his chart.

"Better." She looked over at me, beaming. "Everything's better, Tess."

I felt like crying again, but they would have been happy tears. I leaned down and lightly kissed Coltin's forehead.

"Should I wake him up?" Surral asked. "He'd want to see you."

"No. Let him heal." Rest was more important than a goodbye.

I wished I had something to leave with him, though. Coltin was the one who should have gotten my precious copy of *Tales from the Dark*. "Tell him I'll bring him a book next time. And to work on his math."

Surral chuckled. "Maybe coming from you, that'll work."

I figured he'd be charging around the Dark one day. I wanted him to know how to navigate.

Surral held out her hand, and I slipped mine into hers. She squeezed, and I thought it was a thank-you.

"To Mareeka," she said.

"To Mareeka," I echoed, and we left sick bay to the sound of the first groggy, weak child waking up.

She was asking for food, of course.

CHAPTER

25

"ANNALEE'S NOSE IS ON THE WRONG SIDE OF HER FACE."

Surral and I stopped, both of us turning to a boy with luminous ebony skin, an abundance of tight black curls, big nut-brown eyes, and what looked like a magician's wand in his hand. He was wearing a cape and seemed a little panicked.

"Hi, Tess," he added hastily.

I greeted him back. I'd seen him before, but he was a little young for me to know in particular, although he appeared to know me.

"Excuse me, Thomas?" Surral asked.

He shifted nervously, his eyes darting around so they wouldn't really land on either of us. "We were playing—running—and she tripped and hit the wall. She's crying, and her nose is on the wrong side of her face."

Shit. That sounded dire.

Surral kept her cool, as always. "Lead the way, then, Thomas."

He turned to go, but Surral stopped to give me a quick hug before leaving. "Stay safe. Send news when you can."

"I will." I squeezed her back. "Thank you."

"No, thank *you*. You did so much good here today."

"It wasn't only me. I wouldn't have had anything without my crew."

"Then thank them for me, too." Surral smiled softly in what looked like wonder. "The Mornavail... You can't imagine the questions going through my head right now."

"Believe me, I kind of can," I said.

She started to follow the boy, walking backward to still look at me. "Isn't it strange how you never seem to get sick?" She glanced at my arm. "And I know you didn't inject yourself."

I froze and stared, a surge of blood ratcheting up my pulse. How did she always know everything? It had always been like that. Was she some kind of psychic? Or was I just an open book?

Surral made a locking motion over her closed lips and then threw away the imaginary key. I trusted her with my life, but I also had no doubt that if there was any blood left over after the kids got what they needed to heal, she'd run every test imaginable on it. She could also take samples off my ruined suit—and would—if there was nothing uncontaminated to use instead. Would she find something that Fiona hadn't? Something that could be useful to me?

I'd find out on my next visit, I supposed—assuming I lived.

Surral turned and hurried after Thomas, who was already well ahead of her. I continued toward the office level alone, accepting hellos and giving them back until I'd cleared the residential floors. It was closing in on dinnertime, and there was no one left upstairs.

The cupola was empty and quiet and, to be honest, a little eerie without the usual administrative staff and workday noise.

Outside the windows was pure Dark, broken only by lone twinkles and the occasional cluster of stars. Sector 8 was pretty empty. There was hardly a habitable planet, and the orphanage orbited a barren moon in an equally barren and totally atmospherically challenged planetary system. It was a spacedock, like Flyhole, only without the brigands, extortion, and endless supply lines. Just like Flyhole, we were close enough to the system's star to draw power from it and have light, but not close enough to instantly fry under its harmful UV rays. Perfect—with the added help of the protective filters on every window. Right now, we were on the far side of the moon, though, and it was pitch-black outside.

When I turned down the final corridor to Mareeka's office, everything changed. Color blazed, and the crowning glory of Sector 8 came into view. The Rafini Nebula painted everything outside the long hallway in swirling sprays of purples, pinks, blues, and golds. It was massive and magnificent, and my breath caught, just as it always did.

There was something magical about the nebula, maybe even holy. It went beyond being a cloud of dust and gases. I couldn't get on board with the Sky Mother, but when I saw Rafini's sprawling burst of color spread out like an arm in space, its hand nearly cradling Starway 8, something washed up through me, a wondrous feeling I couldn't explain.

I shivered with it, but it was a warm shiver. It felt like hope.

My bare footsteps made almost no noise, but Mareeka still called out to me before I rounded her door. "Is that you, Tess?"

She got up from her desk when I entered the office, smiling at me.

I moved forward, inhaling the scent of something slightly cinnamony that Mareeka always kept in here. I didn't know what it was exactly, only that it was her scent, and that smelling it brought me home.

"Where's Surral?" she asked.

"She had to take care of a little girl named Annalee. Playing capes and wizards and running in the hallways seem to have led to a broken nose."

"Ah." She nodded. Just another day on Starway 8.

Luckily, that laser instrument in sick bay was a real-life magic wand. Annalee would probably be fine in time for dinner.

"I have a dilemma," I said immediately. We both knew I couldn't stay long.

"What is it?" Frowning, Mareeka crossed her arms and half sat on the edge of her desk, the nebula framing her in brilliant color through the window.

"I have in my possession something that could be considered a weapon. It could potentially turn a good fighter into a great one, a nearly indestructible one."

"Potentially?"

"That's the thing. I'm not really sure what it would do to a person, short term or long term. Think…enhancer."

Mareeka nodded, her expression turning contemplative and a little worried.

"My problem is this: do I turn it over to people who I think—*hope*—would use it to fight for things I would approve of, or do I destroy it, so that no one has it on either side?"

"Does the Dark Watch have this?"

I shook my head. "Not anymore. I don't think so." If they'd had more of the serum somewhere, I didn't think they would have been quite *that* desperate to get their lab back. A potential problem, though, was how many goons they'd *already* enhanced.

"So, you would be giving the rebels something that could possibly help them to gain the upper hand?"

Upper hand seemed like a bit of a stretch, but I nodded anyway. And it appeared we wouldn't be talking in euphemisms tonight. "But like I said, I don't know what it would do to a person. It could corrupt them—physically, mentally… I don't know."

"Do you believe the rebel leaders would impose this *enhancer* on their fighters?"

I shrugged. That was essentially my problem. "I don't know. I don't think I'd take issue with people deciding to try it on their own, but I would have a hard time living with knowing I'd provided something that got forced on anyone." And the rebel leaders were just as capable of fanaticism as anyone else. I didn't personally believe that the end justified any means. I wanted the same thing they did—the fall of the Overseer's imperial regime—but a pendulum that swung too hard one way could also swing too hard in the other direction. I wanted no part of that.

"Could you control the distribution?" she asked.

"If I take it to the leaders, they'll confiscate it. It's what I'd planned on doing, but now…I just have these doubts." I grimaced. "I'm not sure what to do."

"You have a good head on your shoulders and don't

take unnecessary risks—with yourself, or with others."
Mareeka's blue eyes were steady on mine. "Do you
believe this is a necessary risk?"

I wasn't sure what constituted necessary or unnecessary, but I thought Mareeka was probably giving me
too much credit. I could think of a few risks I regretted
deeply. One had sent Gabe and me running in opposite
directions. Another had gotten me a lab full of super
soldier serum and an enormous price on my head. The
latest had landed me in Shade Ganavan's bed.

I ignored the sudden, sharp twist in my chest and
thought about what she'd said. *Do you believe this is a
necessary risk?*

That was it; I couldn't decide. I'd given my blood to
the kids here because I knew it was pure, undiluted with
anything that could hurt them. I was healthy, and contrary
to what my father and his lab technicians had constantly
made me believe, I wasn't a freak of nature, or anything
truly alien. I was only slightly different. The enhancer,
though, was a possibly dangerous piece of chemical engineering made to stick to and mess with a person's insides.
Maybe the result would be good, fine. Maybe it wouldn't.

"I believe we're losing this fight," I answered. "I
believe this could make a difference."

"And what else do you believe?" she asked, clearly
sensing there was something I wasn't saying.

I hesitated and then coughed up the other fear that
was making this a very hard decision. "That suddenly
not losing could cause years of unparalleled bloodshed."

Mareeka uncrossed her arms, stood, and stepped
toward me. "What about winning?"

I scrubbed my hands over my face, wishing I could

wipe away the perpetually icky feeling I had about the serum. "I'm not sure winning is possible, even with this enhancer."

She put her hands on my shoulders and squeezed. "I've never told you what to do, Tess. You were always much too grown-up for that, even at eight years old."

"I know, but...what would *you* do?" I asked. "I'd like to know."

Her pause was very slight. "I would hand it over." She didn't offer a *why*, or any explanation to support her choice.

"But what if it drastically alters people? What if the war spirals out of control?"

"Right now, there technically is no war."

"Fine. What if the current *not*-war we're fighting spirals out of control?" I asked.

"There's always a turning point. And no war is won without sacrifice." She squeezed my shoulders again and then dropped her hands. "What if this is the turning point? Where would we be if no explorer had ever dipped his or her toes into the unknown?"

Probably extinct. On a dead planet. Because, well, nuclear holocaust.

"Make your position clear—that it should be volunteer-based. You are a leader in that world, Tess. You have influence."

I frowned. "I'm not. I'm nothing. I'm just a Nightchaser who runs supplies in and out."

Mareeka scoffed. "Stand tall and speak forcefully enough to be heard, and they will listen."

A hot, prickly feeling grew under my skin. What was she talking about?

"What makes Surral and me able to run this place without ever hitting a child, or even raising our voices?" she asked.

That was an easy answer for someone who'd spent ten years on Starway 8. "Because a disappointed side-eye from one of you is way worse than any lash from a whip."

"Says someone who's experienced the whip," Mareeka pointed out.

I nodded, wondering what she was getting at.

"As a leader, fear will only get you so far, and for so long. Never, in the long history of humanity, has tyranny not ended in revolt. The Overseer would destroy our books and burn our past to hide it, but the outcome is always the same. *Always*, Tess. Some wars lasted days, some centuries. Some spanned regions, others spanned worlds. There is an ebb and flow. Even if we win this day, for our lifetime and maybe beyond, tyranny will rise again. And then revolt. There will always be those who impose. And there will always be those who would die for the right to self-determination."

"It sounds hopeless," I said. "An endless cycle."

"A cycle in the long span of things, but you are alive now, and this is your time to influence events and outcomes."

The pressure suddenly felt heavy on my shoulders, and I hadn't even done anything yet.

"Respect is the key to leadership. You've shown it to others, and the inevitable reward is that you've gained it for yourself." Mareeka leveled her piercing blue eyes on me. "The day you decide to lift your voice, do not be surprised when people listen."

I almost physically recoiled at her implications, somehow mixing in an image of my father spewing his totalitarian crap onto screens across the galaxy. That would never be me, but when I spoke up publicly—*if* I spoke up—not everyone out there would agree with what *I* said, either. I would never expect that.

And part of me felt like I was just out of school, just out of Starway 8 and still muddling my way through the start of adulthood, even though eight years had passed. I didn't want that kind of responsibility. I had it on my own ship, and that was enough. Simply not getting caught or killed was a good day for me, for any rebel space rat. That same part of me wanted to pass off the serum. To get rid of the stuff and make it somebody else's decision.

"My fight is here," Mareeka said. "I might not take up arms myself, but don't think for a second I don't know how many of the children I raise end up in our *not*-war." Her expression didn't sadden at that, for those lost, or maybe lost, like Gabe. She looked like a general, her eyes on the future, her conviction strong. "My part is to show the difference, to demonstrate that the Overseer's way is not, in fact, the only path. Every child who comes through here can then choose what to do with that."

Mareeka was laying things out more plainly than she ever had before, at least in my presence. She wasn't telling me what to do, but she was letting me know that now was the time to step up my game if I wanted to.

"How has this place not gotten destroyed?" I asked. Not every kid reached their majority and went straight out in search of a rebel crew to join, but plenty of them did. And those who didn't... Well, they lived out their constricted lives, but they didn't betray the spirit of this place. Often, I wondered how that was possible, what kind of magic protected Starway 8 beyond loyalty, because even that sometimes wasn't enough.

Mareeka's mouth curved with a subtle smile. "Ask me that again someday. Right now, I fear the answer would betray a trust."

That was cryptic—and not at all what I'd expected. I'd expected her to roll her eyes and jokingly say, *The Sky Mother, of course*, because we both knew what that was worth. Now, I was dying to know what she was talking about, but I knew better than to push.

"Take this," she suddenly said, going over to a key-coded cabinet. She opened it and pulled out a Grayhawk handgun and ammunition clip. "Long story short, it was left here, and I don't want it on the premises."

I took the gun from her and locked in the ammo clip, making sure the safety was on before slipping it under my shirt and into the wide elastic waistband of my borrowed scrubs. The weapon felt cold against the small of my back.

"I'm worth two hundred million in universal currency because of the enhancer I took."

Mareeka paled, her eyes widening. It was no wonder; you could buy a small city on a decent rock for that.

"If anyone comes here looking for me, tell them I came to say goodbye." I thought about Shade Ganavan, money symbols lighting up his mercenary eyeballs. "You can tell them I blew myself up with the stolen goods right outside your window. I'm now one with the nebula." I glanced at the colors outside. That was exactly where I wanted to be when I died.

"You saw the whole thing," I added. "Saddest day of your life."

Mareeka's expression soured. "It certainly was."

I gave her a hug goodbye, refusing to acknowledge that it could be our last. Every departure was the same; we could only hope for a reunion.

"Stay safe." She hugged me back. "No sign of Gabe?" she asked, drawing away enough to look at me again.

It suddenly struck me as odd that everyone would still think I was pining for Gabe. Of course I cared what had happened to him, but it had been years...

I shook my head. "You, either, Surral said."

Mareeka smiled vaguely, seeming sad—mostly for me. "You two... When I think back."

We'd been in love. There was no doubt. My heart still sometimes gave a hard thump when I thought about him. Every now and then, I felt a phantom touch, a memory, and my belly clenched.

Unfortunately, that belly clench had shifted to Shade over the last week, but it was tainted now, a cramp more than a thing of warmth.

CHAPTER

26

I WAS FOUR LEVELS FROM THE *ENDEAVOR*'S DOCK WHEN I heard the firearm cock behind me. My steps slowed at the distinctive sound. Cautiously, I turned.

"I knew you'd come." Nathaniel Bridgebane's words came at me down the barrel of a gun.

My pulse jumped hard. My uncle stood not thirty feet from me. He'd always been tall and handsome, and he'd aged remarkably well. Too bad inside was so much uglier than outside. I remembered when the two parts of him had still matched.

I asked the only question that seemed important to me right now. "Did you infect children to draw me here?"

He didn't even flinch. "No, but I made sure no one came to help. I knew you'd do that yourself."

"How?" I didn't bother telling him that there had been deaths. He wouldn't care.

"Because you came back onto my radar for stealing what you thought were cure-all vaccines. That tells me public health means something to you, and you grew up here…" He shrugged, trailing off.

"Public health should mean something to you! To anyone!" I spat.

"I think I'm beyond that." He sounded toneless. Dead.

What an asshole.

"Put your hands behind your back where I can cuff them," he ordered. "Then turn into the wall and kneel."

Mareeka hadn't said anything about the security cameras coming back online yet. No one was seeing this and would come to my rescue. If Bridgebane had arrived in a discreet, small cruiser, there was a good chance no one even knew he was here. There were guards around, as usual, but they couldn't have eyes everywhere without the cameras. And with the sickness on Starway 8, the sentinels may have been fewer and less vigilant, thinking no one would want to come anywhere near the orphanage now anyway.

I slowly lowered my hands behind me, but I didn't turn. I drew the Grayhawk as fast as I could, cocking it as I leveled it at him.

He left his gun up, too. "And now we're at an impasse."

The problem was, he didn't sound like he meant it.

I tensed a split second before I felt the barrel of a gun press against my back, right between my shoulder blades.

"Easy does it, starshine."

Shade. My whole body clenched.

"Impeccable timing, as usual." My uncle's eyes flicked over my shoulder. "Although I'll have to decide if this technically counts as you bringing her in."

"Lay down your gun and do as the man says," Shade told me.

That sedative obviously hadn't knocked him out for long. Not long enough, anyway. "Fuck you, Ganavan."

"I think we already cov—"

"Shut up!" I snapped.

He did, thank the Powers.

I kept Bridgebane on the other end of my pointed gun. They would have to wrestle the Grayhawk from me.

"How did you even know I lived?" I asked.

"I had no idea what happened to you after you left Starway 8 for good. Not until you announced yourself in Sector 14 after your little heist."

Little heist? "So, I guess you didn't know about my fun stint on Hourglass Mile?" I sank a lot of bitterness into my voice, and to my satisfaction, I could tell my words had stung.

"No." Bridgebane's nostrils flared, but he didn't ask. He didn't ask about my partner, about the mines, about the whips, or about anything that might have happened to me there. "But I pieced that together from your false name."

"Well, aren't you clever. Good job." I ignored Shade and his gun at my back. My raised hand was steady, my weapon level. I felt surprisingly numb. "But that's not what I meant. I meant how did you know I'd survived the Black Widow?"

Behind me, Shade drew in a sharp breath.

"I had a rebel heading to death row on board *DW 12*. I gave him a choice: lethal injection, or the Black Widow in a small cruiser. If he somehow survived and reported back, he was free to go with the cruiser, and I gave my word to clear his name from the system. He chose the Widow. He survived."

"Where did he come out?" I asked.

"Seventeen."

So, the wormhole didn't only lead to Sector 2. I wondered how the Widow chose.

"Did you clear his name?"

Bridgebane's nod didn't surprise me. My knowledge was limited, but the only time I knew of that Nathaniel Bridgebane hadn't done exactly what he'd said he would was the day he brought me to Starway 8.

After all this, he probably wished he'd just offed me when I was a kid, like my father had ordered. "Too bad I didn't die, huh? Hourglass Mile? The Black Widow? Your bounty hunters? Sucks for you... Now you have to decide all over again."

"Quin, I've—"

"You've what?" I interrupted. "Turned into the biggest asshole in the universe?"

"You don't know it, but I—"

I wasn't listening to his crap. Not now. Not ever. "Or am I useful again now that I've destroyed your lab?" I asked.

"You destroyed it?" I think he paled.

Lying was surprisingly easy. I twisted the knife. "I blew that garbage up. *Boom!*"

He cursed. "That was the only thing keeping him from coming after you again," Bridgebane ground out in apparent disgust.

"He thinks I'm dead!"

"No!" His shout nearly blew me back. I might have moved—if not for the gun behind me. "Everything that's happened since Sector 14 is in his records. He *knows.*"

My breath choked off, strangled by the dread

clamping around my throat. I'd used my real name over the com. I'd been talking to Bridgebane, thinking I was about to die, but of course other people had heard me. He wouldn't have been alone on the bridge of that huge warship. But then with the Black Widow, the shock of not dying, the dangerous landing, the repairs, and Shade…I'd forgotten.

I squared my shoulders. I'd think about the Overseer later. Right now, I wanted answers from *Uncle Nate*.

"Did you know we could have saved her? Just a few drops. It's not as though there wasn't enough to spare."

A shadow flickered over his expression. "Lower your gun, and I'll lower mine."

"Well, that's a problem for me, since I have your goon at my back." I kept my arm up, even though the gun was getting heavy. "Now answer me. Did you know?"

"I wasn't there! I came back two days too late." Bridgebane's face twisted, suddenly reminding me of the man I used to know, the one with emotions and a heart. "Don't you remember? I didn't know. I wasn't there."

That was true. I did remember that. "And he didn't care?"

"Your mother was too hard to control." His eyes turned haunted. "Just like you are."

"You threw me to the wolves!" To my dismay, my voice nearly cracked.

"I gave you a life!" he countered.

"And your recent *dead-or-alive* bounty really helps with that," I snapped.

"I made it clear that *alive* was more profitable."

I scoffed. "Well, thanks, Uncle Nate. What a prince."

Suddenly, it *did* seem as though we were at an

impasse. Neither of us spoke. I stared, rage and hurt boiling inside me, anxiety making it all worse, and he stared back, his blue eyes like chips of ice and his mouth a hard line of tension.

After a charged moment, Shade filled our silence. "Uncle Nate? Quin... Tess..." He put it all together in an instant. "Quintessa Novalight? I don't fucking believe this!"

I snorted. "I guess you're not the only one with secrets, asshole."

I ducked, spinning as I elbowed him in the ribs. He turned with me, and my knee came up, hitting him hard in the groin. Shade bent in on himself with an explosive exhale. It wasn't the kick in the balls I'd promised myself, but it was close enough. I slammed the flat of my gun down on his skull with a satisfying crack.

"Fuck! Tess!" Shade stumbled back, shaking his head.

I wasn't anywhere near done. Fury fueled me, and I hauled off, kicking him hard in the gut. He reeled back into the wall, twisting and taking the blow on his arm instead of his back.

"Not the pack!" he wheezed with enough urgency to make me pause.

I kept my guard up. "Why? Got a bomb in there?" I geared up for another kick while his head was still ringing and I actually had a chance of doing some damage.

"Bonk," he said.

I pulled up short. "What?"

Bridgebane put his gun to my head. I stiffened. Either Shade had just screwed me over—again—or...

I didn't know what was going on.

Shade pushed off the wall and stood taller, his eyes darting from me to Bridgebane.

My uncle grabbed my arm and pulled me against him. "I have to produce something, Quin, or the Overseer will set the galaxy on fire trying to make more of what you took." His jaw tightened, visibly flexing. "I wanted to turn over the lab. Without it, I need you."

"Or him," I said through clenched teeth, the barrel cold against my temple. "Why doesn't he use himself? Or is he too much of a coward to get pricked and drained and have his insides stolen from him over and over? Clearly, I didn't get it from Mom, since she died from a fucking fever!"

"Because it's not him, either," Bridgebane said.

"What?" How could that be? Did the anomaly start with me? Then who were the Mornavail?

"I'll do what I can for you," Bridgebane said. "You don't seem to believe it, but I always have."

My bastard of an uncle glanced at Shade. "Cuff her, Ganavan."

Shade moved. He was going to do it, and my stomach hollowed. I'd almost thought for a moment... I swallowed. I'd hoped...

"I don't think so, boss." In the blink of an eye, Shade had his gun right in the center of Bridgebane's forehead.

I inhaled in disbelief. "Shade?"

"Baby, I only ever wanted you to get away safe." He didn't take his eyes off my uncle. "Now take your cat and go."

"Cat?" Bridgebane echoed. His face whitened, turning livid. "*Baby?*"

CHAPTER

27

WHILE BRIDGEBANE STOOD THERE WITH SHADE'S GUN to his head and looking like he'd just been hit by an asteroid, I raised my Grayhawk and hit him hard in the temple. He went down on one knee. My uncle groaned, clutching his head, and I grabbed Shade's hand and pulled.

Shade resisted, the idiot.

"Go!" he shouted, keeping his weapon pointed and cocked.

"You have Bonk!" And Shade had just defied a direct order and threatened a Dark Watch general and the Galactic Overseer's second-in-command with a lethal weapon. He was toast—unless he came with me.

Bridgebane staggered upright again. Neither Shade nor I shot him. I'm not sure why. Maybe we didn't have murder in our blood.

I added my gun to Shade's, keeping my uncle from raising his weapon, if he knew what was good for him. I didn't kill anyone if I could help it. In fact, I'd never killed anyone at all, but I had no problem shooting him somewhere that hurt.

"Where are your goons?" I asked, glancing quickly around.

"I don't bring the Dark Watch here," Bridgebane snapped. "Don't you know that by now?"

"Why?" I asked, an odd tingle creeping up the back of my skull. Did he have something to do with this place? With Mareeka being left in peace?

"We all choose our battles, Quin. Stop being so blind to everything but yourself."

I drew back as if struck. "I'm *selfish* because I don't want to be a lab rat?" I asked.

"You're selfish because you're capable of prolonging war until we're all dead!"

I gaped. "I'm just one person. And I didn't start any of this."

Bridgebane snaked his hand out fast enough to grab my weaponless arm. I yelped, and Shade leaned in, pressing the gun harder to my uncle's head. Bridgebane ignored him and pushed up my sleeve, baring the crook of my elbow where the skin still showed a small bruise and needle mark.

"See?" His eyes cut to mine with an almost frantic edge. "You even do it to yourself. Who will get your blood next, Quin? Where will it stop? When?"

Stepping back, I wrenched my arm from his grip. "I did it for the children! But you wouldn't understand protecting someone other than yourself."

He flinched. Ruthless, implacable Nathaniel Bridgebane flinched like I'd just slapped him across the face.

"I wasn't there." He went toneless again, his face turning blank. "I couldn't help Caitrin, and you and she didn't know what was in the blood."

I hadn't heard my mother's name spoken out loud in years. It ripped through me like a gunshot, leaving a hole in my chest.

"You'd already abandoned us." A tremor crept into my words, and my voice dropped. "Why? Why did you do that?"

Bridgebane ignored the guns between us and searched my face with his eyes. I could have sworn he was looking for something. Maybe understanding, or even forgiveness. "Because I couldn't help you—either of you—and I couldn't stay there and watch."

My heart ached, torn between hate and something I didn't understand, couldn't process. "So you joined the forces of evil?"

"Evil is a perspective, Quin."

"Evil is evil!"

"I did what I could."

He kept saying that, but I didn't believe him. He was from Sector 17. He knew their plight. He'd lived through the destruction. His stepsister had ended up the spoils of war—or a bridge to peace, as the conquering Overseer had liked to put it—and Nate had followed her.

"Mom sucked it up and married that toad." The Overseer had wanted her, and she'd wanted peace. It had been an attempt to heal the galaxy after my father had shown what out-weaponing everyone in all the worlds could do. "The least you could have done was stick by her instead of buying into Dad's crap."

"I. Did. What. I. Could," my uncle grated out, his teeth and jaw not even moving.

"You said you'd kill me!" I yelled, years of anger and betrayal pouring out. "When you brought me here, you said you'd kill me if I ever used my real name or showed myself again."

Bridgebane kept staring at me, searching, something weird and unsettling in his eyes. "I put the fear of the Powers into you so you'd *hide*! And it worked—until you got stupid and stole the lab and then announced yourself over the com into *DW 12*. Why did you do that?"

"I thought I was going to die! I didn't care what I said." Although the sinking sensation inside me told me I cared a lot now that my father knew I wasn't dead. My uncle had a point: handing over the lab would have made the Overseer at least think twice about going on a public, hard-to-explain daughter hunt. Without the lab to give him what he wanted, he'd come after me with everything he had.

"That serum is not worth your life!" Bridgebane shouted. "An unwinnable fight is not worth your life!"

He wanted to protect me? But he'd said he'd bring me in. Without the lab, it was me. He needed to provide something…or the Overseer would go on a rampage to find more type A1 blood. And the Overseer on a rampage was a terrifying thought.

I didn't want to feel anything but hatred for my uncle. I'd loved him once, but he'd ruined that. Now I was confused—about so much.

"You shot my ship!" I accused.

"I tried to disable you! You were about to jump into the Widow!"

"If you take me in, to *him*, what kind of life do I have?" I asked.

"An *alive* one," he ground out.

"No one's taking her anywhere," Shade cut in. His eyes darted to me, a quick flash of brown. "Would you fucking run already?"

Bridgebane suddenly raised his gun again. He turned it on his own head, and my reaction was visceral. Immediate. Horror blasted through me, and a hot flare of adrenaline burned in my veins.

"Would this make you feel better?" He stared straight at me, his finger pulsing on the trigger. "Would Caitrin forgive me then?"

"No!" I reached for him. At the same time, Shade gave me a hard shove back.

"Go!" Shade barked.

I stumbled back. "Uncle Nate?"

He kept staring at me, the veins in his hand turning thick and bulging, his gun smashing his dark hair against the side of his head just where some streaks of gray were starting to show up.

Backing away from him, I lowered my weapon and stuffed it into the waistband of my pants. I had no idea what had happened to this man, why he'd become Bridgebane to me and to everyone else, but I remembered when he'd held me on his lap and played with me. He'd looked like he loved me then. Right now, he kind of looked the same.

Tears stung my eyes. "Don't. That won't earn my forgiveness. Or Mom's." I stopped backing up. "I want you to fight. Stand up and fight!"

He shook his head. "It's too late for that, monkey."

A spasm ripped through my heart. I used to climb all over him. He was big and strong, and I'd been small once upon a time. He'd let me use him like a tree and even found me a book about these extinct furry animals and called me monkey.

I swallowed hard.

He lowered the gun from his temple. "Don't single-handedly ruin what your mother sacrificed herself for."

"Peace?" A chill swept down my spine. "What peace do we have?"

"Have the Outer Zones been annihilated? Has another planet been destroyed? Has your beloved Starway 8 been nuked with everyone inside?"

I drew in a sharp breath, my eyes widening.

"It's give and take, Quin. Choose your battles, or it's all-out war."

I started stumbling back again. "I've chosen mine."

"He'll never let it go!" my uncle bellowed. "You're damning us both. You're making the wrong choice!"

"No! You chose wrong!" I thought Mom had, too. But if she hadn't, would the Outer Zones still have existed today? I wouldn't have existed, but I wouldn't have cared if I hadn't been born in the first place.

Shade's athletic tread raced after me, catching up. I turned the corner, and the first shot rang out.

I skidded to a halt, turning. Shade popped into sight, his body twisting around to return fire. He aimed low. He wasn't shooting to kill. If he had been, I don't think he would have missed.

"Go! Go!" Never stopping, Shade pushed me ahead of him. "He doesn't want to kill you. No problem killing me, though."

We ran, and my uncle stalked after us. The corridor was long but thankfully empty because of the dinner hour. Bridgebane fired, countable seconds between each shot. He wasn't letting off indiscriminate rounds; he was aiming at Shade only.

Shade turned to fire back, keeping me behind him. He grunted, and his steps faltered.

"Where are you hit?" I cried.

"Thigh."

I got under Shade's arm and helped him. Damn, he was heavy. He took most of his own weight back and limped forward. I tried to shield him this time.

"Quin!" My uncle's voice boomed down the hallway. "Don't leave with that man. You have no idea what he's capable of."

"Coming from you, it must be dire," I shouted back.

We needed a shortcut to the *Endeavor*'s dock before Bridgebane caught up to us. I grabbed Shade's gun and shot at my uncle. Bullets pinged around his feet and stuck in the impact-absorbent walls. I looked for a ventilation shaft with a blue keypad on it. Red led up. We needed down, and we needed it fast.

"Come back, or I'll have to find someone else just like you," Bridgebane threatened. "How do you feel about that? The testing? The searching? Maybe I'll test every single kid in this place. How would you like that?"

My stomach clenched at the thought.

Another shot rang out. Shade and I ducked, hurrying our labored steps.

"Come back, Quin. Hand over the bounty hunter, come with me, and I'll tell you everything."

I paused in my steps. What more was there? What did he know that I didn't?

"Seriously?" Shade took his gun back and hammered off a few shots to slow down my uncle and keep him at a distance before pushing me along again. "You're crap in a fight. We really have to work on this."

"I took you down." I angled myself to protect him and had to admit that it was a good thing for both of us that my uncle didn't want me dead.

"I wasn't trying," he said. "And I was worried about Bonk."

The ice in my heart melted a little too much, and a little too fast. It hurt.

"Is he okay?" I asked, anxious. "I don't hear him."

Boom! Bridgebane let off a shot, and I jumped.

Boom! Boom! Shade fired back, pushing us up against the wall.

"He's sedated. I didn't want the bag to freak him out."

The bag was mesh on both sides. Ventilation. I looked up at Shade with wide eyes.

"Come on!" He pulled me forward. "How the hell have you survived so far? Or on the fucking Mile?" he ground out.

"I'm not useless." I was working on getting us out of here, although I wasn't nearly as panicked since discovering that Shade wasn't my enemy, and that my uncle would rather shoot himself than shoot me.

Maybe I was still in shock over both those things.

Shade growled something foul when I stopped again. Ignoring his protest and my uncle's approaching steps, I reached for the blue keypad on the ventilation access panel next to us. I'd created a system-wide code about ten years ago and secretly programmed it to *forever* status—Queen Bee was the password. The overlying code could have changed a hundred times since then, but the lock would still remember me.

"Shortcut," I told Shade as I quickly punched in the numbers corresponding to my permanent password. I stayed in front of him, so my uncle wouldn't shoot. The corridors were monstrously long, the elevators were far away, and Bridgebane would be relentless if he thought he could still catch me without hurting me.

The door to the ventilation shaft swung open. "See? Skills. And on the Mile, I had Jax."

"I'll shoot him in the head, Quin." My uncle was practically on top of us, his gun raised, his finger on the trigger, and Shade in his sights. He'd made up some serious ground the second we stopped shooting to keep him back.

My heart pounding, I covered Shade as he dove into the crawl space, leaving blood on the rim of the panel.

Bridgebane looked livid, but he didn't shoot. He did start to run, his free hand lifting to grab me.

I dove in after Shade, turned, and slammed the door shut, nearly catching Bridgebane's fingers in the crack.

My uncle roared.

I roared back. "See you in hell, Uncle Nate!"

"Quin!" He beat what must have been the butt of his gun against the ventilation shaft door.

To the *thud, thud, thud*, I followed Shade as he started to crawl.

"You've left me no choice," Bridgebane bellowed. "I'll take one. You choose. Mareeka or Surral."

I froze, icing over. Shade stopped with me, turning back.

I suddenly felt light, but that was just the effect of my blood pressure dropping like a stone.

Fighting dizziness, I spoke over my shoulder, spoke toward the door. "No, please don't," I begged.

"I can save you from him," Bridgebane said, his voice tinny through the wall, "but you have to give me something to go on. My position is not a given. If I go, I can't protect you—or Starway 8."

My stomach roiled. I always knew I would do whatever I had to for this place. My whole life was tied up in it. My past. My present. My future. There was nothing that mattered to me more.

"Mareeka or Surral," he repeated. "Who can the orphanage live without?"

Neither. They were the heart and soul of Starway 8.

Tears welled in my eyes, and I screamed, slamming my fist against the tunnel wall.

Shade spun fully around in the tight space and took my face in his hands. I saw the fear in his eyes, illuminated by the low light that ran along the metal shaft.

He shook his head. "No. No, baby. You stay with me."

My breathing turned fast and pounding.

"Just give him some blood," Shade said, still holding my head. "That's what he wants, right?"

I nodded, swallowing hard.

"Blood exchange," Shade called through the wall. "Ten days from now at the Grand Temple on Reaginine. No goons. Six bags of her blood, and you leave the women here alone."

Shade had taken over the negotiation, but he still looked at me for confirmation. It was my blood, after all.

I nodded. What else could I do?

But the Overseer had the formula. He would make the enhancer again.

But now…we had it, too.

A clash of monsters rang before my eyes. The spray of blood I saw in the future sickened me.

"They'll be unstoppable," I whispered. "They have this formula… It makes this super soldier stuff."

Shade swept his thumbs over my cheekbones. His eyes searched mine. "But if they don't have you, can't you make your side unstoppable, too?"

"But what does the wrath of two unstoppable forces make?"

Even in the shadows of the ventilation shaft, I saw the grimness that came over his features. "I guess we'll find out." He turned again. "And I think I just joined the fight."

"Be there, Quin," Bridgebane ordered. "Or I come back here, and one of them goes to Hourglass Mile."

"I'll be there," I growled loudly. After I delivered the enhancer to the rebel leaders. My uncle had just forced my decision. I couldn't destroy the rebellion's chance of making super soldiers while handing over that same weapon to the Overseer.

"And Ganavan! I'm transferring her price to your head. Don't get too attached, Quin. He won't be around for long. And the bounty hunter had better keep his hands to himself!"

I snorted. As if that man had the right to… What? Parent me?

Bridgebane shot at the door. The bullets didn't come through, of course, or even ricochet off. They stuck, because we had really cool walls.

CHAPTER

28

"NOT THAT WAY!" I CRIED WHEN SHADE TOOK MY three-second breather as incentive to strike out first again. He pitched forward and started sliding down a near-vertical shaft.

I grabbed his ankle with both hands and tried to gain traction with my bare feet. His weight dragged us both down. He slipped fully over the edge, and so did my head. A huge fan spun below.

"The sides!" I yelled frantically. "Spread out your arms. There are indents."

Shade spread his arms wide and his fingers found the hollows. They were barely there and hardly visible, but there was enough contour to sink his palms into and stop his fall. I pulled on his leg, and he climbed with his arms, indent after indent. His shoulder muscles bunched, and his triceps bulged under his shirt, standing out from the effort.

Once his hips cleared the edge, he wiggled back, and we flopped down together in the mostly level tunnel, both of us breathing hard.

"Who the fuck builds a shaft like that?" Seeming incensed, Shade adjusted a still-sleeping Bonk. "There are kids in this place."

The depressions along the sides of the steep shaft were a half-assed safety feature for whoever was in a harness every year or so doing maintenance on the fan. The slippery drop over the edge was designed to fool intruders. It didn't seem so steep or different at first, and then, *bam!* You were falling.

"It's a booby trap," I explained, my heart still racing to a panicked beat.

"A booby trap?" Shade echoed, scowling.

"Starway 8 is equipped for war, prepared for just about anything. Except for during those few hours every now and then when the security cameras are undergoing maintenance—like right now," I said a little sourly.

"I wondered why no one questioned me on the docks." Shade snorted softly. "Great timing."

I shrugged. I knew Mareeka well enough to guess at her reasoning. "I only let them know we were arriving five minutes before we got here. They didn't know when we'd come, or even *if* we'd come, and they didn't realize I could be bringing this much trouble with me. Honestly, if it's necessary to take security off-line, what better time to do it than when the news has spread about an awful virus?"

Shade nodded. "It got me to you, so I'm not complaining."

I frowned. "How did you find me? This place is huge."

"Bridgebane *used* to like me. In his way, at least. He sent me his personal com signal the second he located you on Starway 8, hoping for backup." Something rather devilish crept into his expression, despite the strain of worry and injury. "All I had to do was follow it around a few corners before I came up behind you."

"He didn't even look surprised to see you so fast."

"He knows I'm good."

I huffed. "And insanely arrogant."

"Hardly, sugar." He winced, straightening out his wounded leg. "Just telling the truth. Now tell me more about this 'equipped for war' while I bandage my thigh."

"With what?" I asked.

Shade ripped an entire sleeve off his shirt, sat up as best he could in the tunnel, and started to wrap his leg. I moved to help him, and our fingers tangled, reminding me of other times we'd been tangled up together.

Unsettled, I drew back, and he tied off the knot.

"Nothing terrible has ever happened here," I admitted. "But the orphanage is prepared for an invasion, an attack, whatever. Bullets don't ricochet; it would take very heavy weapons to blow a hole in the wall; the entire place is a grid of fifty-meter zones with airtight safety doors that close automatically in case of depressurization. Stuff like that."

We both lay back down rather than sit hunched over while we finished catching our breath. I reached out and touched the furry curve of Bonk's back through the side mesh of Shade's tightly strapped-on pack. Bonk didn't stir, but I felt his little body move as he steadily drew in air.

"Like my uncle said, you'd have to nuke it to destroy it."

Shade gazed at me. "Impressive. Sounds expensive."

I shrugged. "Having a near monopoly on honey

helps." Currency didn't buy medicine, though. It was where you lived and who you knew that counted for that.

"I hope kids don't crawl around in these tunnels," he said.

I'd probably spent a collective two months of my life in these tunnels—at least. "We do evac drills to the pod docks using the ventilation shafts."

Shade looked incredulous. "You can't just take the stairs?"

"What if there's a fire? Or a depressurized zone cutting off a level? Or someone's pumped noxious gas into the residential areas? You never know." We were ready, because we took risks here. Not physical, but intellectual. Emotional. The thousands of children who grew up here were the seeds to every plant the Overseer didn't want blossoming in his galaxy. So far, we'd stayed beneath his notice, germinating far and wide but without him grasping the connection. Partly, it seemed, thanks to Nathaniel Bridgebane.

"That's why it's always lighted through the ventilation system, even though it's a power drain," I added.

"Those vertical shafts are dangerous," he insisted.

"Everyone knows not to take a tunnel if it smells like rose. Even a two-year-old would have avoided it."

Shade hmphed. "I've never smelled a rose."

"Well, sniff, learn it, and steer clear," I said.

Shade inhaled through his nose. "Subtle. I'd hardly noticed it before. Smells good."

I nodded. It did. "There's a scent diffuser on the giant turbine ready to cut you to shreds."

Cautiously, Shade lightly brushed a hand down my arm. "Thanks, starshine."

I nodded, warmth licking through my belly.

"What are you wearing?" he asked, his brow creasing as he plucked at my shirt.

"Surral's scrubs. She had to cut off my spacewalk undersuit to get at the bullet wound."

Shade's hand stopped moving on my arm. He stared at me. "You're scaring the shit out of me right now. When did you get shot?"

"On the Squirrel Tree. Big man? Gun? Remember?"

"I remember," he muttered. "I just didn't know you got hit."

"It wasn't that bad."

"So you decided to go on a spacewalk?"

"Well, someone had to get all those bugs off my ship before we left Sector 2." I didn't bother to curb the bite in my voice.

Shade had the decency to look guilty. "How many were there?" he asked.

"I found three."

"Only one was mine."

"Then it's a good thing I dumped them," I said.

"Did they track you?"

I nodded.

"But you got away?"

"Clearly." I was here, wasn't I?

"Do I want to hear about this?" he asked, sounding wary.

"Probably not." But it warmed me that he cared.

"I'll ask later." Shade's hand swept up my arm again and over my pink shoulder, the tips of his fingers teasing my neck. "Right now, I'm just glad you're okay. And you look good enough to eat."

I grimaced. "I look like candy."

He smiled. "Like I said, good enough to eat."

Before I even knew I was doing it, I smiled back. The heat in his honey-brown eyes made my belly flip.

I shivered when his fingertips skated over my collarbone. "How's your leg?" I asked.

"Hurts like a bitch," he answered. "And you pulling on it didn't help."

My eyebrows shot up. "Should I have dropped you?"

"Maybe," he said a little wryly. "I'm not sure I'd have blamed you."

The warmth I'd been feeling turned into something hot and unpleasant. "Why didn't you tell me the truth?"

Shade took a moment to answer. "Because my head really wanted two hundred million in universal currency, even if the rest of me didn't agree."

Something twisted in my chest. Painfully. "When did you decide?" Or even…had he?

He leaned forward and very slowly, very carefully, gently kissed my lips. "I would never have slept with you and then turned you in."

I didn't kiss him back. I couldn't yet. "I'm not ready to forgive you."

"I know." His eyes were steady on mine, his expression open. "Just give me a chance to earn back your trust. Please."

Bringing Bonk to me was certainly a start.

"You were protecting me on the dock, weren't you? On the Squirrel Tree? You were keeping that bounty hunter from shooting me." I hadn't been able to see it then, hadn't wanted to. The scene looked different to me now.

His open expression hardened into something angry and dark. "He got you, though. I'm sorry I didn't do better."

"He didn't get me until I ran."

"He shouldn't have gotten you at all."

"And I shouldn't have left you there." Not when I'd seen Shade reeling from the tranquilizer that woman had fired off.

He shrugged. "You didn't do anything wrong."

Not sure I agreed with that, I turned and led the way toward the shipping docks. "We've rested long enough. Come on," I said over my shoulder. "Before you bleed to death."

"It's not as bad as all that." Shade still groaned when he got up onto all fours and started moving. He'd already been going more slowly before falling over the Rose Drop, and his lips had seemed cool when they'd touched mine a moment ago. I hoped the pause had done him good, but we needed to keep moving.

"You want me to take Bonk?" I asked, glancing back at him.

He shook his head. "I'm fine."

Right. That was why he'd just flinched.

Instead of continuing all the way down to the docks in the ventilation shafts, I got us out at the next possible exit and helped Shade limp toward the cargo lifts. We had no reason to hide anymore. Bridgebane was gone— assuming he was sticking to our deal, which I believed he would. He was an asshole, but he was an asshole who kept his word.

"Hard to believe, but crawling was easier," Shade muttered under his breath.

"Almost there." I gave his abdomen a reassuring pat,

keeping my other arm around his waist. "If you want, you can still crawl."

He gave me a look that spoke volumes—volumes of *no thanks*.

Even though there was a railing inside the elevator, Shade kept me against his side and his arm across my shoulders in the lift. We exited at the cargo docks.

Across the platform, the *Endeavor* waited with her door open for us. The Dark beckoned beyond, a transparent plasma shield keeping the area pressurized.

"Is Jax going to beat me up?" Shade asked.

My lips twitched. "Possibly."

"Something to look forward to," Shade said.

"Stick around and maybe I'll lick your wounds."

Shade groaned a little, part pain, and part something else. I hadn't said that with any ulterior meaning, but I realized the train of his thoughts when he looked at me with molten eyes. I blushed, my insides going all fluttery and hot.

The *Endeavor*'s stairs were down since Miko and Shiori had been out dealing with the numbers. We climbed them, Shade's steps dragging as we headed up and inside.

"Jax?" I called out, surprised he wasn't waiting for me at the door. Everything seemed strangely quiet, even though the ship was powered up and ready to go. "Fiona?"

Some sixth sense made my heart start to pound. Dread was an actual taste in my mouth, and I swallowed it down, letting go of Shade as I sprinted toward the bridge.

"Miko! Shiori!" I screamed.

No one answered. A cold sweat broke out on my skin. Something was terribly wrong.

CHAPTER

29

"TESS! RUN!" JAX'S BELLOW REACHED ME AS I barreled down the corridor.

I gripped the edge of the open door and swung myself at full throttle onto the bridge. *Oh fuck!*

"Dad?" I froze solid. The Galactic Overseer was on my ship. He had one heavy arm around Miko's chest and a Grayhawk to her head.

Fear erupted inside me. I'd watched my father on screens, but nothing had prepared me for seeing him again in person. Or for seeing that sneer I remembered. He seemed to reserve it especially for me. Others would call his face impassive.

Quickly, I took in the rest of him. Brown uniform, brown hair, brown eyes. Medium-tall. Nothing about him stood out until he opened his mouth and managed to convey such dogmatic fervency that people stopped and listened. They *followed*.

"According to my tracker, Nathaniel just left. Yet here you are. I'm discovering that he's disturbingly inefficient when it comes to you."

Holy Sky Mother. I shook and shook and shook.

Shade came up at my back. He felt warm again—maybe because I'd turned to ice.

"I don't have what you want," I lied. There was a chance he hadn't seen the lab if he hadn't walked around the ship, or that he didn't even know what it looked like. From the outside, it was just a hulking cargo space, and the *Endeavor* was a cargo cruiser. It fit.

"Then you'll provide it again. It's as simple as that."

I darted panicked looks around the bridge. Jax and Fiona were on my left, a few feet from each other. My father and Miko stood right in front of me, near my console. Shiori stayed close to Miko, silent and petrified. Miko was her life and breath.

I didn't think anyone was armed. Only Shade and I were.

And Dad.

His finger was steady on the trigger, and I knew the cold-hearted bastard would pull it unless I gave him what he wanted. Actually, I was terrified he'd pull it anyway.

Miko's small nose flared on sharp breaths.

I held up my hands. "Let her go, and I'll come."

Fiona shouted first. "No, Tess!"

The Overseer whipped his gun toward her and shot.

I screamed. Jax howled in anguish. Fiona flew back against the wall with a crash.

Dad pointed his gun at Miko again. The whole thing took three seconds, if that. I ran toward Fiona.

"Don't move!" the Overseer barked, squeezing Miko until she yipped.

I screeched to a stop, lifting both hands back up. Jax crouched next to Fiona, his face washed of all color and his big hands pressing hard against her shoulder. Blood flowed through his fingers, and Fiona panted, her chest heaving. She clamped her eyes shut but then opened them again, as if she couldn't bear not to see. She was looking at Jax. He looked back before turning his horrified gaze to me.

I faced my father. He was an expert marksman, a military man from the start, but he hadn't taken the time to aim. If he had, Fiona would be dead, a bullet right between the eyes. I'd seen him do it before, to people who worked for him, to people I'd known. I'd seen him just pull out a gun and shoot. Not even out of rage, or in distress, or in defense. Simply, *I'm done with you—boom*.

"I'll back out of the ship," I said, my voice echoing inside me as if coming from far away.

I glanced at Miko. I could hardly hear her terrorized breathing over my own pounding blood. Miko. My Miko had already been through too much.

"Just follow me out," I said, "and leave everyone else alone."

I bumped into Shade as I stepped back. His arm brushed my shoulder as he leveled his gun on my father.

"Drop it," Shade said.

The Overseer jerked Miko more firmly in front of him. Miko cried out, and Shiori bleated an awful, animal sound.

"No! Grandmother, get back!" Miko's pleas went unheeded as Shiori moved, not needing sight to know she was in front of Miko, whose frightened breaths sawed in and out.

Slowly, I turned my head enough to address Shade,

my father still in my peripheral vision. "There are some things I won't ever forgive."

The line of Shade's jaw hardened. "You're my priority."

"I will be nothing to you, *ever*, if he kills someone here because of you."

Shade must have believed me, because after a moment, he lowered his gun to the floor.

"Kick it to the side," the Overseer ordered, nodding toward the empty, right-hand side of the bridge.

Shade kicked the gun, and it slid away, landing in the shadows under Jax's console.

"Why do you need me?" I asked my father, backing up another step to try to coax him off the bridge. I knew what my uncle had said, but I didn't believe I was the origin of type A1 blood. Maybe the Overseer had convinced Bridgebane that he didn't carry it, but I thought he did.

"Why can't you just take what you want from yourself? We both know I didn't get it from Mom. It has to be you. You've got it, too. You've got your own supply of freakish blood."

He laughed a little, the sound dreadful and dark. "You're not mine."

I stared, not understanding. "Not yours?"

"Did you think that when anomalies were found, I wouldn't test? You're not mine, and Caitrin was a lying bitch."

I went cold, then nuclear hot. Relief couldn't happen, considering the situation, but his angry words blew through me like a bomb that leveled all things past.

I looked him right in the eyes, over Miko's head, with her thick black hair catching on the stiff collar of his uniform as she shuddered in fright. "I am so fucking thankful that I'm not yours. That's the best news I've had in my entire life."

The Overseer's expression hardened—a true feat for a man who already had such a stony face.

"No wonder you always hated me," I said, "and treated Mom like crap."

"If I'd known Nathaniel wasn't going to kill you, I'd have done it myself."

"And lose your supplier?" I asked.

"I had enough. You saw what I'd accomplished—when you stole it."

"Who's my father?" I asked.

"I have no idea. Your mother wouldn't tell me, even when I infected her with a fatal disease and held the cure over her head."

All my systems shut down in shock. I couldn't breathe. My vision wavered. My heart stopped beating in my chest. When everything started again, it was with a sickening rush.

"You're a bigger bastard than I ever thought," Shade said. "And my opinion was damn low to begin with."

"I don't know who you are," the Overseer shot back, "but I never forget a face."

"Remember mine, then. Because I'm coming for you," Shade said.

The Overseer brushed that off. He had death threats every day, sometimes more than once. Thinking he was omnipotent helped.

"Attractive, this one," he said, inhaling against the top of Miko's head. "Seems docile enough. I could probably grow you a new hand, my dear, and maybe it's time I shopped for another rebel wife."

Shopping was exactly what he'd done with Mom. Seen. Wanted. Bought—her price being the end of the annihilation of the Outer Zones. He must have loved her in his way, since he'd been willing to bargain. I didn't think she'd ever loved him, but maybe she'd acted out her role convincingly for the good of millions, and especially her home Sector. In any case, she'd kept her word and gone with him, and he'd kept his. He'd finally offered terms to Sectors 17 and 18 instead of sending more explosives. Almost like a bridal gift, their wedding day had been the end of the war.

It would almost have been a romantic tale, if he hadn't been such a narrow-minded tyrant.

I knew the Overseer didn't want a new wife or care what Miko looked like. He wanted to control me and knew that taking Miko meant leverage.

"You don't want her." I took another step back, moving Shade with me and trying to keep the Overseer from even looking at Fiona and Jax again. "Take me instead."

"Yes, you're coming, too, Quintessa." He started pushing Miko forward, plowing Shiori along in front. "I'm sure I'll find uses for you both."

Miko's eyes flared with panic. She'd already been used for sex, and that was what he was implying. But he thought she was docile, which she wasn't—not when trapped.

My heart lurched as I read the transition on her face. Fear eclipsed by wrath. Caution replaced by *No!*

She started fighting. It was wild and powerful and lasted about four seconds before he shot her in the head.

I gasped. Shiori screamed. Miko dropped. Dead.

"Miko!" I lunged forward, but Shade jerked me

back. My back slammed into his chest, and he held me there, his grip too tight for me to break.

My heart pounded in broken beats as I struggled a hand between our bodies and drew my gun. I pointed the quaking barrel at the man who had taken so much from so many. So much from *me*.

He grabbed Shiori as his new shield, and I couldn't shoot.

"Drop it," he said.

"No." I cocked my weapon, and the action steadied my hand.

"Then all three of us walk," the Overseer announced.

He moved to the right, and Shade and I moved left, leaving him room to exit. He backed off the bridge, dragging a comatose-looking Shiori with him. She wasn't crying. She didn't say anything. She looked dead. Upright, but dead, and my heart shattered even more at the sight.

For every step the Overseer backed up, watching me, his gun to Shiori's head, I took a step forward, Shade at my back. Vaguely, I realized how hard I was breathing. But panting was the only thing keeping me from totally losing it, so I just kept wheezing, my breath like a hurricane in my throat.

I glanced back only once, drinking in my last sight of Jax and Fiona. "Stay with Fiona," I told him. She was somehow still conscious, but that was Fiona—tough as nails. "When I'm gone, call Surral."

"Don't go with that man!" Jax pleaded.

"Goodbye, partner." This was the end of everything. I wished the Widow had taken us. Then we'd have all gone together. Our choice.

"Tess…" His voice cracked.

"Save her, Jax," I begged. "*Live*."

His face twisted. It broke. He broke, just like I did.

"Jaxon," Fiona called weakly.

I wouldn't let her slip away when there was still time to save her. I turned and left, walking out on Jax, because that was what I had to do—for him, for Fiona, and for Shiori. Jax and Fiona would be all that was left of us. Maybe they'd start a new family on the *Endeavor*. She was a good ship, meant to be a home.

I walked as if in a trance, raw and aching from the pain and shock of sudden loss. I stepped off the ship and moved across the platform toward a smaller craft in the next bay over, following the man who wasn't actually my father. He never took his eyes off me—or his gun off Shiori's head.

The Overseer climbed the ramp onto his cruiser, dragging a limp Shiori as protection against the Grayhawk I still had pointed at him. He held her in the doorway, facing me.

"Get on," he snarled. "And drop the gun."

"You drop yours," I answered tonelessly.

"Drop the gun, girl, or I'll shoot her in the head."

I threw the gun away from me.

Still behind me, Shade cursed. I wanted to say goodbye to him, to say something, but what was the point? I thought he knew I didn't hate him anymore, that maybe I never really had, and that maybe I'd had hope for us only a few minutes ago.

Shade and Bonk and me in the tunnels. It had felt like a new beginning.

A burning fist gripped my heart and tore. I couldn't

look at Shade. Looking at him would only make things worse.

I continued toward the Overseer's ship, barefoot, unarmed, and a blast of color I hoped would sear that drab-loving bastard's eyes. Life, for however long it lasted, would really suck from now on. I was glad I'd had that night with Shade.

Shots rang out from behind me on my right. The Overseer darted to the side as half a dozen goons jumped out of his cruiser to defend him. They returned fire, some of them falling, while the Overseer scrambled for cover, a look of pure shock and rage on his face.

I scooted to the left, away from the line of fire, and turned to see what had made a hint of fear splash across the Overseer's expression.

Big Guy stalked forward, picking off the goons with perfect aim and avoiding their shots with a slippery kind of swiftness that defied my vision. His terrifying focus never left the Overseer.

Shade dove for my gun. He slid onto his side as he grabbed it and picked off two of the goons from the floor of the dock.

"Novalight," Big Guy growled. With no more soldiers between them now, Big Guy started running for the Overseer, his inhuman speed eating up the space between them in great, angry gulps. He let out a beast-like bellow.

Panic flashed in the Overseer's eyes. He punched his hand down on the door control and then backed away from the huge man racing toward him like a deadly black torpedo. The ramp retracted fast, and Shiori's shock-blank face suddenly took on life again right before the armored door whooshed shut.

"Don't come for me!" she cried. "I forbid it!"

The sliding panels latched together in the middle mere seconds before Big Guy slammed into the closed door with a snarl. The engine fired up, and a thump of heat drove me back a step and made Big Guy throw himself away from the cruiser. A moment later, the ship took off. As soon as it cleared the dock, the cruiser leaped into warp speed and disappeared from sight, taking Shiori from us.

I stared after it, heartsick. How could this have happened?

Big Guy turned to Shade and me. He'd shaved off his beard. He'd also shaved his head. He still looked furious, though not at us.

"You're back." My whole body went heavy and weak, as if I could finally just stop for a moment. Stop and rest.

Big Guy holstered his gun. "Thought I'd help out."

"But...how?" Actually, I didn't care about the answer right now. I was just glad he was here.

Shade hauled himself up and limped toward me. He slid his hands into my hair, cradling my head, and kissed me full on the mouth. Then he wrapped his arms around me and pulled me in close. His heart pounded against mine, and I stood there, absorbing his comfort and warmth, too devastated to do anything else.

When he let go of me, sweat dotted his brow. His mouth was a line of pain, and his pallor was suddenly so evident, even under his suntanned skin, that anxiety twisted through me like a lightning snap. The fog pressing in on me disappeared, and my senses roared back online, all of them flashing code red. Shade and Fiona needed help.

"Come on, Shade. Let's go sit."

He managed a few steps, but it looked as though the adrenaline and fear keeping him going until now had just fizzled out. I tried to steady him, but he sagged too much, and his weight dragged us both down.

"Shade?" I struggled to keep him on his feet.

"Just need to rest," he said.

Big Guy swooped in and heaved Shade up just as he was slipping from my grasp.

"Careful of Bonk," Shade mumbled, and tenderness flooded my chest.

With fingers that still shook, I unclipped the front straps of Shade's bag. Poor Bonk. He'd been jostled around so much.

Big Guy started helping Shade toward the steps of the *Endeavor*, and the pack slipped from his shoulders and into my hands. I unzipped it and looked inside.

A groggy Bonk lay curled up on a crumpled brown towel. He slowly turned his head. His eyes were unevenly open, as if one were heavier than the other. He was just waking up from the sedative and looked small and limp and helpless. He let out a croaky meow when he saw me, and a lump swelled in my throat.

Swallowing it down, I whispered a hello before zipping the bag back up. Bonk probably wouldn't appreciate being confined now that he was awake, but there was no way I was letting him loose until I was sure he couldn't run away again.

I set the Bonk pack down beside Shade on the steps of the *Endeavor* and then looked at Big Guy. "First aid kit," I said. "Under the main console on the bridge." I couldn't go back in there. Not yet.

He nodded and went.

"I'll be right back," I told Shade, giving his shoulder a squeeze.

He nodded without looking up, his head hanging low as he gingerly stretched out his injured leg.

I went to the nearest com station on the wall. I needed Surral, but I couldn't for the life of me remember her bracelet code. I knew Mareeka's, though. She changed it only once a year, to match Surral's age. I typed in fifty-six and waited for her to answer.

"Yes?" Mareeka's voice crashed into me, nearly breaking whatever dams of control I still had in place.

"It's Tess." My voice croaked like Bonk's. "I need Surral on my dock. Two gunshot wounds."

"What!" That was both of them—Surral's voice coming from slightly farther away, where she probably sat across the dinner table from Mareeka.

"Not me. Fiona and...someone else." My next breath shuddered hard in my throat. "And I need a cleaning crew. No children, please. Biological..." I couldn't bring myself to say *waste*.

I fought tears, thinking only of Miko, even though there were also six dead goons on the dock.

"Surral is getting supplies," Mareeka said. "I'm on my way."

I heard them both curse the temporary security black-out before the channel went dead.

I moved back to Shade with purposeful, measured strides, trying to regain some of the numbness from before. I needed it, because right now, every word I said was a battle not to scream, and every step I took was a struggle not to run from the future before us all.

Big Guy handed me the first aid kit, his face reflecting shock and sympathy after what he'd seen on the bridge.

"Is Fiona still alive?" I asked, not wanting to feel my words as they came out. The question scared me too much. For me. For Jax.

He nodded. "Unconscious, but breathing. Your first mate looks like he's about ready to give up on life. Told him you were still with us, and that seemed to help."

Us. Had Big Guy joined the crew, then? I hoped so. His presence reassured me somehow.

I found scissors in the first aid kit and cut off first the makeshift bandage and then the blood-wet leg of Shade's dark combat pants. "Sorry to ruin your clothes, since you have nothing left."

"Got a few spare things in my little cruiser over there." He tipped his head toward one of the other occupied bays on the dock.

As I looked, my eyes snagged on some lumpy shapes in a dark, recessed corner. Five Starway 8 sentinels were on the floor, bound, gagged, and what looked like sedated. With the cameras down, Mareeka *had* posted guards on the open docks. They must have encountered Bridgebane first and maybe known he was somehow connected to the orphanage, so they hadn't put up a fight. Shade hadn't been questioned, and the Overseer would have shot to kill.

"Big Guy? Can you check on those guards over there? Free them and make sure they're all right?" I asked, pointing to the sentinels.

Big Guy nodded and jogged off.

"That'll fit inside the *Endeavor*," I said of Shade's

small ship. It was the two-person craft he'd used to fly me to the beach.

Shade looked up, something in his eyes melting right into me. "Is that an invite?" he asked.

I shrugged. "I guess so."

Where else could he go? The Dark Watch would soon be stalking his place in Albion City, if not torching it to the ground. According to Bridgebane, Shade now had a huge price on his head. And I... I kind of wanted to keep him around.

"Just don't hit anything when you're flying it into the central cargo bay," I said, souring my voice on purpose.

Humor briefly touched his lips. "Wouldn't dream of it, sugar."

I snorted softly. "One more *sugar*, and I'll punch you in the thigh."

"Noted," Shade said.

I almost smiled. The impulse died when I realized the bullet had gone in but hadn't come out. "I'm going to have to dig for it," I told Shade as I inspected his leg. I didn't dare try to take care of Fiona. She needed Surral and trained nurses. This, though, I could probably handle myself.

"Do you know how to do that?" Shade asked.

I glanced back up. "Does having done it before count?"

He looked dubious. "Got any numbshot?"

I shook my head, wishing I could inject him with something to dull the pain, but there was nothing on the *Endeavor* that would help. "We're too poor and not well enough connected for that. We grit our teeth through this kind of thing...cupcake."

Shade smiled, despite the pain he must have been in.

"Or you could wait for Surral," I said. "She'll probably bring some with her, although she rations it out carefully."

"She your doctor here?"

I nodded. "But she needs to see Fiona first."

"How 'bout you take care of me, Tess." He didn't ask, exactly. He just said it. And he used my name, which threw me—and filled me with warmth.

I sprayed his leg clean with a large dose of saline. The wound had almost stopped bleeding, but it started again as soon as I began digging around with a pair of long, sterile tweezers, my fingers gently pulling the hole in his thigh apart.

Shade bit down hard, his molars grinding. After a moment, he tipped his head back so he wouldn't look. I wouldn't have wanted to watch this, either. I *didn't* want to. Big Guy returned and then backed up a step, and my stomach turned over at the pull of flesh and the squish of muscle and blood. I saw a flash of bone and grimaced.

Shade grimaced, too. Often. He was pretty damn stoic otherwise. I finally got the bullet out, and blood gushed from the wound again. I quickly pressed a sterile pad to it, trying to stanch the flow.

"You all right?" I asked, looking up. My eyes crashed into Shade's, and my heart gave an unruly thump. Despite the agony hardening his expression, there was something incredibly soft in his gaze.

He opened his mouth to say something just as Surral raced onto the dock. Mareeka burst out of a different elevator a second later and caught up to her with only a few running steps.

"What happened?" they frantically asked together.

"First Bridgebane," I answered. "And then the Overseer himself."

Their eyes widened in shock.

"But...I don't understand." Mareeka looked around in confusion. "Where are the guards?"

I turned to Big Guy, who answered, "Over there. Sedated, but fine."

Both women glanced quickly toward the sentinels, now propped up in a line against the wall.

"The cameras are going back online now," Mareeka said. "But we have three hours that are totally dark." She sounded as though she'd never regretted a decision more in her life.

"Tell us the situation, Tess," Surral said with urgency.

I didn't want to explain, or to make already horrifying things even more real by saying them out loud, but they couldn't work efficiently without facts. Neither could the nurses and administrative assistants who'd just followed them onto the platform with rubber gloves and biohazard bags.

My throat tightened painfully. I had to force down a breath. "Fiona is unconscious on the bridge. Miko is...dead. Shiori was taken in a bid to get me on board the Overseer's ship, but then Big Guy showed up and chased him off." I waved a hand toward Big Guy. He needed a name—preferably one that fit the only person I'd ever seen the Overseer fear.

I glanced at Shade's leg. "And I need one of those laser healer things to close this up. I already took the bullet out."

Surral produced the healing instrument I needed from her medical kit.

"I can wait," Shade said. "Go to Fiona first." He lifted a corner of the sterile pad to look at his thigh. "It's almost stopped bleeding again."

"Who is this?" Surral asked.

In spite of everything, I felt heat crawl up my neck. "The lying fuckhead," I answered.

"Ah" was all she said.

Shade's wry smile said he totally deserved that. Which he did.

Mareeka didn't ask. She didn't waste time when she knew she'd get the information later from Surral.

"I have two." Surral handed me the medical laser. "Just press the green button until the healing is done. It couldn't be easier."

Shade's and my thanks fell on her back as she immediately climbed on board the *Endeavor* to try to help Fiona. Two nurses went with her while two others went to check on the Starway 8 sentinels. Mareeka started to follow Surral, but I stopped her with a hand on her arm. Surral was the doctor, and I needed to warn Mareeka.

I waited until the administrators had divided themselves between the *Endeavor* and the downed goons in the next bay over before saying, "I think I've put Starway 8 in danger."

She cocked her head to one side. "Why do you say that?"

"The Overseer found me here. He'll think you harbored me. That I come here..." I shook my head. "He could retaliate."

"I know who you are, Tess. I've known since the day your uncle dropped you off."

I stared at her in shock.

"You keep running from that man, and you let me worry about the rest."

"No." It didn't work that way. I wasn't a kid anymore. "I'm responsible for this place."

"You aren't. I am."

I drew back, hurt.

Mareeka softened the verbal blow with a gentle hand on my cheek. "If he decides we harbored you, then destroying us would take away something he could use against you. The Overseer is a lot of things, but stupid isn't one of them. And if Bridgebane doesn't tell him your true connection to Starway 8, the Overseer might not realize the extent of it. Also, there are thousands of people alive in the galaxy right now with a strong sentimental attachment to this place. Attacking us would have the potential to turn public opinion against him."

"And he thrives on adulation."

She nodded. "'Baby Killer' has a terrible ring to it, doesn't it?"

It did. There was a good chance he wouldn't risk that. The Overseer had gotten away with atrocities in times of war, but we were technically at peace. Nuking the galaxy's biggest orphanage for no apparent reason would do more than raise eyebrows. It could raise arms against him, especially considering the type of people Mareeka churned out of this place.

"What about an infection? An epidemic? Something subtle?" I asked.

"And what would be the point of that?" she asked.

"To take you from me." Just like he'd taken Mom. And Miko. And Shiori.

"If he can't glory in his accomplishment, it isn't one. Baby Killer, Tess." She shook her head. "He won't do it."

"Be careful. Be vigilant," I said, not quite convinced. I wasn't sure the Overseer was truly sane, and this line of reasoning required rational thought.

"I will." She hugged me. "I promise."

Mareeka turned and went into the ship. Big Guy followed, having listened to every word. Surral would already be doing everything possible to save Fiona. Mareeka and Big Guy... They'd probably help with Miko.

My heart suddenly hurt. It hurt so hard it burst.

I bit back a sob.

"Baby." Shade reached for me.

"Don't touch me!" I snapped.

He drew his hand back, his fingers curling into a fist.

"Don't touch me," I said more softly, "or I'll break."

"If you break, I'll put you back together."

Emotion ripped through me. I wanted to believe that. "Says the man who tore me apart."

Something flickered in Shade's eyes. "I'm sorry, Tess," he said.

I nodded, acknowledging his words. But I suspected we both knew that the healing I needed now mostly came from the inside, as did forgiveness.

We stared at each other. I didn't hate him. I thought I might love him. I wanted to trust. But it scared me to death—the idea of making the same mistake twice.

"I guess you got your comeuppance." His leg. His whole life...

"I guess I did," he said.

When I didn't move, he nodded toward the instrument in my hand. "Want me to do that?"

His question brought me back to bigger problems than my bruised heart or my fragile new faith in the man I was about to take back into my life.

"Yes." I handed it to him. I had to check on Fiona. "But wait a sec."

I peeled off his soaked compress, relieved to find the bleeding down to a mere trickle again. Then I picked up a scalpel, pulled up the sleeve of my pink scrubs, and cut my inner arm.

"What are you doing?" Shade reached to stop me, and I twisted away from him.

I made four deep slashes, hoping they'd scar. "Miko. Shiori. Fiona." I looked at Shade. "You."

I marked this day onto my skin and then let my blood flow into Shade's wound, mixing it with his.

"I'm guessing I should trust you on this," he said a little warily.

"Let's just say you won't need antibiotics. I'm sparing you a shot."

"Thanks?" He didn't sound quite sure about that. "This is what they want from you?"

"In a way," I answered. "I'm just the base ingredient for the enhancer they developed."

"Is this going to do something weird to me?" he asked, watching my blood flow, watching ours mix.

"No. Your system will flush it out. It's completely compatible."

"Then what's special about it?" he asked.

I was too sad and tired to lie—and not even sure I

wanted to at this point. "I'm life-form A1. Or something like that."

He seemed tired, too. Too tired to look shocked. "What does that mean, Tess?"

"It means I beat you out in natural selection. I heal better and don't get sick."

Shade pursed his lips, absorbing what I'd said. "Should Bridgebane get that blood?"

Worry about the blood exchange we'd agreed to passed between us with a look.

"We had no choice," I said. "They'll alter it with chemicals and drugs and make super soldiers from it. There's no doubt. But they'll make dozens. I still have the lab, and there are *thousands* of injections in it. It was a necessary risk," I said, remembering Mareeka's words from earlier.

Shade nodded, seeming to agree.

I wrapped a compress around my arm, not wanting to drip on everything when I went inside to somehow get my blood into Fiona, questions be damned. Maybe I'd answer them. Maybe I wouldn't. That was up in the air, like everything else.

I started up the stairs. "The super soldier serum? I think Big Guy might be a test."

Shade grunted as though that didn't surprise him at all. "At least I finally know what you stole," he said.

I nodded. I'd even stolen Big Guy, in fact.

"Good for you." Shade powered up the laser healer without saying anything else, and I went inside to face the horror I knew I'd find on the bridge.

CHAPTER

30

IT TURNED OUT THAT SHADE COULD NAVIGATE. THAT was good, since neither Jax nor I really could. We both saw numbers and our minds went blank. It was kind of a curse. I could steer, but I couldn't calculate.

The Fold was no longer where we'd last found it. We got Shade to jump us to eight different systems where we thought we might locate it, all without a result. No one was willing to tell Shade what we were looking for or why we appeared to be leaping willy-nilly around Sector 17, which frustrated the hell out of the guy who was setting the coordinates. We kept searching, anxiety and fatigue growing. Shade did what we asked and didn't press too hard for information, although I could tell he was damn curious. It was obvious we weren't ready to trust him with a big secret yet, and he respected that.

Big Guy stuck around this time when I asked him to, bringing his personal cruiser on board the same way Shade had. He finally gave us a name—Merrick Maddox. He'd been captured and experimented on, imprisoned for six months while scientists and machines monitored the serum's effect on his body and blood. The result of making someone with a rebel's heart faster, bigger, and stronger than everyone else was apparently an escaped prisoner who could find a secret lab and nearly blow it up.

The charges he'd been setting when I came along and stole the lab were still hidden under the refrigerated shelves. That unexpected news made me understandably nervous, but Merrick assured me that the bombs were controlled by a remote that he'd deactivated—after he'd decided he could trust us with the serum.

He'd initially wanted to bring the enhancer to the Fold but hadn't had any means of getting the lab to the rebel leaders or contacting them with only a stolen military cruiser and a bunch of goons hot on his tail. No wonder the Dark Watch had popped up all over the place around the lab just after we'd stumbled upon it. They'd been after Merrick, not us. But then we'd nabbed the lab—and their intense focus.

We'd been willing to die to keep the serum away from the Overseer, and that had made us okay in Merrick's book. He'd figured the Black Widow would do as well as his bombs to destroy the lab when the Dark Watch had cornered us once and for all in Sector 14, so he hadn't set off the explosives. When we'd gotten away, he'd left to try to contact his friends but had kept an eye on us, spying to see what we'd do with the serum. If it was bring it to the Fold, then all the better—we had a cargo cruiser to haul it there. If it was something else, he still had that remote.

I remembered the prickle to my senses, that feeling of being watched, as I'd walked the streets of Albion City.

Apparently, Merrick had been that itch on the back of my neck.

I wished he'd been more straightforward with us, although I couldn't be too angry, since he'd saved my life by keeping us in his sights.

I gave him a requisite stink-eye and strongly urged him to remove his tracking devices from inside my ship and find all his charges. I also did a thorough sweep, inside and out, to make sure I hadn't missed any trackers during my frantic spacewalk—and that none had been added while the ship had been docked on Starway 8.

I didn't find anything, and Merrick put his bugs and bombs in our secure weapons chest while I wondered about his confrontation with the Overseer. Everyone knew the Overseer, but why did the Overseer know Merrick? Had he monitored the tests on him? Or was there something else? Something more?

Fiona didn't wake up for three days. It was part blood loss, part heavy sedation, and part probably not wanting to wake up and face a reality without Miko and Shiori in it. I understood. I longed for the temporary escape of deep sleep myself. And I would have it—after I found the Fold.

Shade's cruiser was inside the main cargo hold next to Merrick's, but unlike Merrick, who'd taken up residence in the bunkroom, Shade was living out of his little ship. When I laid my head on my pillow for brief periods of rest and stared numbly at the wall, I wanted his arms around me. When I got up and saw him again, my heart jerked with uncertainty and doubt. But I also warmed all over with anticipation, and attraction, and the memory of his touch. The confusing mix kept crashing together and just hurt.

Shade looked at me as though he wanted to comfort me, and that just made everything both better and worse.

Bonk stuck mostly to the bridge and to my room, seeming completely fine after shaking off Shade's sedative. He gave out affection like he had an endless supply, bumping his head into any leg he could find and snaking his little body under any hand that reached out to touch. Without him purring against me most of the time, the panic and desolation growing inside me might have eaten me alive.

Jax stayed almost constantly with Fiona until she opened her eyes. I could hardly get him to eat, and he looked like a ghost. Or maybe he was seeing ghosts. Alone in the heartbreak that had never left him, he sat there and watched.

When she finally woke up, he kissed her on the forehead and then went to bed. I wasn't sure he slept. His face looked too battered for that when he eventually emerged again, his eyes still bloodshot and stark.

In the meantime, I looked for the Fold. And looked, and looked, and looked.

Merrick knew more than any of us about finding the pocket between the stars. Unfortunately, not even he could locate it. But the time we spent searching together gave me a chance to ask how he'd survived so well in the lab for three full days. It turned out he'd had food and water in a small pack and used empty biohazard bags for those bodily functions I'd wondered about.

On day *four* of wandering the Dark, I gripped my console, growling and wanting to give the damn thing a good shake.

"I can't find it!" I had to get what was left of my crew to safety, finish drawing six bags of blood, and then get to the Grand Temple on Reaginine before Bridgebane's ten days were up. If he survived the Overseer's wrath about letting me get away—*again*—my uncle would expect the deal to stand. If I didn't pay up, he'd take either Mareeka or Surral to Hourglass Mile, I had no doubt.

"Then finally tell me what we're looking for!" Shade whipped his head around. "I can't navigate without coordinates."

"It moves," I said. "There are no coordinates."

"It *what*?" he ground out in frustration.

I pressed my lips together. *Fuck it.* "The Fold."

"The what, baby?"

A ripple of awareness shivered over me every time he called me that. Shade was like a goose-bump-raising plague. "The Fold. The rebel hideaway. Our safe zone."

He frowned. "Well, it must be big. A huge space-dock. Or on a planet, right? Why can't you find it?"

"Because it doesn't exist on this side of things."

His face went blank. Yeah, I'd lost him there.

"You have to fly through an almost untraceable gateway to get there. The others say it hurts like hell."

"The others?" he asked, frowning again.

"I don't feel it," I admitted to him. I never had.

"A1?" he asked.

Shade's question was a good one. I'd often wondered that myself, although before I'd been using the Overseer's words for the differences in me—*freak, alien, mutant.* Really positive stuff.

I shrugged. "Maybe." Among us, we'd always chalked it up to the vagaries of the Fold, and I'd let the crew think it was a quirk in the gravitational warp and not a quirk in me.

But now, I'd done it. I only had one secret left, and that was the blood exchange Shade and I had agreed to. Otherwise, I'd told everyone here everything—called a fucking powwow in the kitchen as soon as Fiona could walk and spilled my guts. Because fuck it, we needed the truth here. We needed to protect each other and survive. Because fuck, fuck, fuck!

"Where is it?" I yelled, giving the base of my console a kick that hurt me more than it.

"Look for denser Dark," Merrick said. Again.

"I am! We all are!" We had been for days. At this rate, I was going to have to leave the *Endeavor* and the serum in the relative safety of the Outer Zones while Shade took me to Reaginine in his cruiser.

That would be fun to explain to the others. Just sit tight for a day or two while I hand over a weapon to the enemy.

And being trapped in a tiny starcruiser with Shade was sure to go well.

I glanced at the man in question. We hadn't spoken about anything that had happened before the attack on the Squirrel Tree. Or touched. Or been alone together. We hadn't talked about *us* at all.

I went back to glaring out the bridge's windows. *Deep breaths. Focus.*

First the Fold. Then Reaginine. Then I'd figure out how to get Shiori back.

I fought the growing ache in my chest. Her screamed "I forbid it!" haunted me, but how could I not?

"What if it's not here?" I abruptly asked. "We've

scoured all of Sector 17, so what if it's in 18 instead?" Just because the Fold was almost always somewhere in Sector 17 didn't mean that it *had* to be. It could have been anywhere in the Outer Zones.

Merrick looked pensive. After a moment, he nodded. "Look around the Tarrah System first. It was there about fifteen years ago. That's the last time I heard about it being outside of Sector 17."

It suddenly seemed really handy to have a rebel older than Jax, Fiona, and me on board. None of us knew anything about where the Fold had been hanging out a decade and a half ago. Hell, we couldn't even find it now.

"Shade." I glanced at my navigator. "Set coordinates for the Tarrah System."

Shade nodded, raking his gaze over me before turning back to his controls.

Something quivered in my belly. Despite neither of us addressing the giant elephant in the spaceship, there was no doubt in my mind that Shade Ganavan was more than just my navigator. The only time in the last few days he'd come anywhere near my personal space, he'd inhaled deeply enough to stir my hair. Without even touching me, he'd made me want everything we'd had back on Albion 5.

I forced my eyes away from him.

"Coordinates set," Shade said, swiveling back around.

Wow, that was fast. He was good at that. He was good at a lot of things.

I looked around. We were all on the bridge, even Fiona for once. Everyone was seated. Bonk was curled up on a cushion where he'd be safe.

"Prepare to jump," I said, sitting as well.

I pressed the button to activate the hyperdrive myself instead of handing the honors over to Jax, as I often did. Instantly, the *Endeavor* shot through interstellar space, so fast we left time behind, and our bodies seemed to collapse in on themselves before inflating back out.

Hundreds of thousands of kilometers away but only moments later, we slowed, and the Tarrah System loomed before us. I looked for stars with long stretches of pure darkness between them.

"Let's poke around," I said, my insides still reeling from the jump. "See if gravity gives us a thump."

"I thought you didn't want a planet," Shade said.

"I don't."

"Then how do you expect gravity to give you a thump?"

I think we both knew we weren't heading into a star, because that would suck.

"What's invisible except for gravitational force?" I asked.

Shade's eyes narrowed. "Are you talking about dark matter? Because no one's really—"

"Figured that out?" Yeah, maybe that was why the Fold was still hidden, right inside a pocket of it.

Or maybe it was something else. What did I know?

"It's not like a black hole. It's much subtler than that." I shrugged, at a loss to explain the inexplicable. There were scientists getting things wrong every day for that. "Just keep an eye on the scanners. If something strange happens, you'll know it."

Something strange finally did happen. It took fourteen more hours of searching, but then the darkness between two stars suddenly felt like a sticky wall when we got close enough.

My pulse accelerated, and I forgot all about my gritty eyes and about being so tired I got dizzy every time I blinked. I moved us in closer and felt the Fold's familiar tug start to lightly rattle the ship.

"Starshine?"

Shade sounded nervous. Basically, a big patch of nothing was shaking us and pulling us in.

"Sit tight," I told him, glancing up from my controls. "It'll be all right."

I hoped. The Fold wasn't nice to everyone, but I had a feeling that Shade would make the cut. And if he didn't, that meant he had no place on my ship, or in my life.

Trying not to think about that, I turned us straight into the gluey gravitational warp.

The *Endeavor* rattled harder. The point of no return was fast approaching after all these days of combing the Dark. Every single one of us lurched when the Fold finally grabbed us and sucked us in with sudden, jarring force.

The others started screaming like banshees the second the Fold really latched on to us, contorting in pain, and pressure, and I didn't really know what else.

Merrick and I looked at each other, both of us fine.

"A1," I said, almost like a bitter toast.

"A1," he echoed, but he didn't sound like it had ruined his life. "This used to hurt."

Well, that was bad news. "You know what that means?" I asked.

"The serum is even more dangerous than we thought. Its A1 base must somehow negate the Fold's defenses."

I thought about Susan's book on the Mornavail. In the first paragraph, it said the Mornavail had made their home in the "deep pocket of the Fold." Did they—*I*—originate here, and that was why passing through the warp didn't hurt?

"Anyone they've shot up with the enhancer can get in here." I swallowed that piece of bad news as I said it, and it tasted like a bitter pill going down my throat. Who knew how many people the Overseer's scientists had already experimented on with some form of the enhancer, or even with the finished product? It could have been hundreds of willing goons, maybe even thousands. There were also captives, like Merrick.

And I would still hand over my blood to Bridgebane in just a matter of days, allowing our enemies to arm even more people with the means to invade the Fold. I just hoped the rebel leaders never found out. They were as kind to traitors as the Overseer was.

"At least they'd have to find the Fold first," I said, more as self-reassurance than anything else. Spinning words to allay my guilt didn't make them any less true. In terms of protection, the Fold's cloaked appearance and shifting whereabouts were almost as effective defenses as massive pain and possible death.

I glanced at Shade. He did not look good. Neither did Fiona, but neither was quite as bad as I would have thought. After the initial shock, they'd turned white-knuckled and started groaning through gritted teeth, their eyes squeezed shut against some kind of awful compression that remained a mystery to me. Jax, who'd done this dozens of times, was in worse shape, still contorting in terrible pain and uttering noises that I'd never tell him about.

In the body, red blood cells lasted about four months, while white blood cells only lived for a few weeks. Were Shade and Fiona benefitting from my immunity, even to this sickness, but to a far lesser extent? The dose I'd dripped into their wounds had been much larger than the small injection both Jax and Fiona had gotten at the orphanage. And my blood was still fresh and alive inside them, not needing whatever was in the serum to make the benefits last.

The gravitational warp spat us out on the other side of whatever the hell that really was—and into wherever the hell we really were now. The shouting and moaning abruptly stopped.

"What...was that?" Shade asked, his breaths still heaving. He looked pretty freaked out. First-timer and all that.

The Fold defied explanation, and a long time ago, I'd decided to just go with it. I gave him a reassuring smile. He'd have to get used to it—assuming he stayed.

My stomach sank with a feeling I didn't want to analyze. He and I probably needed to have a talk one of these days.

Steering was more important right now, and the Fold was as packed as ever, with ships zooming all over the place. The main structures spread out in an ever-expanding, floating strip of metal and lights—a dozen immense spacedocks, all connected, all busy like a hive, and all powered by the big, bright stars of the Tarrah System. For the moment, at least.

I flew us toward the towering constructions, avoiding the heaviest traffic by taking a lower approach. The buildings didn't orbit anything. They just hung there, the Fold's own gravity holding them in place and taking them wherever the concealed pocket went. The Fold didn't have borders. It simply fit whatever was in it at the time, and I wondered what in the past it had sheltered, and what in the future, when we were all dead and dust, it would decide to protect.

I almost felt sorry for all the millions of people who didn't even know it existed. It was like a living thing, a hidden treasure, and part of me was absolutely certain it held the key to unlocking the secrets of the universe.

But that was for someone else to discover.

I gave our identity to the technicians on the first docking area with a vacancy indicator above its plasma-shielded platforms. The series of passwords I had was slightly out of date, and the guards got twitchy until Fiona figured out that the head technician was her friend Macey's cousin, and she knew him. He sent us on to a better dock, closer to the center of the Fold's structures.

I zipped off before he could change his mind, since an inner dock would significantly cut down the walk when I had to approach the rebel leaders about the serum. I couldn't wait to get rid of that stuff.

At the same time, the thought of people using it also made me feel sick.

Ignoring the churning that kept bubbling through my gut, I manually guided us through the shield pressurizing the platform we'd been assigned to and then slowly flew us toward the back wall where we could plug in. The docks here were too closed in for a natural recharge, so we had to rely on stocked energy from the solar panels on the Fold's main constructions to boost our power levels back up.

The moment the *Endeavor* was docked, I shut down the propulsion system and sagged in my chair. I hadn't slept in more than fits and starts for days. I hadn't showered since…

I grimaced. A lot had happened since then.

But we were safe. I could breathe again. I could mourn Miko, knowing her body had been incinerated and given to the Rafini Nebula by now. That was what Starway 8 did with its dead. It was our burial place, beautiful, ashes and colors swirling through the heart of space.

Tears welled in my eyes, and I stood up, getting off the bridge as quickly as I could.

When the door whooshed a second time right behind me, opening and then closing again, I knew Shade had chased after me. Merrick had no reason to follow, and these steps were lighter than Jax's but heavier than Fiona's.

I kept walking, but Shade stopped me by quietly calling my name. There was almost a question in the way he said it, an uncertainty that made my heart ache.

"I'm going to shower," I said, halting but not turning around.

After a moment, he said, "I could use a shower."

Warmth curled through me. My voice dropped to a rasp. "I'm sure you can use Jax's once the water recycles."

Shade's pause was longer this time. "I'd rather use yours." His voice had turned husky as well.

I stood there, vacillating. Hardly breathing. My heart beat hard, my body heated, and my mind screamed at me because I didn't know what to do, and a captain always decided.

Abruptly, I turned. The talk had come, even if I wasn't ready for it.

"What are you doing, Shade? What are you *going* to do?" I asked.

He had his cruiser. He could leave. He could blab about the Fold, although I didn't think he would, or I wouldn't have brought him here in the first place. And he'd made it through the sticky part without dying, so I figured the Fold must have thought he was okay, too.

Some people totally ruptured on the way in, suffering from sudden, violent aneurysms. They inevitably turned out to be people we wouldn't have wanted in here anyway. The Fold destroyed her foes, or *ours*, I supposed, which made us fairly confident about those who got through. And while I couldn't be certain, I didn't think Shade had enough type A1 blood in his system to truly invalidate the Fold's defenses.

He still looked bad—as haggard, tired, and disheveled as the rest of us—but also determined. His eyes snagged mine and held. "I chose you, Tess. I want you. All you have to do is want me back."

Emotion knotted around my heart, squeezing. I wanted him back, but I was afraid.

Shade's gaze stayed steady on mine. He was asking me to accept the things he'd done before we met—and what he'd almost done after. To accept and forgive.

Could I do that?

"I think…" I swallowed, my heart hammering out of control. Shade had proven himself to be on my side in the end, and wasn't that what mattered from now on? I believed in second chances. I'd needed some myself.

"I think my shower is probably big enough for two," I said.

His eyes flared, the desire in them flushing me with heat. Hesitantly, I lifted my hand to Shade's chest.

His hand covered mine, pressing until I felt the thud of his heart against my palm. "I want to comfort you, Tess."

Warmth washed through me, along with the ever-present pain of loss. I wanted his comfort. I probably wanted it too much.

"Fair warning," I said in a voice I hardly recognized. "The water might run out."

"Then you need bigger tanks."

"I do. I could never afford them."

Shade looked aghast. "Showers are sacred. I'll fix that."

I felt myself smile. It kind of broke my face, but it also brought some relief, as though now that I'd done that—smiled after Miko's murder and Shiori's abduction—I could take the next step toward moving out of the heaviest part of grief.

"With what?" I asked, wondering how he planned on paying for improvements. "Is there a big stash of universal currency in that little cruiser of yours?"

"I have more than two hundred million units spread over eight different untraceable accounts, and all my pass codes memorized, despite them being annoyingly complex and long."

I blinked. "Why in the galaxy do you have that much currency?" I asked, tugging my hand out from under Shade's.

I didn't need to ask how. The Dark Watch obviously paid its elite bounty hunters well. It was possible I had acquaintances in prison because of Shade, and the fact that I was ignoring that sat like a chunk of ice inside me that wouldn't melt.

He leaned against the wall, rubbing the back of his neck. He winced, as if the words were hard to get out, and it made me worry that things were even worse than I thought.

"I've been trying to buy back an empire I lost after my parents died in a freak shuttle accident," he finally said. "It turned out my father was really, really in debt to an asshole named Scarabin White. That's the person you met on the dock of the casino—the one who gave me the silver money clip with the engraved bird's head."

I remembered. I'd wanted to wash my hand after that man had touched it. It hadn't been hard to see that he was rich, powerful, and used to getting his way.

"White owns that whole place—the resort and casino—and my father...liked to gamble, it turned out. I had no idea until ten years ago, when his debt suddenly transferred to me. It was... It felt overwhelming. I'd just lost my family, and I wasn't used to running things. I'd just finished my engineering studies and had come home a few days earlier. Instead of trying to work off the debt like I should have, I went for a quick fix. I went to that stupid casino and gambled him for everything. I bet it all—and lost."

"Oh, Shade..." I could imagine the devastation of that, how he must have felt, especially right after losing his parents. It must have been doubly awful, because he didn't seem like the kind of man who made reckless, impulsive decisions.

Although maybe he did. He'd thrown it all away to protect me, hadn't he?

"So, he got what you—what your *father*—owed him?"

"Oh, he got ten times what I owed him," Shade said bitterly. "But that was the only deal he would make, and I just wanted it over. I was young and an idiot and figured I couldn't lose, since I'd never really lost at anything."

I was starting to piece together the picture. The golden boy. The privileged life. The shock of loss and a bad decision. Bad decisions made a person grow up fast—and maybe do things they would never have previously considered.

Shade shook his head, obviously still disgusted with himself, even after all these years. "I got White to sign an agreement, though, before I threw the dice. I made him promise to sell for a certain price—a huge but mostly fair price for all that—no matter when, if I had the currency to pay him one day. After ten years of hunting down the Dark Watch's most-wanted criminals and doing important retrievals, like finding abducted officials and officers—real under-the-radar stuff—I was more than halfway there. Your bounty would have finished it, and then some."

I swallowed. Well, that sucked.

Standing there, Shade looked so dejected that I began to reevaluate our situation, thinking that maybe I needed to comfort him, too. I didn't agree with the things he'd done, but I couldn't fault his motives. In fact, I understood them more than I probably should have and was in no position to judge. What wouldn't I do for Starway 8? I was about to give my blood to the enemy and allow them to re-create the serum just to keep two people safe. Was that a wise choice? Probably not. But I was making it anyway.

Shade had been working toward something on Albion

5, and now there was a good chance he'd never set foot on his home planet again, let alone reclaim his family's legacy. His was now a life on the run, probably forever—or for as long as it lasted. There was no way out of this.

Unless we somehow overthrew the Galactic Overseer and defeated the Dark Watch, and what were the chances of that?

CHAPTER

31

SHADE FELT LIKE AN ASSHOLE, STANDING THERE IN the hallway, confessing his sins. Tess even looked sorry for him, which made his gut twist. He didn't deserve her sympathy.

"It's the docks, isn't it?" she asked. "All the towers?"

He nodded, not surprised she'd picked up on his knowing more than was typical about the history of the docks, their prices and quality... Yeah, he knew exactly what he'd lost.

"Every single one on Albion 5—and on the rock under construction next to it."

She made a strangled sound. "Great Powers, that really is an empire. I can't believe you gave that up."

Shade felt himself go rigid. "I didn't give it up. I lost it. Like an imbecile."

"No." She shook her head. "Not then. I mean now... not even a week ago."

That decision? It had been hard—until it had been as simple as taking his next breath.

Reaching out, he swept Tess's bangs back from her

face and tucked them behind her ear. His fingers trailed down the side of her neck, and he felt her little shiver.

"I'm not going to lie to you, starshine. I agonized over the choice for a week. But I kept working on your ship, and helping you sell books, and wanting you every second I saw you. I was hell-bent on getting you away safely; I wanted to hold on to you and keep you with me; and I wanted the damn bounty. It was like a three-way war inside me. But then you came to me that last night on Albion 5, and you turned into the easiest decision of my life."

Her lips parted on a surprised inhale. Her always-fabulous blush sent a hot bolt of lust through him.

"Me?" she asked in a tempting whisper.

"You." His voice dropped, thickening.

"Was my door really half price?" Tess's eyes narrowed. The sultriness disappeared from her voice, replaced by suspicion.

Wariness blew a hole in the warm haze wrapping around him. Shade cleared his throat. "Yeah, it was half price."

"Because you paid for the other half?" she asked.

He hesitated. "Might've," he eventually said.

Would she hate that? She'd been determined to pay him what she owed and had even sold her precious books to Susan for it, probably for a mere fraction of their true worth. What he'd done to provide a solid door for the *Endeavor* hadn't been charity in his mind. This was Tess. He did what he needed to.

She fisted her hands in his shirt and abruptly pulled him close. The fire that had only been banked inside him roared to life as his hands clamped down on her waist, and she went up on her toes for a kiss. There was nothing hesitant about it. Her lips devoured his, pushing, moving, parting, and then her tongue swept into his mouth for a fuck-me lick that nearly made his knees give out.

Shade released a guttural sound. He didn't care if he came across as needy or weak. She made him both. He was about to spin her up against the wall and show her just what she did to him when Tess drew back, breathing hard. Shade could barely see. Want pounded through his blood.

"Shower?" Her breathless question went straight to his groin.

Right. She'd wanted a shower. He could do that. Get her all soaped up and slippery and...

Tess grabbed his hand and pulled. Shade followed. This was going to be fast.

She led him to her room and shut the door, yanking off her boots as she locked it. Her now-wrinkled pink scrubs and skimpy underclothes hit the floor before he could even reach for her, and the sight of her naked body thumped through him like a beat of deep percussion, resonating in his chest. The heavy thud of his heart told him things he already knew. *Tess. Mine. Us. Want.*

She moved toward him and grabbed his shirt, lifting it up and over his head. Shade's abdomen tightened, and anticipation made his cock grow thick and hard. A wave of warmth surged through him when Tess's fingers fell to his belt.

He let her undress him, helping only to toe off his boots. Her blue eyes landed on his erection and then roamed greedily over the rest of him. The way she looked at him was so fucking generous and sexy. No holds barred. She'd take a mile and give two. They stood together in nothing but skin, and Shade was more than ready to leave the shower for later and drag her into bed.

But Tess turned and moved toward her washroom, beckoning for him to follow. He stepped into the shower with her. It was tight for two. No matter; he'd make do. He couldn't wait to be closer to her, so close they were joined from top to bottom, inside and out.

"Here goes," she said, drawing in a deep breath.

It seemed like an odd thing to say and do, but Shade was beyond caring about anything other than getting inside her. He wanted her. And he wanted to show her, to prove to her... He wasn't sure what. Whatever it was men proved.

Tess turned on the water. A timer beeped on, and an ice-cold spray hit him square in the back.

Shade jumped. "What the fuck?" he yelled.

"Go!" she cried. "Four minutes and seven seconds before the tank runs out."

She pushed past him and slipped under the frigid stream, scrambling to get herself wet. She leaped back out again and went for the shampoo.

Shade followed her lead, breathing in short, pained bursts laced with muttered curses.

"Swearing your head off won't make the water warm," she said tartly.

"I'm going to punish you for this," he told her through gritted teeth. His lust had died a cold death, and it was all he could do just to move.

"Switch!" Tess yelled out.

They waltzed in a circle, and she gasped when the

water hit her head. She got the shampoo out of her hair, scrubbed her face with her hands, and then jumped back out and grabbed the soap.

Shade rinsed his hair and quickly exited the stream of death while Tess rinsed off, shivering, her nipples hard peaks, and her teeth chattering audibly. He soaped up like a madman, she got out of the way, and he started to rinse off just as the countdown began, a tinny electronic voice announcing that the tank would run out in *five, four, three, two, one…*

The water stopped.

Shade stood there, dripping wet, covered in goose bumps, his shoulders hunched in, and his cock the smallest it had ever been. Tess was in so much trouble right now.

He growled. "You are—"

He stopped talking when she grinned. Her reddish-brown hair was slicked back, and her freckles stood out in her pale face. She looked at him through dark lashes spiked with moisture, her brilliant-blue eyes glittering like the brightest of stars and blinding him to everything but her light.

"—fucking adorable," he finished, smiling back.

Tess jumped into his arms, all naked, cold, and wet.

He swept them both out of the cubicle of doom and then reached for the towel he saw hanging on the wall. He rubbed Tess dry, quickly swiping the cold drops off her skin and then making a mess of her hair as he scrubbed her head extra hard in payback for the torture he'd just endured. She laughed, batting his hands away.

"Detail your water situation for me, Captain," he demanded, turning the damp towel on himself.

Fuck, that was cold.

She answered as she ran her fingers through her hair, shaking it out. "One four-minute and ten-second tank for showers. It takes two days for the water to recycle and clean itself. Another slightly smaller tank for sinks and laundry."

Shade gaped at her. "That's it?"

Tess nodded. "Water's expensive. So are tanks."

"And none of it heats?"

She shook her head.

He'd been taking care of the minimums of personal hygiene on his cruiser—with water that quickly and easily heated up. It wasn't equipped for showers, though.

"Clothes get cleaner with warm water," he said, glancing at their discarded apparel.

"Cold gets rid of blood," she answered with a shrug.

She said it so matter-of-factly, like *such is the rebel's life*.

Shade frowned. He wasn't sure how much blood he could stand to see her lose. None already seemed like enough.

"Does this fold sell tanks and water?" he asked, herding her into the bedroom.

"*The* Fold," she corrected over her shoulder. "And yes."

"Permission to make a few changes to the system?" He grabbed a big sweater off the foot of Tess's bed and dropped it over her head.

She wiggled into it, getting her arms through the sleeves and pulling her hair free from the neck. "Permission granted."

"Permission to get on your bed?" He gently tugged her right over to the edge of it.

Her cheeks flushed a gorgeous pink. "Permission

granted," she said again, her eyes dipping over his naked body as she reached for him, her fingers feathering against his waist.

Shade captured her hand, his skin jumping at her cold touch. "Oh, no you don't." He pulled back the covers on what was really a one-person bed, making a curled-up Bonk lift his head. Still freezing, Shade got in and guided Tess down next to him. When they were curved together like spoons, he covered them both up.

She went still in his arms. "Shade?"

He gripped her tighter and then threw his leg over hers, embracing his inner caveman when it came to pinning her down. That would suffice for now. Later, he'd use other methods to get her underneath him and keep her there.

"I need to recover from that ordeal you call a shower," he grumbled. "And you're tired. I'll still be here when you wake up."

It wasn't something he could see from behind her, but he thought she smiled. There was a change in her body language that gave it away, even though she didn't say anything or turn around.

Settling in, Shade nuzzled the back of her neck, inhaling the scent of her damp hair and clean skin. Tess sank into him, relaxing against his chest in a way that sent satisfaction blazing through him.

Holding her as tightly as he dared, he rubbed a lazy thumb back and forth over her stomach. It must have soothed her, because Tess fell asleep fast. A few minutes later, Bonk picked his way over Shade's thigh, angling for a spot in between Tess and him. He wasn't about to let that happen, and the tabby finally gave up and went back to where he'd been before, warming Shade's back. Bonk started purring, his paws pressing into Shade's shoulder. Knead, knead, prick.

Shade was worn out like he'd rarely been before, but he didn't want to close his eyes just yet. As he lay there in between Tess and Bonk, he felt something he hadn't felt in a long time. The last time a similar feeling had barreled through him, he'd been young and cared for, with loving parents and what he'd thought was an easy future ahead. Now, he wanted to be the provider, the protector, but nothing about the future looked easy to him.

There were a thousand differences, but the core of the feeling remained the same: family.

He just hoped Tess felt it, too.

Finally giving in to fatigue, Shade let Bonk push against his shoulder and cradled Tess as she slept.

CHAPTER

32

SHADE WAS ASLEEP. HIS BREATHING WAS DEEP AND even, his body relaxed. He was nice and warm now, and I didn't move, not wanting to wake him up.

I let him rest, leaving my thoughts to carry me away. After an hour of lying there nestled against his warmth and strength, my imagination had taken me all over—to some places we'd already been together, and to a whole bunch of others I still wanted to explore with Shade.

Desire coiled low in my belly, and I started to ache for his touch.

To hell with it; he could sleep later. I turned in his arms.

Shade opened his eyes as I half sat up and pulled off my sweater.

His lips parted. "Excellent choice of wake-up," he murmured in a gravelly voice.

I nudged him onto his back and eased on top of him. His hands found my waist and then skimmed up my bare ribs.

I kissed him hungrily, licking and nibbling his bottom lip. "I'm dying to feel you inside me again."

His expression sharpened. All trace of sleepiness vanished from his eyes, and he flipped us over, his gaze turning hot.

Disturbed by the sudden movement in the narrow space, Bonk jumped off the bed—probably for the best.

Shade looked down at me, his arms caging my head and his legs between mine. I slowly drew my knees up.

"Clean or dirty?" he asked, his voice dropping so low it sank right into me and teased my sex. "Slow or fast?"

Heat unfurled between my legs as tiny muscles clenched. "Do I have to pick just one?"

Shade chuckled. He dipped his head, his mouth brushing my cheek in a slow caress of a kiss. In my ear, he whispered, "That's my Tess."

The possessive affection in his voice sent pleasure fluttering through me. "You mean your Captain," I teased.

"In bed, I steer the ship." A mischievous glint lit his eyes when they met mine again.

My mouth twitched. "Is that so?"

He nodded. "I have to press all sorts of complicated buttons. You're the copilot. All you need to do is grab the handle and pull."

I burst out laughing. "Like this?" I asked, snaking my hand between our bodies.

His hips shifted away from my questing fingers. "Careful, baby. That's a delicate instrument. No replacement parts available."

Still smiling, I reached for his hard length again and gave it a gentle stroke from base to tip.

"Believe me"—I lifted my head and sucked on his earlobe—"it's in my best interest to not damage the tools."

Shade's husky laugh turned into a groan when I stroked

him again, squeezing this time. He rocked into my hand. Our eyes met, and the need I saw in his gaze was like a gravitational pull, drawing me in, body and soul.

Angling my hips up, I guided him inside me. Shade's broad shoulders bunched with tension, and a slight vibration rolled down his back. Even after an hour of working myself up in my head, he still had to push his way in slowly. I was so hot and throbbing that I wanted him to move faster and satisfy the ache inside me, but I was also—

"So tight," Shade muttered, sounding pained.

I tilted my head back on an exhale when he stopped, finally seated fully within me. My body adjusted to him quickly.

"I want to do this every day," I said.

"Baby, we can do this ten times a day, upside down, tangled up, and hanging from the ceiling if you want."

I smiled. All that sounded promising.

He flexed his hips back and then thrust deep between my legs. I gasped. It felt so good. He did it again, harder, and stars burst behind my lids.

Shade lowered his head and kissed me so completely that I almost couldn't breathe. "Tied up. Tied down. Blindfolded. Hands and knees. Whatever the fuck you want," he said, pumping into me with each promise.

The possibilities flashed before me. So much to explore. I started to pant and writhe, arching into sensations that were building almost too quickly. I chased them, greedy, even though I wanted this to last.

Shade thrust harder, his movements less controlled now. I rose up to meet him, matching his pace and driving him on.

I whispered his name. Shade groaned mine. I locked my legs around his waist and gripped his back. He was sweat-slicked and trembling and so hard inside me that he felt like hot steel and smooth rock.

"Not gonna last, baby," he said. "Not when you're so wild and hot."

I grabbed his short hair and pulled.

"Yes…" He panted against my neck.

Shade shifted his weight to one arm and then palmed my breast. The pad of his thumb found my nipple, and he pressed, the steady pressure traveling straight to my core and tightening the quivering muscles there. Abruptly, he gathered the taut bead between his fingers and pinched. I yelled and came like a nuclear blast.

Shade followed me over the edge, his hips moving in hard jerks. The tension in our bodies slowly unraveled, and we sank into the mattress together, both of us breathing hard.

"Holy Sky Mother," he finally mumbled. "I think you wiped me out."

I laughed. "I hope not. You promised we could do that again."

He grinned, lifting some of his weight off me. I pulled him back down, enjoying the press of him against my skin.

Shade gave in to my unspoken demand while still making sure he didn't crush me. "I would suggest another shower after that, but there's no fucking way I'm going through that again."

I clamped my lips together, trying to keep my smile to a minimum. I probably should have warned him about that.

"May I have permission to make another change, Captain?" Shade asked.

Warmth swirled through me. "Permission to *ask*, Bedroom Captain."

The corners of his mouth curled up. "Does this fold have a mattress that would fit both of us?"

My heart fluttered a little wildly. "*The* Fold has everything."

Shade rolled over, dragging me mostly on top of him and trying to keep us both comfortable on my narrow bed. His hand swept down my back and stayed on the curve of my bottom.

"Then how about a bed for two?" he quietly asked.

I lifted my head, something clenching in my chest.

The brown eyes searching my face darkened with sudden hesitation. "I don't want to assume…"

I leaned forward and kissed him. "Spoil me. I'm game."

The words *blood money* popped into my head, but I pushed them aside.

"Good." Shade gave my rear end a light squeeze.

His touch stirred sensations that were still alive inside me, and I almost told him I was game for more right now, but Shade looked exhausted.

"What's that secret smile about?" he asked, his eyes narrowing on me.

"Nothing." I kissed him again. "Just rest."

He grunted a little suspiciously but then got comfortable with me beside him, relaxing like a man utterly ready for sleep. I threw my leg over his, making sure he didn't go anywhere. Or fall off the bed.

A secret sort of smile suddenly curved *his* lips.

"What?" I asked.

"Nothing, cavewoman. Go to sleep."

"Cavewoman?"

Still smiling, Shade didn't explain, and I *hmphed*, letting it go.

A moment later, Bonk jumped back onto the bed. He took the spot above our heads, commandeering most of the pillow. We both wiggled down, making room for him.

"Make that a bed for three," I said, not even remotely kidding.

"Noted." Shade kissed my temple, brushing his lips against my hair and skin and breathing me in.

A contented sigh whispered out of me, and I closed my eyes, knowing I would easily drift back to sleep. Later was for dangerous serums, filling more blood bags, meeting with the rebel leaders, and facing what came next. Now was for Shade and me.

Paws started kneading the top of my head. A little engine revved up.

I smiled, revising my earlier thought. Now was for Shade, me, and, apparently, Bonk. Which was perfect.

EPILOGUE

THE FOLLOWING DAY...

MY BOOTED FOOTSTEPS RANG OUT LOUDLY ON THE grated metal flooring of Spacedock 1, the innermost station of the Fold. Shade, Jax, Fiona, and Merrick strode next to me, turning us into a veritable chorus of thuds.

I had five vials of the super soldier serum in my pack and a lead weight on my chest.

Would the enhancer help us to even the odds? Maybe even give us an edge?

Or would turning it over to the rebel leaders just send everything spiraling out of control?

Nothing came without a cost. I just wondered who would be paying up.

Possibly everyone.

I glanced at Shade. He caught my eye and gave me a quick nod back. Reassuring. A little grim. He understood the stakes.

Rebel Command Center loomed before us, blocked by a huge, guarded door I'd been through only twice before.

Maybe we needed to lose control. Maybe that was

what it would take to bring the Overseer down, not just be a thorn in his side.

I figured we'd find out soon, because I was about to light the fuse on enough explosives to blow the galaxy apart.

ACKNOWLEDGMENTS

This novel was so much fun to write, and I couldn't have done it without the support of a fabulous group of people. Many thanks to my agent, Jill Marsal, to my editor, Cat Clyne, and to the whole team at Sourcebooks Casablanca for their talent and expertise.

Readers, reviewers, bloggers, authors, and anyone who picks up my books or takes a moment to help spread the word about them—you're the best, and I'm so grateful!

I also couldn't do this without my amazing family and some very dear friends. I'm so lucky to have the help and support of my husband and children, my parents and sister, and a great group of readers and writers that I'm privileged to know, including Callie Burdette, Lynn Latimer, Katerina Papasotiriou, Adriana Anders, Chelsea Mueller, Grace Draven, Jeffe Kennedy, Jennifer Estep, and Darynda Jones. Your encouragement means the world to me. Thank you.

STARBREAKER

"An out-of-this-world blend of
sci-fi action and sizzling romance."

—JENNIFER ESTEP, *New York Times* and *USA
Today* bestselling author of *Kill the Queen*

Captain Tess Bailey and Shade Ganavan never intended
to become heroes. But when Tess handed over the stolen
goods, she may have given the rebel leaders the power to
bring down Galactic Overseer Novalight and his oppressive
regime. Now, revolution is in the wind and the galaxy on
the brink of catastrophic war.

Tess, Shade, and the remaining crew of the *Endeavor* are
still the galaxy's Most Wanted. With the Dark Watch—and
every bounty hunter known to humankind—scouring the
galaxy for them, the situation couldn't be more desperate.

The clock is ticking. As their attraction builds and
secrets are revealed, Tess and Shade must decide if they
trust each other enough to plan their next move together.
They could change the course of history…or at least bring
hot water to the showers aboard the *Endeavor*. They'll just
have to tackle one crisis at a time.

COMING SPRING 2020

  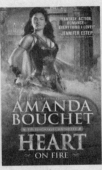

"A heart-pounding and joyous romantic adventure."

—NALINI SINGH,
New York Times **bestseller**

"Simply brilliant."
—*Kirkus Reviews* **starred review**

—DARYNDA JONES, *New York Times* bestseller

"Give this to your Game of Thrones fans."
—*Booklist* **starred review**

For more Amanda Bouchet, visit:
amandabouchet.com

Also by Amanda Bouchet

THE KINGMAKER CHRONICLES

A Promise of Fire

Breath of Fire

Heart on Fire